Rushed to the Altar

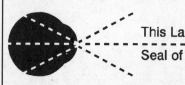

This Large Print Book carries the
Seal of Approval of N.A.V.H.

THE BLACKWATER BRIDES

RUSHED TO THE ALTAR

JANE FEATHER

THORNDIKE PRESS
A part of Gale, Cengage Learning

GALE
CENGAGE Learning·

Farmington Hills, Mich • San Francisco • New York • Waterville, Maine
Meriden, Conn • Mason, Ohio • Chicago

GALE
CENGAGE Learning®

Copyright © 2010 by Jane Feather.
The Blackwater Brides Series.
Thorndike Press, a part of Gale, Cengage Learning.

Thorndike Press® Large Print Romance.
The text of this Large Print edition is unabridged.
Other aspects of the book may vary from the original edition.
Set in 16 pt. Plantin.

LIBRARY OF CONGRESS CATALOGING-IN-PUBLICATION DATA

Feather, Jane.
   Rushed to the altar / by Jane Feather. — Large print edition.
     pages ; cm. — (Thorndike Press large print romance) (The Blackwater Brides series)
   ISBN 978-1-4104-7176-5 (hardcover) — ISBN 1-4104-7176-4 (hardcover)
   1. Nobility—England—Fiction. 2. Prostitution—Fiction. 3. Impostors and imposture—Fiction. 4. Inheritance and succession—Fiction. 5. Mate selection—Fiction. 6. Large type books. I. Title.
PS3556.E22R87 2014
813'.54—dc23   2014017224

Published in 2014 by arrangement with Pocket Books, a division of Simon & Schuster, Inc.

Printed in Mexico
1 2 3 4 5 6 7 18 17 16 15 14

Rushed to the Altar

PROLOGUE

London, 1761

The air in the room was thick with the smell of incense from the candles burning on every surface. The fire was built so high the heat was almost suffocating and the three men standing within the curtains at the foot of the great canopied bed were sweating. The candles threw long shadows onto the ornately papered walls, the dark carved moldings echoed in the carvings of the bed and the heavy furniture. Thick velvet curtains at the long windows deadened the sounds from the street below and the heavy Turkey carpet muffled the footsteps as one of the three men moved backwards out of the stiflingly close confines of the bed curtains.

"Where's Jasper?" The querulous voice coming from the high-piled pillows at the head of the bed was a thin thread in the heat and the gloom. Immediately one of the two men still beside the bed hastened to his side. He wore the plain black clothes of a lawyer or man of business.

"Where indeed?" muttered the man who had moved away from the bed. He was tall and lean, the candlelight reflecting off a head of golden hair, drawn smoothly back from a wide forehead and fastened at his nape with a black velvet ribbon.

"He'll be here, Perry." The speaker bore a striking resemblance to the golden-haired man. He stepped away from the bed to join him. "You know Jasper. He's never in a hurry."

"If he doesn't get here soon he'll be too late, and we'll all be the sufferers," Peregrine stated, his voice still low. "The old man won't settle anything without Jasper, Sebastian, you know that as well as I do."

Sebastian shrugged. "So be it," he said, casting a quizzical glance at his twin brother. Physically they were alike, but temperamentally a world apart. Sebastian was troubled by little, regarding the vicissitudes of life with a cheerful insouciance. Peregrine took everything seriously, to the point of obsession on occasion as far as his twin was concerned.

"I don't need the damn leech, Alton. I need my damned nephew, damn his eyes."

Irascibility lent strength to the voice from the bed and an outflung arm swept dismissal at the black-clad figure hovering at his head. The face on the pillows, framed in thin locks of white hair, had the yellowish cast of infirmity and age, the skin creased and brittle, the blue eyes pale and blurred with cataracts. But nothing diminished the sharp intelligence of their expression. The long, skeletal fingers of a blue-veined hand twitched restlessly over the ivory beads of a rosary.

"I'm glad to hear you in such fine fettle, sir." A new voice, smooth and mellow with a hint of slightly caustic humor in its depths, spoke from the doorway. Sebastian and Peregrine swung around, looking towards the door. Jasper St. John Sullivan, fifth Earl of Blackwater, resplendent in a suit of deepest blue velvet, an amethyst glowing in the froth of Mechlin lace at his throat, came into the room, closing the door behind him.

"Sebastian . . . Perry . . ." He greeted his younger brothers with a cordial nod as he approached the bed, one gloved hand resting negligently on the hilt of the sword at his hip. "Ah, you're here too, Alton." He nodded at the black-clad man who had straightened at his arrival and was now fixing him with an anxious gaze. "I suppose the presence of my uncle's lawyer means we are here to do business."

"You know damn well why I summoned you, Jasper." The invalid was sounding stronger by the minute, struggling up against his pillows. "Help me up."

Jasper leaned over and propped the pillows against his uncle's back. "That better, sir?"

"It'll do . . . it'll do," the old man said, and then was convulsed in a violent coughing fit, pressing a thick white napkin against his mouth as his shoulders heaved. Finally the spasms ceased and he fell back against his pillows struggling to catch his breath. He looked at the faces around his bed. "So, the crows have come to the feast," he declared.

"Hardly that, sir, since it was you who insisted upon our presence," Jasper said amiably, tossing his bicorne hat onto a nearby table. He was as dark as his brothers were fair. "I doubt any one of us would impose ourselves upon you had we not been obeying an apparently urgent summons."

"You always were an insolent puppy," the bedridden man declared, wiping his mouth again with the napkin. "Well, now you're all here, let's get on with it." He drew the rosary up to his chest. "Tell 'em, Alton."

The lawyer coughed discreetly into his fist and looked as if he would rather be anywhere other than where he was. His gaze darted from brother to brother and then finally came to rest on Jasper. "As you know, my lord, your uncle Viscount Bradley has recently returned to the bosom of the church."

"A fact that lies between my uncle and his conscience," the earl said with a touch of acerbity. "It hardly concerns my brothers and myself."

"Ah, there you're wrong, m'boy," the viscount declared with a chuckle. His faded eyes had taken on a shimmer of amusement in which just a hint of malice could be detected. "It concerns all three of you most nearly."

Jasper drew a japanned snuffbox from the deep pocket of his coat and flipped the lid, taking a delicate pinch. It was hot as Hades in the chamber, but much as he longed to fling a window wide onto the cool night air of early autumn he refrained. "Indeed, sir?" he said politely.

"Aye." The old man's smile was almost smug. "You want my fortune, and you shall have it, three even shares, if you abide by my conditions. Tell 'em, Alton."

The three brothers exchanged glances. Jasper leaned back against a carved bedpost, his arms folded. "You have our attention, Alton."

The lawyer coughed again and took up a sheaf of documents from a table beside the bed. He began to declaim. "It is so stipulated in Lord Bradley's will and testament that his entire fortune be divided equally among his three nephews, Jasper St. John Sullivan, fifth Earl of Blackwater, the Honorable Peregrine Sullivan, and the Honorable Sebastian Sullivan on condition that before Lord Bradley's death they each have taken to wife a woman who is in need of salvation, and that by bestowing on that woman their name and fortune, they are the means of said woman's conversion to the paths of righteousness."

There was an instant's stunned silence, then Peregrine demanded, "What in heaven's name does that mean? *In need of salvation? Paths of righteousness?*" He turned in bewilderment to his older brother.

Jasper's shoulders were shaking with silent laughter. "Sir, you have outdone yourself," he stated, bowing with mock humility to the figure in the bed. "I expected something out of the ordinary, but never in my wildest dreams could I have come up with this."

"Then, nephew, I shall eventually go to

my Maker well satisfied," the viscount declared, his fingers busy on his rosary, although his eyes still retained the gleam of amusement. "You are a trio of reprobates and you shall see not a penny of my fortune until you have each taken to your hearts and reformed some poor lost soul. It is my fervent hope and prayer that in the process you will find your own reformation."

The twin brothers were silent, Peregrine still staring in a degree of openmouthed astonishment, and even Sebastian for once looking nonplussed. Jasper thoughtfully tapped his mouth with his fingertips. "Well, I'm sure your goal is a worthy one, sir. And, while I can't speak for my brothers, for myself I am humbled that you should have such a care for my immortal soul. I take it that should you succumb to your illness before we have accomplished this task, the will is void?"

The viscount chuckled and closed his eyes. "Believe me, dear boy, I have no intention of meeting my Maker until you three are well and truly leg-shackled to women who satisfy my terms. Alton will explain the rest." He waved a hand at them. "Go away now, and send in that crow Cosgrove. I have some writing to do."

Alton gathered up his papers and scurried

13

to the door. Sebastian and Peregrine followed; only Jasper remained. He looked down at the old man, who was breathing in shallow gasps, the parchment skin seeming to grow more yellow as the candlelight flickered. "You old fraud," he murmured. "Of course you've no intention of dying on us any time soon. But I will say this, Uncle. Of all the tricks you've perpetrated on the world and your fellow man over your long life, this one takes the crown for sheer hypocrisy."

Another cackle of malicious amusement ended in a bout of coughing, and the old man waved him away. "Get out, dear boy. I need to preserve my strength . . . indeed, you three should be more than anxious to ensure that I do." He lay back against the pillows, his eyes glittering as they rested on his nephew's countenance. For an instant, the old man's mouth moved in the semblance of a smile. "You're more like me than you'd care to admit, dear boy."

"Oh, I don't deny it, sir." Jasper chuckled softly. As he turned from the bed a thin angular figure slipped into the room in the black garments of a priest, the weighty gravity of his expression belying his youth.

"Father Cosgrove." Jasper greeted him pleasantly.

"My lord." The young priest bowed.

"Get over here, Cosgrove. I have another installment to write and time is running out." The invalid's irascible tones made Father Cosgrove wince slightly, but he hastened to the bedside with a murmured, "At once, my lord."

Jasper shook his head, feeling sorry for the young priest whose role as amanuensis to Viscount Bradley could not have been an easy one . . . certainly no easier than his role as personal priest and confessor. Not for the first time Jasper wondered what project could so involve his uncle in the last months of his life.

He left the bedchamber and joined his brothers, gathered with the lawyer in the antechamber to the bedroom. Sebastian said without preamble, "Is the old man mad? Can we credit anything he has said?"

"Oh, I think so, Seb, yes," Jasper observed. He strolled across to a sideboard and picked up a decanter of sherry. "This seems to be all that's on offer. May I pour for you?" He didn't wait for a response but filled two glasses and passed them to his brothers. "Alton, for you?"

"Uh, yes, m'lord. Thank you." Alton fumbled uneasily with his folder of papers as he took the glass handed to him.

15

Jasper filled one for himself and then crossed the room to the fireplace that was mercifully empty. He put one foot on the fender, rested his free arm along the mantel, and regarded his brothers and the lawyer with the hint of a smile. "So, we have much to discuss, it would seem. No, Perry . . ." He held up an arresting hand as Peregrine began to say something. "Let me speak for a moment and try to present this as I see it."

Peregrine subsided and perched on the arm of a sofa, staring fixedly at his elder brother. The lawyer sat stiffly on an armless, straight-backed chair, clutching his documents with one hand and his sherry glass in the other.

"First, there's nothing wrong with our uncle's mind. In fact I'd say it was working more sharply than ever." Jasper shook his head. "I imagine he's been planning this diabolical little scheme for months. Certainly since before he decided to have his road-to-Damascus epiphany." His smile was sardonic as he took another pinch of snuff. "You may choose to take that at face value if you wish. I for one don't believe a word of it; however the whys and wherefores need not concern us. The fact is plain enough. Our uncle is an extremely rich man." He glanced at the lawyer. "Do you have a figure, Alton?"

"Uh . . . yes, yes, my lord." He began to shuffle the papers but without looking at them. "Viscount Bradley's estate is worth in excess of nine hundred thousand pounds."

Jasper contented himself with a raised eyebrow, although Peregrine drew breath sharply and Sebastian gave a low whistle.

"A goodly sum indeed," Jasper said after a moment. "Certainly worthy of a nabob of my uncle's ingenuity. And he could reasonably assume that since his nephews don't have two pennies to rub together they would be more than willing to fulfill any conditions he might lay down for their inheritance."

"You have rather more than two pennies, Jasper," Sebastian pointed out without rancor.

"Yes, I inherited a heavily encumbered estate in Northumberland and an equally mortgaged mausoleum in town, and more debts of our father's than I can ever imagine settling," Jasper returned, equally without rancor. "And somehow or other our family name seems to create the expectation of largesse to every devout and poverty-stricken family hanger-on."

"You need the money too," Peregrine

agreed hastily.

"Precisely. And our uncle knows that perfectly well. He has no one else to leave it to —" He stopped as the lawyer cleared his throat.

"If I may interrupt, my lord. Lord Bradley has specified that if you and your brothers do not meet the criteria for inheritance before his death his entire estate will go to a convent . . . a silent order, I believe . . . in the Pyrenees."

Jasper laughed with rich enjoyment. "Oh, has he, indeed? The old fox." He went to refill his glass, bringing the decanter to his brothers, still laughing. "Well, my dears, it seems we either each comb the streets for a fallen woman and steer her into the paths of righteousness, or we settle for poverty at best and debtor's prison at worst." He took an armchair, lounging with one velvet-clad leg crossed over the other. Candlelight glimmered on the silver buckle of his shoe as he swung his foot indolently.

"I don't see what you find so amusing, Jasper," Peregrine said.

"Oh, don't you, Perry? I do." Sebastian gave his twin a twisted grin. "Jasper's right. It's a stark choice."

"Alton, give us the gory details," Jasper instructed the lawyer with a nod.

"Well, my lord, first of all, all three of you must satisfy the terms of the will before any one of you can inherit." Alton shifted a little in his chair. "The weddings must all take place, as you know, before the viscount's demise. And the estate is to be divided equally, after all the mortgages have been paid on Blackwater Manor, and on the London property, Blackwater House."

Jasper nodded in appreciation. "So the old man has some family pride left. Go on. Tell us about our prospective wives. How are they to be described?"

The lawyer consulted his papers again. A flush adorned his cheekbones as he began to read. " 'Each prospective bride must be plucked from a situation that is injurious to her immortal soul. Each prospective bride must be without means to provide for a conventional existence. It goes without saying that each prospective bride will not be found in the conventional social circles in which my nephews customarily move, although such a bride may be found in the less acceptable social circles which I'm certain they also frequent.' "

"Oh, clever," Jasper murmured. He chuckled again in admiration. "The old man really has outdone himself. Ever the family outcast himself, he's determined to force the high sticklers of Sullivan convention to accept into the family women they wouldn't allow to touch their dirty laundry. Such a neat revenge for all the slights he's endured over the years. Can you imagine the outrage among the aunts? I can hear them now." He shook his head, still chuckling.

"That would appear to be the gist of the viscount's thinking, my lord," Alton concurred, looking even more uncomfortable.

"I can't believe even Uncle Bradley would come up with such a diabolical revenge," Peregrine murmured. "You're the head of the family, Jasper, they'll have to acknowledge your wife however much it galls them." He subsided, shaking his head gloomily.

"You have it in a nutshell, Perry." His elder brother smiled into his sherry glass.

The lawyer coughed again. "There is one other thing, gentlemen." He turned over a page. "His lordship has made available to each of you immediately the sum of five thousand pounds to facilitate your pursuit of a suitable bride. He understands that you are all, for whatever reason, somewhat short of funds."

"And never did man speak a truer word," Jasper murmured. He regarded his brothers. "Well, gentlemen, despite the obvious difficulties, do we agree to this joint venture?"

Sebastian shrugged. Then he came forward, hand outstretched. "I do . . . Perry?"

"Yes . . . yes, of course." Peregrine jumped to his feet, his own hand extended. "But it's a damn smoky business, whatever you say."

"Of course . . . what else did you expect from Uncle Bradley?" Jasper inquired, taking his brothers' hands in turn. He raised his glass in a toast. "Here's to the success of our enterprise."

CHAPTER ONE

The Earl of Blackwater moved through the crowd of drunken revelers outside the Cock tavern in Covent Garden and strolled in leisurely fashion along the colonnaded Piazza. His black garments would have been somber except for the rich luster of the velvet and the soft cream of the lace at his throat and wrists. He wore no jewelry, only the blood-red ruby embedded in his signet ring. His black hair was confined at the neck with a simple silver clasp and he carried a black tricorne hat, its brim edged with gold braid.

He paused to take a leisurely pinch of snuff as he gazed idly around the thronged scene. It was midafternoon of a glorious green and gold day in early October and folk were out in force, men and women of every class and occupation. Dandies lounged with painted whores on their arms. Covent Garden was a market where the main commodity was flesh, whether offered by fashionably dressed ladies accompanied by their footmen, or their less fortunate sisters standing in the doorways of the coffeehouses and the wooden shacks that crowded the outskirts of the central court, lifting ragged petticoats to display the invitation of a plump thigh.

Jasper set his hat on his head as he walked, one hand as always on the hilt of his sword, both mind and body alert. The nimble fingers of a pickpocket were all too frequently encountered in Covent Garden and anywhere else in the city where crowds gathered.

He had just been visiting Viscount Bradley and felt the need to breathe some fresh cool air after the viscount's overheated bedchamber. He had found his uncle as irascible as ever, but out of bed and seated by a blazing fire, imbibing, liberally and against his physician's orders, the rich ruby contents of a decanter of port. Father Cosgrove, quill in hand, sat at the secretaire in the window embrasure, and the rather pathetic relief he had evinced at the earl's unannounced arrival earned Jasper's sympathy once more.

A slight smile touched his lips as Jasper recalled his uncle's response to the offer his nephew had made to have his body transported to the family mausoleum at Black-water Manor on his death — a response that had caused poor Father Cosgrove to seek the instant comfort of his rosary, his lips moving in silent prayer.

I don't want to rot in the company of those sanctimonious, holier-than-thou ancestors, nephew. I've lived my life and paid for my sins, and I'll lie with other good, honest sinners in a good, honest churchyard.

He had then demanded to know how far Jasper had progressed in his search for a wife, a question that had reminded the Earl of Blackwater of his negligence thus far. He had left his uncle's house and was now strolling in Covent Garden, mulling over what seemed an intractable problem. He had no desire to marry anyone, let alone some forlorn creature in need of spiritual salvation; he had enough need of that for himself. But without his uncle's money, he was eventually facing debtors' prison and a pauper's grave, not to mention the irretrievable loss of everything the Blackwater family held dear. And, he had to admit, he had enough pride in his family's name and lineage not to view its loss with sanguinity.

He realized his footsteps were taking him towards a pieman. The tray slung around the lad's neck was laden with golden offerings, fragrant steam rising from the puffed crusts. Only then did Jasper recognize his own hunger. He hadn't eaten since the previous evening and the scent set his juices running. He was reaching for the leather pouch of coins he kept in an inside pocket of his waistcoat when something ran headlong into his midriff.

A few minutes earlier Clarissa Astley had been weaving through the mass of people thronging the Great Piazza, trying to keep her quarry in view. Fortunately Luke was a tall man, and he wore a high-crowned beaver hat that made him even easier to keep in her line of sight. At nine o'clock that morning her weeklong vigil had been rewarded. Luke had left his house on Ludgate Hill, walking with a purposeful air along High Holborn. Clarissa had followed, easily keeping a discreet distance, ducking in and out of the busy traffic on the thoroughfare.

She had no idea where he was going but could only hope that he would take her to her brother, or at least to somewhere that would give her a clue as to where Francis was being held. Luke's destination had become clear after a few side turns, and shortcuts down alleyways and through shadowy courts. He was making for Covent Garden. So, she had come full circle, Clarissa reflected wearily. She had left King Street in Covent Garden early that morning and was now back there a mere four hours later.

She ducked into the colonnade of the Great Piazza, keeping him in view. He was walking more slowly now, glancing at the pamphlets on display in the booths lining the Piazza, and she realized almost too late that he had stopped dead outside one famous for its particularly obscene offerings. She just managed to stop herself from running into him and dived sideways, head down. She was brought up short when her lowered head met resistant flesh, and her shoulders were grasped ungently by a pair of hard hands.

"Oh, no, you don't," an annoyed voice declared. "Believe me, miss, I'm more than up to the tricks of a pickpocket."

Clarissa raised her head and stared in incredulous indignation at the man holding her.

"Let go of me." She tried to wriggle her shoulders free of his grip.

"Why should I? You were about to rob me," Jasper pointed out almost affably.

Her voice, although clearly furious, was

surprisingly melodious and he could detect no hint of a London twang. He scrutinized her intently. His hands were curled in a tight grip over a pair of slim shoulders. A pair of jade-green eyes gazed up at him in surprise and anger, and they belonged to one of the loveliest countenances Jasper had ever encountered.

"I most certainly was *not,*" Clarissa declared, outraged. "Why would I want to rob you?"

"Why would you not?" he asked mildly. Covent Garden held all sorts of ruffians and mountebanks of both sexes, and despite this girl's beauteous countenance and the delicacy of her accent, there was nothing else about her to set her apart from the rest of the rogues in the Piazza. She was clad simply in a countrified linen gown and apron. Her hair was tied back in a kerchief and he could see only a few stray reddish-gold tendrils on her forehead. It was enough however to make him want to see the rest of it.

His anger was gone, replaced with curiosity and the most definite stirrings of a more personal interest. "I doubt you have much coin about you, which is the general case with pickpockets." It was a guess but one he hoped might elicit more information.

"You've no right to make such an assumption," she declared. "What I have and don't have is my business."

"As long as you don't have anything of mine, I would agree with you." He frowned down at her. "If you weren't attempting to rob me, what were you doing bumping into me in that deliberate fashion?"

Her attention seemed to have wandered, he realized incredulously. Instead of giving him an answer, she was peering around him with an air of acute frustration, ignoring the hold he still had on her shoulders. "Now I've lost him," she muttered.

"Lost whom? Answer me, if you please. Whom have you lost and why did you so deliberately bump into me, if you were not intending to pick my pocket?"

"I was trying to hide from someone," she explained impatiently. "And now, by detaining me, you've ruined everything."

"My apologies." His voice was dry. "Maybe one day I'll understand the logic of that. As far as I can see, I haven't revealed your presence to anyone with apparent interest in it." He looked pointedly around. The crowd went about its heedless way as always, and he could detect no suspiciously attentive glances in their direction.

"Why do you need to hide from someone?" Jasper was unwilling to release his grip on her shoulder, although she tried again to wriggle free. He was certain she would be off into the crowd before he could draw another breath and he wasn't prepared to lose her just yet.

"That's none of your business either," she said. "Just let me go, please. You have no right to detain me."

"Are you from one of the nunneries?" he asked, hazarding a guess. It would explain her presence in the Piazza. Possibly she was running from an unwelcome proposition. She was certainly lovely and fresh enough to attract only the best custom, and he could well imagine any one of the pimps and madams who ran the many such establishments in and around Covent Garden would find her a valuable acquisition. Her simple dress didn't indicate a top-class establishment, but judging by her accent someone had gone to some trouble to eradicate the rougher edges to her speech in preparation for a higher class of client, so maybe she was being groomed to take her place among the ranks of the elite courtesans in a good house.

Something flashed across the green eyes but he couldn't read it. Then she said, "Maybe, maybe not. What's it to you, sir?"

Her eyes narrowed suddenly. "Why, are you in the market for a little play?"

It was almost as if she was issuing a challenge, Jasper thought. She hadn't said one way or the other, but the obliqueness of her answer had to be confirmation of his suspicions. And then the obviousness of his next move made him laugh out loud.

The laugh disconcerted Clarissa. She was already regretting the ridiculous impulse that had prompted that last question. Sometimes the devil seemed to run her tongue and she was always having to deal with the unintended consequences of a glib statement or question.

"What's so funny?"

"Oh, just a rather delightful conjunction of supply and demand," he said. "I think you'll do. Oh, yes, I think you'll do very well."

"Do what?" She looked up at him, unease replacing her anger.

"A little job I need done," he said.

"What job?" She took a step back, but he tightened his hold on her shoulder.

"If you come with me, I'll explain."

"You must be mad. Let me go or I'll call the beadle."

He shook his head. "No, if anyone's going to call the beadle it'll be me. And whom do

31

you think he'll believe?"

Anger flashed again across the jade eyes. "That's not fair."

"No," he agreed. "But little in this life is. What's your name?"

"Clarissa." She had answered before she could stop herself and could have bitten out her tongue.

"Well, Clarissa, I suggest we go and find a glass of wine and something to fill our bellies and I will make you a proposition."

"I have no interest whatsoever in any proposition you might make . . . whoever you are." Her voice was as haughty as she could make it, acutely conscious as she was of the vulnerability of her position. He had the advantage in every way, as he'd just pointed out. No one would believe the word of a seemingly powerless, friendless girl roaming the colonnades of the Great Piazza against that of a powerful gentleman oozing wealth and privilege.

"Jasper St. John Sullivan, fifth Earl of Blackwater, at your service, madam." He smiled down at her, and the smile illuminated his expression as if lamps had been lit behind his eyes. "Would you do me the honor of dining with me?"

Clarissa blinked once and her gaze was suddenly both speculative and calculating.

Was there an opportunity here? If her present quest had taught her anything it was never to overlook the possibility of an opportunity. This gentleman could be a most powerful friend, and if anyone needed a friend at present it was she. And if the encounter turned sour, she could look after herself. She had proved that several times already.

Besides, there was something about the man, something about those black eyes, that pulled her to him. She wanted to know more about this proposition; maybe if what he wanted was something she could supply easily enough, she could bargain for his help in exchange. And besides, on a more mundane plane, she realized she was hungry. It had been a long time since dawn, when she'd broken her fast.

"Very well," she said, throwing caution to the wind. "The Angel has venison pie on Tuesdays."

"Then venison pie it shall be." He released her shoulder but instead took her arm, slipping it through his, and Clarissa felt as firmly if less obviously captured as before. It made her uneasy but she was in the most public venue, surrounded by folk who would surely come to her aid if she screamed for help. And then again, of course they wouldn't, she reflected wryly. But she knew how and where to place a knee to best advantage, and she had sharp teeth, and she could run faster than a man with a sword at his hip. She could vanish into the crowd before he'd realize which way she'd gone.

With such spurious comfort, she allowed herself to be led into the Angel tavern. It was dark, noisy, and crowded. At first glance she could see no empty space at any of the long tables and ale benches but her companion steered her effortlessly through the crowd to a small secluded table in a nook beside the fireplace. The two men sitting there glanced up as they approached, then, without a word spoken, they got up, took their tankards, and plunged into the fray in the center of the room.

The unspoken power of wealth and privilege again, Clarissa thought. "Amazing," she murmured. "They vanish at a look. It must be quite something to have such power, my lord."

He hooked a stool forward with his foot and gestured for her to take it. "Oh, one grows accustomed to it." A smile glimmered in his eyes again as he took the stool opposite her, and Clarissa realized that he was probably a match for any attempts to puncture his complacence with sarcasm.

Jasper glanced over his shoulder and beckoned imperatively at the tavern wench threading her way through the crowd, two overfull tankards spilling over her hands as she held them high above the throng. She responded with a nod, deposited the tankards on a table already wet and slippery with spilled ale, and weaved her way across to the nook, wiping her hands on her stained apron. Her quick glance took in the elegance of the gentleman and the rather drab appearance of his companion.

"What'll it be, sir?"

"Two dozen oysters, two tankards of Rhenish . . . and then the venison pie with a bottle of mine host's burgundy . . . the one he keeps in the back. He'll know which one."

The girl looked at him with a degree of admiration. "Yes, m'lord." She didn't bother to look again at Clarissa, who assumed rightly that the tavern wench had decided she'd seen her like before and knew exactly what commercial arrangement existed between them. "Jake don't usually let them bottles out in 'ere. Keeps 'em for private parties an' the like."

"I think you'll find he'll make an exception." Jasper took a pinch of snuff, then dropped the silver embossed box back into his deep coat pocket and regarded Clarissa with a speculative gleam.

"So, Clarissa, how long have you been in London?"

"What makes you think I haven't been here all my life?" She was somewhat taken aback by the question.

"Oh . . . just something about you . . . about your voice. You don't speak like a native Londoner."

"But neither do you, my lord," she pointed out.

"No, but then I too have my roots elsewhere in the country and count London as a place I visit."

"But you have a house here?"

"That is true. So, how long have you been in London?"

"A few months," she prevaricated, by no means ready to confide any personal details until she had established whether the earl could be of service to her.

"What part of the country are you from?" He leaned forward, sweeping crumbs off the table with his glove, before resting his forearms on the surface. His black eyes looked closely at her, but there was nothing unfriendly or dangerous in the look, Clarissa decided.

"Bedfordshire way," she said with a shrug. "I came to make my fortune." It seemed a reasonably vague explanation, one that could mean either any number of things or nothing at all. A throwaway comment. She laughed. "A fond hope, you might say."

"Not necessarily." He paused as the tavern girl leaned over his shoulder to put a platter of opened oysters in the middle of the table, the pearly gray mollusks glistening against the opalescent shells. She put two pewter tankards of golden wine beside the platter and backed away.

"Oysters are supposed to be an aphrodisiac," Jasper remarked, slurping one from the shell, savoring the liquid as it slipped down his throat. "But of course you know that." He reached for his tankard, drank deeply, watching his companion the whole time.

Why would she know that? Clarissa wondered, taking an oyster from the platter. It certainly wasn't a fact either her mother or her governess had felt necessary to impart. She sucked the oyster neatly from the shell with a flick of her tongue, and then took another. She paused with the shell held close to her lips, wondering why he was looking at her so closely, before flicking her tongue again and sucking the fishy morsel out of its shell.

Jasper was momentarily mesmerized. It was the most audaciously seductive gesture, and if she was setting out to capture a wealthy client she was going about it in a very skilled fashion. But for some reason the seductiveness, which in another woman would have amused and enticed him, didn't suit this one, and he realized that he did not like it one bit.

"What's the matter?" she demanded, setting down the empty shell and reaching for another. "Why're you looking at me like that?"

"Oh, don't play the innocent with me." He laughed with a touch of scorn and took another oyster. "I prefer my women to be straightforward, and my . . ." He hesitated, looking for the right word. "My arrangements . . . shall we say . . . to be equally so. A commodity is for sale, a price agreed, and all parties are satisfied."

Oh, sweet heaven, why in the world had she thought her response a clever way of dissipating curiosity? *She'd come to make her fortune.* How had she expected him to interpret that? It was time to bring an end to this charade; she was out of her league and just digging herself deeper and deeper into the cesspit.

She spoke with quiet vehemence. "I'm sure *your* women are more than happy to satisfy your demands, sir. *I,* on the other hand, don't come into that category and have absolutely no interest in them." She pushed back her stool, preparing to get up, but his hand shot out, pinning her own hand to the table.

"Just a minute, Clarissa. We both know what this is all about, so let's not play games. Believe me, if you hope to increase your price with such artifice it won't work. I don't find it amusing or appealing."

Clarissa, incredulous, stared at him in silence. But her incredulity was directed more at herself and her own stupidity. Of course she should have expected a proposition on these lines. He'd found her wandering the Piazza among the whores; she had not exactly denied that she lived in one of the nunneries — well, in honesty that would be hard to deny, but the circumstances were so different. She had to extricate herself as quickly as possible.

"Let me go, please."

He didn't move his hand, merely said impatiently, "My dear girl, you came with me to discuss a proposition. I could only have meant one kind of proposition, so don't pretend to be insulted."

Clarissa reached with her free hand for the tiny oyster fork and a second later the Earl of Blackwater, with a bellow of pain, brought his bleeding hand to his mouth. Clarissa was gone on the instant, her stool clattering to the floor with the violent speed of her exit.

Jasper stared after her, then with an oath he jumped to his feet, nearly colliding with the tavern wench bearing a crusted bottle of burgundy and a venison pie. He paused long enough to throw a coin on the table, then pushed his way through the taproom and out onto the Piazza. He searched the crowd looking for the girl and thought he caught sight of her disappearing around the corner of the colonnade. He set off in pursuit, his long stride eating up the yards.

He saw her as soon as he'd turned the corner from James Street. She was some way ahead and once paused to look back. He ducked behind a pillar and when she started off again, he followed, keeping his distance. He didn't know why he was bothering with this girl; there were plenty like her in the city. But he'd never come across one with quite such an arresting countenance, he amended. And there was something about her spirit, a quickness of wit that would make her the ideal player in the charade. And he was piqued by her quixotic behavior. Why would she treat a potentially well-paying client with such discourtesy? He rubbed his throbbing hand, conscious of a vengeful impulse to get his own back. She'd deprived him of his burgundy and venison pie into the bargain.

She had reached her destination. He stood in the doorway of a bagnio and watched as the girl disappeared into a discreet house on King Street. It was a nunnery run by one Mother Griffiths. A top-flight brothel catering to the highest class of client, certainly, but a house of ill repute nevertheless.

So much for Mistress Clarissa's protestations of innocence. Jasper smiled to himself. Whatever game she was playing, he could deal a better hand. He strolled across the street and lifted the brass knocker on the front door.

CHAPTER TWO

Clarissa entered the square hallway and heard the steward close the door behind her with a little sigh of relief. She felt exhausted, as if she'd just run from a pack of hounds. She had made a big mistake, somehow believing that she could look after herself in this depraved and bewildering city. What on earth had made her think she could tangle with a man like the Earl of Blackwater? Enter some kind of bargain with him?

Sounds of laughter, soft voices, and the faint strains of a pianoforte came from behind double doors leading off the hallway. Some of the girls must be entertaining already, although it was early in the day for their work to start. But most of them had regular clients whom they entertained with all the gracious hospitality of a lady of the manor. It was a very strange business, this matter of selling flesh.

She made her way up the broad stairs to

the wide second-floor landing, and then up a much narrower stair to the attic floor, where she had her own sanctuary, such as it was.

It was a small chamber high under the eaves with a dormer window looking down onto King Street. It was a maid's room, furnished simply enough with a cot against one wall, a rickety-legged dresser on which reposed a cracked basin and ewer, and a low chair by a small grate, empty now, but she would have to pay for coal once winter set in, pay for it and haul it up three flights of stairs from the basement coal cellar.

But by the time winter came, she and Francis would be settled somewhere safe and secluded, far away from the city. Clarissa sat down on the cot to untie her kerchief and kick off her shoes. Really she should have been back on the streets searching for a more salubrious lodging, but her feet ached after her round-trip trek to Ludgate Hill, and for the moment she couldn't summon up the energy. At least here she was alone and unthreatened, however inappropriate the environment.

Clarissa had found her present garret just after her arrival in London by responding to an advertisement in one of the pamphlet shops in the Piazza. Of course, with hindsight she should have realized that rooms for rent in Covent Garden were intended for a particular type of lodger, one who was expected to pay her rent on her back. After this morning's debacle, it seemed she still hadn't learned the facts of Covent Garden life.

Mother Griffiths, after her initial astonishment at being applied to by a young woman who was clearly not a prostitute, had laughed heartily and agreed to rent the garret if Clarissa paid the same as the working girls the house. Tired and alone in a city that scared her as much as it confused her, Clarissa had been comforted by her landlady's friendly disposition and accepted the arrangement. But now she knew she couldn't continue to stay there. She had already had several difficult encounters with stray clients on the stairs, and the prospect so unnerved her that she found it hard to garner the courage to leave her chamber in the evening.

And now, like some naïve idiot, she had given the impression to a strange man that she was open to any proposition that would be acceptable to any of the usual inhabitants of the bagnios and nunneries lining the Piazza. Well, it had been a narrow escape and another lesson well learned. And she'd lost Luke into the bargain. Although she thought now that it was unlikely his destination in Covent Garden would have revealed anything about Francis's whereabouts. Luke had had pleasure of some kind in mind; why else visit the Piazza?

In the morning she would renew her watch on his house and hopefully she would have better luck then. Until then, there was a whole afternoon and evening to get through, listening to the squeals, the bangs, the creaking beds, the occasional cry, footsteps up and down the stairs, all the sounds of a lively brothel at night.

She lay back on the cot, trying to ignore the fact that she was hungry. Two oysters didn't go far and she could find it in her to regret missing not only the rest of the oysters but the venison pie and the burgundy. Maybe she should have pretended to listen to the earl and at least enjoyed a good meal in return. She closed her eyes.

Was Francis hungry?

All desire to sleep vanished and Clarissa sat up abruptly. How could she forget why she was here, even for a second? She was no closer to finding her little brother than she had been a week ago when she'd first arrived. And one thing that was becoming abundantly clear . . . she wasn't going to find him without help. The city was such a heaving, confusing monster of a place, a maze of twisting lanes and alleys, strange dark courts filled with shadows, and everywhere people, all hurrying, noisy, and rough. Every corner seemed to hide some danger, some sinister threat, and each time she ventured forth, Clarissa had to steel herself.

She got up from the cot and went to the leather chest that contained the few possessions she had brought with her to London. This was never intended to be an extended visit. Once she had Francis in safekeeping, she would shake the dust of this grim city from her heels and they would find a safe haven, somewhere where they could hide for the next ten months. Kneeling in front of the chest she lifted the lid and took out the letter. It was an ill-written, misspelled scrawl, but the message was clear enough. If only she could find the anonymous messenger . . .

The steward who answered the Earl of Blackwater's imperative knock at the door bowed deeply. "My lord. May I say what a pleasure it is to see you?"

"You may." The earl handed him his hat and cane as he strode into the hall. "Is

Mistress Griffiths at home?"

"Yes, my lord. I'll tell her you're here at once. Would you wait in the parlor?" The steward opened the door onto a small, pleasantly furnished chamber, where gentlemen callers were accustomed to await their ladies. The room was empty and Jasper walked across to the window, looking idly out into the street, his hands clasped loosely at his back.

The door opened again in a very few minutes. "Why, my lord Blackwater, this is a rare pleasure indeed." A woman in a billowing sacque gown of a startling shade of yellow, her hair piled high beneath the folds of an elaborate striped turban, closed the door behind her and regarded her visitor quizzically. "Dare I hope you are come to do business at my humble establishment, my lord?"

Jasper turned from the window, a slight smile on his lips. He bowed. "Good afternoon, Nan." He put up his glass and remarked, "You are in remarkably good looks, madam."

"Oh, flatterer." She waved a hand at him. "I'm fagged to death if the truth be told. Will you take a glass of Madeira?"

"With pleasure." He took a seat in the corner of the sofa, regarding her still with that faint smile. Margaret Griffiths, known to her intimates as Nan, was a woman of a certain age whose heavily painted face did little to hide the ravages of a life lived at the edge of debauchery. Her gown was suited to a much younger woman and the bubbling swell of an overripe bosom lacked the pristine creaminess the deep décolletage was designed to show off. But no one would make the mistake of dismissing Mother Griffiths as a raddled old hag past her prime. She was one of the sharpest business-women in the city.

He swung his quizzing glass idly back and forth as he asked, "So, talking of business, how is it these days?"

"Oh, well enough, as always." She handed him a glass and took a seat opposite. "There are always customers for the commodity I am selling, in good times and in bad." She sipped her Madeira. "But you, Jasper, have not been one of them, at least not since you attained your majority."

Jasper smiled slightly. He was remember-ing his first visit to Mother Griffiths's establishment at the age of sixteen, escorted by his uncle Bradley on one of the viscount's rare returns to England from his business empire in India. Lord Bradley had been horrified to discover that his nephew was still a virgin and had set about repairing the omission with a dedicated enthusiasm. That, of course, had been quite some years before his lordship had decided to return to the fold of the Catholic church. And Jasper was still unconvinced of that particular conversion.

"Yes, you did enjoy your visits then," Mistress Griffiths said, reading his mind and the significance of the reminiscent smile. "What was her name, that young filly who took your heart? Meg . . . Mollie . . . Millie . . ."

"Lucille." Jasper corrected with a dry smile. "Lucy."

"Oh, yes, I remember." She nodded. "Took your heart and broke it too, as I recall."

"I was a naïve simpleton." Jasper shook his head. "It never occurred to me, foolish lad that I was, that a lady of the night couldn't afford to let her emotions confuse the transaction."

"And you've avoided such ladies ever since, as I understand it." She lifted an eyebrow.

"I prefer these arrangements to be exclusive," he agreed. "And that, my dear Nan, brings me to the point of this visit . . . not, of course, that your company alone isn't incentive enough."

She laughed. "Such pretty words, m'dear; you always did have a smooth tongue, even as a stripling." She reached for the decanter beside her and refilled their glasses. "So, to the point."

"I came across one of your young ladies in the Piazza a short while ago."

"Oh?" Her eyes narrowed. "I wasn't aware anyone had left the house thus far today. For the most part they're either still abed getting their beauty sleep or preparing themselves for the evening. Only Anna and Marianna are entertaining in the salon."

"This is a rather unusual young lady," Jasper said slowly, taking a sip of his wine. "Rather plainly dressed, but far from a plain countenance. By the name of Clarissa, I believe."

Nan Griffiths's face was abruptly swept clear of all expression, something Jasper remembered from the past. When it came to discussing and negotiating business, Nan Griffiths had the ability of the most gifted gamester to conceal her thoughts.

"Clarissa," she murmured. "Yes . . . very fresh . . . a newcomer . . . a country girl."

"So she said."

"You spoke with her at length?"

"I tried to, but something I said offended

her." He glanced ruefully at his hand. An ugly bruise was developing around the two tiny pinpricks of the oyster fork. "I'm not sure whether it was *what* I said, or the manner in which I said it. Either way, she reacted somewhat vehemently. I had been intending to make her a proposition but she ran from me before I could begin. I followed her here."

"Did she . . . did she say she worked here?"

He shook his head. "Not in so many words, but as I said I followed her. I saw her come in and assumed . . . unless . . ." He stopped, frowning. "Is she in domestic service . . . a maidservant?"

"No . . . no, not that." Nan tapped her painted fingernails against the wooden arm of her chair. "You wished to make her a proposition . . . what kind of a proposition?"

"I would prefer to make that directly to Clarissa," he said. "Forgive me, Nan, but it's a rather delicate matter. I would, of course, pay your usual commission."

"And her services would be exclusively yours."

He nodded. "Without question."

Nan rose to her feet. "If you'll excuse me for a few minutes, Jasper." She sailed from the room, her loose train flowing behind

51

her. She went upstairs and into the small chamber that served as her office, closing the door firmly. She sat down at the secretaire and gazed into the middle distance. She had never turned down the opportunity to make money and she didn't intend to turn down this one. But the girl in the garret was not one of her employees.

Nan was well aware that that astonishing beauty compounded by a fresh-faced innocence would attract the very highest bidders. It was inevitable, of course, that she would lose the innocence, but there were plenty of sophisticated buyers who would then pay a small fortune for an experienced courtesan with that elegance of form and beauty of countenance. Mistress Clarissa could have a satisfactorily long career if she played her cards right. But Nan had sensed that the girl was not alone in the world, for all the vulnerability of her present position, and natural caution had kept her from attempting to persuade, or coerce, her into the harlot's life until she had found out more about her.

But this put a different complexion on things. Jasper St. John Sullivan, fifth Earl of Blackwater, was the kind of protector any girl would be lucky to have. He had no deviant appetites, unless he'd developed them in the last ten years, and he was known to honor his commitments. He would pay the procuress well, and the girl would be well looked after for the duration of whatever arrangement Jasper had in mind.

Nan made her decision. She left her study and climbed the stairs to the attic. She knocked once sharply on the door to Clarissa's chamber and entered on the knock. "Ah, good, you're here." She closed the door and regarded the startled Clarissa with an assessing eye. "How old are you, my dear?"

Clarissa had jumped to her feet at the sound of the knock. Startled, she stared at her visitor. "I have twenty summers, ma'am, but what is that to do with anything?"

"Quite a lot," Nan stated. "It means you're no child, for all your countrified innocence."

Clarissa flushed with mingled embarrassment and annoyance. "I may be innocent in some things, ma'am, but I can have a care for myself, believe me."

"Well, we shall see." Nan went briskly to the dilapidated armoire in the corner of the room. "Do you have another gown, something a little less plain?"

Clarissa stiffened. "No, but what if I had? Why does that interest you, ma'am?"

"You have a visitor, my dear. A very important visitor who is most anxious to have speech with you. I believe you met him in the Piazza this afternoon."

Clarissa swallowed, drawing herself up to her full height. "I met a gentleman certainly, or at least he appeared to be a gentleman; his behavior indicated otherwise."

"The Earl of Blackwater is a gentleman in every respect." Her landlady contradicted her briskly as she riffled through the scant collection of garments in the armoire. "And he is downstairs waiting to speak to you about a proposition he would make you."

"But I stuck an oyster fork in his hand," Clarissa exclaimed. "Why would he want to talk to me now?"

"You did what?" Nan, who was rarely surprised by anything, could not hide her astonishment. She spun around to stare in disbelief at Clarissa.

"Well, he insulted me," Clarissa stated, trying not to sound apologetic. She had nothing to apologize for. "It was instinctive . . . I didn't think. Is he here to haul me off to the justice of the peace for assault?"

"Oh, I don't think that's what his lordship has in mind." Nan chuckled, turning back to her examination of the contents of the armoire. "Vindictive he is not. But perhaps, to make amends, you should listen to his proposition. No one will compel you to accept it." This last was said into the contents of the armoire and Clarissa barely heard it.

"This is a mite prettier than that dull old thing you're wearing." Nan brought out a simple gown of bronze muslin. "Change into this, dear, and then run along downstairs and talk to him. You owe him an apology at the very least."

"Maybe I do, but I don't need to change my dress for that," Clarissa declared. "And neither do I need to listen to any proposition. But I will, in courtesy, apologize for hurting him." *Even if it's just to prove that I am more mannerly than an earl.* But that she kept to herself, adding instead, "He owes me an apology too for being so insulting. And so I shall tell him." She sat on the cot to put her shoes on again. "Where is he, ma'am?"

"In the small parlor to the left of the front door." Nan wisely gave up any further attempt to work on her lodger, sensing that it would be useless at best and put up her defenses at worst. She followed Clarissa out of the chamber and downstairs.

Clarissa ran lightly down the two flights of stairs, in a hurry to be done with this awkward business. She had no desire to be always looking over her shoulder for a vengeful earl at her heels, so a quick apology for the injury, and it would be over and done with. She tried to ignore the flicker of curiosity about the proposition. What did a man in the earl's position offer a harlot? It would be interesting to know in a general kind of way. But then, ruefully remembering the old adage about curiosity and cats, she reflected that her curiosity had always been a besetting sin and had led her into more trouble than she cared to revisit.

She laid a hand on the latch of the door, telling herself that she was safe enough here, much less vulnerable in the house than on the open street, and there was a certain sense of security, whether false or not, imparted by the presence of Mistress Griffiths and the steward, standing sentinel in the hall behind her.

Jasper stood up as she entered. His first thought was that her hair, no longer hidden by the kerchief, was every bit as magnificent as he'd expected. It swept from a widow's peak above her broad forehead in a glistening red-gold cascade to her shoulders, and his fingers itched to run themselves through the luxuriant silken mass. She stood with her back to the door, and her green eyes, fixed upon his countenance, held a distinctly militant spark. Her mouth was set in a firm line and a frown creased her forehead between fair, delicately arched eyebrows.

"I understand you have something to say to me, sir." Her voice was cold, and there was nothing about her posture that indicated she accepted any differences in their social status, nothing that indicated she was the seller and he was the buyer, she the commoner and he the aristocrat. Jasper was intrigued. He had never before come across a Covent Garden denizen who behaved as if she was anything else.

"You left me somewhat abruptly earlier." He moved a chair forward for her. "I would like to renew our conversation. May I offer you a glass of Madeira?"

She shook her head and remained standing by the door. "No, thank you. If I didn't feel guilty about hurting your hand, I wouldn't be here at all. So, as a form of apology I will hear you out, but please don't take long about it."

Jasper rubbed his hand reflectively, contemplating her in silence for a minute before asking, "What did I say that upset you so?"

She shrugged impatiently. "It matters little now. Could you please say what you came to say and then go?" A thought suddenly struck her and she wondered irritably why she hadn't thought to ask as soon as she walked into the room. "How did you find me here?"

"I followed you." He smiled, and again it was as if a lamp had been lit behind his eyes, it so transformed his expression. He extended his hands palm-up in a gesture of surrender. "My dear girl, could we cry truce? I beg your pardon for insulting you earlier, although I have to confess I don't quite understand how I did. I was merely drawing an assumption from the obvious." He moved an expressive hand around the room. "You'll have to forgive me if I point out the obvious, but you do live here, under the protection of Nan Griffiths."

And the sooner she moved out the better, Clarissa thought grimly. Without revealing her true circumstances, and she couldn't possibly do that, she had no choice but to leave him with his assumptions. "Can we conclude this conversation now? I have things to do."

"You still haven't heard my proposition," he pointed out. "Would you please take a seat?" There was a touch of impatience in his tone now and his eyes had lost their earlier warmth. He indicated the chair he had brought forward for her, and Clarissa, after a moment's hesitation, sat down.

"Now, we will drink a glass of Madeira together and begin afresh." He handed her a glass and resumed his seat in the corner of the sofa again. "To come straight to the point, I need you to marry me."

Clarissa choked on her wine. She just managed to set down the glass before it spilled everywhere, then succumbed to a violently spluttering fit of coughing. She fumbled in vain for a handkerchief in the wide lace-edged sleeve of her gown.

"Take this." An elegant square of Mechlin lace was dropped in her lap and she mopped at her streaming eyes.

"Thank you." She dabbed her mouth with the handkerchief and then crumpled it into a ball in her hand as she raised her pink face and stared at him with damp and reddened eyes. "I must have misheard you."

"Oh, I doubt that," he said with a shake of his head. "I'm sure you heard me correctly, but if you promise not to choke again I'll repeat it if you wish."

She held out a hand as if to ward him off. "No, don't do that, I beg you. What an absurd thing to say."

He seemed to consider the matter before saying, "I can see how you might think that. But you haven't heard all the details as yet."

"Spare me the details." Clarissa began to

get up. "I don't see why you should wish to make game of me, but now you've amused yourself so thoroughly at my expense I will take my leave."

"Sit down, Clarissa."

The peremptory tone was so unexpected she dropped back into her chair and stared at him again. "I don't understand."

"No, of course you don't. But if you'd give me a chance to explain I hope to enlighten you."

Clarissa continued to regard him with all the fascination of a paralyzed rabbit with a fox. She remained in her seat, unsure which of them was mad but certain one of them was.

"I wish you to play a part for a few months. It will enrich you beyond your wildest dreams if you can play it convincingly enough, and I can safely promise you that you will never have to earn your living in places such as this again."

"But I d—" Clarissa closed her lips firmly on the denial. Some devil prompted her to hear the full insanity of this scheme. She clasped her hands over his handkerchief, then let them lie easily in her lap and tilted her head in a composed invitation for him to continue.

Jasper chuckled. "Oh, I can see you playing the part to perfection," he murmured. "I had the feeling from the first moment of our meeting that you were rather more than you appeared." He leaned forward. "Listen carefully."

Clarissa listened in incredulous silence. In order to claim a fortune for himself the earl needed a harlot who would pretend to be in love with him, give up her evil ways, and embrace a life of strict convention and morality in order to marry him. In return, after the wedding the earl would settle upon her a munificent sum that would enable her to live her life exactly as she chose.

"It would probably be better if you chose to live abroad, at least for a time, after the formalities are concluded," Jasper finished. "As I said, you will have an easy competence that will enable you to go anywhere you choose."

"Is this marriage to be legally binding?" Clarissa was so fascinated by this rigmarole that she found herself responding as if it was a proposition to be seriously considered.

"It will have to be." Jasper spoke briskly. "But after a certain length of time we will have the marriage annulled."

"On what grounds? It is to be a Catholic ceremony, as I understand it. There are no acceptable grounds."

"Non-consummation," he informed her drily. "That is generally sufficient."

Clarissa felt herself blush a little, much to her annoyance. "Just how would you go about this charade?"

"Quite simply." Jasper rose and brought over the decanter. He filled Clarissa's glass and she was too absorbed in the wild tangle of her thoughts to stop him. He filled his own and sat down again. "We will begin in the usual way. I will become one of your clients, and will request of Mistress Griffiths your exclusive services. This will involve a contract to which all three of us will append our signatures."

She ought to interrupt, to tell him he was laboring under a terrible misunderstanding, but somehow the words would not come to her lips. She looked down at her clasped hands in her lap and let the earl's plan take shape around her.

"And then I will set you up in a house of your own and you will become my public mistress. We will be seen at the theatre, dining in the most select venues, and eventually you will be introduced to society. Once society has accepted you, then the marriage can take place and the conditions of my uncle's will satisfied."

He leaned back and regarded her with a

questioningly raised eyebrow. "So, what do you say, Mistress Clarissa?"

"Is society likely to accept a known harlot as one of its own?"

"It's been done before. Courtesans have become the acknowledged mistresses of princes of the blood and on occasion the wives of aristocrats. You have the requisite beauty, and I will provide the necessary training in the courtly arts to ensure that your previous existence will cease to be relevant."

Oh, will you? Clarissa lowered her eyes so that he wouldn't see their flash of scornful indignation. *What right had he to assume she lacked such an education?* But then she had to admit that her present circumstances probably gave him, if not the right, at least the excuse to assume so. Whereas in fact she had had a rigorous education in all such matters at the hands of a mother who based her own station in life on her position as the third daughter of an earl, whose marriage to a country squire, albeit a wealthy one, had been something of a comedown. It had been a love match, and remained so throughout her mother's life, but Lady Lavinia Astley had decided that her daughter should form a union that reflected her maternal lineage and had educated her accordingly.

Lady Lavinia would be turning in her grave if she could see her only daughter now, discussing such a proposition in the parlor of a Covent Garden brothel. Or would she? The proposition would make a countess of her daughter. Suddenly the absurdity of the paradox was too much. Clarissa began to laugh and once she'd begun she couldn't stop.

Jasper stared at her, wondering if he had a hysterical woman on his hands. He was about to summon Nan with smelling salts and water when the paroxysms ceased and she leaned back in her chair, his handkerchief pressed to her eyes.

"I fail to see what's so amusing." He took a sip of wine, unable to disguise his annoyance and what he had to admit was chagrin. "I offer you an opportunity any other woman in your position would give her right hand for, and it sends you into whoops of laughter."

"I do beg your pardon," she managed to gasp after a moment. "It was most unmannerly of me. But I happened to think of something and it just set me off."

"Enlighten me, pray."

She glanced across and saw that she had seriously offended him. Short of putting him right as to her position there was little she could do about it. "Something you said made me remember something from long ago, something I'd forgotten all about. I'm truly sorry. It was very discourteous."

Jasper frowned at her. Once again he had the unmistakable impression that all was not what it seemed with this Titian-haired, dewy-eyed beauty. "Well, do you have an answer for me?" he demanded.

Clarissa realized that she did have an answer. Somewhere during this extraordinary hour or so she had come to half a conclusion, and it was by no means one she'd expected to reach. "I would ask for a little time to consider, my lord." She rose from her chair. "Will you grant me that?"

"If I must." He rose with her. "I will return at noon tomorrow . . . oh, no, that will be too early for you, of course. You'll be unlikely to seek your bed before dawn."

"No . . . no, that will be a fine time. I do not anticipate a busy night," she said with a smile, amazed at herself. "I'm expecting no regular clients tonight." *It was true,* she told herself firmly.

"Then at noon tomorrow." He bowed as she moved to the door. "I bid you farewell, Mistress Clarissa."

"And I you, my lord." She curtsied and

slipped from the room.

Nan Griffiths materialized in the hall the minute Clarissa had closed the door behind her. "Well, my dear. What was his lordship's proposition?" Her shrewd eyes scrutinized the girl's countenance looking for clues.

"Perhaps he should explain that to you himself, ma'am." Clarissa moved to the stairs.

"And did you accept it?" Her voice sharpened.

"Not as yet. I asked for time to consider. His lordship will come for his answer at noon tomorrow."

"I see." Nan looked thoughtful. "Is there anything you need this evening, my dear, to help you make your decision?"

Clarissa didn't stop to think. It was almost evening already and she'd eaten two oysters since her dawn breakfast. "I own I am very hungry, ma'am, and thirsty. I have much to think of and would prefer not to go out to find my supper."

"I shall have supper brought up to you, my dear. And maybe you'd care for a bit of fire in the grate . . . the evenings are drawing in."

"That would be lovely, ma'am. I'm most grateful."

"Oh, don't give it another thought. Go

along upstairs and it'll be taken care of immediately."

Clarissa ran up the stairs, astonished at herself. She seemed to be becoming someone she didn't know at all. In the quiet of her own chamber she closed the door and went to the window. As dusk fell over the city the night sounds of Covent Garden grew ever livelier as the hummums in the Little Piazza opened their doors and music and laughter poured forth from the taverns and bawdy houses of the Great Piazza.

She was filled with a strange energy, almost a vibration of the senses, as if she stood on the brink of some life-altering experience. A knock at the door startled her from her intense reverie.

A manservant came in with a laden tray followed by a girl, little more than a child, struggling with a scuttle of coal. The child laid the fire and produced flint and tinder from her apron pocket, while the manservant set the tray on the dresser.

"That be all, miss?" The man looked sourly at her, obviously unaccustomed to waiting upon young women in the servants' garret.

"Thank you." Clarissa smiled warmly, turning to the girl. "And thank you, too, my dear. The fire is doing well."

They left her and she examined the contents of the tray. Roast chicken with a compote of mushrooms, crusty bread, cheese, and an almond tart would certainly compensate for her missed venison pie, and the flagon of burgundy would go some way to compensate for the loss of the fine burgundy in the Angel.

She filled a goblet from the flagon, then took that and her platter to the small chair beside the now cheerful glow of the fire. She ate with relish and, finally replete, put her platter on the floor, took up the goblet, and stretched her feet to the fire. Now it was time to think as clearly as she had ever thought in her life.

CHAPTER THREE

It had been a glorious May day when Clarissa's father died. He had been sick since the beginning of the year, but in his usual stalwart fashion had refused to acknowledge it. His old friend, the village doctor, had given him physics that he'd refused to take, had advised rest that he'd refused to take, had forbidden riding to hounds, to no avail. For as long as the ground was soft enough, the hounds eager, and his hunters champing at the bit, Squire Astley would not miss a day's hunting across the glorious Kent countryside.

The orchards had been in full bloom, the County truly earning its title of the garden of England on that afternoon when Clarissa stood by her father's chair in the library and realized that at some point in the last hour, since she had left him peacefully reading, he had slipped away. His book had fallen to the floor and automatically she bent to pick it up. She had been expecting his death but it still stunned her and she felt winded, as if struck in the stomach. She had sensed the emptiness of the room the moment she had walked in; the presence that had been her father was no longer there, and now she stood for long minutes trying to grasp the reality. His skin was still warm, his hair still thick and lustrous as it had been in life, but she was alone in the room.

Alone in the room and, for the first time in her twenty years on earth, on her own. No longer would she have the knowledge of her father's strength at her back, his sometimes sardonic humor hauling her back from the more emotional flights she had taken during her childhood and young adulthood, his humorous but nonetheless powerful intercessions between the ambitions of his wife for their daughter and Clarissa's own frequently conflicting wishes.

Francis Astley had always been behind his daughter, his love a constant in her growing. And only now, in the great void left by his absent spirit, did she realize how much she had relied on that love, on that strength.

Clarissa wasn't sure how long she stood there but finally she pulled the bell by the fireplace. Hesketh, the butler, answered the summons immediately. He glanced towards his late master's chair and with instant comprehension said he would summon the physician.

"Yes, that would be best." Clarissa knew she sounded vague and distant. She would deal with her own grief later, but now she had to break the news to her little brother. Francis was ten and five years earlier had lost his mother. Lady Lavinia had died giving birth to a stillborn babe, and the squire's enduring grief had cast a pall over the little household until finally he had returned his attention to the living. The bond then between father and son had grown stronger than ever, and while Clarissa had tried to prepare the child for the squire's imminent death once she herself recognized its inevitability, she was not convinced Francis had taken it in.

Any more than she had, she thought. Knowing something was going to happen was one thing, the reality after the fact quite another.

Now she left Hesketh to deal with the practicalities and went in search of her brother. She found him, as she expected and hoped, in the stables with one of his favorite people, Silas, the head groom. Silas was generally a taciturn man but he never showed any irritation or impatience with the child's nonstop chatter and endless questions. He would be an invaluable support when it came to helping Francis come to terms with his father's death.

They had buried Squire Astley a week later. He had been well loved in the County where he'd served as Master of Hounds and Justice of the Peace for most of his adult life, and the church and the graveyard had been so full of mourners Clarissa had given orders that tables should be set up upon the lawns to host the crowds who came up to the house to pay their respects to the grieving family.

That afternoon the family lawyer, another close friend of the squire's, had solemnly read the will to the only surviving members of the family: the squire's two children, Clarissa and Francis, and his brother, Luke.

Luke . . . so very different from his older brother. Where the squire had been powerfully built, bluff and hearty, always straight in his dealings with his fellows, Luke was tall, thin faced, with angular features and small, deep-set eyes that never met another's gaze. Hard and cold as little brown stones, they slithered away from all contact even as he smiled and honeyed words dripped from his lips.

Clarissa had always disliked and distrusted

him, although he had never given her overt reason. Her distaste for his company was instinctive, although her father treated his brother with the same courtesy and consideration he afforded to everyone and Luke was always a welcome visitor to the gracious redbrick manor house that had been his own childhood home. He visited rarely, however, and Clarissa was convinced he only came when he needed something from his brother, or, she suspected, when he was running away from his creditors.

On that May afternoon the four of them had gathered in the library. Clarissa could even now hear again the sound of voices drifting in from the lawns beyond the mullioned windows that stood open to the soft air perfumed with blossom from the surrounding cherry orchards. She could feel the gentle breeze that lifted tendrils of her hair on the nape of her neck, and she could hear Lawyer Danforth's dry tones as he read the will.

" 'I, Francis Evelyn Astley, being of sound mind, do hereby leave my fortune and estate to my son and heir, Francis Charles Astley. To my daughter, Clarissa Elizabeth Astley, when she attains her majority, I leave, in addition to her inheritance from her mother, the sum of ten thousand pounds. My children will be in the guardianship of my brother Luke Victor Astley until my daughter attains her twenty-first birthday. Upon reaching her majority, my daughter will assume the guardianship of my son. Until that time my daughter is to receive the same quarterly allowance from the estate as she has hitherto.' "

Clarissa could see Luke standing in front of the empty grate, his eyes on the richly hued carpet at his feet. Francis was sitting on the window seat swinging his nankeen-clad legs, his solemn little face still puffy and tearstained. When the lawyer finished reading Luke raised his eyes and cast one long speculative look at the child on the window seat, then his gaze flickered across his niece's countenance before he resumed his examination of the carpet. He said nothing but Clarissa was aware of a stab of dismay.

The lawyer cleared his throat and continued to read the list of minor bequests, but he'd lost the attention of his audience. Clarissa had known that she should not have been surprised at her uncle's guardianship. On paper it was the most logical, reasonable disposition for her parent to have made. She would not gain her majority for a year and could not assume responsibility for Francis until then. But she had hoped in her heart that her father would have left his children to the nominal care of one or both of his dearest friends, the doctor and the lawyer. He had known that she was perfectly capable of looking after Francis, running the house, and even conferring with her father's agent on estate matters. She could have looked to either of her father's old friends for advice. But Squire Astley would not have wished to offend his brother, and such an oversight would have looked strange to the world.

Luke returned to London almost immediately after the reading of the will, and for the next month, life continued along its usual paths. Francis began to come to terms with his father's death, although he became very dependent on his sister, needing to know where she was at any given moment. He continued to study with his tutor in the company of the vicar's children and Clarissa continued to run the household as she had done since her mother's death.

There had been no communication from Luke and Clarissa was beginning to think that the ten months remaining before her twenty-first birthday would continue unaffected by his guardianship . . . until one morning. She remembered coming downstairs, light-footed as always, ready and eager to start the day. She'd entered the breakfast parlor and all her optimistic anticipation vanished under a wash of disquiet. Luke was sitting at the breakfast table. His eyes were bloodshot and he looked thinner and paler than ever, his hand curled around a bumper of brandy, an untouched platter of sirloin in front of him.

"Why, Uncle, this is a surprise. We weren't expecting you."

His eyes slithered away from her startled gaze as he said, "I left London at dawn. I'm here to take Francis back to London with me. I'd like to leave within the next couple of hours, so could you get him ready and see to his packing?"

Clarissa protested, trying to keep her tone courteous and reasonable. "But, Uncle, you can't just tear a child from his home, without any warning. Francis is only just getting over Father's death. Why would you want to take him to London?"

Luke had drunk deep of his brandy before saying, "You are forgetting, Clarissa, that I am the boy's guardian. My brother left him to my care and it is my responsibility to honor his wishes. I can best do that by keeping Francis under my roof and supervising his education. It's time he had a decent tutor instead of the childish lessons he gets in the vicarage schoolroom."

"But . . . but my father thought it was adequate," she said, hearing how defensive she sounded.

"Sadly my brother was too ill in his last months to make the necessary decisions for his son." Luke's voice had a syrupy sweetness to it. "Believe me, my dear niece, I have only the child's best interests at heart. He is my nephew and I love him dearly."

A spurt of orange flame shook Clarissa free of her journey into the past. She sat up, her eyes focusing on the fire. It was dying down rapidly. She shoveled more coal onto the ashy embers and stirred it with the poker until the flame caught again, then she refilled her goblet. It was a painful journey she was making, but it was by no means done. The worst, that which had brought her to this extraordinary place, remained to be examined.

Poor little Francis had been distraught at the prospect of leaving his beloved sister. In the ten short years of his life he had lost his mother, then his father, and now was about to lose both his home and the last loving figure in his world. Clarissa tried to comfort him, promised she would visit him soon.

She fought to keep back her own tears, knowing they would only distress him further, but once the child had been bundled unceremoniously, weeping and struggling, into the carriage, the door firmly closed on his wails, her tears flowed freely. Luke had barely given the boy time to make his farewells to the people who formed his world: his nurse, the housekeeper, Silas, Hesketh. They all stood on the circular drive waving forlornly as the carriage, bearing its howling burden, disappeared through the stone gateway.

In the next week Clarissa wrote daily to her brother, and each day passed with no answer. She wrote to her uncle then and had a letter back telling her that Francis needed time to settle down in his new home and her letters upset him too much, so they were being withheld from him.

She found that impossible to believe but didn't know what to do about it, until the next letter from her uncle. Luke informed her that he had placed his ward in the family of a very well-regarded tutor who was educating several other boys of Francis's age. The boy was settling in well with his new companions and she should have no qualms.

Clarissa felt again the sickening sense of

helplessness with which she had read that letter. She wrote back instantly asking for her brother's address. Again her uncle had responded by telling her that communication from his sister upset the boy too much and destroyed all the good that had been done. Francis was doing well, eating well, and the tutor had only good report to make of his progress.

She remembered now the despair, the dread, that had crept over her as the days went on. Something was very badly wrong, but she was helpless to do anything about it. She could go up to London, demand her uncle take her to see her brother, but if he refused, and she knew in her heart that he would, then she had no redress. He was Francis's legal guardian, and, indeed, hers also. He had every right to do as he saw fit. At least for the next ten months.

She consulted her father's friends, and although they listened in kindly sympathy they both treated her fears as the natural consequence of grief over losing first her father and then the company of her little brother. It was ridiculous to imagine some melodramatic plot of their guardian's to cause harm to his nephew. And, of course, it was high time Francis had a more formal education in the company of his peers.

No one mentioned that Luke would inherit if anything happened to Francis. Somehow Clarissa hadn't felt able to point this out to her father's old friends. They must both have been aware of it, and it was such a gothic idea, it would make her anxiety look even less credible than it already did.

She stood up now and with sudden energy went to open the leather chest, withdrawing the letter she had been looking at earlier. She took it back to the chair by the fire and unfolded it. *The lad's bin took to a babby farm. 'E'll not live long, they gets rid of 'em quick. Best find 'im quick.*

And that was all. She guessed that even such a brief message had been a supreme effort for the writer, but surely he could have included an address. But maybe he didn't have one.

Clarissa folded the letter carefully. It had been opened and refolded so many times it had almost come apart at the fold. She knew about baby farms; everyone did. They took in the unwanted babies, the illegitimate, the burdensome, whose existence threatened to ruin their mothers. No one monitored the care these children received and for the most part they died sooner or later of neglect. Disease and poor, inadequate food took their toll. But Francis was strong and healthy. He was no dependent babe. It would take a long time for him to die of neglect.

She bit her lip hard to keep the tears at bay. She had been telling herself this for over a week now, ever since she'd received the letter. She'd left for London immediately, telling only the servants that she was going to visit her uncle and see Francis. She had deliberately refrained from confiding in anyone who might question such a journey, and had taken the mail coach from the neighboring village, stepping down in the yard of the Crown and Anchor in Southwark that evening, without the faintest idea what she was going to do next.

The first thing was to find a bed for the night before it became dark. The coaching inn seemed like the obvious choice. She had plenty of money sewn into an inside pocket of her gown, more than enough for a private bedchamber and a decent supper.

The landlord, reassuringly, had shown no curiosity about this lone woman traveler and merely showed her to a reasonable bedchamber and offered to have supper brought up to her if she didn't want to eat in the Ordinary downstairs with the other customers. In the morning he had directed her to the ferry stop that would take her across the river into the city.

After a few wrong turns and a lot of directions from passersby Clarissa found her way to Ludgate Hill. Her uncle's house was in the shadow of St. Paul's in a narrow street running off Ludgate Hill. It was a tall, narrow building, not particularly impressive, and Clarissa wondered whether her uncle's circumstances were even more straitened than she had sometimes suspected. He would have had some inheritance from his parents, but as the second son it would not have been substantial; the lion's share, as always under the laws of primogeniture, went to the oldest son. She was fairly certain her father had been more than generous with his brother when asked, but now that he was no longer there, where would Luke turn if he needed an urgent injection of funds?

Or was he counting on a permanent solution?

She hovered in the shadows, watching the house until she became aware that she was drawing attention to herself. A couple of unsavory characters were watching her from a doorway across the street and she realized that she must present an easy target, a well-dressed young woman loitering alone in a quiet street.

She turned and walked briskly away, not slowing or looking behind her until she reached Ludgate's busy thoroughfare. Ignorance of the city, and a need to find somewhere not too expensive to stay where she wouldn't draw attention to herself, had led her to Covent Garden and a brothel on King Street. And subsequently to the Earl of Blackwater.

Clarissa, suddenly restless, got up from her fireside chair and went to the window. The Piazza was in full night guise now, crowded with men and women in their bright colorful garments. She opened the window and leaned out. Laughter and music filled the streets; the toothsome smells of hot pies, spiced ale, and mulled wine scented the cold night air, drowning the less salubrious odors of rank bodies, ordure-filled kennels, the decaying corpses of cats and dogs. It was a carnival scene, Clarissa thought, and once again she felt that sensual vibration, the surge of energy. She wanted to be a part of it. After a lifetime of country quiet . . . of country tedium . . . she was ready for this excitement, this edge to life.

But that was not why she was here. She had to find Francis. She drew the window closed and turned back to the room. One thing she had learned in her fruitless search thus far: She needed help. She had visited Luke's house every day this week and until this morning had seen nothing. And then this morning her uncle had left the house while she was watching. She'd followed him, hoping he would lead her to Francis, but then, of course, she had run headlong into the earl and had lost her quarry. So she was back to square one.

She could, of course, simply bang on the door and ask to speak to her uncle, but wisdom — or was it cowardice? — prevented her. If he was trying to do away with Francis, he would hardly direct her to where her brother was being kept. And there was no knowing what steps he would take if he realized Clarissa's suspicions.

No, she needed help, and powerful protection, if she was going to tangle with Luke. Jasper St. John Sullivan could provide both the help and the protection. He wouldn't need to know it, of course, but there could be a quid pro quo to his proposition. Once she had Francis safe, where better to keep him hidden than in London, right under her uncle's nose? Under the unwitting protection of the Earl of Blackwater? She was to have a house of her own while she lived under the earl's protection, and she could keep her little brother with her under that roof. Luke would never in his wildest nightmares imagine that his sheltered niece was living the life of an earl's mistress. Even if he looked for her once he discovered she was no longer in Kent, and once he discovered that Francis was gone, as was inevitable, he would never find either of them.

The earl was interested only in the charade that would bring him his uncle's fortune. He had no interest in who or what she really was. As long as she fulfilled her side of the bargain, he would be satisfied. How hard would it be for her to play that part?

But there was a snag of course. What else would he expect? Would he expect her really to play the part of his mistress? He believed her a whore; why wouldn't he expect her to service him in the same way? He'd said he would pay Mistress Griffiths for an exclusive contract, and of course he would expect some of the benefits of such a contract. Of course he would. What red-blooded male would not?

Clarissa sipped her wine and gazed into the fire. How could she legitimately and rationally refuse to give him her body when he'd paid for its exclusive use?

She couldn't tell him she was a virgin

because then she would no longer suit his purposes. He needed a fallen woman. And Clarissa Astley had fallen nowhere. Oh, she'd exchanged a kiss or two with the sons of local gentry under the mistletoe at Christmas. And there had been one particular summer, hot and sultry, when she had imagined herself head over heels in love with a university friend of a neighboring squire's son. They had indulged in some moments of what had seemed like a grand and illicit passion, but it had not gone beyond intimate fumbling and inexpert kisses.

Maybe to start with she could come up with an excuse for delaying consummation. Perhaps the earl would be sympathetic to the idea that she would like some respite from selling her body. Maybe he would agree that she needed to concentrate on the part he would have her play and understand that the sex would be a distraction.

She was clutching at straws, Clarissa decided. But what else did she have to clutch at? She could start by trying to set her own rules. She would agree to the charade, but to nothing more intimate. If he was as anxious to have her play the part as he appeared, maybe he would be willing to agree. He hadn't after all expressed any physical interest in her thus far.

It was worth a try. And it was comforting to have a plan at least, something that offered a glow of light in the darkness. Clarissa put more coals on the fire and went to bed, where she lay in the dark, listening to the faint sounds from the Piazza and watching the comforting flicker of the fire.

Five miles away in a house in Bethnal Green, Francis Astley coughed miserably, shivering under the thin blanket that reeked of urine and vomit. All around him he heard coughs, the moans of the very small children, the cries of the babies. Every now and again the woman, or one of her girls, would come in and pour spoons of clear liquid from the brown bottle down the throats of the little ones and the babies, and they would stop their cries and moans. Francis always hurled the spoon away. The liquid tasted foul and smelled even worse. At first they had hit him, and tried to hold his head to force the stuff down his throat, but he'd kicked and bitten and finally they'd left him alone. So he coughed and tossed on the straw mattress, and tried not to think of food. The thin porridge twice a day did nothing to assuage his appetite, and the occasional crust of bread made little difference. He couldn't understand how he had ended up in this approximation of hell. And he couldn't understand why Clarissa hadn't come for him yet.

But that was only when he was feeling feverish and so miserable he couldn't think clearly. In his lucid moments he knew perfectly well that his uncle Luke was keeping Clarissa from him, but eventually she *would* find him. This conviction buoyed him through the bad times, even if his misery was so overwhelming at those times that he couldn't acknowledge it.

CHAPTER FOUR

It was midmorning the next day when someone knocked on the door to Clarissa's bedchamber. It was such an unexpected sound that she jumped. Her landlady yesterday had been her first visitor since she'd taken up residence there. "Who is it? Come in."

The door opened to reveal two young women in lacy dishabille standing on the threshold. "You should be up and dressed by now," one of them said, shaking her head at the sight of Clarissa, still in her shift and night robe, perched on the edge of the bed.

Clarissa realized that she'd been sitting in the same place unmoving for what seemed hours. She'd awoken before dawn and managed to rekindle the embers in the grate, after which she'd sat on the bed and stared numbly into the fire. For some reason, she'd been unable to summon either the will or the energy to do more than feed the fire. All her resolution of the previous evening had vanished with the first light of dawn and getting dressed had seemed impossible.

"Probably I should be," she returned. "I don't mean to be rude, but why should it matter to you?"

"It doesn't," the second one said cheerfully. "But Mother Griffiths sent us up to see how you're doing. She's sent you up a gown. She wants you to wear it when his lordship comes." She stepped into the room and laid a gown of sprigged muslin on the bed. "Pretty, isn't it?"

Clarissa stared at it. "Where did it come from? I have clothes of my own; I don't need this."

"Well, Mother said you don't have much in your armoire, and this'll suit you when you meet with his lordship." The girl grinned. "She always likes us to dress up for a contract. Lucky you, snagging Blackwater. He's one big catch, isn't he, Em?"

"That he is," her friend said.

It seemed the entire house knew of it, Clarissa thought. She'd never been introduced to any of the other inhabitants, indeed had barely seen them except occasionally as figures disappearing through a door in a silken rustle. Now it seemed they were ready to embrace her as one of their own.

"Let's see what we can do with your hair." Em had a pair of curling tongs in her hand. "Fetch the hairbrush over here, Maddy."

"No." Clarissa recoiled as the two approached the bed. "I don't even think I'm going to meet with the earl."

Her visitors stopped in their tracks. "Lord, you must be daft in the head. You can't say no to Mother Griffiths."

"I most certainly can." Clarissa stood up. "And while I appreciate the offer, Em . . . Emma . . . Emily . . . ? I can also dress myself in my own clothes."

"It's Emily," the girl said. "What's yours?"

"Clarissa."

"Clarissa." Emily nodded. "Is that your real name, or one you use for the business?"

"How long have you been in the business?" Maddy chimed in.

"I'm *not* in the business and never have been." Clarissa could hear a note of desperation in her voice.

Disconcertingly they both laughed. "Oh, we all say that at first," Emily said. "We all think, *It's only for a week, it's only to get over this rough spot,* but then you realize you've been at it for months and it's really not so bad after all. This is a good house. We're looked after, no rough stuff unless you're willing."

"And Mother Griffiths will only have the best class of client through her door," Maddy added. "And when she negotiates a contract, it's always fair. We get our fair share. She keeps a good table, plenty of good wine, and there's regular health inspections, so if you get a dose of the clap you take the physic and don't have to work until the physician says you're clean."

" 'Tis nice to have a rest once in a while," Emily chimed in. "We none of us mind that bit, do we, Maddy?"

Clarissa was torn between fascination at this insight into a world she knew next to nothing about and revulsion at the idea that as far as these two women were concerned she was as much a part of it as they were.

She was about to put them right in no uncertain terms, then stopped, swallowing the hot denial as it came to her lips. If she wanted the earl's protection he had to believe she was a harlot. Which meant that everyone must believe it. Walls had ears after all.

"I'll wear my bronze muslin," she stated. She was not going to wear a gown that came from God knows where. And she was not going to be beholden to Mistress Griffiths in any way. It seemed, however, as if her earlier paralysis had dissipated. She went to the armoire and drew out the gown, laying it on the bed.

"Oh, the sprig muslin's much prettier," Emily said, tilting her head as she compared the two. "This is rather prim, don't you think, Maddy?"

It was true that the neckline of the sprig muslin was much lower than Clarissa's own gown, but there wasn't much call for daring décolletage in the country. "That may be, but it's mine and I intend to wear it." She cast aside her night robe and stepped into the bronze muslin, lacing the bodice. "Thank you for the offer, but I truly don't need your help. I've been dressing myself since I was five years old."

They both looked disconcerted. "We always help each other when it's an important meeting," Maddy said. "We're all in this together, Clarissa. You'll realize soon enough that you need friends."

"Oh, leave her be if she's too good for us." Emily walked to the door.

"No . . . no, forgive me." Clarissa spoke in a rush, realizing abruptly how much she did need friends in this strange world and how ungracious she had been. "I am truly grateful for your help. This is all new to me, and I really don't know what to expect."

"You really are new to the business?" Emily looked astonished. "How could you have attracted Blackwater if you haven't been around?"

"An accident." Clarissa improvised quickly. "I was hoping to find some custom in the Piazza because Mother Griffiths had said I could have the room but none of the house services until I could pay her a proper rent. I needed to find some regular customers of my own. And then . . . well, while I was walking I suppose I took the earl's eye, because he followed me back here and made an offer for me."

She was astonished at how easily the story tripped off her tongue. And she could see that it had satisfied her visitors.

"Oh, that's all right." Maddy put a reassuring arm around her. "We all know what it's like at first. But you struck lucky first time, so let Em do your hair. She's a magician with the curling iron. Your hair's a gorgeous color, but it needs a touch of curl, don't you think, Em?"

Emily was already heating the curling iron in the fire's glowing embers. Clarissa had often wondered how she would look with curled hair; now might be the time to find out. She sat back on the bed. The faint smell of singeing hair perfumed the air while Emily worked, but after a few moments she stood back and declared, "There now. Lovely, isn't it, Maddy?"

"Beautiful," Maddy agreed. "Are you sure you won't wear the sprigged muslin, Clarissa? Those ringlets would look lovely drifting over your shoulders. They'd draw the eye to your boobies just perfect."

Clarissa was about to protest that drawing the eye to her rather insignificant bosom had never been the primary purpose of her wardrobe choices, but then reflected that since she was playing this charade, she should probably make it as authentic as possible. "I'll try it," she conceded, unlacing her bodice.

The sprig muslin was unlike any gown she possessed. It was laced at the back, and by the time Maddy had tugged and tied until Clarissa could barely breathe it fitted like a glove. She looked down at the pronounced swell of her breasts over the lace edging to the neckline, if, indeed, you could call it a neckline; it was so low it barely concealed her nipples. She felt almost naked. Her breasts were quite small, but in this gown they seemed the most prominent aspect of her appearance.

"I don't know," she muttered doubtfully. "I don't feel like myself."

"You're not supposed to. Wait here."

Maddy disappeared and reappeared in a few moments with a mirror of beaten copper. "Now look, see the ringlets against your skin . . . it's so white."

Clarissa looked. She thought she could get accustomed to the ringlets — they did frame her face in an attractive manner — but she was not happy with the expanse of flesh exposed by the gown. She shook her head firmly. "No, the hair's nice, but not the gown. I'll wear my own." She reached behind to struggle with the laces.

"I think it's a mistake, but if you insist . . ." Doubtfully Emily helped her loosen the bodice and Clarissa stepped out of the gown with a sigh of relief. She stepped into the bronze muslin again, laced it up, then looked at her reflection in the copper mirror.

"That's better; I least I can recognize myself. But thank you." She smiled at the two young women. "I do appreciate your help."

"We'll see you later then." Maddy gathered up the rejected gown, smoothing it over her arm with a rather regretful air. "I expect the earl will buy you an entire wardrobe of gorgeous gowns."

"And jewels too," Emily put in as she went to the door.

"Yes, but once he's tired of you, he'll want those back," Maddy declared matter-of-factly. "So enjoy them while you have them." The sound of their footsteps on the stairs receded and quiet once more descended upon the attic.

But not for long. Mother Griffiths bustled in a few minutes later looking distinctly annoyed. "Why wouldn't you wear the gown?"

"It's not mine," Clarissa said simply. "And it didn't suit me. I prefer to wear my own clothes."

The woman raised her eyebrows and examined Clarissa's appearance with disapproval. "That gown's all very well for a vicarage tea party, but it won't attract a man's interest."

"I think I've already done that," Clarissa returned.

Mother Griffiths frowned. Then her eyes narrowed, her expression sharpened. "So, how will you answer his lordship? I'll tell you now, you'd be a fool to turn down such a proposition."

"I won't turn him down."

Nan's expression relaxed. "Now that's a sensible girl. But in that case I really think you should dress to please him."

"The earl didn't express any objections to the gown I was wearing yesterday," Clarissa pointed out. "Maybe he was in the mood for something different."

"I suppose it's possible. Men do take some strange fancies on occasion. Well, if he's in the mood for a little virginal innocence, I'm sure you can supply it, my dear. Maybe his lordship fancies a little schoolroom play; they do sometimes." She nodded her head. "Just play it by ear, dear, and give him what he wants. The earl is one of the easy ones to please. He won't make any unpleasant demands."

"I'm relieved," Clarissa murmured. Once again she felt as if she were living in someone else's world. What she was doing was ridiculous, and yet it wasn't. If she was to protect Francis in this vast city she needed more resources than she alone possessed. If the earl should question the sudden appearance of a small boy in the house occupied by his mistress, she could concoct some story about a lost child, a stolen child, that would wring the heart of the most hardened individual.

In fact, it could be her own child. Now that would really tug the heartstrings. And the existence of an illegitimate baby would make her whoredom even more convincing. It would provide the perfect excuse for her arrival in London, and it would sail close enough to the truth to make her deception all the easier to carry off. But that wouldn't work, of course, since she couldn't possibly have a ten-year-old child; however, she could come up with something along those lines.

"Come down now. You should wait for his lordship in the parlor." Nan went to the door. "You'll leave the contract negotiations to me. There'll be no need for you to say anything, and his lordship won't expect you to."

She had plenty to say, Clarissa reflected, following her landlady downstairs, but she would bide her time; no point antagonizing Mother Griffiths at this point.

"Now, there's sherry and Madeira; his lordship is partial to both." As they entered the parlor, Nan indicated the decanters on the sideboard. "And some savory tarts. You will offer the hospitality of the house while I deal with the business side of the matter. And then once everything's settled I'll leave you to his lordship. He'll tell you then what he wants of you."

Clarissa murmured something vaguely appropriate and went to the long windows that looked out onto the street. After the night's boisterousness King Street was quiet, deserted except for a beggar limping alongside the kennel turning over garbage with his stick. A mangy dog rushed at him, barking, before snatching up a piece of rotting meat and disappearing into an alley.

A slatternly woman emerged from a doorway pushing down her skirts and a man stepped out behind her, fastening his britches. The woman dropped a coin into her bodice and without exchanging a word, she turned up the street and he turned down it towards the Great Piazza.

Clarissa suppressed a shudder. Then she stiffened. A familiar figure was strolling towards the house swinging a silver-knobbed cane. For a moment she reveled in the indulgence of the unseen watcher. She could take in his appearance now without distraction, and it was an appearance every bit as attractive as she remembered. In fact, even more so. Everything about him bespoke wealth and privilege, from the green striped silk of his knee britches and full-skirted coat to the gold edging on his black tricorne hat. But despite the elegance of his clothes, and the leisurely fashion in which he strolled down the street, everything about the Earl of Blackwater, about his physique and his manner, warned that this was not a man to tangle with. His free hand rested on his sword hilt; his posture was alert, his eyes sharp and quick, missing nothing. She hadn't noticed before quite how powerful his shoulders were, but the close-fitting coat set them off to perfection, as plain dark stockings did for a pair of well-muscled calves.

A little frisson of excitement crept up Clarissa's spine. She turned from the window, saying calmly, "His lordship is coming down the street, madam."

"Good, punctual as always. Stay here, I will greet him in the hall." Nan examined her reflection in the mirror above the fireplace, deftly pinched her cheeks to produce some color, and ran a dampened fingertip over her eyebrows before hurrying from the room.

Clarissa sat down and then stood up, nervous now and unsure how she wanted to present herself. She heard the door knocker and the earl's composed tones greeting the steward. Then the door opened and the earl came in with Mistress Griffiths. He bowed to Clarissa, smiled, his black gaze sweeping over her.

"Good morning, Mistress Clarissa."

She curtsied. "Good morning, my lord."

He laid his hat and cane on a pier table beside the door and extended his hands to her in invitation. "You have an answer for me."

Clarissa dampened her suddenly dry lips. She glanced at Mistress Griffiths. "Madam, I wish to talk with his lordship alone. Afterwards I will leave you to do business as you see fit, but there are some things I wish to discuss first that concern only Lord Blackwater and myself."

Nan looked astounded, put out, and was about to expostulate, when she remembered that this lodger was not one of her usual girls. She was neither destitute nor seemingly experienced in the ways of whoredom. It would do no good to badger her when she could simply walk out of the house if she chose.

She looked at Jasper and shrugged. He nodded. "Perhaps you'd be good enough to leave us, Nan."

Nan glanced once at Clarissa, then with another shrug left them alone.

"So, what is it that we must discuss?" Jasper sat down, smiling amiably. "Mistress Griffiths is not accustomed to being excluded from these delicate matters."

"No, I daresay she's not. Sherry or Madeira?" She lifted the decanters in turn, suddenly more sure of herself now that she was alone with the earl.

"Sherry, please." He took the glass, and a mushroom tartlet, and leaned back in his chair regarding her with a wary amusement. She seemed different now, older than she had previously, strangely determined. "So, let's hear it."

Clarissa kept her back to him as she took a quick fortifying gulp of sherry. Then she said, "You want me to play a part in a charade. I would like it agreed between us that that is *all* I will do. I will play the part of your mistress, but I will not *be* your mistress in any real sense." She felt her cheeks warm as she said this. She'd never had such an awkward conversation with anyone before.

Jasper frowned at her averted back. He hadn't really given much thought to the physical aspects of this contract, but it had never occurred to him to question his right to whatever he wished in that area. He certainly found her physically appealing, and at the back of his mind had lurked a degree of anticipation at the prospect of bedding her. Now she was laying down conditions that caused him puzzled chagrin.

"I'm not sure I understand. You will *play* my mistress, but you won't *be* my mistress?"

"Exactly. No one will know except you and me, but we will not have a . . . a physical arrangement." The words seem to stick in her dry throat. How could she expect him to agree to such a condition? He believed her a whore.

"May I ask why?"

"I . . . I would like a respite from . . . from all this." She gestured vaguely at her surroundings. "Is that so difficult to understand, sir?"

He considered. "No . . . no, I suppose it's not."

"I believe you said you would wish for my exclusive services. If I restrict those services to the one you really want from me, then we both get what we wish for."

Still she didn't look at him and didn't hear him come up behind her, soft footed on the thick Aubusson carpet. She gave a startled gasp when he put his hands on her shoulders from behind, moving his fingers up the deep groove of her neck in a strangely soothing gesture. She could feel the heat of his body against her back and trembled.

"I would find that quite a sacrifice," Jasper murmured, lifting a ringlet, twisting it around his finger. His breath was warm against her ear. "It seems a somewhat uneven bargain, to buy services that will not be available to me."

She remained motionless, almost rigid

with a paradoxical mixture of apprehension and anticipation. "I will perform the service you want from me. I will enable you to inherit your uncle's fortune. Can you not think of me purely as an actor, someone you pay to play a part?"

"But how convincingly can either of us play that part if we are not sharing the pleasures that are essential to our roles?" After not giving the matter much thought, he found that he now cared *very* much about this issue. She was a whore whom he had offered to rescue from a harlot's life and instead of gratitude she was making insulting conditions.

"Believe me, my lord, you will have no cause for complaint." Her voice shook a little.

He turned her to face him and she forced herself to meet his frowning gaze. "I am going to pay Nan Griffiths for your exclusive services. It seems to me that I have the right to dictate those services."

Clarissa looked him in the eye. "You offer me the means to get out of this life, sir; as I understood it that was the incentive for me to join with you in this charade, but you still want to keep me in whoredom, for *your* benefit. Illogical, wouldn't you say, my lord?"

He pressed finger and thumb against the bridge of his nose as he frowned at her. She was right, of course, but it had never occurred to him Mistress Clarissa would consider she had the right to dictate terms. "That may be if you look at it from a certain perspective. But it could also be said that until you are finally free to take charge of your own life, you must continue to do what you are accustomed to doing to earn your bread. I need a whore for this task and I fail to see why you would refuse to undertake all aspects of the task. Unless, of course, you find me repulsive?" An eyebrow lifted in question.

That would be an easy way out, but for some reason it wasn't one Clarissa could imagine taking. "No . . . no . . . it's not that," she said hastily. "I don't find you repulsive. But I would like a respite from this life. I don't know why that is so difficult to understand."

He threw up his hands. "Let us leave it at that for the moment. I will complete negotiations with Mistress Griffiths, and then we will pay a visit together." He went to the bell rope by the fireplace and pulled it. "The sooner we start, the sooner we will finish."

And that, thought Clarissa, sounded like a most heartfelt wish. But how could she blame him? The man was paying for something that he wasn't going to get. Although the caveat *for the moment* wasn't too reassuring. It didn't sound as if he was resigned to such a condition at all. But she'd cross that bridge when she came to it. It occurred to her that there were rather a lot of bridges she was leaving to be crossed when she came to them.

Nan came in almost before the sound of the bell had faded, and Clarissa guessed she had been waiting outside the door. "So, my lord, are we ready to do business?" She spoke to the earl but her sharp gaze was on Clarissa.

"I believe we are." Jasper nodded and his own gaze flicked to Clarissa standing still and silent by the window. Puzzlement lurked in his dark eyes. "The usual terms apply, I assume, Nan?"

"Unless you have any unusual requests, my lord." Nan set out a sheet of parchment on the secretaire and smoothed it with her palm. "There is no need for you to remain, Clarissa. I'll ring for you when we're ready for your signature."

"You are all consideration, ma'am, but I believe I'll stay." Clarissa sat down with an air of composure that she didn't feel. "I am, after all, most nearly concerned in the business."

Nan looked as if she was about to protest but Jasper said, "Indeed you are, Mistress Clarissa. I have no objections to your presence. Let us continue, Nan."

Clarissa listened in silence as she was bought and sold. It was the most extraordinary sensation to hear herself, her worth, discussed like some kind of commodity. Nan drove a hard bargain in the interests of her commodity, and listening to her demands Clarissa understood what Emily and Maddy had meant when they'd said Mother Griffiths looked after her own.

Nan considered Mistress Clarissa to be worth a house in Half Moon Street, with a cook-housekeeper and maid. In addition she was to have a quarterly dress allowance, and the unlimited use of a sedan chair and carriage. In return, the Earl of Blackwater was to have her exclusive services.

Jasper made little demur to the list of requirements and for the most part listened in silence, with the occasional nod of agreement.

"And my commission is as usual, my lord," Nan finished briskly, sanding the parchment on which she'd been writing the contract.

Clarissa longed to ask what the whore mistress expected as her usual commission. She'd done little to earn this particular one, short of a moment's kindness in renting a servant's garret to a naïve country chit.

"As always." The earl sounded impatient, as if he wished to be done with the formalities. He rose from his chair and went to the secretaire, taking the quill from its pot and signing the sheet. He inverted a candle and dropped wax below his signature, then pressed his signet ring into the soft wax. "You now, Clarissa." He spoke over his shoulder.

Clarissa went over and took the quill. She glanced down at the closely written sheet. Nan Griffiths had signed above the earl. She hesitated, suddenly terrified that she was about to sign her life away. Could she really expect to be a match for these two sophisticated city people? What would be the penalty for breaking this contract? Because in ten months whether the agreed marriage had taken place or not, she was going to break it, there were no two ways about that. Could she be accused of theft, even if she took nothing with her when she left? Would she be a fugitive for the rest of her life? But that was ridiculous. She wasn't important enough for these two to give a damn about her. They'd be annoyed and the earl might demand his money back from Mistress Griffiths, but surely it wouldn't be the first time a contracted whore had broken her contract.

"What are you waiting for, girl?" Nan's voice was sharp and Clarissa had an inkling of what it would be like to run afoul of the whore mistress. She knew she'd better make certain she was far, far away when Nan discovered her perfidy.

Slowly she dipped the pen in the inkpot and carefully signed: *Clarissa Ordway*. At least she could keep her real name unknown as an elementary precaution. She sanded the wet ink and stepped back, feeling oddly light-headed. "So, what now, my lord?" Her voice seemed to come from very far away.

Jasper turned to look at her, and there was something about this scrutiny that was quite unlike any other look he had given her. It was possessive, as if he was sizing up a recent purchase. As, indeed, he was. "I need you to dress in a manner a little more indicative of your profession," he said slowly. "At least for the visit we will be paying this morning. I'd like you to change into one of the gowns you wear for entertaining your clients in the evening. Something a little more revealing, if you please."

Clarissa glanced at Mistress Griffiths, who said swiftly, "Of course, my lord. Come, Clarissa." She beckoned imperatively as she went to the door. "We will be but a few minutes, Lord Blackwater."

Clarissa followed her, feeling as if she was being escorted to the steps of the gallows.

CHAPTER FIVE

"You should have heeded me earlier, Clarissa," Nan scolded her as she preceded Clarissa upstairs. "I told you to wear the sprigged muslin then. Believe me, I know what our gentlemen like in their girls."

Clarissa said nothing. She'd signed away her right to insist on the modesty of her own wardrobe. If the Earl of Blackwater wanted an exposed bosom, then an exposed bosom is what he would get. She would learn to become accustomed as she would learn to act her part in the charade.

She moved to the attic stairway and was surprised when Nan said, "No, this way. I've had your chamber changed. Now that you're one of us, for as long as you remain under this roof, you will sleep on this floor with the others. I expect it will take several weeks for his lordship to make arrangements for a house for you."

She opened the door onto a large and very

comfortably furnished chamber. "Should his lordship wish you to entertain him in the house, then this is where you may bring him. The servants will bring you anything either of you desires. You may dine or bathe à deux, if that is his lordship's wish. The gentlemen frequently like to watch their ladies in the bath; for some reason it stimulates desire."

Nan shrugged as if there was no accounting for taste as she hurried to the substantial armoire. She flung it open and reached for the sprig muslin gown that hung there in lonely splendor beside Clarissa's two other countrified gowns. "You'll have no need for those others," she declared with a dismissive gesture. "I daresay his lordship will have the milliner and the seamstress visit you here to have your wardrobe made up. But in the meantime we must contrive as best we can." She laid the sprig muslin over the back of the daybed. "Now, make haste and take off that gown."

Resigned, Clarissa unlaced the bronze muslin and hung it up in the armoire. She was not prepared to have her own clothes dismissed with such contumely and she was equally determined that they would follow her to Half Moon Street. Unfashionably prim and proper though they may have been, the material was good and the work-manship as fine and delicate as the most expensive garment from a London dress-maker.

Nan laced her tightly into the sprigged muslin, then adjusted the décolletage with little tugs and twitches that served to reveal even more of her breasts than earlier. She arranged the ringlets artfully over Clarissa's shoulders, then stepped back to examine her handiwork. "Yes, very pretty, very entic-ing. His lordship will be pleased. You had better hurry down to him now."

Clarissa dropped an ironic curtsy, fairly confident that the whore mistress would fail to detect the irony, and returned to the parlor. The earl was standing with his back to the door as she entered and turned swiftly. She offered the same ironic curtsy and saw from the quick flash in his eye that he had not missed the slight tilt of her head, the challenge in her eye that turned the courtesy into a parody.

He looked her over deliberately. "Much better but still not enough" was his eventual pronouncement. "I need you to look the part. My uncle is expecting a whore, and I would give him one." He rang the bell again and when Nan reappeared instructed, "Powder and rouge, a touch on the lips, oh . . . and on the nipples."

Clarissa gasped, looking down at her bosom. Instinctively she put her hands over her breasts. "No," she protested. "I won't have it."

"You will do whatever pleases your benefactor," Nan stated. "I will fetch the paint box." She hastened away, leaving the door ajar.

Jasper regarded Clarissa with a quizzically raised eyebrow, a question in his eye. "I confess that in general I don't care for paint either, but you are surely accustomed to men who do?"

"I have not been in London for many weeks," she improvised, "and the men who seem to find me appealing seem to prefer at least an assumption of innocence." Clarissa was astonished at how easily the fabrication tripped off her tongue.

Jasper inclined his head in acknowledgment. "I can see how that would be, but we are going to visit my uncle and if he is to be persuaded of the importance of your conversion he must see how far you have fallen from chastity's tree. The more you look like a harlot now, the more impressed will he be by the eventual transformation."

It's just a charade, Clarissa told herself. *No different from the charades they played at*

Christmas house parties. She had loved playacting for as long as she could remember. As far back as her nursery days she remembered co-opting the nursery maid and anyone else on the staff willing to act in her elaborate reconstructions of nursery rhymes. Later she'd tried her hand at writing her own plays, encouraged by her governess and rather less ably assisted by her schoolroom companions. She'd always felt Lawyer Danforth's and Doctor Alsop's children lacked a proper imagination.

Nan returned with a box of rouge, powder and brushes, and a small bowl of water. She set to with brisk efficiency, brushing white powder on Clarissa's cheeks and then dabbing a piece of cotton into the water before dipping it into the rouge. She applied the red paste on the cotton to Clarissa's cheekbones and then lifted her nipples from the décolletage with a finger and painted them dark red, before arranging the neckline so that they were clearly visible above the lace edging. As a final touch she took a stick of rouge from the box and traced the line of Clarissa's lips.

"Will that do, my lord?" She stepped away from her subject so that the earl could take a look.

"Admirably." He lifted a ringlet from one

creamy bare shoulder. "I didn't think your hair could be improved upon, but the ringlets are delightful."

Clarissa was too conscious of the cold air on her exposed breasts to be flattered by the compliment. She'd seen enough painted and powdered ladies in the Piazza to make a fair guess at what her face must look like, dead white with two deep red patches and a shining red mouth. Utterly hideous; he couldn't possibly be expecting her to walk the streets like this. "I cannot go out without a cloak."

"A shawl, certainly," he agreed. "There's a chill wind."

"I'll fetch my cloak."

She turned to leave but Nan forestalled her. "I have the perfect shawl, my dear. Just in the cupboard in the hall, no need to go upstairs." She went out as she spoke and returned almost immediately with a shawl of Indian figured muslin. She draped it carefully over Clarissa's shoulders, still managing to leave most of her neckline bare. "There, that will keep the wind off."

It was better than nothing, Clarissa reckoned, but if she'd had her way she'd have been smothered head to toe in her own woolen cloak, the hood pulled close around her face. But it was clear that she was not going to have her way at present, at least not while Nan Griffiths was around. Nan knew whores and as far as she was concerned she had one in Clarissa. But as soon as they were out of the house she would draw the shawl tightly across her chest.

"I have a present for you, Clarissa." Jasper was smiling as he reached into the deep pocket of his full-skirted coat. "A small gift to seal our compact." He handed her a slim silk-wrapped packet.

He must have been confident of her agreement, Clarissa thought. She hesitated for a moment, feeling somehow that the simple act of taking the gift would morally commit her to honoring the contract to its bitter end. She realized they were both looking at her expectantly. She couldn't continue to hesitate; taking the gift was merely part of the contract and she'd leave it behind with everything else when this was over.

"You are too kind, my lord." She took the packet and untied the ribbon, opening up the silk wrapping to reveal an exquisite fan with sticks of delicately painted mother-of-pearl and painted leaves of ivory vellum depicting a carnival scene. She opened it slowly; it was so delicate, so fine in every detail, it seemed out of place with the base crudity of her present appearance.

"I cannot accept it," she said softly, closing it and holding it out to him. "It's too beautiful."

"Don't be ridiculous." Jasper moved her hand aside. "It's a beautiful fan for a beautiful woman, my dear girl, and I wish you to use it. Come, now, let us go." He picked up his hat and cane and extended a hand to her. "Madam, will you come?"

Clarissa yielded, feeling that she was in the grip of a wave that would not release her until it finally washed up on the beach, but she was momentarily reassured by the firm warmth of his clasp as he folded her fingers into his.

They left the house and Jasper raised his cane at a pair of chairmen loitering in the shadow of the colonnade. They picked up their chair and came over at a run.

Jasper gave Clarissa a hand into the chair, then, having directed the chairmen to the Strand, walked companionably beside the open window. There was nothing companionable about his conversation, however. It was more a series of instructions.

"I should warn you that Viscount Bradley is an irascible old man, but he was a libertine in his youth, indeed into his later years, and still has an appreciative eye for female pulchritude. He'll expect a certain boldness from you. He's never had time for innocence, pretend or otherwise, so don't imply it. Be a little vulgar, flirt, be as seductive as you know how, show off your charms. He'll know why *I* find you appealing just by looking at you. You may find some of his remarks near the bone; he comes of a different age, when men said what they meant without honey-coating, so if you can match that, he'll enjoy your company."

Clarissa absorbed this in stunned silence. How on earth was she to behave like a vulgar prostitute, flirt seductively with an old man, presumably flash her painted nipples at him? It was ludicrous. It bore no relationship to the charades of her past. She flipped open the fan and closed it again with a snap. Nevertheless she could do it. She *would* do it.

"Are you clear? Do you have any questions?"

Thousands, but she didn't say so. "It sounds rather intimidating" was all she managed.

"Yes, he is an intimidating old bastard." Jasper laughed shortly. "But he happens to hold my salvation between his hands, so I need you to act as you've never acted before. Imagine he's a client, if that helps, one with particular tastes. I'm sure you're accustomed to acting out all sorts of roles for your customers; just imagine you're in the nunnery entertaining an old gentleman of less than refined tastes."

Clarissa was afraid she was going to start howling with laughter again at the lunatic absurdity of the whole situation. She bit down hard on her lip, then remembered the paint and hastily rubbed at her front teeth with her fingertip. She leaned towards the open window on the far side of the chair, away from the earl, and concentrated fiercely on the busy street until certain she had the unruly impulse under control. And then all desire to laugh vanished. Luke was walking briskly along the street a few yards away from her chair but in the same direction. She leaned back, away from the aperture, her heart thumping.

What were the odds of seeing him like this? But they were not that bad, of course. The London she and Luke were inhabiting was a very small area, maybe three square miles in all. She couldn't follow him now, but as soon as she was free of the earl later this morning, she would return to Ludgate Hill. If Clarissa Astley, the well-bred, refined, carefully educated daughter of Squire Astley and Lady Lavinia Astley, could fool an irascible libertine of an old nobleman into believing her to be a prostitute, she could present herself at Luke's kitchen door as someone she wasn't. An itinerant gypsy, perhaps, or a beggar maid, a girl down on her luck for some reason. Surely someone in Luke's household would have had dealings with the little boy before he'd been packed off to whatever hellhole held him now.

Suddenly the charade took on a different patina. If she could play one part, certainly she could play another. And the better she played the one, the better she would play the other.

Suddenly emboldened Clarissa leaned forward, resting an arm on the edge of the window, once again looking for Luke. She allowed the shawl to slip open to reveal her bosom. Even if Luke saw her he would never recognize her in her present guise and beneath all the paint and powder. He wasn't expecting to see her anywhere in the city, so it would never occur to him that this painted, half-dressed harlot could have anything at all in common with his niece.

He was still walking on the far side of the thoroughfare, swinging his cane, his gaze flickering from side to side. He glanced into the street at the passing traffic and for one brief instant his eyes met Clarissa's. She forced herself to maintain an air of indifference as she looked past him, giving the impression of an idle interest in the street scene. Her body thrummed with the suspense, with the dread that she was wrong and he would recognize her and give chase, but his gaze lingered on her only briefly, and even for that short time Clarissa recognized the lascivious nature of his cursory inspection. It was oddly comforting that Luke of all people should see a whore instead of his virgin niece.

"I don't appear to be holding your attention," the earl remarked, laying a hand on the edge of the window beside him.

"Oh, forgive me, I thought I saw someone I know." She gave an unconvincing little titter and turned her eyes on him again. "You were talking of your uncle . . . ?"

"Actually, I was not," he said drily. "I was talking of my twin brothers, whom you might well meet at the viscount's house. It is imperative that you don't reveal to them that you know about our uncle's will and even more so about our little arrangement. Those details must be kept strictly between the two of us. Is that clear?"

Clarissa gave him a smile of bland innocence. "Perfectly. It is for you to make the conditions, my lord. I am merely your servant."

"Your understanding of the situation is a weight off my mind," he observed as drily as before.

Clarissa wondered if she had overstepped the line but had no time to ponder the question because the chair had come to a halt and the chairmen were setting it down outside the imposing front door of a double-fronted mansion. Jasper paid the chairmen and handed her out.

He escorted her up the short flight of well-honed steps and lifted the big brass door knocker. In a few minutes the sound of scraping bolts heralded the door's opening. An elderly retainer in powdered wig and brocade livery bowed as he held the door wide.

"Good morning, my lord."

"Good morning, Louis." Jasper urged Clarissa ahead of him into a large, square hall with a beautiful frescoed ceiling and ornately gilded molding. A magnificent horseshoe staircase rose from the rear to a galleried landing. "How is his lordship this morning?" He handed his hat, cane, and cloak to the retainer. "Is he receiving?"

"He is always happy to receive you, Lord Blackwater." The man laid his burdens on a highly polished settle and glanced curiously at the earl's companion.

Clarissa had instinctively drawn the shawl close around her shoulders as she'd stepped into the street but now Jasper twitched it out of her grasp and away from her body. "You won't need this, it's always too warm in the viscount's apartments." He handed the shawl to the retainer, who took it without a word, but with a surreptitious glance at the expanse of white skin its removal revealed.

Clarissa felt as naked as if she had no clothes on at all but she resisted the urge to adjust the lace of the gown's neckline to cover her nipples, telling herself firmly that she was in costume for a charade, no more, no less.

"I'll announce myself, Louis." The earl moved towards the staircase, easing Clarissa in front of him with a hand on her arm. The warmth of his fingers penetrated the thin muslin of her elbow-length sleeves. "There's no need to be nervous, Clarissa, I won't leave you alone with him."

"I'm not," she denied, realizing that in truth she was more curious about this devious, degenerate old man than nervous. Besides, he was a bedridden invalid; what harm could he do her?

Jasper opened a set of double doors along

the landing. They gave onto a thickly carpeted antechamber. Clarissa looked around, noticing the richness of the furnishings; the gold and silver ornaments, some elaborately carved; and the array of delicately painted porcelain figurines. "Is the viscount a collector?"

Jasper glanced around the room. "He's always been an acquisitive tyrant. Much of the treasure in this house, and particularly the gold and silver, he brought from India, and God alone knows whether it was honestly acquired. I would guess not, myself." He crossed to another set of doors in the far wall and knocked once.

"Stay in here until I call for you." He opened the doors and stepped into the room beyond.

Clarissa wandered around the antechamber examining the objets d'art. They were ornate and beautiful for the most part. A gold pedestal urn in particular caught her eye for the elaborate engravings that adorned it. She examined it closely and then jumped back with a startled gasp. Innocent though she may have been, she'd have to have lived in a silent order in a convent all her life not to recognize the obscenities depicted. The figures were engaged in multiple forms of carnal intercourse, each one connecting to the one in front. Fascinated now, she bent closer, turning the urn as she followed the progress of the figures around the pedestal. She was so absorbed she didn't hear the door opening again.

"Amusing, isn't it? Hard to believe such positions are actually possible."

She stepped backwards guiltily, her cheeks flushed as if she'd been caught in some unsavory activity. The earl was standing so close behind her she stepped on his foot, her body coming up hard against his.

"I beg your pardon . . . forgive me . . . I didn't hear you," she stammered, trying to move sideways away from him, but he put an arm around her, pinning her in place against him.

"Don't move, I'm enjoying this." There was a chuckle in his voice and his breath was warm on the nape of her neck. His hands slid up from her waist, lightly cupping her breasts, his fingers moving over the dark red nipples above the lace.

"*No,* please don't," she exclaimed, her body stiffening. "Let me go, my lord, *please.* We had an agreement."

"Did we? I don't remember agreeing to anything more than putting the matter on hold for a while."

"So, you'd stoop to rape, would you, my

lord?" Her voice shook with fear-fueled outrage as she realized that in this house she could not stop him from doing anything he wished with her.

His hands dropped from her as if she were a burning brand and he thrust her almost roughly away from him. "Don't ever accuse me of that again."

Clarissa turned to look at him. His expression was dark, his eyes black and unreadable. "You frightened me," she said softly. "Can't you understand how helpless I feel, here alone with you?"

His expression became one of acute exasperation, although his voice remained low. "Good God, woman, you're a whore. How could I possibly have frightened you? You know what to expect. You signed an agreement; don't tell me you expected that to include nothing more than pretty clothes in a pleasant house in exchange for a little playacting?"

There was nothing to be said, given that the truth was an impossibility. She turned away, saying dully, "Is your uncle receiving?"

Jasper didn't immediately respond. He looked at her in angry puzzlement, once again wondering what it was about this young woman that set him back on his heels at every turn. He knew what she was, so why did her behavior seem to deny it? There was nothing to be gained by the denial, not in his company anyway. God's blood, he'd seen the way she ate an oyster, the most seductive act he'd ever witnessed. She lived in a whorehouse, she'd signed a whore's contract. And the plain fact of the matter was that he wanted her. Perhaps she was holding him off in order to get more out of him. That was a whore's trick, one he knew well. It had been played on him several times before — not with any success, mind you, but it had certainly been tried.

That made sense of her paradoxical come-hither, go-whither behavior, and she'd learn soon enough that he was no gull.

"He's waiting for you," he said, his tone curt. He went ahead of her to the far door that still stood ajar. "Allow me to introduce Mistress Clarissa Ordway, sir." He reached for her wrist and drew her up beside him as he entered the chamber.

Clarissa blinked in the dim light. The curtains were partially drawn across the long windows, shutting out the crisp autumn sunlight, and a fire blazed in the massive hearth. Wax candles burned around the room and the faint odor of a sickroom lingered in the stuffy air. An old man in a fur-trimmed robe, fur rugs wrapped around his knees, was ensconced beside the fireplace, a glass of wine held in a surprisingly graceful hand, the slender, white-skinned hand of a much younger man. He raised a quizzing glass and examined Clarissa as she stepped hesitantly towards him.

"Well, come closer, girl, I don't bite," he rasped.

Clarissa came within several feet of him and curtsied. "Good morning, my lord."

"Hmm." He raised his quizzing glass again. "So, you're my nephew's latest piece. Not bad . . . not bad at all. Nice bubbies; a bit small, but shapely enough."

"La, sir, you flatter me. I believe them to be insignificant." She curtsied again, flicking open her fan, smiling at him over the edge, fluttering her thick golden-brown lashes.

He laughed. "Don't shortchange yourself, girl. Which nunnery are you from?"

"Mistress Griffiths's, sir."

The old man cackled. "Nan's still at it, is she? Well, she always did run a fine establishment. Jasper, over there" — he gestured with his head to where his nephew stood — "he lost his virginity in that house when he was a lad of sixteen. God alone knows how he managed to get to such an age with his cock untried, but that father of his was a namby-pamby, and as for his mother —"

Jasper interrupted him, his voice mildly remonstrative. "You may cast as many aspersions as you wish upon my lamentable lack of physical education, sir, but I beg that you will leave my mother, at least, out of the conversation."

Clarissa was much amused. She ought to have been shocked by the old man's language but instead found it entertaining; it was so unlike anything she'd ever been exposed to before. Amazingly, she thought, she could probably manage to hold her own.

"Oh, your mother was a milksop." The viscount waved a dismissive hand but refrained from any further mention of his brother's wife. "Go away, Jasper, and leave me with this charming creature." He patted the ottoman beside his chair. "Sit here, my girl, and tell me all about yourself. How long have you been at Mother Griffiths's?"

Clarissa took the seat, arranging her skirts carefully and making sure the old man had a good view of her bosom. "Just a few weeks, sir. I came to London to make my fortune."

"Oh, you and half a hundred other girls," the viscount declared with a chuckle. "And not many of 'em will make it." He leaned

131

closer, examining her again through his glass. "I'd lay odds you will though. Cosgrove, you black crow, fetch a glass for this pretty creature. I insist you take a drink with me, my dear."

Clarissa hadn't noticed the other inhabitant of the darkened chamber. A tall, thin, angular man in the black robes of a priest appeared suddenly from the shadows by the bed curtains and stepped soundlessly across the room. A heavy cross hung from his neck, his rosary beads at the waist of his cassock. He regarded Clarissa with an expression of alarm and she thought sympathetically that the poor young man had probably never expected to find himself waiting upon a whore, any more than she had expected to act the whore.

"My secretary and confessor, Father Cosgrove," the viscount said with a vague wave between them. "Fetch a glass, man."

The priest slid back into the shadows and returned with a wineglass that he set down on the table beside the viscount's chair.

"Well pour, pour for the lady, man."

He filled the glass and handed it to Clarissa, who thanked him with a smile that Mistress Clarissa Astley would have bestowed upon her own parish priest. He looked momentarily reassured, before fading into the background once more.

"So, what d'you think of my nephew, then, Mistress Clarissa?" the viscount demanded with a glint in his eye. "It's all right, he's left us, so you can speak freely. How's his swordsmanship?"

"I couldn't say, sir." Clarissa was genuinely surprised at the question. "I've never witnessed it."

"*What?* You mean the blackguard's not bedded you yet? What's the matter with him? Lost his gumption . . . lost his starch?"

Clarissa struggled to recover from her mistake. She laughed, trying to sound insouciant. "I was funning, sir. A stupid jest, of course. It's true I have never witnessed my lord Blackwater on the dueling field, but in other matters . . ." She gave him a bold smile, remembering that Jasper had told her the viscount did not like false innocence. "I have no complaints, my lord."

He nodded and drank from his glass. "It's been a few too many years since I had a woman in my bed. Old age is the very devil. But I've had my moments." He glanced towards the shadows by the bed. "Haven't I, Father Cosgrove? I've had my moments indeed."

"Yes, my lord" came the mumbled response.

"Father Cosgrove, for his sins, is hearing my life's confession," the old man informed Clarissa with a wickedly beatific smile. "Not only is he hearing it, but he is writing it down for posterity. If such an account of one man's wicked ways can serve to deter another after him, then my work is well done. Isn't that so, Father Cosgrove?"

"If God so wills it, my lord."

"Bring the book here, man. I would take a look at the last chapter."

The priest returned to the fireside carrying a bound sheaf of papers. He laid them on the arm of the old man's chair. "If you have no further need of me at the moment, my lord, I will go to my devotions now."

"Send my nephew in to me." The viscount sat up straighter and took the papers onto his lap. "Put a rug around my shoulders, my dear, over there on the chair. I've no desire to contract a quinsy." He patted the papers in his lap and chuckled. "Father Cosgrove finds my confessions require that he go frequently to his devotions to cleanse his soul from the taint of debauchery."

Clarissa wondered why the old man took such malicious delight in discomfiting the priest when, judging by the rosary on the table beside him, he belonged to the same church. She fetched the fur-trimmed rug from the chair and arranged it over the old man's shoulders. He reached up to adjust it, a massive ruby carbuncle glowing in the candlelight against the slender white fingers. A thick gold signet ring adorned his other hand.

Jasper came into the chamber, closing the doors behind him. "You wanted me, sir?"

"Aye, I wish to talk to you alone. Send the whore into the antechamber."

Clarissa's nostrils flared at the sudden hostility in the old man's voice. A moment earlier he had been laughing with her, paying her compliments, and now he was dismissing her as if she were a piece of flotsam in the kennel. She rose to her feet and without so much as a glance in the viscount's direction stalked from the chamber before Jasper could reach the door to open it for her.

"Was that necessary, sir?" Jasper asked, his voice even but his eyes glittering with anger.

"Hardly necessary, dear boy, but what does it matter? The woman's a whore, a gold digger. Prettier than most, I grant you. You're a meal ticket as far as she's concerned. Why did you bring her to me? You don't ordinarily parade your whores for my inspection."

"I had thought to make Mistress Ordway my project for conversion, sir." Jasper took a deep chair with earpieces on the opposite side of the hearth. He crossed his legs and regarded his uncle with a sardonic smile. "Unless, of course, you don't consider her suitable."

The viscount chuckled. "A whore is a whore, and if she's under Mother Griffiths's protection then that's what she is. Let's see if you can persuade society that a whore can see the error of her ways and become a model of Christian propriety and a devoted wife." He shook his head. "You'll have your work cut out for you. I've met many a fallen woman in my time, and none have managed to get up from the gutter for long; the life gets into their blood, they don't understand honest emotion, they're always looking for a trick of some kind."

He began to riffle through the papers in his lap. "There's many an example in here, all the beautiful women who've crossed my path; some even lingered awhile, but they all proved faithless in the end."

He looked up and across at his nephew with a malicious gleam in his old eyes. "You know what I have here? My life story, my life's confession. By the grace of God and Father Cosgrove I shall go to my death when the time comes well shriven." His laugh was a cackle that turned into a violent fit of coughing. He struggled to catch his breath, the papers falling in a shower to his feet. Jasper hurried to him, ringing the handbell on the table beside his uncle before helping him to sit forward.

A liveried servant came into the room. "I'll take care of his lordship now, my lord." He carried a brown apothecary's bottle and poured a dose into a small cup, holding it to the viscount's lips. "Swallow this, sir. You know it'll help."

"Foul muck, it'll poison me more like," the old man gasped through a spasm, but he swallowed the mixture and after a moment it seemed to bring him ease. He fell back in his chair with a sigh and closed his eyes.

Jasper remained for a few moments, then, thinking his uncle asleep, he bent to pick up the scattered papers, trying to put them in order. As he did so, a passage caught his eye and he read on, turning the pages slowly, his eye scanning the lines. He forgot for a moment where he was, so absorbed was he in his reading, and then, after a minute, he looked up.

His uncle was watching him, a knowing gleam in his eye. "Makes titillating reading, don't you think, Nephew?"

"I'm not sure that's the word I would use, sir." Jasper put the papers together and placed them carefully on the table. "But I can find it in me to feel pity for Father Cosgrove." He bowed and moved to the door. "I'll leave you to your rest."

CHAPTER SIX

Clarissa was pacing the antechamber, still struggling to regain her composure. She couldn't imagine what had caused that insulting volte-face and she wanted only to shake the dust of this ornate palace from her shoes and have nothing more to do with either the house or its vile owner.

She had almost made up her mind to walk out and find her own way back to King Street when the sound of voices from the gallery outside gave her pause. She stopped pacing and listened. Men's voices, cheerful and interspersed with laughter, were drawing closer. Instinctively she moved into a far corner of the room, half-concealed behind an easel-mounted painting of a black-eyed, dark-skinned odalisque.

The door opened and two young men entered, flaxen haired, blue eyed, tall and slender, almost impossible to tell apart except for their clothes. One was dressed in a flamboyant suit of crimson and gold lace, his tight-fitting striped waistcoat a riot of scarlet satin; jewels sparkled off the heels and buckles of his shoes, and he carried a tricorne hat sporting a magnificent ostrich plume. The other was more soberly clad in a suit of plain dark blue, with a cream-colored waistcoat; both buckles and heels of his shoes were as unadorned as his hat.

"So, do you think Jasper's started on his rush to the altar yet, Perry?" the flamboyant one asked, going to a sideboard on the far side of the chamber away from Clarissa and examining the decanters through his quizzing glass. "Lord, you'd think the old man could run to a decent port or cognac once in a while, wouldn't you? Nothing here but sherry."

"I suspect he keeps the decent stuff for himself. I haven't seen Jasper for a couple of weeks; who knows what he's doing? But I'd lay odds he's not letting the grass grow." The speaker wandered over to the fireplace, kicking at a falling log. "You know our esteemed brother, Seb."

"Jasper's all right," Sebastian said. "He's always stood by us."

His twin raised his hands in a defensive gesture. "I never implied otherwise. He's a great gun. Oh, thank you." He took the glass of sherry his brother handed him. "Might as well fortify ourselves before we enter the den. How's your search progressing?"

Sebastian's smile tried to be secretive. "Oh, little by little," he said vaguely, but his brother was not fooled.

"Come, Seb, tell. You can't pull the wool over *my* eyes. Where have you found your sow's ear?"

"I'm not ready to divulge that yet, brother." Sebastian grinned. "But unless I'm much mistaken, this sow's ear will make a most elegant silk purse."

Clarissa looked desperately for a way to get out of the chamber without these two, clearly Jasper's twin brothers, knowing she had been eavesdropping. If only she'd had the sense she was born with and stayed clearly visible. If she'd been wearing her own clothes, it would never have occurred to her to hide. Perhaps she could sidle behind the easel and along the paneled walls to the door, keeping in the shadows. There were so many objects in the room, maybe a flicker of movement wouldn't be noticed.

And then the door from the viscount's chamber opened and Jasper came out. "Seb, Perry, how are you?" He greeted his brothers without much surprise. "You've timed a visit to the old man rather poorly, I'm afraid. He's in one of his worst moods, irascible and ready to insult anything that moves. Talking of which . . ." He looked in puzzlement around the antechamber. "Where . . . ? Oh, there you are. Why are you hiding behind an odalisque?"

"I wasn't hiding." Clarissa denied it with as much dignity as she could muster as she emerged. "I was looking at the paintings."

The twin brothers were looking at her in ill-concealed amazement, then Peregrine came to his senses and bowed. "Madam, forgive us, we were not aware of your presence, otherwise we would have introduced ourselves. Peregrine Sullivan at your service."

Clarissa curtsied, remembering just in time her adopted name. "Clarissa Ordway, sir."

Sebastian moved forward, offered a bow. "Sebastian Sullivan at your service, Mistress Ordway."

She curtsied again. "Sir." The ritual was so comfortingly familiar that for a moment she forgot her appearance, but then Sebastian's fascinated gaze fixed upon her bosom brought it back to mind with unpleasant reality. She looked at Jasper. "Are we ready to leave, my lord?"

"Certainly," he said pleasantly. "If you

would go down to the hall, I will join you in a few minutes." He held open the door and Clarissa took her cue and left, hearing the door close quietly behind her.

Jasper turned back to his brothers. "So, my dears, questions?"

"Where did you find her, Jasper?" Sebastian sounded awed. "She's delicious, so beautiful, so perfect for Uncle Bradley."

"I believe Mistress Ordway has all of those qualities," Jasper agreed with a complacent smile. "Let us just say that we ran into each other."

"Where is she established?"

"Nan Griffiths's nunnery." He poured himself a glass of sherry and regarded his brothers with an ironic smile. "For what it's worth, I think our esteemed uncle has two quivers to his bow with this diabolical scheme. I think he's searching not only for revenge on the family, but also for his own redemption through our efforts."

"How so, Jasper?" Peregrine, perched on the deep windowsill, regarded his brother with an air of uncertainty.

"Take a look at his *confession* when you get the opportunity." Jasper chuckled. "Father Cosgrove has all my sympathies."

"What d'you mean, Jasper? No, seriously, you can't walk away and leave us with that."

Sebastian was indignant as his brother set down his empty glass and appeared ready to depart.

Jasper laughed. "Our reprobate uncle is writing of his past indulgences and iniquities in the most graphic, intimate detail, and our innocent Benedictine novice is transcribing each and every one. It's Bradley's idea of a final confession, so that he will meet his maker properly shriven. And by paying us to save a lost soul apiece, he has the twisted idea that he will achieve his own redemption."

"You've read this confession?"

"I glanced at a few pages that had fallen to the floor. It was enough, believe me." Jasper regarded his brothers with a flickering smile. "So, how are your bride searches progressing?"

His brothers exchanged glances, then looked at him, their discomfort obvious. "Not as well as yours," Sebastian confessed. "I have a lady in mind, but she's proving hard to land."

"And I have yet to find my quarry, let alone bring her to the bank." Peregrine shrugged. "I don't like it, Jasper. We're playing a game of our uncle's. He's baited the hook and he's playing us like trout. For two pins —"

"For two pins, Perry, you'd leave us all floundering in the quicksand," Jasper interrupted, his voice harsh. "Are you prepared to see the Sullivan name sink into infamy? Blackwater Manor collapsing in ruins? Everything this family has stood for over the generations lost to memory because our father gambled away every last hectare? There are generations of Blackwater tenants dependent upon us — upon me — for the roof over their heads and the bread on their tables. I will *not* pass up the opportunity to put that right, and neither will *you,* Peregrine, neglect your family duty. Find yourself a wife. I don't give a damn how you do it, but do it you will. Is that understood?"

Peregrine was ashen as he listened to his brother's cold, hard statement. He glanced at his twin and saw no reassurance there. Sebastian was pale but resolute. Slowly Peregrine nodded. "Understood," he said.

Jasper nodded. "Come to dinner next week, both of you." It was an instruction rather than an invitation and his brothers murmured an assent.

Jasper left them. He found Clarissa waiting in the hall below, tapping an impatient foot. "Forgive me, I needed a few words with my brothers," he explained as he ran down the stairs. "Find us a chair, Louis,

145

will you?" The servant went off at a run, a whistle in his hand. "Why *were* you hiding, Clarissa?" Jasper came up beside her.

"I wasn't," she said, denying it again. "Your brothers caught me unexpectedly while I was looking at a painting behind the odalisque. They were already in the middle of a conversation and I couldn't find the right moment to step out and make myself known."

"And what was their conversation?" he inquired, draping the shawl across her shoulders before taking his hat and cane from the bench.

She shrugged. "I don't know, just chat between brothers, I suppose."

He looked at her with narrowed eyes but let it go. "It's long past noon, and I for one am hungry. I suggest we return to the Angel and see if we can reproduce yesterday's dinner, which we so abruptly abandoned."

Was it only yesterday? So much had happened in the last twenty-four hours, Clarissa wasn't sure she was still the same person, but she was sure she was hungry and her present appearance would draw no attention in the Piazza, so, with a nod, she acceded.

Louis returned slightly out of breath. "Chair's outside, m'lord."

The chair stood before the door, two sturdy chairmen at the poles. Jasper handed Clarissa in and then walked beside the chair as the chairmen trotted back to Covent Garden.

The deserted quiet of the morning was a mere memory, and the Piazza was as crowded as ever, business being transacted on every street corner and behind every colonnade. Raucous voices floated on the steam billowing from the bathhouses and outside a tavern a man was selling his wife. He had set the woman on a rickety table, a rope around her neck, as he called out the bidding to the crowd of jeering carousers surrounding them. The woman's expression was one of desolate desperation.

Clarissa closed her eyes, feeling sick. She unfurled her fan and plied it vigorously, trying to shut out the noise and the image. Jasper glanced into the chair and frowned. "Are you unwell? You're very pale suddenly." Indeed, even beneath the white powder, her pallor was noticeable.

"No . . . no." She waved her fan at him but still didn't open her eyes. He looked around, wondering what had affected her. He could see nothing out of the ordinary.

The chair stopped outside the Angel and Jasper handed her down. The tavern was thronged but the tavern wench recognized the earl immediately and came over to them. "You want that special burgundy now, sir? 'Cause if 'n you do, Jake says as 'ow you should 'ave it in the back room." She jerked her head towards a door at the rear of the taproom. "Can't 'ave everyone after it. We've a good mutton stew to go with it, and as many oysters as you can eat."

"Then lead the way." They followed the girl into a small deserted chamber behind the bar warmed by a fire in an inglenook hearth.

"I'll bring oysters then, shall I?"

"And a flask of Rhenish." Jasper tossed his hat and cane onto the pine bench beneath the small window. "Come to the fire, Clarissa."

She obeyed, huddling into her shawl, trying to rid herself of the chill that had struck deep at the sight of the wife sale in the Piazza. Jasper frowned at her crouched figure, bending to the fire, hands outstretched. The bright red spots of rouge on her cheeks stood out as if she were in the grip of a fever.

He went to the door and beckoned to the wench, who was filling a flagon with Rhenish wine at the bar. "Bring a towel and a bowl of water, girl."

"Aye, sir." She set the flagon on the bar and went to satisfy this strange requirement. She set them down on the deal table against the wall. "I'll bring the Rhenish and the oysters now, sir."

He nodded, intent on the task at hand. He dipped the towel in the bowl and came over to Clarissa. "Let me get this stuff off your face, you've no need of it now." He tilted her chin and scrubbed vigorously at the rouge on her cheeks. It came off with some difficulty, then he soaked the cloth again, but before he could apply it to her lips, Clarissa took it from him.

"Thank you, my lord, but I can wash my own face."

She sounded much stronger, so much more like herself that he relinquished the cloth and went to pour the wine that the tavern wench had just brought.

Clarissa was scrubbing at her nipples, an expression of such acute distaste on her face that Jasper was startled. There were women all around them dressed and painted as Clarissa had been. But it wouldn't be necessary again, he decided. He certainly didn't care for it, particularly on a woman as youthful and fresh faced as she was. She was right to dislike it, to know that it didn't suit her. But it had served its purpose.

Clarissa became aware of his gaze as she scrubbed at her bare breasts and realized with a shock that she had thought nothing of washing her nipples in front of him. What was happening to her? She seemed to be changing into someone else without volition. Hastily she tucked her breasts back into the gown, pulling up the neckline, then swathing herself in the shawl. Instantly she felt more like herself.

"Oysters?" Jasper inquired, having watched this hasty readjustment with interest. He gestured to the table.

Clarissa sat down and took an oyster. She picked up the oyster fork and caught his quick glance. Her eyes went to the bruise on his hand. "You wouldn't let me go." She speared an oyster and popped it into her mouth.

"No, I suppose that's true." He speared one himself. "So, can we agree to bury that lamentable incident far in the past, and start a new chapter?"

Clarissa sipped her wine, rolling the golden flowery liquid around her tongue. It warmed her and she felt some of the tension slide away, a tension that had been a part of her since Luke had appeared in the breakfast room at Astley Hall that dreadful morning.

"When will I move to the house on Half Moon Street?" The question was sufficient answer to his question.

It was, however, a slightly awkward question for Jasper. His present mistress was still in situ. Their understanding had been drawing to an acrimonious close for some weeks now as his suspicion that she was sharing her favors with rather more than himself alone became undeniable fact. But as a matter of courtesy he needed to confront her before evicting her. "It will take me a few days to have it refurbished for you," he temporized.

Clarissa speared another oyster. "I'm sure I don't need a newly refurbished house, sir. My tastes are simple. Isn't it important that we begin this charade as soon as possible?"

Jasper thought of the house as Gwendolyn had it furnished. It was an ornate muddle of opulent swags, gilded furniture, a bed so deep in feathers he felt he was drowning whenever he joined her in it, and he had regretted giving her carte blanche with it from the moment he had first walked through the front door, although in the early days of their lustful passion he had deliberately ignored his reservations.

But lust had faded as it so often did, and his own sense of obligation to his mistress had ended abruptly when it had become abundantly clear to him that she had not the same sense of loyalty to her protector. He had dismissed the early whispers as malicious gossip, and somehow, probably because of his apparently nonchalant understanding, Gwendolyn had decided that he was a blind fool, to be used and manipulated as she chose. From then on the vulgar opulence of his so-called love nest had irritated him beyond bearing. Thus far, indolence had stopped him from confronting his mistress and dealing with the resulting unpleasantness. He had had no mistress to put in Gwendolyn's place, so it didn't really matter, but now the situation was very different.

Half Moon Street would become a love nest that would suit Clarissa Ordway, a woman so unlike Gwendolyn Mallory it was almost impossible to imagine them in the same room.

"It is important," he agreed. "But before I establish you there are other steps to be taken. First your wardrobe . . . you need clothes, fashionable clothes that don't smack of the nunnery, if society is to accept you. Nothing too modest, of course, nothing like that bronze muslin or the gown you were wearing yesterday, but —" He broke off as the tavern maid came in with a cauldron, which she set on the table. She lifted the lid and fragrant steam rose from the contents.

They didn't resume the conversation until she'd ceremoniously set a crusted bottle of burgundy on the table with two goblets, which she wiped over on her grimy apron; bowls; and utensils. "There y'are then. That'll do you, I reckon."

"It will, thank you." Jasper gave her a nod of dismissal, then lifted the ladle. "Pass your bowl."

Clarissa did so, wondering how many elegantly dressed earls ladled mutton stew from tavern cauldrons as a matter of course. Jasper St. John Sullivan certainly seemed to know his way around a ladle and a mutton stew. He filled her bowl, selecting choice pieces of meat and vegetables, and discarded anything with fat or gristle. He passed the bowl back and then helped himself.

Clarissa took a small spoonful, watching with a degree of amusement as he ate with relish, breaking bread into the gravy and eschewing all the finer points of table manners. Although there was nothing distasteful about his table manners, they were just the straightforward, hungry conduct of a man at a country table. She'd seen her own father eat with such enjoyment after a day hunting or in the fields with his tenants. And it made her instantly comfortable. She dipped again into her bowl and gave herself up to the sheer pleasure of good plain food.

Until she remembered Francis. Her spoon drifted down to her bowl and she crumbled her bread between her fingers, fighting back tears.

"What is it, Clarissa?" He leaned over the table. "You look stricken, what is it?"

She bit her lip. "A memory, a bad memory. Forgive me, my lord. It intruded." She gave a tiny unconvincing laugh. "They do, on occasion."

"Certainly they do." He looked at her closely. "Will you not tell me what it is?"

It was too soon, too soon even to give him the fabrication she had finally developed of her own child lost in childbirth. "A piece of history," she said lightly. "Nothing to concern us." She forked a piece of mutton and smiled at him.

Jasper was unconvinced, but he was also convinced that at this point he had no right to probe. Of course the woman had a past, of course she had complications in her life; everyone did. He didn't need to know them, understand them, or attempt to solve them. He was paying her to perform one part;

everything else about her was of no interest, unless it interfered with her ability to perform satisfactorily.

"As you say," he conceded, refilling his glass. "And to get back to your wardrobe . . . after we've eaten I will escort you to a milliner I know, a very skilled woman with a good eye. She'll know what to do for you."

"It's just possible, my lord, that I will know what to do for myself," she said, her tone sharp. "I haven't lived my life in a byre."

"No, of course you haven't, I never intended to imply such a thing," he denied, somewhat startled by her vehemence. "But you cannot know anything much about prevailing town fashion; it's not as if you've been frequenting fashionable London these last weeks. What is appropriate for the Piazza will not do in society's salons and drawing rooms."

Clarissa flushed with annoyance. "I am well aware of that, sir. Credit me with some sense."

He held up his hands in a gesture of surrender. "Enough said. We will go and visit Madame Hortense and you may share your views with her."

Clarissa frowned. "Must it be this afternoon?"

"I see little point in delay. Why, do you have something else, something more important, to do this afternoon?" He raised an interrogative eyebrow as he leaned over to refill her wineglass.

He sounded as if it was impossible that she should have. Clarissa, still frowning, stared into the ruby contents of her glass. He'd want to know what it was that was so important she couldn't spend the afternoon in his company, and she could hardly tell him she was impersonating a Bow Street Runner whenever she wasn't impersonating a prostitute. But to let a day slide by without furthering her search for Francis seemed like the worst betrayal. "I'm rather fatigued," she said finally. "I would like to rest this afternoon."

Jasper regarded her for a moment, wondering why he was unconvinced by such an excuse. It was not unreasonable; her life had turned topsy-turvy since the moment she had run into him the previous day. She probably needed some time to herself. And yet he had the feeling she was not telling him the truth. However he merely nodded. "As you wish. I'll send a carriage for you in the morning to take you to Madame Hortense's establishment."

"Thank you." Clarissa set down her

spoon. "If you'll excuse me now, my lord, I would return to King Street. I have no need of an escort. It's just around the corner." She pushed back her stool.

Jasper rose to his feet, observing drily, "You seem to have the habit of unceremonious departures from the dinner table, Clarissa. But I do insist that I accompany you to your door. Wait here while I settle up with mine host."

"I would not take you from your dinner, sir."

He dismissed her protest with a brusque gesture and went into the taproom. Clarissa grimaced; she couldn't really blame him for being annoyed. But in truth she didn't think she could face another mouthful of food or another moment of inaction. She wrapped herself in her shawl and went into the taproom.

Jasper turned from the bar counter, where he was talking with the landlord. "Come along then." He ushered her through the noisy crowd and out into the Piazza. His displeasure was obvious and he walked so fast that she almost had to trot to keep up with him. At the house he sounded the knocker and waited, tapping his foot until the door was opened by the steward. "Until tomorrow then," he said with a curt nod, then turned on his heel and left her on the doorstep.

Clarissa took a half step after him, then thought better of it. He was angry and entitled to be so by her discourteous haste to be rid of him. On the morrow she would try to make amends. She waited until he had disappeared around the corner onto Bedford Street, then entered the house, intending to fetch her cloak and coin purse before setting out for Ludgate Hill.

Jasper walked briskly, the crisp air cooling his temper somewhat. He was not accustomed to being dismissed so abruptly by anyone, let alone someone in his employ, and there were no two ways about it; he had paid good money for the services of Mistress Clarissa Ordway. He realized after a while that he was walking to Half Moon Street without having made a conscious decision as to his destination. Well, in his present mood, he would relish the inevitable confrontation with his mistress. It had to come sometime in the next day or two.

It was a longish walk but it served to clear his head and restore his equilibrium, so that he was once more his calm, dispassionate self when he unlocked the front door of the pretty little house where he kept his mistress and entered the small square hall. The maid who looked after Gwendolyn came through the baize door that led down to the basement kitchen regions as the earl closed the front door behind him.

She bobbed a hasty curtsy and her eyes darted side to side as if she were afraid to meet his gaze. "My lord . . . we wasn't expectin' you. I'll run up and tell madam."

"No, don't bother, Sally," he said. "I'll announce myself." He walked to the stairs and then paused, his eye falling on a hat, cane, and gloves on the bench by the door. The girl followed his eyes and stepped hastily in front of the bench.

"Madam gets powerful cross, my lord, if I don't announce folks."

Jasper crossed the small space. He reached out and indolently caught the girl's chin in his palm, tilting her face so that he could examine her countenance. He shook his head gently. "Sally, your loyalty is admirable but quite unnecessary. You may return to your work. I will take these to their owner." He released her chin, picked up the hat, cane, and gloves from the bench, and continued on his way upstairs.

Outside the door to the drawing room he paused, listening to the subdued murmur of voices within. A grim smile touched his lips as he identified the voice of Gwendolyn's visitor. He opened the door without ceremony.

Gwendolyn and the Honorable Henry Lassiter were sitting cozily on the daybed before the fire. Too cozily for mere friendship.

"Good day, my dear." He entered the drawing room, a smile on his lips that came nowhere near his eyes. "Lassiter, yours, I believe." He dropped his burdens onto a chair. "There's a chill wind, you will need them."

It was clearly a dismissal and the Honorable Henry, who had jumped up from the daybed at the earl's entrance, looked at the woman as if for an answer to his next move. He looked back at the earl, standing impassively holding the door open.

"Perhaps I didn't make myself clear," Jasper said amiably. "I bid you farewell, Lassiter."

"You have no right to dismiss my visitors, Jasper." Gwendolyn rose to her feet, her countenance flushed. "As it happens I wish Henry to remain."

"And I wish him gone, my dear." The earl's voice was as pleasant as ever, but his eyes were cold and hard. "I believe it to be my prerogative to decide whom I wish to entertain under my own roof. Just as it will be my pleasure to assist your guest down the stairs should he so wish it."

Lassiter went swiftly for his belongings. He cast one last glance at Gwendolyn, who was still standing beside the daybed, her expression a mixture of dismay and anger, then left, sidling past Jasper, who was still holding the door.

Jasper closed the door at his back and surveyed his mistress with that same smile. "Do sit down again, my dear. May I pour you a glass of Madeira?"

"No, I thank you." She sat down, arranging her taffeta skirts carefully. "That was very discourteous, Jasper. It's unlike you."

He inclined his head. "Do you really think so? I think most men would show a degree of incivility when their possessions are usurped."

She flushed. "I am not your possession."

"No, indeed you're not, my dear. But this house is and I retain the right to decide who spends time under its roof." He stood before the fire, resting an arm along the mantel as he looked at her. She was a very handsome woman. But even so she could not hold a candle to the lovely Mistress Ordway. Gwendolyn was older in many ways but that added to her appeal. She was well versed in the ways of the world and knew how to please him where it mattered. But she had no loyalty and he had long ago sworn to himself that he would never be duped by a woman again. Once was enough. He must be the only man in her life for as long as their arrangement lasted.

"You are free to do as you please, Gwendolyn," he continued, watching the color ebb and flow in her cheeks. "But you are not free to live under my protection and enjoy the favors of other men." He shrugged. "You may consider me old-fashioned in my need for an exclusive arrangement. So be it."

"What are you saying?" She stood up again, her hands restlessly opening and closing her fan. "Are you telling me it is over between us?"

"Yes, I believe that is what I'm saying. You may take whatever you wish from this house but I would like you to vacate it by the end of the week. I'm sure Lassiter can find a suitable property for you in the next few days. Unless, of course, there is someone else who might be preferable?" His tone was as cynical as his raised eyebrows.

Gwendolyn was very pale now. "I will promise never to see Henry again."

He shook his head. "Much as I would like

to believe that, my dear, I know how impossible you would find it. I know you too well. You need variety, the excitement of new conquests. Leave the house by the end of the week, if you please." He moved to her and lifted her hand, lightly brushing a kiss across the back. "I have enjoyed our association, Gwendolyn, but it's time to bring it to a close before things become ugly."

Releasing her hand, he bowed and walked quickly from the room.

CHAPTER SEVEN

Clarissa tentatively approached the rear steps at her uncle's house on Ludgate Hill. She couldn't decide whether she dared risk a direct approach to the kitchen door at the base of the steps. Someone had sent her the note, and it seemed a reasonable assumption that that someone lived in the house, or was intimate at least with the household. But she risked exposure if she asked questions of the wrong person, a member of the household loyal to his master.

The door below suddenly opened and lamplight poured forth into the small gloomy yard at the base of the steps. Although it was still only midafternoon the sky was heavy with cloud, making the basement kitchen even more in need of lamplight.

Clarissa moved hastily away from the top of the steps as voices rose in cheerful farewell and an elderly packman emerged into the yard. He carried a basket on his back and a tray around his neck displaying his selection of pins, ribbons, pieces of lace, buttons, and other trifles.

"Don't be a stranger now, Bert," a voice called from the kitchen.

"Never fear, Clara, I'll be back for more of that there mulled ale an' lardy cake," the peddler shouted back as he made his way up the steps to the street.

Clarissa darted across the road before he reached the street. It seemed, judging from what she'd overheard, that he was a frequent visitor to the back door and a welcome one. Whenever he visited he would be offered refreshment as he laid out his wares to the entire household gathered in the kitchen, and he would hear the household gossip. It might be safer, with less risk of Luke hearing of it, if, instead of approaching her uncle's household directly, she talked with someone who visited often. She knew from her own experience that the packmen who made their regular rounds peddling the trifles and trinkets necessary to the smooth running of a household and to the pleasure of servants who had little enough to please them were au fait with the most intimate details of some of their habitual households, as were the tinkers, cobblers, and knife grinders who paid regular calls.

She glanced up and down the street, wondering if her uncle was in the house, looking from a window maybe. But perhaps he hadn't returned from wherever he had been going that morning, which meant that at any moment he could turn the corner of the street on his way home. He couldn't find his niece loitering outside his front door.

The packman was shuffling his way up the hill towards the bulk of St. Paul's, a dramatic edifice against the darkening sky. It was getting colder, a hint of early frost in the sharp wind, and Clarissa huddled into her thick woolen cloak as she hurried half running after him. He heard her quick footsteps and turned round, his expression startled.

"Forgive me, I would like to talk to you for a moment." Clarissa reached him, slightly out of breath. "You were visiting Master Astley's house just now."

"What if I was?" He looked at the hooded, cloaked young woman in surprise.

"I was wondering if anyone ever mentioned a young boy living in the house . . . or if you'd ever seen him. A lad of about ten, Master Astley's ward."

The peddler frowned. "Who wants to know?"

"I will tell you that, if you'll answer my question first," she said, her eyes wary.

"Maybe I 'ave 'eard summat . . . maybe I seen a lad. Like I said, who wants to know?"

"His sister. I work for her, she sent me to see how her brother was doing." It was a gamble but one worth taking.

"Where's your mistress now, then?" The peddler still looked suspicious.

"Back at the inn. She doesn't want her uncle to know she's in town."

The packman seemed to consider this before he nodded slowly. "Well, you tell your mistress the laddie's with a baby farmer in a house near the stairs at Wapping."

Clarissa's heart leaped. "Did you send my mistress the note?"

"Maybe I did, 'n' maybe I didn't." He looked anxiously down the street. "I'm saying nothing . . . more than my trade's worth."

Clarissa nodded impatiently. "Tell me the address. Is Wapping in London?"

"Course it is, down the east end, on the river. But I don't know the street, just it's by the stairs."

How big was Wapping? "What stairs?"

He gave her a pitying look. "River stairs, of course."

167

Of course. "How will I . . . my mistress . . . how will she find it?"

" 'Tis a house hard by the Eagle an' Dove. If she asks around, someone'll tell 'er." He hesitated, then said, "Best if she gets 'im out of there quick. He's doin' all right, but there's infection an' all sorts around there." He hoisted his pack further up his back and started off again up the hill.

"Just a minute . . . please . . . just one more question." Desperately Clarissa ran after him. "How do you know he's all right? Have you seen the boy?"

"Aye, a few days ago. Gave 'im some gingerbread."

She grabbed his arm. "Could you take me there?"

He shook his head. "Not on my rounds for another month, girl. But you tell your mistress what I said an' to find him quick." His expression softened a little. "Nice little lad, 'e is. Don't know what that uncle of 'is thinks he's doin', but he's a bad one and no mistake." He spat into the kennel, then continued on his way and this time Clarissa let him go.

Wapping? How was she to get there? Would a chair take her? It didn't sound like the kind of place frequented by chairmen. She looked around helplessly and then froze. A hackney carriage turned into the street at the bottom of the hill and drew up outside Luke's house. She moved closer into the shadow of a house, watching as her uncle descended from the carriage, paid the jarvey, and disappeared into the house. Only then did she breathe easily.

The hackney was coming up the street towards her and she moved out of the shadows, raising a hand. The jarvey pulled his horses to a halt and scrutinized her with the eyes of experience. In general respectable women did not hail hackneys alone. But this one wore a good cloak and good shoes. "Where are you bound, mistress?"

She hesitated. Could she tell him to take her to Wapping, to a tavern called the Eagle and Dove hard by Wapping Stairs? But it was growing dark and she would be wandering alone in an unknown and more than likely dangerous part of the city. She couldn't help Francis if she was lying in the street with her throat cut. It would have to wait until daylight.

"Covent Garden." Her voice was haughty, the set of her head arrogant, as if defying him to draw any conclusions from her destination.

He looked at her again, his eyes narrowed. "Show me your coin."

Clarissa controlled her anger at his insolence and withdrew her purse from the deep pocket of her cloak. She selected a silver sovereign and held it up. "I daresay this will compensate you for your trouble."

He nodded and grinned down at her. "Aye, that it will, missie. Take you anywhere for that. Hop in."

Clarissa climbed into the dirty, stale-smelling interior and sat gingerly on the stained leather squabs. The jarvey cracked his whip and the horse moved off, the iron wheels bouncing over the cobbles. She caught a faint whiff of perfume from the leather behind her head. It was Luke's; she'd smelled it many times before. Her hands clenched inside her muff and she shifted to the far corner of the bench. It wasn't going to be sufficient simply to rescue Francis; somehow the man had to be brought to account.

The bright lights of the Piazza with its attendant sounds and smells soon penetrated the uncurtained window aperture of the carriage. She leaned out of the window. "You may set me down here, jarvey."

"As you wish." He reined in his horse and Clarissa jumped down, thankful to be out of the insalubrious interior of the hackney. She handed up a shilling, saying calmly,

"You know as well as I do that a sovereign is daylight robbery and you can be fined for extortion. But while I doubt the journey was worth more than sixpence, I'm prepared to pay you a shilling."

He took the coin with a muttered imprecation, spat his disgust to the cobbles, and urged his horse forward. Clarissa had made him set her down on the corner of Russell Street and the Great Piazza. It was a only short walk to 32 King Street and she reached the house in a few minutes. As she was about to raise the door knocker, the door opened under her hand and she found herself looking up into the Earl of Blackwater's disgruntled countenance.

He stared at her. "There you are. Where have you been? You said you needed to rest." He was clearly put out and Clarissa realized for the first time what it meant to be living under the protection of a man who considered he had paid for her to be at his beck and call.

"Forgive me, my lord, but I didn't fully understand that I was to have no freedom of movement under this arrangement," she said stiffly. "Am I to be confined within doors waiting until you choose to seek out my company?"

The anger in her jade eyes would have

scorched a lesser man. But Jasper only drew back for a second from the heat and returned to the fray now with the utmost good humor. "Of course not, but I felt sadly deprived. I was certain you would be here as you had said you would be, and how was I to know you had changed your mind?" He made his tone plaintive as his eyes smiled at her.

He hadn't realized how pleased he would be to see her. Her cheeks were pink from the cold, the anger in her eyes made them shine like emeralds, and he wanted more than anything to strip the thick folds of her cloak from her and let his imagination savor that dainty figure in the thin muslin gown.

"I needed some fresh air," Clarissa said, mollified by both the conciliatory tone and the appreciative gleam in his eye. "What did you want with me, my lord?"

"I wished to sup with you, in the peace and solitude of your own chamber," he responded. "So far every attempt I've made to enjoy a meal in your company has been somewhat truncated. I thought if it were on your own terms, as it were, we might even manage to savor dessert. I seem to remember that Mistress Griffiths's cook makes a most delectable syllabub."

"Does she?" Clarissa took the opportunity

to step past him into the hall as he moved slightly to one side.

"You haven't tasted it?" He sounded astonished, following her back into the house. "None of your clients has —"

"If you don't mind, my lord, I would prefer to leave the subject of my other clients out of our dealings," she declared. "After all, it's agreed I shall have no others for the duration of our arrangement."

"That is true." He began to divest himself of his cloak and hat. "Well, now you are returned, we may resume our plan to sup together."

"*Our* plan, sir? I don't believe I had any part in its making." She moved to the stairs. "You will forgive me if I decline the invitation. I am fatigued and would seek my bed early."

"No, I will not forgive you. The invitation is not yours to decline, Clarissa." His voice had changed, hardened. "I will sup with you this evening."

Clarissa stood with one foot on the bottom step, her hand resting on the banister, as she contemplated her response. Before she could say anything, however, Mistress Griffiths came into the hall from the salon. "Ah, Clarissa, there you are. His lordship was desirous of supping with you. You told no one where you were going when you went out."

Clarissa sighed. "I didn't realize it was mandatory to do so, madam. I have explained to his lordship that I would prefer to seek my rest early tonight and I beg his indulgence."

Nan looked at her sharply. Either the girl was getting cold feet, or she was playing another game altogether. Nan suspected the latter. The readiness with which she had accepted the earl's offer of protection had convinced her that, whatever she would have others believe, Mistress Ordway was no virgin and had not arrived on her doorstep by accident.

"In this house, Clarissa, we do everything to please our clients. You will, if you please, go up to your chamber and ready yourself to receive his lordship. Your supper will be served whenever you ring for it." Her voice was icy, but she was all smiles as she turned to Jasper. "If you will wait for a few minutes in the salon, my lord, Marianna is playing the pianoforte and I have a particularly fine claret if you care to sample it. Clarissa will be ready for you directly."

Jasper bowed his acquiescence and went into the drawing room. He slightly regretted Nan's involvement, which he knew would include coercion if necessary, but at the same time he wasn't prepared to play ducks and drakes with Clarissa.

"Go along upstairs, girl. I don't know what this nonsense is but it had better finish here. Tidy yourself up for his lordship. You'll find something suitable in the armoire." Nan gave Clarissa a nudge up the stairs and for a moment Clarissa had to resist the need to push her back, to stand tall and tell her who and what she was, the daughter of Squire Astley and Lady Lavinia Astley, no penniless whore without friends or family. But she couldn't do that. Not yet, not until she had Francis safe.

Without a word, she went up the stairs to the chamber that had been allotted to her. Wax tapers were lit, rich velvet curtains drawn against the encroaching night; a fire burned in the grate. A round table was set for two in the window embrasure, a decanter of wine in the center. Her eyes darted to the bed. The bed curtains were drawn back, the coverlets turned down in clear invitation. She went cold. How was she to stop this?

Slowly she peeled off her gloves and shrugged out of her cloak. The muslin gown had lost its pristine crispness since the morning; the lace edging to the décolletage was limp and lifeless, the folds of the gown hanging creased and formless over a starched petticoat that had lost its stiffness. She was beginning to understand why ladies of fashion changed their gowns so frequently.

She went to hang up her cloak in the armoire and looked in disbelief at the taffeta chamber robe hanging beside her own clothes. Presumably that was what Nan had meant by *something suitable.* Suitable for entertaining gentlemen in one's bedchamber à deux. She fingered the material, which was a rich deep emerald with a delicate tracing of pale gold leaves; long, full sleeves ended in lace ruffs, and a series of tiny ribbon bows fastened the gown at the front. Where had it come from? Did Mother Griffiths keep a costume room to cover all eventualities?

She took it out and laid it on the bed. The robe was altogether delightful, surprisingly tasteful, and Clarissa could find nothing about it to object to beyond the immutable fact that it wasn't hers.

Thoughtfully she unlaced the sprig muslin and hung that in the linen press, where with luck the creases would hang out. She poured water from the ewer into the basin on the washstand and washed her face and hands, surprised at how grimy she felt. A day spent in taverns, crowded streets, and dirty hackney carriages would do that to you, she reflected with a wry grimace. Her hair, so carefully curled that morning, was rapidly returning to form, hanging now in a straight curtain to her shoulders. But at least it still shone. She pulled her hairbrush through it with slow, almost dreamlike strokes, wondering how on earth she was going to get through this evening intact.

She sat down to take off her shoes and stockings, and wriggled her bare toes in the warmth of the fire, then stood up abruptly. She couldn't pretend she could stop the world turning just by doing everything so slowly. She needed a strategy for the evening, a way to keep the earl at arm's length.

She slipped into the chamber robe, fastening the little ribbon ties down the front. The garment hung in loose pleated folds from a waistline set just beneath her breasts; the lace-trimmed neckline was square cut and higher, she was relieved to find, than that of the sprig muslin. She looked at her reflection in the long pier glass. She presented a most elegant figure, and not in the least provocative, except for her bare feet.

A brief knock at the door made her jump

and she turned to face it, her heart thudding against her rib cage. She still had no strategy.

Jasper stepped into the chamber. "I trust I'm not intruding, madam." He bowed formally even as his eyes assessed her, a glow of appreciation in their depths. For a moment his gaze lingered on her bare feet and he smiled slowly. "How delightful. How utterly charming, my dear." He closed the door behind him and stepped up to her.

Clarissa stepped back. "My lord, *please*. May I pour you a glass of wine?"

He looked at her, his eyes narrowed. "You intend to refuse me?"

"I thought I had explained . . . explained how I would like some respite." And then it came to her. She clasped her hands, regarding him earnestly. "My lord, just once I would like to have a proper liaison, one conducted with some grace. I would like us to progress as . . . as ordinary people do in the world outside this . . . this . . ." She waved an expressive hand around the hushed and silken chamber of lust. "I would like to be able to believe that we are not in a bordello."

She let her clasped hands fall against her skirts and offered a tentative smile, her head slightly tilted. "Can you not grant me that one wish, sir?"

Jasper scratched the bridge of his nose. He looked at her in momentary incomprehension, then he said, "You would be courted then? You would have me woo you?"

Slowly she nodded. "It will be new for me. I have never been courted."

He began to laugh, softly but with deep amusement. "Oh, my dear Clarissa, if that is your wish, then I will put aside my admittedly rampant desire and play the game of courtly love. If I can remember how," he added with another chuckle. "It's been a long time since I went a-courting. But if those are your terms, then I accept them."

He strode to the table and filled the wine goblets, bringing them back to the hearth. He handed her one, then linked his arm through hers, bringing his glass to his lips as she raised her own. "To courtship, Mistress Clarissa."

"To courtship, Lord Blackwater." She drank, filled with a heady sense of relief, but also excitement, realizing for the first time how much she enjoyed being with him, how she seemed to be more of everything in his company. Brighter, quicker, prettier even, despite the edge of antagonism that sharpened their exchanges. His body was so close to hers now, she was enveloped in his heat, and she could somehow feel every line of her own body clearly delineated as he would feel her against him beneath the delicate taffeta robe.

Jasper disentangled their arms and took Clarissa's glass, setting it down with his own. He slid an arm around her, drawing her up against him as with his free hand he tipped up her chin. "Kisses are perfectly acceptable courtship behavior," he murmured, and brought his mouth to hers.

Clarissa was momentarily startled, momentarily dismayed, and then she was aware of nothing but the sensation of his mouth on hers, his body against hers. This was a kiss unlike any she had experienced before. The clumsy fumblings of her earlier forays into the world of passion bore no relation to this masterly caress. She could feel the hard muscularity of his thighs against her own, the steady beat of his heart against her own breast. His lips were firm and pliable, and the scent of his skin, earthy with just the slightest hint of lavender, seemed to envelop her. Her arms found their way around him, her hands on his back, because where else were they to go when it came to this business of kissing, and everything seemed perfectly right, perfectly natural, indeed utterly inevitable.

When he released her and stepped away she felt bereft and had to resist the urge to pull him to her again. "Courtship is a time of slow and gentle pleasures," Jasper said, smiling. "I think I'm going to enjoy it." He took her hand and drew her to the fire. "Are you hungry? Shall I ring for supper?"

Clarissa glanced towards the bed, glaring in its invitation. "In a moment, if you please." She went over and swiftly pulled the curtains around the bed, closing it off from the room.

Jasper hid a smile, saying with mock gravity, "Well, that makes it plain enough." He reached for the bellpull before picking up his wineglass and taking one of the armchairs on either side of the fire.

Clarissa took up her own glass, sat opposite, and commenced civilized drawing room conversation. "I trust you spent an enjoyable afternoon, my lord?"

A look she couldn't interpret crossed his countenance, to be instantly dismissed. He said blandly, "I accomplished a disagreeable but necessary task." He sipped his wine. "And you, Mistress Clarissa? A pleasant walk, I believe you said."

"A fruitless errand," she improvised. "I wished to purchase some ribbon, but unfortunately I could not find the particular shade I need. It's to trim a bonnet," she added, astonished at her powers of invention.

"When you visit Madame Hortense in the morning, you will be able to see if she can be of assistance," Jasper said. "Of course, you should feel free to direct my coachman to take you anywhere you wish. You might find what you seek in one of the silk warehouses. What is the exact shade you require?"

Clarissa's lips twitched. It was all too absurd. Jasper, Earl of Blackwater, engaging in a discussion of ribbon trimming for a nonexistent bonnet. "A straw color," she murmured, her voice quivering with laughter. "A most particular blond tint. It must be exactly right, you understand, sir, other—"

Her sentence ended in a squeak as he leaned forward, seized her hands, and abruptly pulled her across the intervening space to land on her knees in front of him. "You have something of the devil in you, Mistress Clarissa," he declared, his eyes alight with laughter. He pulled her up a little so that she was kneeling against his knees and lightly kissed the corner of her mouth.

At this auspicious moment the door opened to admit two manservants with heavy trays. Their well-trained eyes took in the fireside scene in one quick glance, and then silently they set out their platters and serving dishes on the table and melted from the chamber.

"Good lord," Clarissa breathed in astonished admiration. "I suppose they're accustomed in this house to entering a chamber and politely ignoring a couple in flagrante delicto."

Jasper looked at her oddly. "Of course they are. Why would you sound surprised? You must be used to the convention. They come in when they're called and leave as if they were never here."

Clarissa realized her mistake. She seemed constantly to be making them, which was hardly surprising in the circumstances. Fortunately, for the moment anyway, Jasper was so convinced of her position in Mother Griffiths's establishment that even while he seemed surprised at some of her innocent remarks, it hadn't occurred to him to dig deeper.

"I suppose I never really thought of it before," she said with a light shrug. "Usually I was too busy to notice."

He seemed to accept this and, slipping his hands beneath her arms, lifted her to her feet as he stood up himself. "I for one am sharp set, so let us see what delectations await us."

There was a dish of baked crab, a roast duck with a compote of apples, and a dish of buttered salsify. A fresh decanter of wine had also appeared on the table.

Jasper held Clarissa's chair for her and then took his own. He unfolded his linen napkin and took up his wineglass, smiling at her over the lip. "I trust I'm not overly optimistic in hoping that this meal we can enjoy to its conclusion?"

She caught her lower lip, biting back the urge to defend herself. On both occasions he had adopted a tone that somehow reduced her to a possession, a person of much less value than himself. She was prepared to accept that it was inadvertent, simply springing from an assumption he considered accurate and comprehensible. But she wanted to put him right and she couldn't.

"I see no reason why not, my lord." She helped herself to baked crab and took a hot roll from the breadbasket.

Jasper helped himself, broke his bread, and asked, "What brought you to Mother Griffiths's establishment, Clarissa?"

"I told you, my lord, I came to seek my fortune." She took a sip of wine.

"Yes, a little too glibly, I feel." He cast a

quick searching glance across the table. "But let's assume that's so; did something other than the desire to make your fortune drive you from the country . . . where was it you said you were from?" Studiously he spread butter liberally on his roll, his eyes on his task.

Clarissa thought quickly. What had she said? "Oh . . . Bedfordshire way," she muttered, disguising the falter with a cough, reaching hastily for her wineglass.

"Yes, I remember now. So what drove you from Bedfordshire?"

She looked up at him, once more composed. "Need, sir. Certain personal circumstances make it necessary to earn my bread."

"And may I inquire what those circumstances are?"

"No, my lord," she stated. If this was to be another truncated meal so be it. He'd gone back to his old ways.

Jasper's eyebrows disappeared into his scalp at this flat negative, but he controlled the swift rise of his temper and paused for thought. He had agreed for whatever lunatic reason to court this woman before bedding her, and he was probably not going about it in quite the right way.

He changed the subject, offering her a smile as he reached across the table to lay his hand over hers. "Can we dispense with the formalities, Clarissa? I have a given name; I would like you to use it."

"Jasper," she said, accepting the olive branch. "I like the name."

He chuckled. "That's certainly fortunate. May I carve you some duck?"

"Thank you."

Throughout the evening Clarissa's thoughts veered wildly between the need to concentrate on her companion, the pleasure she took in his company even if it required her to keep on her toes, and planning for the morrow, when she would find Francis. How would she get her brother away undetected? Where would she take him at first? It would be so much easier if she were already situated in the house on Half Moon Street. At least there she would be to some extent her own mistress.

"Do you have a better idea now when exactly I will be able to move into the house on Half Moon Street?"

Jasper blinked at the abrupt non sequitur. He'd been describing a particularly interesting play he'd seen just recently and had thought her attention showed signs of wandering, but not quite so thoroughly.

"Why? Are you in a hurry to be gone from here?" He spooned salsify onto his plate. "It

186

seems comfortable enough."

"I am anxious to do what has to be done," she replied. "Particularly after this morning. I must tell you, my lo . . . Jasper . . . that I did not care for your uncle."

"No, I can hardly blame you, my dear. He doesn't care whom he offends. But take heart, he offends everyone equally regardless of status or relationship. And I believe he rather took to you."

"He has a strange way of showing it."

"That is certainly true. And to answer your question, the house will be ready for you on Saturday."

CHAPTER EIGHT

Jasper took his leave shortly before midnight, indulging only in a decorous kiss. He went on his way smiling at the reflection that delaying the consummation of this liaison added a rather exciting frisson of anticipation. It made him feel younger, somehow. And unless he was much mistaken Mistress Clarissa Ordway found him a suitable object for her own desires. He had felt her hesitation when he'd first kissed her, a tentative instant when she'd drawn back a little, but although it had been a good many years since he'd had need of a whore's services, in his experience of such commercial encounters, kissing was one intimacy they generally withheld from their clients, so Clarissa's initial withdrawal was natural enough.

But it hadn't lasted and there was nothing artificial about the little thrill that had run through her when his lips met hers, or the quick flush of her cheeks when his hand lightly brushed across her breast. He wanted to see her naked, to feel her body moving beneath his, responding to his touches as he knew she would, but in the meantime he would sharpen his appetite with anticipation and allow his imagination full rein.

If he could have seen Clarissa at this point he might have been a little less complacent. Jasper was the last person on her mind. She had, rather cleverly she thought, orchestrated the perfect excuse for delaying the inevitable, and having resolved that issue at least temporarily she put it from her mind and turned all her attention to planning for the following morning.

Her mind raced as she prepared for bed. She would need transport to Wapping, as much as anything because she hadn't the first idea how to get there. She knew where east was, since the sun rose there every morning, but if the East End of London was anything like where she was now it would be a convoluted tangle of narrow streets and dark alleys. She would never negotiate them alone.

She exchanged the seductress's chamber robe for her own rather plain but warm woolen one and snuffed the candles on the mantel, leaving only the one by the bed burning, then went to draw back the heavy curtain at the window. She needed a few inches of morning light to penetrate, otherwise she was afraid she might sleep until noon. As she pulled the thick velvet aside, she had her second brilliant idea of the night.

Of course. The river. That was the obvious way to reach her destination. The watermen went anywhere accessible along the mighty thoroughfare of the Thames, and she needed the river stairs at Wapping. They would take her right to her destination. From there she would ask in the Eagle and Dove about a woman who took in babies. If the baby farmer was hard by the tavern as the peddler had said, then she should be easy to find. But how to make her approach?

She turned back to the chamber, deep in thought as she shrugged out of her chamber robe and tossed it at the foot of the bed. She climbed into bed, propping the pillows up behind her. The deep featherbed was a vast improvement on the narrow maid's cot in the garret and she had a moment of pure indulgent pleasure settling herself under the feather quilt. Of course, the comfort of the bed was for the added pleasure of the nunnery's clients rather than the cosseting of the inhabitants themselves, but for the moment that did nothing to inhibit her hedonistic enjoyment as the firelight flickered on the ceiling and the bedside candle cast a soft golden pool onto her pillow.

How to approach the baby farmer? Who would ordinarily approach such a woman? People who needed to dispose of an unwanted child, obviously. Supposing she pretended to be a pregnant lady's maid, desperate not to lose her situation? She needed to make arrangements for the child's care after its birth so that she could continue to work.

That was the perfect story to tell a baby farmer. It would get her into the house at the very least. What happened next was in the lap of the gods, but now that she knew where Francis was, Clarissa felt the dreadful sense of powerlessness slide away. She was in control of her life, of her brother's life, again.

She leaned sideways to blow out her candle and lay in the flickering dark as her eyes grew heavy and for the first time in weeks she fell into a deep, dreamless, restful sleep.

She awoke with the sound of the first iron-wheeled cart rolling over the cobbles beneath her window. The light was gray, promising another chilly and overcast day, but such considerations were unimportant. Clarissa allowed herself to wake slowly, listening to the sounds of the house around her, except that there were no sounds of life, only the creakings and settlings of a sleeping house.

Early mornings were not well known to the inhabitants of 32 King Street, who rarely found their beds before dawn. Even most of the servants, out of the same consideration, started late.

Clarissa swung herself out of bed and sat on the edge, pushing her feet into her slippers. She reached sideways for her chamber robe and wrapped it around herself. Her first order of business was breakfast. She let herself out of the chamber and stepped into the deserted hallway. Sconced lamps burned low along the wall as she made her way to the staircase.

A sudden blast of cold air swept the hall as the front door opened and a child with chapped cheeks and hands came in with a pail of dirty water and a scrubbing brush. She stared mutely at Clarissa, the door banging shut behind her.

She must have been scrubbing the steps, Clarissa thought with quick sympathy. She didn't look more than ten years old in her down-at-heel clogs, holland pinafore, and grimy apron, her hair caught up under a mob cap. Her nose was running, which added to the general air of desolation.

"Is anyone up below stairs?" Clarissa asked gently.

The child nodded. "Cook an' the scullery girl."

"Have you had breakfast?" Clarissa tried a smile.

The child shook her head, sniffing vigorously before wiping her nose on her sleeve. "Not till I done the fireplaces, mistress."

"*All* of them?" There must have been at least half a dozen in the downstairs reception rooms alone.

Another nod and the child trailed off towards the grand salon, dragging her bucket.

Clarissa headed for the back stairs. She found the cook stirring pots in the kitchen and the scullery maid scrubbing pans in the scullery. No one else had yet made an appearance. "Good morning, Cook." She greeted the woman as she would have greeted her own cook at home at Astley Hall. "Would you mind if I help myself to a piece of bread and cheese?"

"Aye, miss, that I would," the woman declared bluntly. "I'll send you up a proper breakfast and a pot of hot chocolate directly."

"But no one's up yet," Clarissa protested. "Indeed I am perfectly happy to take care of myself."

"Not in my kitchen, miss. You go back to your bedchamber now."

Clarissa knew better than to interfere in a cook's territory and with a smile of thanks returned upstairs. She was half-dressed in her own countrified linen gown and apron when a scratch on the door produced the scullery maid with a tray of fried eggs, toasted bread, and a pot of hot chocolate.

"Cook says this was all she could manage at present." The maid set the tray on the table and scurried away before Clarissa could even express her thanks.

She ate hastily, wondering if her early morning encroachment on the kitchen regions would reach the ears of Mistress Griffiths. It seemed unheard-of for an inhabitant of the above-stairs regions to visit the below. But on Saturday she would be out of this place and her own mistress once again.

Her appetite satisfied, Clarissa examined herself in the mirror. How to make herself into a convincing lady's maid? Pregnant, a little down at heel . . . ? She had to look like someone else so that Luke would not be able to recognize his niece from any description. Her hair was her most obvious feature. She pulled it back from her face and plaited it tightly, pinning the plait into a coil at the nape of her neck, and then tied a kerchief around her head, so that not a single distinctive red-gold strand was visible. Her eyes seemed larger than usual without the softening of her hair. Experimentally, she dipped a finger into the ash in the grate and smudged the skin beneath her eyes, giving them huge dark shadows against her cheekbones. It was an amazing transformation. But not quite enough.

She looked around the chamber, then her eye fell on one of the small, round cushions on the daybed. She picked it up and went to the mirror, experimentally tucking the cushion against her stomach beneath her cloak. It produced quite a convincing little bump, not enough for an instant recognition of pregnancy, but sufficient proof if someone knew she was carrying a child. She hauled up the skirt of her gown and pushed the cushion into the waistband of her petticoat, tying the drawstring tightly over it, then dropped her skirt down. She threw her cloak around her shoulders, drawing it tightly around her, then examined her reflection again in the mirror. She really didn't look in the least like herself. She drew her hood up, hiding as much of her face as she could, and hunched her shoulders a little, as if she was trying to hide the shameful evidence of her pregnancy. The transformation was complete; she barely recognized herself.

She let herself out of the house without encountering another soul. The streets were cold, empty, and piled with the debris of the previous night's entertainments. She stepped gingerly over a pile of vomit, holding her skirts high, and made her way around the colonnades of the Great Piazza, heading for the river. She threaded her way through the streets leading to the Strand and from there down Savoy Street to the water steps on the embankment at the end of the street.

There were more people around here and the river was already busy with skiffs darting between the larger barges laden with goods. The watermen kept up a constant whistle as they touted for custom on both banks, poling their craft up and down along the embankment.

Clarissa descended the stairs to the small platform that jutted out over the water. A skiff with two oarsmen came up immediately. They shipped their oars and one of them leaned out to seize a rope hanging from the platform. He hauled on it, bringing the little boat tight into the platform. He held it steady as Clarissa stepped in.

"Wappin' Stairs." Her voice was a little muffled, her accent that of the Kentish countryside. It was an accent she had heard all her life and she felt reasonably confident she could keep it up as long as she didn't say too much.

The waterman nodded, finding nothing remarkable in either his passenger or her destination, and as soon as she was seated on the narrow thwart pushed off from the bank with his oar and he and his partner took the skiff into the mainstream. It was cold on the river and Clarissa huddled closer into her cloak. Her nervousness grew as the skiff moved swiftly towards her destination. She rehearsed over and over in her head what she would say to the baby farmer, concentrating on getting the vowel sounds authentic, remembering to drop the final *g* at the end of certain words. If she was word-perfect the disguise would be easier to maintain.

The hulking bulk of the Tower of London loomed up ahead of them after almost an hour. Clarissa was frozen by this time. She'd had no idea it would take so long and guessed now that it would have been quicker by land under horsepower. But it was too late for second thoughts. The watermen brought the boat close to the forbidding Traitor's Gate, a grilled gate giving onto a dark hole leading into the gray stone of the edifice. She shuddered, thinking of all those who had disappeared into that darkness never to reappear.

They went beneath Tower Bridge, the rowers carefully steering between the great stone pillars that were sunk deep into the riverbed. The river eddied swiftly at their bases and many a boat had come to grief caught in the swirling currents. They passed Alderman's Stairs and Tower Bridge wharf, and finally Wapping Stairs came up on the north bank of the river.

The jumble of buildings along the embankment looked like warehouses. The watermen brought the skiff against a long pier jutting into the water. Steps led from there up to the embankment. Clarissa paid them the shilling fare and stepped out onto the pier.

The landscape was alien, threatening in its strangeness. Porters darted hither and thither along the pier with great baskets balanced on their heads, raucous shouts filled the air, children struggling bent double under the weight of heavy sacks staggered past her to the barges waiting to be loaded at the end of the pier, and above her loomed the great stone warehouses on either side of the steps. Her only comfort lay in the fact that everyone was too occupied with their own affairs to cast so much as a glance in her direction.

She climbed the steps, which were wet and slimy with green weed at the lower level where the river at high tide covered them. Once she reached the top she breathed a sigh of relief. The air felt lighter, fresher, although it was still redolent of fish and tar, and the crowded buildings blocked the daylight. She looked around, searching for the Eagle and Dove tavern. It was supposed to be hard by the stairs.

Tentatively she approached a woman, carrying a basket of laundry on her head. " 'Scuse me, mistress, I'm lookin' fer the Eagle and Dove?"

The woman barely glanced at her and hardly broke stride. "Corner o' Scandrett."

And where or what was Scandrett? Clarissa looked around again helplessly. It must be a street close by. She set off along the muddy lane that stretched behind the warehouses, picking her way through evil-smelling puddles. The powerful, vile reek of a tannery made her catch her breath as she passed one building, and then there was the more familiar and certainly pleasanter smell of a livery stable a little further on with a narrow alleyway running alongside it.

A stable lad came out of the livery stable leading a brown cob and Clarissa accosted him. "I'm lookin' fer Scandrett Street."

He looked at her as if she'd walked out of Bedlam. "Y'are standin' on it."

Clarissa looked behind her up the alleyway. "This is it?"

"Aye, where you from, then?"

"Not around 'ere," she said shortly. "I'm wantin' the Eagle and Dove."

"Up top." He jerked his thumb at the alley and continued on his way.

Clarissa followed direction and ventured into the alley. There were houses on either side, the street so narrow that their rooftops almost touched across the lane. It was dark and dank and strewn with rubbish. How could Francis possibly survive in one of these filthy hovels? Anger burned deep within her, giving her strength. Luke would pay, and he would pay dearly.

The Eagle and Dove was at the far end of the alley as the boy had promised, and to Clarissa's pleasant surprise the alley opened onto an expanse of green, with the tavern sitting on the edge of it. It was as if suddenly she found herself on a village green in the countryside, and her spirit lifted a little. Maybe Francis wasn't buried in those reeking alleys. Maybe he was in one of the cottages scattered along the sides of the green.

Emboldened, she pushed open the door of the tavern below the creaking sign depicting an eagle with a dove in its talons and found herself immediately in a small taproom, heavy with the odor of spilled beer and the sea coal that burned sullenly in the fireplace.

The taproom was deserted and she went to the counter. "Landlord?"

An elderly man shuffled through a door in the rear wall and peered myopically at her. "Who wants 'im?"

"Me. I'm lookin' fer a woman what takes in babies around 'ere. Is there one?"

His eyes became mere slits as he took in the slight swell beneath her cloak. He began to rub the stained countertop with a filthy rag. "Depends on who wants 'er."

"I does, sir." Clarissa decided she would get what she wanted more quickly if she went straight to the point. "I've coin t' pay for the information." She huddled closer into her cloak, turning slightly sideways, laying a hand on her belly.

The old man's eyes took on a calculating gleam. "Let's see yer money then."

Clarissa slipped her hand into the pocket of her cloak and felt in her coin purse. She didn't dare bring it out into the open in what was inevitably a den of thieves, and she didn't dare give the impression that she had more than a few meager coins. She identified a sixpence with her fingertips and laid it on the counter, letting him see it before covering it with her hand. "Where will I find her?"

"Dundee, next street along the green." He reached for the coin but she kept her hand over it.

" 'Ow will I know the 'ouse?"

He grunted and blew his nose copiously on the filthy rag he'd been using on the countertop. Clarissa controlled her revulsion and waited. Finally he said, "Third 'ouse down on the right."

Clarissa lifted her hand off the sixpence and it disappeared in an instant. "Is she the only one 'ereabouts?" She gave him a pleading look, her hand stroking over her belly. "Please, sir. I need 'er real bad."

He grunted again, and seemed to consider his answer, before he said grudgingly, "Nobbut our Bertha on Dundee."

"Thankee, sir." She gave him what she hoped was a pathetic smile of gratitude and left the taproom, heaving a sigh of relief once she was out in the fresh air again. The stench of stale beer and tobacco smoke seemed to be stuck in her nostrils. But she had the information she needed.

She found Dundee Street easily enough; the name on a wooden plaque was actually screwed into the wall of the first house. At the third house, she stopped, her heart racing. It was a house like any other on the mean street, its crooked tiled rooftop almost touching the one opposite. There was no knocker on an unpainted door opening directly off the street, and the tiny windows were ill fitting, their frames slightly askew.

She touched the shape of the cushion, making sure it was firmly in place. It would be a disaster if it drifted loose during the coming interview. Then she raised her hand and banged vigorously on the door.

It seemed to take a long while before the sound of bolts being drawn on the far side of the door told her someone had heard her knock. The door opened a crack and a small girl peeped out at her. "Yeah?"

"Is Bertha 'ome?"

"Who wants 'er?"

It seemed to be the first question anyone

asked around her. Clarissa said firmly, "Me. Is she 'ome?"

The child leaned back and yelled with surprising power into the gloom behind her, "Mam, someone's 'ere."

"I know that, yer daft biddy. Who is it?" The yell was loud enough to bring down the rafters and Clarissa winced. Francis hated loud noises. A woman appeared behind the child before the echo had died. She cuffed the child across the head. "Get back inside, yer lazy good-fer-nuthin'. See to that babby what's cryin'."

Clarissa could hear a baby's thin cry now coming from somewhere above. The woman stood in the doorway drying her hands on a dirty apron, treating her visitor to a thorough scrutiny. Her eyes lingered on the swell of her belly. "Best come along in, then," she said eventually, turning away from the door, leaving Clarissa to follow her. "Shut the door, we don't live in a barn."

Hastily Clarissa did so and found herself in a narrow dim passage. She could hear sounds of children now, cries, whimpers, murmurings, all coming from above her head. She could hear them through the ceiling, where cracks of light showed through the gaps in the floorboards of the room above. It was cold, drafty, and damp in the passage, but the woman was heading for the rear and Clarissa followed, wondering how she would discover if Francis was among the children upstairs.

The kitchen was warmer at least, although it smelled of boiling clothes and fried onions. A man in his shirtsleeves sat in a rocker by the range, a tankard in his hand, his stockinged feet propped on the andiron. He glanced incuriously at the visitor and growled, "Fetch me another jug o' gin, Nancy."

"Jem says as 'ow 'e'll not give you 'nother without threepence." A girl, older than the one who'd answered the door, materialized from a shadowy corner. She carried a baby against her shoulder.

"Eh, mother, give the girl threepence," the man demanded of Bertha.

"Give it to 'er yerself," she retorted. "I'm sick o' keepin' you in gin with me own 'ard labor."

The man was out of his rocking chair in a trice and came at her, fists clenched. She backed away. "All right, all right. Just one, mind. An' 'tis only to keep you away from the babbys' bottle. Nancy, take threepence from the jar, an' hurry back. 'Tis time to give that lot upstairs their dosin' or they'll be screamin' all afternoon."

The girl handed over the baby, picked up a jug from the dresser, and disappeared through a back scullery and out of a back door, presumably heading for the Eagle and Dove.

Bertha sat down at a deal table, the baby propped against her shoulder. "So, what can I do fer you? In trouble are you?" The baby began to whimper and she rocked it.

Clarissa nodded, keeping her shoulders hunched, her face slightly averted. "Aye, someone said you'd 'elp. I can't keep the babe, someone'll 'ave to to care for it after." She kept her hand on the cushion beneath her cloak.

Bertha nodded. "Aye, thought as much. When're you due?" The baby's whimper turned into a shrill cry and with a muttered execration she got up and went to the dresser. She took a brown bottle and a spoon off the shelf and sat down again with the baby held against her arm. She poured clear liquid into the spoon and pushed it between the child's lips.

Clarissa smelled the powerful aroma of gin and a wave of nausea swept over her. She pressed the back of her hand to her mouth. She had heard of poor mothers feeding their babies gin because they couldn't afford milk, but this woman was paid to care for these babies. Dear God, was she giving gin to Francis?

"So, when're you due?" the woman demanded again as the baby went quiet and limp against her arm.

"Dunno, really. About five months give or take." Clarissa tried to inject a note of desperation into her voice even as she fought her horror. There was no child, but how did all those women feel who had no choice but to give up their own children to this woman's gin-soaked mercies? "I can't lose me position, 'tis a good one. I've a good mistress but she'll not keep me if she finds out about the child."

"You'll be showin' good an' proper soon enough," Bertha said matter-of-factly. " 'Ow d'you expect to 'ide that?"

"I won't 'ave to. Me mistress is going abroad fer six months and she don't need me to go with 'er. I'm to be sent to the country 'ouse, where me mam's 'ouse-keeper. I'll 'ave the child there and bring it to you when we gets back to London. That way I'll be able to visit it sometimes." She managed a pathetically hopeful smile.

"Oh, they all says that," Bertha said with a degree of scorn. "But soon enough it's outta sight outta mind. You'll be no different, mark my words."

Clarissa felt as if she herself were being so categorized and had to fight down a surge of resentful anger. She took a deep breath. "Will you take it?"

"Aye, there'll be room enough. 'Tis sixpence a week. You can do that?" Her gaze sharpened.

Clarissa nodded. "Just about. I 'ave some savings too. I wonder . . . d'you . . . d'you ever take children as well as babies? I've a friend who's in need of a caregiver for 'er boy, 'e's around ten. She's 'ad a good offer from a good man, but 'e won't take another man's child."

Bertha nodded. "Aye, I've a ten-year-old lad 'ere now. Nuthin' but trouble 'e is." She stood up and put the now quiescent baby into a basket by the hearth, muttering, "That'll keep 'im fer an hour or so."

"Where d'you keep the older ones?" Clarissa looked inquiringly around the kitchen.

"Oh, we puts 'em out as 'prentices soon enough," Bertha said. "Soon as someone wants a likely lad or lass, most times we 'ave one t' suit. Chimney sweeps fer the most part wi' the lads; lassies go fer scullery maids or down to the wash'ouses."

Clarissa had a vivid memory of the child scrubbing the steps at King Street that morning, with a dozen fireplaces to clean before she'd be given breakfast. Rage filled her and she had to force herself to keep still, to nod as if what she was hearing was only to be expected.

"The boy you 'ave now . . . is 'e goin' fer a 'prentice? Me friend would like 'er son to be 'prenticed to a good trade." She offered an ingratiating smile, as if she didn't know that such a trade condemned a child to a tortured existence and an early death, if he were lucky.

Bertha gave her a sharp look. "None o' your business, mistress. His keep is paid, an' there's no 'urry to 'prentice 'im out. But if your friend wants the best fer 'er lad, then she'd best come and talk to me 'erself."

"Yes, o' course." Clarissa offered another placatory smile. "I'll be off then an' tell me friend to come 'erself. I'll bring the babe when 'tis born."

Bertha nodded, then said casually, "There's ways to stop that 'appening, you know."

"Stop what?"

"Babbies bein' born. I can put you in the way of a woman who knows 'ow t'do it. Safe as 'ouses, it is. It'll cost you, mind."

Clarissa felt an extraordinary attachment to the cushion. "I don't 'ave that kind o' coin, mistress." She began to move to the door. "I'll let meself out." As she reached the door a loud shriek came from above followed by the sound of a piece of furniture clattering to the floor.

Bertha got heavily to her feet. "Wretched tykes, always fightin' over summat. I'll larn 'em." She grabbed a broomstick and pushed past Clarissa into the passage.

Clarissa followed her and when Bertha went up the stairs, hauling herself up against the rickety banister, she followed a few steps behind. The woman was so intent on her mission she didn't seem to notice she had company.

Clarissa kept three steps from the top, but she still had a clear view of a narrow attic space scattered with cots and mattresses. It was a cacophony of infant bellowing and the shrill cadences of fighting toddlers.

She saw Francis. He was standing on a chest, his arms hugging his body, as if protecting himself from the chaos exploding around him. He was pale, peaky, thinner, but he was on his feet and his eyes were gauging the scene around him with the same swift intelligence he had always shown.

Clarissa stood motionless. She couldn't take him out of there now. She had no way to combat the opposition of the fearsome

Bertha and the gin-sodden man in the kitchen. But her heart swelled with relief at the sight of the boy. He was a long way from succumbing to the death trap that held him. And there was no immediate danger of his apprenticeship to a chimney sweep, not between now and Sunday, certainly. But she wanted him to see her. To know that she was there.

She made a tiny movement with her hand, willing him to take his watchful eyes off the chaos around him for just a minute, just enough for a quick glance to the stairs. And it happened. He did. Francis, still in his protective stance, glanced across the room, over the scene where Bertha was wielding her broomstick to devastating effect, sending weeping children scattering to the corners of the attic, and he saw Clarissa.

He stared at her blankly for a moment, then a look of uncertainty crossed his face. His brow wrinkled, his mouth pursed. And she realized with a shock that he wasn't recognizing her. She reached up and pulled the kerchief from her head, looking him straight in the eye, and then his face lit up.

Hastily she pressed a finger to her lips and his expression changed. The guarded awareness in his eyes made her want to weep for what had been done to him. He stared at her, still frowning, the hope that had sprung into his eyes now vanished. She tried to give him a reassuring smile even as she was terrified Bertha would suddenly turn and see her standing at the top of the attic stairs.

Francis's expression cleared abruptly. He put a finger to his own lips, which moved in a tremulous smile. His sister nodded vigorously as if to answer an unspoken question and the child swallowed hard and nodded in response.

Clarissa forced herself to turn away, to descend the stairs as silently and swiftly as she could, tying the kerchief back over her head. Bertha was still wielding her broomstick and bellowing as she restored a semblance of order to chaos when Clarissa let herself out of the house.

Without looking back, she hastened down the alley and back to the water stairs. She licked a finger and wiped the smudges of ash from beneath her eyes as she went. She couldn't go into 32 King Street looking quite so haggard.

Francis had seen her; she hugged the thought to her. He knew now she would get him out of there. That knowledge would give him the strength to survive that hellhole for a couple of days. On Sunday she would have him safe.

CHAPTER NINE

Jasper adjusted the ruby pin in the snowy lace of his cravat while his valet hovered at his elbow. "Does that meet with your approval, Simmons?" the earl asked as he shook out the froth of lace at his wrists.

"Of course, my lord. Always, my lord." The valet bowed and stepped back. "But may I suggest the black striped waistcoat with the red silk coat?"

"You may, Simmons." Jasper stepped away from the mirror and allowed his valet to help him into the black and silver striped waistcoat and the full-skirted coat of dark red silk. The valet lovingly smoothed the silver lace that adorned the wide turn-back of the sleeves. He took his master's appearance a great deal more seriously than did the earl himself.

Jasper's appearance interested him for as long as it took him to dress in the morning; after that he gave it not a second thought.

His thoughts this morning were on the next step in his wooing of the elusive Clarissa. He had met with the decorator before visiting Clarissa the previous evening and work on Half Moon Street would begin this morning. He would stop by the house and see how the work was proceeding, after which he would visit Clarissa to discuss her morning's appointment with the milliner.

He was at breakfast when his butler with an apologetic bow told him his coachman waited to speak with him on a matter of some urgency.

Jasper looked up from his deviled kidneys with a quick frown. It was already eleven o'clock and the coachman had a morning's work that would take him until well past midday. "I'll see him now."

The coachman bowed in the doorway, his cocked hat held tight to his liveried chest. "Forgive the intrusion, m'lord, but the young lady wasn't there." Jasper set down his knife and fork. "Mistress Ordway was not at King Street when you got there?"

"No, m'lord."

"Where was she?" He took up his ale tankard.

"Well, no one seemed to know, sir." The man looked as miserable as if Mistress Ordway's absence could be laid at his door.

"No one?" Jasper set down the tankard and dabbed his lips with his napkin. "Mistress Griffiths was unaware of Mistress Ordway's whereabouts?"

"Aye, m'lord. And, if I might speak so bold, she seemed mighty put out, sir, at the lady's absence."

"Yes, I imagine she might." Jasper frowned into his tankard. "What time did you arrive at King Street?"

"Ten on the dot, m'lord."

"And Mistress Ordway had left the house already?" It was a rhetorical question. "Thank you, Baker. I won't need you again until this evening."

"My lord." The coachman bowed himself out.

Jasper finished his breakfast. He could see no point in rushing around to King Street until he was good and ready. Either Clarissa had reneged on the contract and disappeared, or there was some explanation for her failure to make the rendezvous with his coachman.

An hour later he ordered his curricle and drove to 32 King Street. Nan Griffiths greeted him with a flood of excuses and apologies. "I daresay Clarissa had some errands to run, Jasper. Let me offer you a glass of claret, a particularly fine claret."

215

Wreathed in smiles she ushered him into the parlor. "I believe she left the house very early . . . indeed, before anyone was up." She laughed. "Such energy, such vitality. She even went to the kitchens for her own breakfast, would you believe?"

Jasper found he could believe it perfectly well. "Do we know where she went at that hour? Did she take a chair . . . a hackney?"

"Unfortunately, my lord, no one saw her leave." Nan fanned herself vigorously. "But, there is good news. She left all her possessions behind."

"So we can assume she's not decided to renege on the contract?" Jasper leaned back in his chair, crossing his ankles. He frowned at his silver-buckled shoes. "Or maybe not. Is it possible she left nothing she needed to take with her?"

Nan's fan worked harder. The Earl of Blackwater knew nothing of Clarissa's arrival at 32 King Street, or of the accommodation arrangements that had been made. He had no idea that the girl had presented herself as a tenant of unimpeachable virtue in search of lodging, which she was able to pay for. It struck Nan as possible that Clarissa, still in possession of an independence of some kind, had decided she didn't care for the arrangements she'd agreed to. It also occurred to Nan that perhaps Jasper, Earl of Blackwater, had done something the previous night when alone with his mistress that had so disgusted Clarissa she had left without a word.

"Was everything all right last night, Jasper?"

A quick frown crossed his eyes. "What do you mean, Nan?"

She snapped closed her fan. "Why, only that if something happened to . . . to dismay Clarissa, maybe she took fright."

Jasper laughed. It struck him as inordinately amusing that Nan should imagine he had somehow abused the woman who had told him that in order to win her he had to court her with all the leisurely artistry he could muster.

"No, Nan. Nothing that occurred last night could have dismayed her. Nothing could have caused her to take fright."

Nan looked curious. "You did not — ?"

"Some things, Nan, are best not spoken of." He was still chuckling as he got to his feet. "Well, let us wait and see what happens when Mistress Ordway returns from wherever she is."

Nan rose with him. "You are very forbearing, Jasper. I doubt she deserves the consideration."

Jasper shook his head. "There's a deal more to Mistress Clarissa Ordway than meets the eye, Nan." He walked into the hall just as the front door opened and Clarissa came in on a blast of cold air, rubbing her gloved hands together, her cheeks pinched with cold.

"Ah, and here we have the truant." He bowed to Clarissa with a flourish of his plumed hat. "Mistress Clarissa, we were missing you."

Nan bustled forward, her cheeks pink with indignation. "Where've you been, Clarissa? You knew his lordship was sending his carriage for you. How dare you leave the house at dawn without a word to anyone?"

Clarissa withstood the tirade, holding herself slightly hunched, her arms crossed over her body as if trying to warm herself. She was trying to conceal the bulge of the cushion beneath her cloak, since she had no idea how she would explain that if challenged. Her gaze found Jasper's and she read there curiosity but no anger. "Forgive me, my lord, but I confess I forgot our arrangement," she said when Nan paused for breath.

"And what could possibly have caused you to forget such an important arrangement?" Nan demanded. "Such consideration on his lordship's part, to furnish you with a wardrobe, and you disappear without a word to anyone?"

"I have my own wardrobe," Clarissa snapped, momentarily pushed beyond caution. "I have no need of any other. And if I choose to leave this house, madam, at any time, I will do so." She took a step to the stairs, wanting only to get rid of the cushion before it drew unwelcome attention.

Nan looked shocked. No one spoke to her in that fashion. Jasper stepped into the breach. "I believe there's no need to say anything further, Nan. This lies between Clarissa and myself and I beg you to leave it there." Smiling, he gestured to the stairs, where her own sanctum lay.

Nan gave Clarissa one shrewd all-encompassing stare, then with a quick nod at Jasper said, "As you wish, my lord," and went upstairs, brushing past Clarissa.

Clarissa kept her body half-turned to the stairs as she pulled at her gloves. "I need to take off my cloak, my lord. I'll come down in a minute."

"What on earth do you have under your cloak?" he asked as she took a step onto the bottom stair. "That bump?"

"It's just some extra padding to keep out the cold," she replied, improvising desperately, hearing how utterly unconvincing it was. "If you'll excuse me for a minute . . ." And she fled up the stairs.

She'd attained the relative safety of her own chamber and had just managed to haul out the cushion and toss it onto the daybed when the door opened again without ceremony, and the earl came in, a puzzled frown in his dark gaze.

She turned her back hurriedly, unclasping her cloak, surreptitiously smoothing down her rucked-up skirts at the same time. Only then did she turn back to face him. "So, my lord?" She realized she sounded defensive as well as challenging.

"So, Mistress Clarissa?" He raised an eyebrow, a humorous quirk to his mouth. "What was so important that you forgot our arrangement?"

"Nothing that need concern you, sir." Belatedly she remembered the kerchief and the severity of her hairstyle beneath. She untied the kerchief and went to the mirror, unpinning the tight knot of coiled braids. She ran her fingers through the loosened plaits, untangling them, then scooped the thick hair up into a full, looser knot on her nape, pinning it roughly. Tendrils of hair drifted softly around her face once more.

Jasper watched her with a mixture of

amusement and puzzlement. Why the devil had she set out to make herself look as unattractive as was possible for someone so naturally beautiful?

Satisfied that her appearance was now in order, Clarissa began to recover her composure. Her anger at Nan's chastisement had been fueled by her anguish over Francis. But a cooler head prevailed. She had to maintain this charade for her brother's sake. In two more days, she would descend upon that filthy hovel with all the power she could muster, emboldened by the silent and unwitting power of the Earl of Blackwater. And Francis would be safe.

"Maybe it need not concern me, but I would still like to know." His tone was equable but his gaze was sharp. "I find it difficult to believe that between midnight last night and dawn this morning something so important arose that you completely forgot my coachman was coming for you at ten o'clock."

"Well, it did," she said flatly. "And I am sorry for it, but my reasons are my own. I apologize for any inconvenience caused to your coachman, but I owe no one an explanation." She faced him across the chamber, challenging him to question her further.

He nodded slowly, his arms folded, a

question still in his eyes as he regarded her. His silence unnerved Clarissa and she fought the urge to fill it with a rush of contrived explanations. After what seemed like a very long time, he let his arms fall to his sides and shrugged. "Well, let us go now. My curricle is outside and I don't wish to keep my horses standing too long in the cold."

He picked up her cloak from the chair where she'd dropped it. "What kind of padding did you use to keep the cold at bay? It seems a strange solution to a cold wind."

Clarissa cursed her improvisation. "Just a shawl around my waist," she said vaguely. "Are you suggesting we visit the milliner now?"

"Yes, in fact I believe I'm doing rather more than suggesting it." He set the cloak around her shoulders, turned her to face him, and fastened the clasp at her throat. "I feel a certain desire to assert myself for once . . . unless, of course, you have some further pressing business that absolutely cannot wait for a couple of hours . . . ?" A mobile eyebrow flickered.

Clarissa shook her head, her gaze for an instant riveted on his mouth. She hadn't noticed the fullness of his bottom lip before, or the most attractive curve at the corners.

He must spend a lot of time smiling, she thought distractedly. And then he kissed her and she had no further thoughts, lost once again in the pure sensation of his mouth on hers, firm yet pliable, the scent of his skin, the feel of his hand cupping her cheek. And when at last he raised his head she felt bereft, wanting only to pull his face down to hers again.

He smiled into her upturned face and lightly traced the shape of her mouth with his thumb. "This wooing business is quite appealing, I find." He turned her to the door as he spoke, his arm around her shoulders as he ushered her out.

His groom was walking the horses down the street as they emerged, and brought the curricle up at a smart trot as soon as he saw them. Jasper handed Clarissa up and swung himself onto the seat beside her. "Let go their heads, Tom."

The groom released the horses and jumped up behind as they plunged forward. Clarissa considered herself a more than adequate whip, having been taught by her father, who was as skilled with the reins as he was on the hunting field, so she watched Jasper's hands with considerable interest. As he feathered a tight corner in the path of an oncoming phaeton she acknowledged she was in the hands of a master and settled back to enjoy the ride.

Jasper didn't take his eyes off the road ahead as he said with a slight laugh in his voice, "I'm glad to see you've relaxed. I had the impression my reputation as a whip was on the line just then."

Clarissa decided it would be too dangerous to respond. He must already be wondering about a prostitute who presumed to cast a critically appraising eye over his driving skills. She waited anxiously for him to press further, but to her relief he said nothing more, although that flickering smile, which she now knew denoted a degree of internal reflection, continued to play over his mouth, and she had a feeling she'd been granted only a temporary reprieve.

He drew rein outside an elegant bow-windowed establishment on Mount Street. It had a discreet sign above the door, MODISTE MADAME HORTENSE. He tossed the reins to his groom and swung down, reaching a hand up to assist Clarissa to the road. She stepped down beside him, looking curiously up and down the street. So far her experience of the city consisted of the ribald street amusements of Covent Garden, the more businesslike areas around Ludgate Hill and St. Paul's, and, as of this morning, the sweat and grime of wharfside Wapping. The streets they had traversed on this drive were lined with graceful houses with gleaming windows and white honed, iron-railed steps leading up to wide entrances adorned with glowing brass doorknobs and knockers. Mount Street was no different.

"Walk 'em, Tom, we'll be an hour or so."

"Right y'are, m'lord." Tom jumped onto the driver's bench and clicked his tongue. The horses moved off at a sedate pace.

Jasper escorted Clarissa up the steps to the front door and pulled the chain of a bell to the right of the door. The door was opened instantly by a maid who curtsied and stepped aside to let them enter a square hall. "Is Madame Hortense expecting you, sir?"

"She was expecting Mistress Ordway earlier," Jasper told her, drawing off his driving gloves and laying them with his driving whip on a bench beside the front door. "Be good enough to offer Mistress Ordway's apologies for our late arrival. If Madame Hortense is unable to accommodate us now, I will, of course, understand."

The maid hurried away and Clarissa gazed around the hall, deciding to ignore what was clearly an implicit rebuke. Jasper was probably entitled to something since he was the one who'd made the appointment, and it was hardly just that their tardiness be laid at his door.

The maid returned almost before she'd left, curtsying again. "Madame Hortense is delighted you were able to keep the appointment, my lord. She is ready for the young lady immediately."

Jasper nodded. "Thank you." He crooked a finger at Clarissa, who was looking over her shoulder at him as she stood in front of a painting on the far wall. "Shall we go in? Or should we delay a little longer?"

She glared at him, but saw that he was laughing, and shook her head in exasperation as she came over to him. She wanted to ask what he found amusing, but she didn't want to open up the discussion about where she'd been that morning, or what she'd been doing, so bit her tongue and allowed him to ease her ahead of him through a set of double doors into a large salon.

If this was a shop, it was unlike any Clarissa was accustomed to. She found herself in an elegantly appointed drawing room, and the woman who came to greet her was a vision of fashionable elegance in a *contouche* gown of lavender silk, ornamented with dark green velvet bows. Her hair was unpowdered and molded smoothly into the shape of her head, with a few curls clustered on her brow. Beneath the powder and paint, Clarissa reckoned she must be in her late forties, but there was nothing matronly about her appearance.

"My lord, you are welcome." Madame Hortense curtsied and the earl bowed with a flourish, his hat at his chest.

"Hortense, delightful as always. You look charmingly."

"Another woman might simper and say you flatter," the lady said with a smile. "I, as you should know, my lord, am impervious to flattery. And I believe you speak the truth anyway."

Clarissa warmed instantly to the woman. She caught the swift exchange of knowing smiles between Jasper and Hortense and wondered if at some point they had had a liaison.

"So, Hortense, I need you to dress Mistress Ordway." Jasper gestured to Clarissa. "Her present attire is too countrified for the town." As he spoke he divested Clarissa of her cloak.

Hortense looked her over. Her gaze was the disinterested assessment of a modiste with a client and Clarissa relaxed. Hortense was not concerned about Clarissa's position vis-à-vis her previous lover, if they had indeed had an affair, but only how best to do her job.

The modiste walked slowly around her and then said, "She's lovely, Jasper. She will be a pleasure to dress. I assume we're talking society, the opera, the ballrooms of the Upper Ten Thousand, and all that goes with that?"

"Most definitely."

"Carriage dress, walking dress, of course. Ball gowns, evening gowns." She was ticking items off on her fingers. "Riding habit?"

Clarissa, who was beginning to feel like an insensate doll, spoke up. "Yes. Definitely."

Jasper looked at her. "How well do you ride?"

She was about to tell him that her father had put her on her first pony almost before she could walk, and she had hunted some of the hardest country in Kent, before she caught herself and said only, "Well enough."

"A sedate trot around the tan in Hyde Park?"

No, a gallop over any terrain you choose. "I'm sure I could manage that."

He nodded. "Then, yes, Hortense. Riding habit as well. I'll find a well-mannered lady's mount." He caught Clarissa's quickly smothered grimace and frowned. *If she did know how to ride, how had she learned? Or, more to the point, where?*

Hortense rang a handbell on a small table and two young women in plain black gowns entered. "This is Bella and Amanda, Mistress Ordway. If you would go with them they will take the necessary measurements . . . My lord, will you take a glass of Madeira? Or would you prefer claret?"

"Claret, Hortense." He moved with her to a sofa over by the fireplace and Clarissa followed the two young women out of the room.

They took her into a small, cheerful parlor where a fire burned brightly. "If you'd undress to your chemise, Mistress Ordway?" Bella produced a tape measure.

Clarissa did so, standing in chemise and stockinged feet as the two apprentices took careful measurements. It was a painstaking process, and one quite new to her. The milliner in her village at home did good enough work, but the measurements were nowhere near as accurate or as extensive as those Bella and Amanda were taking. For some reason the circumferences of ankle, wrist, and throat were as important as the usual measurements.

"If you'd care to put this robe on, Mistress Ordway." Amanda held out a silk chamber robe. "We'll return to the salon, where Madame Hortense will show you designs and materials." Bella set a pair of embroidered slippers at Clarissa's feet.

Clarissa acquiesced, undeniably fascinated by this process. She had squashed all reservations about allowing a man to pay for her clothes on the grounds that they were necessary if she was to play the part she had agreed to play for him. She had no intention of keeping them when it was all over, but it was a charade, a stage play, no more than that. The only time she didn't feel as if she were living in some dream world was when she was in search of her little brother. And then, in its dreadful reality, she inhabited a nightmare world.

Jasper and Hortense were standing side by side, apparently examining bolts of rich materials that had somehow appeared on a long table beneath the window where the daylight fell full on them. There was an intimate connection between them that only a blind person would miss, Clarissa thought as she and her two helpmeets came back into the room. The easy way they stood so close together, their bent heads almost touching, shouted a deep and comfortable familiarity. She wondered abruptly if they were still involved in a liaison. It was not a thought that she liked in the least. But what business was it of hers? She was simply playing her part in a charade. Jasper was experienced in the ways of the world; it was inevitable that he had had lovers and highly likely that he still did.

Hortense turned to examine Clarissa with the same clarity as before. Jasper took his glass of claret to a deep armchair by the fire and sat down, watching the proceedings with interest.

Hortense pursed her lips, nodding to herself. "Now, my dear, I think, because you are so slight of frame, that we should for the most part use lighter fabrics. We can deal with the cold with woolen undergarments, or petticoats of a heavier cloth. A light-colored velvet might do for the riding habit, and for a walking dress, but we want nothing to disguise your figure, and everything must complement your wonderful hair . . . such an unusual, vibrant color." She glanced across at Jasper. "Do you agree, Lord Blackwater?"

"You know best, Hortense," he said with an easy smile. "And I'm sure Mistress Ordway knows she's in the hands of an expert."

"I do have that impression," Clarissa murmured, running her hand over a bolt of embroidered ivory damask. "This is pretty."

"Yes, and admirably suited to your coloring." Hortense held a fold of the material up to Clarissa's hair. "Over a rose velvet petticoat, I think." She moved along the table, selecting materials. "This will make a splendid riding habit." She touched a dark green wool. "Trimmed with gold lace, with a cream waistcoat."

Clarissa followed in her wake, listening, nodding, and only once objecting when a floating muslin was selected for an afternoon dress. "I don't care for that particular shade of yellow. It makes me look sallow."

Hortense looked at her with interest. "Does it . . . why, yes, I believe you're right." She lifted a fold of the bolt and held it up to Clarissa's face. "So right, my dear. In fact I suspect yellow is not your color at all."

"I tend to avoid it," Clarissa said.

Jasper sipped his claret, musing gently on what circumstances had permitted Mistress Ordway to pick and choose the colors of her wardrobe.

Finally they were finished to Madame Hortense's satisfaction. She set down the last bolt of material. "I will have everything made up in the latest fashions, adapted, of course, to Mistress Ordway's particular frame. Some prevailing fashions will not look well on her at all. But I dare to believe, my lord, that you and Mistress Ordway will be well pleased."

Jasper nodded. "I don't doubt it. But before we leave, Hortense, do you have anything to hand that could be adapted for Mistress Ordway to wear now?"

"Her own gown is sadly outmoded," Hortense said, nodding her agreement. She frowned, looking closely at Clarissa, still in the peignoir. "I think I might have the very thing. Bella, bring me the apple green robe à l'anglaise . . . the one we made up for the little Heron heiress before she ran off with the ensign."

Bella disappeared and Clarissa wondered how she was to avoid wearing yet another secondhand gown. But she allowed them to dress her in the pale green gown, which opened over a pink striped petticoat. And when, after some minor adjustments to the neckline, they set her free, she looked at her image in the long glass and saw someone she was very happy to see.

She had never worn anything so modish, so exactly suited to her coloring, to every curve and indentation of her body. It seemed to require no adjustments, flowing easily over her. Her shoes were a little too sturdy and practical to complement such a frothy garment, but they would have to do. It seemed now as if she had truly entered another world: the world of kept women, gorgeous gowns, and fantastic entertainments.

"Well, my lord." She turned to Jasper and swept him a curtsy, realizing just a moment too late that she had treated him to the perfect execution of a courtesy that could only be produced by someone well trained in the art.

He smiled, and Clarissa was already beginning to distrust that smile. The Earl of Blackwater was no fool. But if she soldiered on playing the game, maybe he wouldn't challenge her.

"It's very well, Clarissa," he said, picking up her cloak. "Thank you, Hortense. As always you have exceeded all expectations." He draped the cloak over Clarissa's shoulders. "When everything is ready, have it sent to the address on Half Moon Street."

Hortense nodded her understanding. The earl had changed mistresses. "I anticipate a week, my lord."

Jasper nodded. "That will be perfect. Mistress Ordway will be in residence from Saturday. If you need her for anything, I'm certain she'll make herself available." He looked at Clarissa as he said this.

"Of course," she murmured, drawing on her gloves. She smiled at the milliner, sketching a curtsy. "I thank you for your time, Madame Hortense. And your most excellent eye. Now, if I could just have my own garments back . . ."

"Of course. Amanda will fetch them for you." Hortense nodded at the girl, who hurried away, returning in a few minutes with a neatly wrapped parcel, which she presented to Clarissa.

Jasper said very little on the drive back to King Street; his gaze seemed fixed on the road ahead, and he hummed a little to himself, a pleasant tune that Clarissa guessed, judging by the tiny private smile on his mouth, suited his reflections. It made her, on the other hand, rather uneasy.

"Are you and Madame Hortense lovers?" she asked abruptly, wanting to divert his thoughts.

She succeeded. He stopped humming and looked at her sharply. "Why do you ask?"

She shrugged with apparent nonchalance. "Just a feeling I had, watching you together. You seem very close."

He inclined his head in acknowledgment. "We have been close — very close — in the past."

"But not now?"

"We are friends, very good friends."

"How long ago were you lovers?"

He frowned at her. "Why so curious?"

She felt herself blush a little. "I don't know. I'm not really. I just wondered. She's a very handsome woman."

"Oh, yes, she is certainly that." A reminiscent smile hovered on his lips.

"She seems a lot older than you." Clarissa wondered why she was pursuing this, but once she started it seemed impossible to stop.

He nodded, shooting her a glance of amused inquiry as he said teasingly, "What an inquisitive one it is. But yes, Hortense is older than I. She taught me much about the ways of love and lust, for which I shall always be grateful."

"I expect your other lovers are too."

Jasper gave a shout of laughter. "Let's leave the matter there, shall we, before you find yourself hip-deep in indiscretion?"

Clarissa subsided, now only too happy to let the subject drop. Jasper kept his eyes on the road ahead and said nothing more, his mind fully occupied. Was this innocence of hers a ploy of some kind, or could it possibly be genuine?

CHAPTER TEN

"Who did you say?" Luke Astley stared with jaundiced eye at the manservant. A long night at the gaming tables and copious quantities of brandy had left him with a pounding behind his temples, blurred vision, and a woolly brain that seemed unable to absorb anything. "Well, speak up, man."

The servant was familiar with his master's temper at these times and stood prudently by the door of Luke's bedchamber, his hand on the latch ready to make a speedy escape. Luke himself was sitting up in bed, the waxy pallor of his complexion further evidence of his condition.

"A Master Danforth, sir. A lawyer, he said. Wishes to speak with you on a matter of some urgency, sir."

Luke's countenance seemed if possible to grow more pallid. "What the devil does he want?"

"A matter of some urgency, he said, sir,"

the man repeated, slowly lifting the latch at his back as he readied himself for the explosion that seemed imminent.

"Well, you may tell him I'm indisposed . . . not receiving visitors at present." Luke glared at the servant. "Well, go on. What're you waiting for?"

The man slipped backwards through the door and Luke flung himself against his pillows. What could Danforth want with him? He didn't know the man, had met him only once at the reading of the will. Was this something about the will, some clause that had slipped past at the initial reading, some vital bequest he had forgotten to mention?

Whatever it was, it boded ill. Lawyer Danforth had no ordinary business with his old friend's brother and no reason to pay him a friendly visit. Luke's head began to throb even more fiercely and he felt a wave of nausea wash over him.

He reached for the tumbler of brandy he kept ready by his bed for these morning emergencies. His hand shook so much the glass knocked against his teeth as he took a steadying gulp. It steadied his hand and the nausea faded, but the pain in his head didn't abate and his vision was blurred as he stared down at the quilted counterpane, trying to focus his eyes on the intricate oriental pattern. He had liked the pattern at first but too many mornings like this one had made him loathe the thick, bright reds, blues, greens, and golds of the plumaged birds and exuberant flora.

"What is it?" he growled at another knock at the door.

The manservant entered again. "Master Danforth, sir, says he would be happy to wait upon you in your bedchamber, sir. Or he will wait below until you are ready to join him."

Luke closed his eyes for a moment. "Tell Master Danforth that I will be down to join him within the hour."

"Yes, sir. And should I offer the visitor refreshment?"

"Of course, you idiot."

"Should I bring your breakfast up, sir?"

The thought of food brought a fresh wave of nausea. "No. Just refill the brandy decanter and bring up hot water."

The man took up the empty decanter and hastened from the room. Luke lay back against the pillows willing himself to swing his legs over the side of the bed. With a groan he managed to maneuver himself to the edge of the bed, the room spinning around him. He was on his feet, somewhat shakily but at least upright, when the servant returned with a jug of hot water and the recharged brandy decanter.

"Should I shave you, sir?" The servant glanced knowingly at his master's shaky hands.

"Get on with it, man." Luke sat down at the washstand. "But pour me a glass of brandy before you start. It steadies my nerves."

It was hardly his nerves that needed steadying, the servant reflected as he brought the glass over to his master before sharpening the razor on the leather strop.

Luke closed his eyes and let the man do his work. The warm water and the soothing strokes of the razor restored some measure of physical well-being, and by the time he was dressed he felt sufficiently clearheaded to face his visitor.

He allowed his manservant to tie his cravat, however, unsure whether his hands were steady enough to achieve the delicate operation himself, and when he examined his reflection in the long glass found it satisfactory. His tall, thin figure had a certain natural elegance, lending itself to the lavish brocades, gold braid, and giant buttons that Luke affected. His rather scrawny calves did not show at their best in the clocked stockings that were all the fashion, but that was a minor sartorial detail. A man must be in fashion, after all. He took up a fan of painted chicken skin with ivory sticks, adjusted the pomander at his waist, tweaked his cravat one final time, and sauntered down to the parlor.

Lawyer Danforth was a patient man and had occupied himself while waiting for his host in examining the contents of the room. The books and periodicals he judged to be lightweight, of interest only to a fashion-obsessed flibbertigibbet who felt he needed to be able to discuss the latest *on-dit* in the fashionable world. The artwork was mediocre, the various objets d'art similarly so. It was as if the present inhabitant of the house had furnished it with a job lot from some auction. It had a distinctly temporary feel to it. The location of the house itself had struck Danforth as oddly out of the truly fashionable area of the city, the five square miles occupied by aristocratic London. He had concluded that Master Astley was not a man of means, but then he had been the younger son so it was hardly surprising. But there were ways for even younger sons to augment their income. Marrying an heiress was the most usual, and there was nothing in Master Astley's pedigree to render him an unsuitable match.

He set down a small figurine as the door opened behind him and turned to greet his host with a bow. "Master Astley. I give you good morning. I am sorry to disturb you when you're indisposed, but the matter is of some urgency."

"So I understand, Master Danforth." Luke sounded a trifle petulant as he returned the bow. "Did my servant bring you refreshment?"

"I asked for coffee, sir, and he was obliging enough to bring me a pot." Danforth gestured to the coffeepot on the sideboard.

"Pray sit down, sir, and tell me what I can do for you. Is this something to do with my brother's will?" Luke sat down, tapping his closed fan against his knee.

The lawyer chose to remain standing, his feet planted firmly slightly apart, his shoulders square to the fireplace. "I understand Clarissa is visiting you and her brother," he stated.

Luke felt a cold sweat on his brow. He offered a noncommittal smile and flicked open his fan, plying it languidly.

"However according to your servant, she's not under your roof," Danforth pointed out. "Clarissa explained that you had placed Francis with a tutor and his family. Could she perhaps be staying there with him?"

Luke ignored the question for the moment. "I judged it right and proper that the boy should receive the education fitting his status, and should have the company of other boys of good family." Nothing in his composed expression indicated the frantic racing of his muzzy brain.

"Yes, I would agree with you there. We all would." Danforth rocked slightly on his heels, his hands clasped at his back. "I don't believe even Clarissa would quarrel with you on that score."

Another noncommittal smile while Luke waited to hear something that would tell him exactly what he needed to know in order to deal with this situation.

"Clarissa left home just over a week ago. She told her household that she was coming to stay with you and visit Francis. She's been very anxious about him. I understand her letters to him have gone unanswered." Danforth continued his steady rocking, his shrewd eyes fixed upon his host.

"I explained to my niece that her letters upset Francis. His tutor agreed with me that it would be best to withhold them from him initially until he had settled down." *Clarissa was supposed to be here with him? So where was she now?*

Danforth nodded slowly. "I would very

243

much like to see Clarissa. She left in such a hurry and without a word to anyone but her own household. Her friends are somewhat concerned. It's most unlike her to be thoughtless where her friends are concerned. She would know we would be worried."

"I daresay she was only thinking of Francis," Luke said, feeling his way with growing confidence. "She arrived in some agitation . . . indeed, she came very close to accusing me of ill-treating her brother and deliberately keeping her away from him." His smile was benign. "Of course I understood the natural agitation of a recently bereaved daughter, and took no offense. She visited Francis and I gave permission for them both to accompany his tutor, with his family and Francis's fellow pupils, to Bath on an educational visit. Roman history, I believe, is considered a most necessary part of a classical education."

The lawyer scratched his head, then the tip of his nose. He could fault none of this, but unaccountably he was still uneasy. It went so against the grain for Clarissa to give no thought for the anxiety of her friends. She had been too well schooled in the courtesies for that. Even if she felt no affection for her father's old friends, she would treat them with respect. And Master Danforth knew perfectly well the degree of affection in which Clarissa held both him and Doctor Alsop. They took the place of her beloved father, although the lawyer would be the first to acknowledge that they were inadequate substitutes.

The bond that had existed between father and daughter had been extraordinarily strong, more so than the one between Clarissa and her mother. Lady Lavinia had been too anxious that her daughter make the kind of marriage suitable for an earl's granddaughter to spend time on actually getting to know the girl. If she had, Danforth reflected, she would have given up trying to mold her daughter in her own image. Clarissa was, and always had been, very much her own person.

Maybe they had failed her by not taking her worry about her brother seriously, but surely she would have pressed them harder if she had really thought something was wrong. He looked around the parlor again, looked at his host, could see nothing amiss except the sense of a certain hand-to-mouth existence . . . the servant's less-than-pristine livery, the meager accommodations on Ludgate Hill, the stale coffee.

"When do you expect them to return,

Master Astley?"

Luke offered a vague wave of his fan. "I do not interfere in my ward's education, Master Danforth." There had been an unmistakable emphasis on *my ward,* clearly intended to remind the lawyer where the power lay. "Clarissa, also, is my ward, as you know." He laughed, gave a little shrug. "But I would not consider it right to curtail the freedom my brother, her father, accorded her. I might disagree with its scope, but . . ." Another shrug. "She will be her own mistress in a little under ten months."

"Quite so." Danforth frowned at his feet. "Well, I must ask you to forgive me for disturbing you, sir. I hope you will trust the natural anxiety of your wards' friends." He allowed his own slight emphasis to weight the description. Master Astley must not be allowed to consider he had no observers.

"But of course." Luke rose to his feet, prepared to escort his visitor to the door. "When Clarissa returns I will ensure she understands the unnecessary journey her lack of thought obliged you to make."

"I beg you not to make too much of it." Danforth waved the issue away as he was ushered rather swiftly to the front door. "I had other business in town anyway."

The waiting servant had the door open as

he reached it and he stepped out, bowing to his host with a politely doffed hat.

Luke bowed, stepped back, and the door closed. Only then did he allow himself a deep breath of relief. But it was only temporary. He'd managed to get rid of the troublesome lawyer, but where the hell was Clarissa? She hadn't shown her face at his door, hadn't written to him for weeks . . . in fact he couldn't remember when he'd received her last letter. He'd simply consigned them to the fire instantly, the ones to him and the ones to her brother. He had a little under ten months to ensure he inherited the Astley fortune and estates. But if that wretched girl was snooping around somewhere . . .

How could she be? She knew nothing of London. She couldn't take care of herself here, and obviously she hadn't sought the help or protection of friends. So if she managed to make the journey alone without coming to grief, she was somewhere lost in the depths of the city. And if that was so, she'd be no trouble to him. She was probably lying in an alley with her throat cut, or worse.

Luke felt somewhat restored. He'd handled the lawyer well, he thought. Clarissa was unlikely to be a problem. If somehow she managed to turn up on his doorstep he would deal with her then. She could disappear without a trace and everyone would assume an accident had befallen her in the lanes and alleys of this dangerous city. But to settle the last niggle of anxiety he yelled for the manservant as he reentered the parlor.

"Send a message to the livery stable at the top of the hill . . . fetch that stableman, Ed, down here. I need him to do something . . . oh, and tell Clara to make me breakfast . . . sirloin, bread, eggs."

"Aye, sir."

Luke kicked a fallen log back into the hearth.

He was at his breakfast half an hour later when the servant brought Ed into the dining room. "You wanted me, sir."

"Yes, I did." Luke buttered a slice of bread. "Help yourself to ale." He gestured to the jug on the sideboard.

"Thankee, sir." Ed filled a tankard and drank deep. He was a youngish man, with the shoulders and huge hands of a prizefighter. The muscles of his thighs swelled against the leather britches, and the buttons of his leather jerkin strained across the breadth of his chest.

"I want you to go back to the house in Wapping . . . check on the boy. Find out how he is. You told me he'd not last above a month. I need to know how long it's going to be."

The stableman nodded slowly. "If'n 'tis takin' too long, sir, you could always send 'im up the chimbleys."

Luke shook his head. He couldn't do that; the risks were too high. Chimney sweeps died all the time, it was true, but it was always possible the death of a child would cause an inquiry if it happened in the house of some nosy do-gooder among the gentry, and the trail could lead back to him. It was unlikely but not worth the risk. Whereas a quiet death of infection and malnutrition could not be laid at his guardian's door. He'd have the child in a closed coffin before anyone could question the cause of death. There'd be an elaborate family funeral, and it would all be over.

But where in hell was Clarissa? He couldn't be totally easy until he knew. He took a draft of ale and said through a mouthful of sirloin, "Ask around, too. Find out if anyone unusual's been seen . . . anyone's been snooping. Understand?"

"Aye, sir. 'Tis clear enough." Ed set down his tankard. "But I'll be needin' the fare. Costs a pretty penny to get to Wapping, even on the river. I'll be needing a shilling."

Luke grimaced. "A shilling, that's daylight robbery."

" 'Tis what it costs." Ed regarded him steadfastly until Luke fumbled in his pocket and finally laid a shilling on the table. He pocketed it with a brief nod. "I'll be back later."

"See that you are." Luke dipped some bread into his egg yolk and waved an irritable dismissal.

Jasper escorted Clarissa to the door of 32 King Street after their visit to the milliner. "I will return for you at three o'clock, Clarissa. It's the hour when fashionable London is walking and driving in the park. One must, after all, see and be seen at least once a day."

A touch of scorn had entered his voice but when she gave him a curious glance he continued blandly, "So we'll join the throng on a drive in Hyde Park, but we'll not stop for conversation and introductions, however anxious people seem to be for them. The object of this exercise is to arouse curiosity and set the gossips' tongues wagging."

"Hence my new gown," Clarissa murmured.

"Hence your new gown," he agreed. "And it becomes you, my dear," he added. "As I believe you are well aware." An amused smile accompanied the comment and she couldn't help an answering chuckle.

"It is a particularly fine gown. And I thank you, sir."

"Oh, you'll earn its price," he said lightly. "I have no doubt about that."

Clarissa contented herself with a raised eyebrow. "I applaud your confidence, my lord."

He laughed, tilting her chin for a quick kiss as the steward stood waiting in the open door. "At three o'clock sharp. Mind."

"I'll be ready." She hurried past the steward, giving him a quick smile of thanks as he closed the door behind her. She had reached her own chamber and was struggling with the laces of the new gown when someone knocked at the door. She had no desire for visitors, and most particularly not Nan Griffiths, and went to open it with ready excuses on her tongue. Maddy and Emily stood on the threshold, a group of young women behind them.

"We have to know the story . . . oh, what a beautiful gown." Maddy bubbled into the room and the rest came after her. "Mother Griffiths won't tell us a thing, and she's normally quite happy to discuss the girls' good fortune." She perched on the bed, swinging her slippered feet. "Come on, Clarissa, tell all. What's he like, the earl? Is he good? Gentle . . . rough? What kinds of things does he want?"

Clarissa shook her head in momentary bewilderment. How was she to answer any of this? They were all exclaiming at her gown, feeling the material, discussing it as if it were on a dressmaker's dummy instead of a living person.

"Yes, Clarissa, you can't keep anything from the rest of us," Emily chimed in. "What's the earl like in bed?"

Clarissa took a deep breath. She had no idea how to invent a description that would satisfy these women who knew all there was to know about men and their proclivities. She said, "I don't know, because it hasn't happened yet." An astounded silence fell over the group. They gazed at her in awe. "You . . . you refused him?" Maddy said eventually.

"No . . . not exactly. I asked him to wait a little . . . to . . . to court me." It sounded so unlikely, even to her ears, that she was not surprised when as one they burst into gales of laughter.

"Oh, give over, Clarissa," Em exclaimed through her laughter. "Of course you didn't. Tell the truth now."

"I am," she said calmly. "Would one of you help me with these laces?"

A rather mousy-looking girl stepped forward at once and swiftly unlaced her gown. Clarissa stepped out of it and shook out the folds. "It is pretty, isn't it?" she said with a mischievous smile.

"Far too pretty for a gift from an unrewarded lover," one of the other women declared. "We don't play games here, girl. You're new and we make allowances, but there are rules, and one of them is we share what we know about clients. It gives us all a degree of protection. The more you know about a man, the better able you are to deal with him and the whole tribe of 'em. So, tell us the truth."

Clarissa wondered if there was a hint of menace in the demand. The woman was something of an Amazon, a rather brawny, freckle-faced woman with big hands. Before responding she put on her own chamber robe, taking her time as if completely unthreatened by her audience. "As it happens, this is the truth. I decided I would fix the interest of the earl more securely if I made him wait. If I played the game of a little now, a little later, but always the promise of everything in the end."

"And he agreed?" There was a universal

wide-eyed gaze of astonishment.

"Apparently," Clarissa said calmly.

"Probably he can't get it up anymore," the Amazon hazarded. "No red-blooded male would contract with Mother Griffiths for a girl's services and then not use them. He must be trying to hide the fact that his sword's lost its steel by pretending to have a mistress."

Clarissa wondered how Jasper would react if he could hear this matter-of-fact discussion of his manhood. She felt rather as if she had betrayed him in some way, which was absurd.

"I don't have that impression," she said. "He seems red-blooded enough to me. I think he enjoys the game . . . the suspense of it. I'm going driving with him later this afternoon."

"Well, if you really are keeping him dangling, you'd better not push him too far," the Amazon said. "Things could become nasty . . . take a rough turn. We've all been there."

"I'm on my guard," Clarissa said. "But I thank you for the advice. It's well heeded, I promise." It seemed to placate the woman and she gave a short nod of acknowledgment.

"Does Mother Griffiths know the game

you're playing?" Maddy asked.

"I haven't told her," Clarissa responded. "I don't consider it her business. If Lord Blackwater chooses to tell her, that's no concern of mine either."

"Best hope that he keeps his mouth shut," the mousy one declared. "Or there'll be trouble. Mother Griffiths doesn't take kindly to us setting our own rules."

"True enough. You're playing with fire, girl. You take my word on it." The Amazon was moving to the door as she spoke. "We've a card game to finish." The others left with her except for Emily and Maddy.

"She seems rather intimidating," Clarissa observed, sitting at the dresser to brush her hair.

"Oh, don't take any notice of Trudy. She's got a big heart underneath it all," Emily said. "You'd be surprised how many men like a bit of bullying. Trudy does very well by them, scolds 'em, then babies 'em until they don't know which way is up. They love it . . . keep coming back for more. Mother Griffiths thinks the world of her."

It seemed there was always something new to be learned about the world inhabited by the ladies of the night, Clarissa reflected, pulling the brush through her hair with rhythmic strokes.

"You want I should curl it for you before you go out with his lordship?" Emily inquired. "Won't take but a minute."

"Would you really?" Clarissa smiled gratefully. "That's very kind of you."

"Not a bit of it," Emily said cheerfully, and went off to fetch the curling iron.

She was halfway through her hairdressing when Mistress Griffiths came into the bedchamber without ceremony. She carried a hatbox and a wrapped parcel and spoke as she set her burdens down on the bed almost as if she was carrying on a previous conversation. "Oh, that's good, Emily. A little curl never goes amiss. The gentlemen do like it." She surveyed Clarissa critically. "Yes, the curl softens your face, my dear. Now, see what has just been delivered for you."

"Who from?" Clarissa turned on the stool as Emily suspended her operations.

"I believe it was Lord Blackwater's footman." Nan swiftly unfastened the ribbons around the hatbox. She lifted the lid and took out a cream straw hat with black velvet ribbons. "Oh, very modish." She held it up. "His lordship had always the most exquisite taste. Try it on, my dear, and Emily can arrange the ringlets to cluster around your ears. It will look charming."

Emily took the hat before Clarissa could

reach it. She turned it around between her hands, examining it carefully. "It is very pretty, and the black velvet will be a most fetching contrast to your hair." She set the hat on Clarissa's head and deftly tweaked the ringlets to frame her face beneath the brim. She tied the velvet ribbons beneath Clarissa's chin and then stood back with a nod of satisfaction.

"Yes, delightful," Nan declared, unwrapping the other parcel to reveal a pair of dark green kidskin half boots and matching gloves.

The hat, boots, and gloves would go beautifully with Hortense's apple-green gown, Clarissa reflected. Jasper had clearly given much thought to the matter of her costume for her first exposure to the polite world. He was surprisingly knowledgeable about fashion, but perhaps that wasn't surprising. Hortense had probably educated him in more ways than those of a good lover. She fetched the gown from the armoire and laid it on the bed beside the boots and gloves.

"Very pretty." Nan nodded her approval. "I hope you realize how fortunate you are, Clarissa, to have attracted such a notable and generous protector."

"Oh, believe me, madam, I am all too

aware of my situation," Clarissa murmured, untying the ribbons of the hat. "I am to drive with his lordship in the park at three o'clock. I daresay he wanted to be sure I was suitably dressed to reflect well upon him."

Nan's eyes widened. So this was to be a public affair. They were unusual in her business, reserved for affairs of the heart, not the purely commercial liaisons that were her stock-in-trade. But Jasper could not have fallen in love with the girl, not in such a short time. He was too experienced in the ways of the world to allow that to happen.

"Well, make sure you look your best, and don't keep his lordship waiting." With which parting shot, she sailed from the chamber.

"Does she never knock on a door before entering?" Clarissa asked.

"Only if we're with a man," Maddy responded. "If we're alone she just comes in when she wishes."

"It is her house," Emily pointed out.

"That should not excuse discourtesy," Clarissa pointed out.

They both looked at her as if she'd taken leave of her senses. Since when did courtesy have anything to do with the lives they led? "Where were you before you came here?" Maddy asked.

"In the country, working for a family," she improvised. "They treated me well enough until their youngest son said he was in love with me and wanted to marry me. They threw me out then, and I wandered around London for a few days earning my keep as best I could, then ended up here." Her new-found ability for invention never ceased to amaze her.

"You were lucky then," Emily stated. "You could've found yourself in a lot worse places."

Clarissa merely nodded and changed the subject before they could come up with any more awkward questions. "I haven't eaten since dawn and I'm famished."

"Ring for something." Emily pulled the bellpull on her way to the door. "The servants are quite used to serving food at different times. I had a man once who wanted dinner at three in the morning . . . a real dinner, mind, three courses, each one served by liveried footmen." She grinned. "We sat at table as naked as jaybirds, with nothing to cover us but a table napkin on our knees."

She laughed, Maddy with her, and Clarissa joined them. There was something indomitable about the way these two saw their lives. Instead of seeing themselves as the bond slaves they were, bought and sold to service men's needs, they managed to see the good things, to find blessings in the most unblessed situation.

Emily laid a hand on the latch. "Come on, Maddy, you promised to help me sew the torn flounce on my red gown. I need it for tonight. I'm expecting a visit from that young man I told you about, the one who starts sobbing just before he goes off the top. He's always finished almost before he's begun and the red dress always gets him so excited I can get rid of him even quicker. See you later, Clarissa." The door closed behind them as they went off chattering.

CHAPTER ELEVEN

Promptly at three o'clock Jasper's curricle drew up at the door. Clarissa had been waiting in the parlor, looking out onto the street, and as soon as she saw him went out into the hall. The steward opened the door for her.

Jasper jumped lightly down from the curricle. "I approve of punctuality," he said with a smile. "And I'm glad I was right about the hat. It suits you to perfection."

"I can only commend your taste, sir." She gave him her gloved hand as she stepped up into the vehicle. "I trust it won't become too chilly. I thought you would probably not wish me to hide my expensive finery from inquisitive eyes under a cloak, so I'm prepared to shiver if that is your pleasure." She settled on the bench, smoothing down her skirts as she spoke, her teasing tone matching the somewhat mischievous smile she cast him.

"Indeed, madam, I have no desire to see you suffer," he returned with mock gravity, the gleam in his black eyes matching her own. He reached under the bench and drew out a fur-trimmed rug, which he wrapped around her legs. "There now; you should know, madam, that your comfort is always at the forefront of my mind."

Clarissa went into an involuntary peal of laughter. His tone was so sanctimonious, his expression so earnest, it was irresistible. He was so instantly responsive to her moods, so more than ready to match her point for point when the urge to say or do something provocative overtook her. And she realized suddenly that she felt more comfortable in his company than she had ever felt in anyone's outside her own family.

The realization stunned her, and her laughter died. Jasper shot her a quick, questioning glance. She looked surprised about something, he thought, plaiting her gloved fingers against the lap robe as if it were the most absorbing activity.

She looked up, aware of his regard, and a faint flush highlighted her cheekbones. "Is something the matter, my lord?"

"No, except that as I've pointed out before, I have a name, and I would like you to use it." It was a dry comment. He took up the reins, flicked the whip lightly, and his horses set off, the groom jumping up on the box behind.

"Sometimes *my lord* comes more naturally to my tongue." The dryness of his tone enabled Clarissa to reclaim her equilibrium, banishing whatever fanciful reflections she'd been having, or at least putting them in abeyance. "It seems more suited to the true nature of our relationship."

His lips thinned and a quick frown creased his brow, but this time he chose not to fence with her. Nothing further was said as they trotted down Piccadilly and turned into the park. The driveway was graveled; alongside it ran the tan, a broad path of packed earth where riders showed off their horses and their own form. Pedestrians for the most part strolled along the grassy edge between the driveway and the tan.

Clarissa watched the scene with fascination. It was clearly a parade . . . a spectacle. The ladies in the latest fashions, taking delicate little steps in their high-heeled shoes, their *cicisbeos* accompanying them, flourishing gold-knobbed canes and pomanders. The Earl of Blackwater bore little resemblance to any of these fashion plates, she thought, sneaking another surreptitious glance. There was nothing about his appearance to attract attention, but perhaps that was exactly what set him apart. A certain understated elegance, a certain carelessness to his manner as he drove, as if he had no interest at all in being a part of the display around them. She watched his hands, long and slender, on the reins, the infinitesimal movements that directed the horses, the occasional deft flick of his long driving whip.

"Jasper . . . Jasper, don't you dare pass me as if I didn't exist," an indignant voice called from the tan. A rider on a showy chestnut caught up with them.

Jasper gave a mock sigh of resignation. "Ah, brother, how could I ever overlook you?" He regarded his brother's mount with a raised eyebrow. "How much did you pay for that hack? Too much, I'll lay odds."

"Well, there you're wrong, Brother. It's not mine, I paid not a penny for him. I'm riding him as a favor for a friend . . . schooling him, you might say. Although I doubt it's worth my trouble." He looked disparagingly at his mount. "Never mind, one does what one may for one's friends."

His gaze fell on Clarissa and he bowed from the saddle. "I'm delighted to renew our acquaintance, madam. Do you consider my brother a fair whip?"

"More than fair." Clarissa smiled as she tried desperately to remember which of the twin brothers this one was.

"I'm Sebastian," Sebastian said with a quick and complicit smile. "Don't feel badly, ma'am. Few people can tell us apart if we're not together."

Clarissa warmed to him immediately. "You are kind to take pity on me, sir."

"Not at all." His gaze was appreciative as he smiled at her again. "May I say how well that hat becomes you?"

"You may, sir, but the compliments should go to your brother," she returned with her own smile. "He is responsible for the garments on my back, for both the choice and the expense. I have had nothing to do with it."

His eyes widened in surprise at this swift rejoinder. He glanced at Jasper, saw that his brother wore an air of mild resignation, and he laughed. "Jasper, my friend, you may just have a winning hand." He doffed his hat with another bow to Clarissa. "My congratulations, Mistress Clarissa Ordway."

"What did he mean by that?" Clarissa asked, watching as the young man set his horse to high-step down the tan. "What hand have you won?"

Jasper set his pair in motion again. He said

evenly, "Sebastian clearly thinks that you have the ability to play the game to its conclusion. He does not, of course, know that you're a party to the game. I would ask you again to ensure he stays in ignorance."

"Of course," she agreed. "But why would it matter?"

"Because I'm cheating," Jasper stated. A look of distaste crossed his features. Since earliest childhood he had been taught to despise even the remotest hint of cheating. A gentleman did not cheat, any more than he failed to honor his gaming debts. But on this occasion, he had decided that his uncle's loathsome bargain deserved an equally loathsome response.

"How are you?" She had little difficulty interpreting his look of distaste at the idea of dishonorable behavior; she had been educated in the same school. Her father would have taken a horse whip to a cheat.

He said curtly, "For the agreement to run true, the women in question must be saved out of love."

"Women?"

"Yes, in order for us to inherit from our uncle, my brothers must also achieve their own miraculous conversion of a lost soul." His tone was as sardonic as his words.

Clarissa absorbed this for a moment.

"What's to stop them coming up with the same idea as yours?"

"Nothing. I hope they do," he said shortly. "It offends me to think of any one of us dancing to my uncle's obscene tune. The only answer is to play him at his own game. Now, coming up along the drive towards us is a carriage with three ladies. I would like you to keep your eyes straight ahead while I bow as we drive past."

"Very well." Clarissa kept her eyes on the middle distance as the carriage came abreast, but she could feel three pairs of eyes scanning her even as they responded to Jasper's bow with smiles from behind their fans.

"So, why could I not look at them?"

"Mystery, my dear. I wish to create mystery that will stimulate gossip. By this evening the speculation as to your identity will be running riot in the salons and around the dining tables all over town."

"Are people so very interested in your doings, then?" She looked sideways at him. "Are you such an important person?"

"If that's intended as a snub it went wide of its mark," he informed her. "I don't consider myself to be important, but a man of my age, lineage, and supposed fortune is an eligible bachelor in the eyes of every lady on the marriage mart and her mother. If I'm seen with any woman, they're going to wonder what kind of competition they have. Believe me, I will be glad when the notice of our engagement is sent to the *Gazette*."

Clarissa frowned. "I thought you had no fortune, that's why you have to play your uncle's game."

"That's right. Without my share of Viscount Bradley's estate, the Blackwater estates will go under. But most people are unaware of that, including, with the exception of my brothers, most of my own family, who are always expecting some kind of handout from me. Most people see only the title, the London house, the estates, and a wretchedly uncomfortable but impressive family pile in Northumberland and assume there's a fortune to match."

"If you put them right on that score, then surely you would no longer be plagued by matchmaking mamas and their debutante daughters," Clarissa pointed out.

He gave a short laugh. "What a simpleton you are. If the truth about my lack of fortune were to become known, my dear girl, I would be hounded by every one of the long line of creditors I inherited from my father. I'd probably find myself in the Fleet prison by nightfall."

Clarissa rather resented being called a simpleton, but it seemed in this case that she really was ignorant of life's realities. "Have you never been tempted to take a wife, then?"

He cast her one of his sharp sideways glances. "I've never felt the need to subject a woman, particularly one I might like sufficiently to share my life with, to that life of aristocratic penury."

"That's very noble."

He shrugged. "Not in the least, and believe me, my dear girl, I have not suffered from the lack of a wife. There are substitutes, perfectly pleasant ones."

"Mistresses, you mean?"

"That is exactly what I mean."

She thought she could detect a faint note of warning in his voice. The conversation was over. She held her tongue and for the remainder of the drive they passed the bows, the waves, the smiling nods of acknowledgment from their fellow travelers without pausing. Jasper responded to the greetings with polite half bows from the driver's seat and noncommittal smiles. Clarissa kept her eyes straight ahead and her tongue still.

When they drove out of the park an hour later, Jasper said casually, "We will dine together. I've a mind to advance my wooing a little."

Clarissa swallowed. *What did that mean? Advance it how far?* But she couldn't refuse to dine with him even if she wanted to. In this instance she was as much a bond slave under contract as any of the other women under Mistress Griffiths's roof. Her company was bought and paid for. "If you wish it, sir."

"I do most certainly wish it." He frowned at her. "Do you not, Clarissa?"

She did, of course. And in her own world, nothing would give her more delight. Except that in her own country backwater, she would not have attracted the attention of Jasper Sullivan, fifth Earl of Blackwater. She would never have come within his sphere.

If her mother had lived, of course, it might have been different. Lady Lavinia would probably have insisted on a formal coming-out Season for her daughter in the hopes she would catch herself a good husband, but after Lavinia's death the squire had mentioned such a Season only once, and when Clarissa had dismissed the idea, he had seemed relieved, and she had forgotten about it.

There was more than enough to keep her occupied with running the household and looking after Francis. She had inherited her father's passion for all the country pursuits, hunting, riding, even hawking, and had thought herself content enough with the local County society. Now, however, she questioned that contentment. It seemed with hindsight that she had been drifting in some kind of trance, oblivious of the static nature of her life.

Somehow she had to find a way to keep her growing enjoyment and involvement in the game she had orchestrated separate from its final goal, a goal she must not lose sight of for an instant.

"Where will we dine?" she asked in neutral tones, as if it were a matter of indifference even though she was hoping against hope that he would select some other rendezvous, somewhere less private, a chamber less redolent than her own of the activities that went on under Mistress Griffiths's roof.

"Tonight we will dine in my house. Now that we've been seen in public, it's time for your association with King Street to come to an end. I will no longer visit you there, and on Saturday you will move to Half Moon Street. Your position as my mistress will then be an open secret."

His house? Was that better or worse than King Street? She didn't know. But Clarissa knew she would find out soon enough.

Luke was dozing by the fire, sleeping off the last of his headache before going forth for another night's entertainment, when Ed returned. The man stood in the doorway twisting his cap between meaty hands. "The boy's there all right an' tight, sir."

Luke heaved a sigh of relief. Even though it seemed an impossibility, he had been plagued all day with the thought that Clarissa might have found her brother and spirited him away. "How's he doing?"

"Peaky."

"Ill?" His heart leaped.

"Not as such, sir. But he'll come down wi' summat soon enough. They always does."

Luke nodded. "All right." He waved a hand in dismissal before remembering something else. "Have there been any strangers around there, anyone asking questions?"

Ed shook his head. "No one in particular, sir. No one who didn't have business there. Landlord at the Eagle and Dove had a woman in —"

"What woman?" Luke sat up abruptly.

"Pregnant girl, sir. Lookin' fer somewhere to dump the child afore she loses her place.

A maid of some sort, landlord reckoned. Bertha didn't think nuthin' of it, she gets 'em all the time, girls in trouble."

Luke bit at his thumbnail, staring into the fire. It didn't sound remotely like Clarissa. No one in their right mind would ever believe Clarissa was a maidservant. And besides, she wasn't pregnant. Anyway, how could she ever from the depths of the Kent countryside have heard of a baby farm in Wapping? She led such a sheltered existence, she probably didn't even know such establishments existed.

No, he decided, there was no possibility that such a description could fit his ward. Clarissa had not been seen around Wapping Stairs. He spat a piece of thumbnail into the fire and glanced up at Ed, who was still standing there. "Why are you still here?" he demanded of the burly figure.

"Took me three hours from me work, sir, runnin' that errand." Ed didn't move. He had had the measure of Luke for some time and knew him for the skinflint that he was. If you wanted fair play from him you had to fight for it.

Luke sighed heavily and heaved himself from his chair. He unlocked the drawer in the desk and felt in the coin purse it contained. "Here . . . for your trouble." He tossed the shilling across the room.

Ed caught it deftly, glanced at it, and then gave a scornful grunt as he pocketed it. He left, the door slamming behind him.

Luke stood for a moment chewing his lip. He couldn't afford to antagonize his accomplice. Ed could turn on him in a blink. He'd have to pay him off more substantially. Maybe if he won at the tables tonight he'd have sufficient to part with a decent sum.

The curricle drew up outside a double-fronted mansion on Upper Brook Street. Sconced lanterns on either side of the double doors illuminated the railed steps leading up to the house. Lamplight showed in the long windows on either side of the doors and in the fanlight above them. Such a quantity of light was an expensive business, Clarissa reflected. It was difficult to believe the earl's tale of penury.

She stepped down to the pavement, looking up at the handsome building. "It's very grand, my lord."

"Suitably so for an earl's residence?" he responded with a quizzically raised eyebrow.

"Certainly, but is it suitable for a poverty-stricken earl, I ask myself?"

"I am living on my expectations," he declared in a lofty tone. "Come into my parlor, Mistress Clarissa."

A butler opened the door before they'd mounted the last step. They walked into a marble-floored hall, lit by a massive chandelier, the crystal pendant drops sparkling and dancing in the light of myriad candles. A grandly ornate staircase rose in a graceful curve from the center of the hall.

"I think champagne is in order." Jasper handed his caped driving coat to a waiting footman. "Bring it to the library, Crofton. And we'll dine in an hour in the small dining room."

"Yes, m'lord." The butler moved in stately fashion across the hall to open a set of double doors at the rear. They opened onto a pleasant, book-lined room, candlelit, filled with comfortable, well-worn furniture and warmed by a brightly burning log fire.

It was a room rather similar to the library at home in Kent, Clarissa thought, finding the space instantly comforting and reassuring. There was none of the chilly grandeur that the outside of the house had led her to expect.

"What a cozy room." She went to the fire, drawing off her gloves, bending to warm her hands at the blaze. "I expected something a little more formal."

"Oh, there are those rooms too." Jasper

took the gloves from her and set them aside. Slowly he untied the ribbons of her hat and set that beside the gloves. He smoothed her hair, twisting the ringlets around a finger, a thoughtful look in his eyes. Then he took her hands in his, and a glint had replaced the thoughtfulness.

"I use only those parts of the house that meet my needs. It's a way for a poverty-stricken earl to economize without broadcasting his condition. Most of the reception rooms are shrouded in dust covers and except for an annual spring cleaning never see the light of day."

"That seems a pity," she said lightly, trying to slide her hands out from his. "I'm sure they're beautiful."

"They are." He tightened his fingers. "Don't try to wriggle away, Clarissa." He was smiling, but there was a hint of determination in the dark gaze. "I agreed to seduction, and I will honor my promise. But you must honor yours."

When she said nothing, leaving her hands limp in his grip, a frown darkened his gaze, and his voice was suddenly harsh. "If you find me repulsive, if the thought of being touched by me disgusts you, then tell me now."

She shook her head. "No . . . no, it's not that."

"Then what is it? If this is a game to increase your price, I'll tell you straight, it will not work. It's been tried many —" He broke off at the horrified expression on her face. "It's not that, is it?"

"Of course not. How could you think such a thing?" Taking advantage of his momentary distraction she snatched her hands free. "What kind of loathsome person would —"

"You'd be surprised," he said with a cynical smile. "But let us agree that you are not of their ilk." He turned as the butler came in and in the quiet bustle of opening and pouring the champagne, Clarissa steadied her nerves.

Crofton left the room as discreetly as he'd entered it, and Jasper handed Clarissa a glass of straw-colored wine. "Let's begin again." He raised his glass in a toast and took a sip, then sat down on a worn upholstered sofa at one side of the fire, patting the seat beside him.

She sat down, and he slipped an arm around her shoulders, drawing her against him. There was something so comfortable, so unthreatening about the position that Clarissa leaned into him, her head resting against his shoulder. His hand found the

277

swell of her breast, and a finger lightly teased the nipple beneath the silk of her gown. To her momentary embarrassment she felt the nipple prickle, harden, press against her bodice, but then, when his mouth teased her ear, his teeth nibbled her earlobe, she lost all sense of embarrassment and her body seemed to move and respond to its own music.

He kissed her, his probing tongue demanding entrance, and her lips parted with an involuntary sigh of pleasure, as she tasted the sweetness on his tongue, felt the muscular presence exploring her mouth, dancing with her own tongue, running along her teeth, into the soft flesh of her cheeks, tasting her. Her nipples rose hard and insistent and she half turned so that she was lying sideways across his chest, reaching against him.

He slipped a hand beneath her, lifting her further onto his lap, turning her fully sideways as he kissed her more deeply and her breasts pressed hard against his chest. She felt a hardness beneath her too, a strange pressure against her hips, and an even stranger sensation in her lower belly, a sinking, plunging feeling that was as delightful as it was strange.

And then reality landed like a bucket of

icy water. If she didn't stop this now, the inevitable would happen, and while part of her at this moment of intense sensation didn't give a tinker's dam if she lost her virginity, some cautious little part of her brain that had not succumbed to pure physical need reminded her that if she let this happen, he would know she had been lying. She was a virgin, and losing the maidenhead was a painful and bloody business, or so she'd heard. She would not be able to disguise her virgin state and a virgin was of no use to the Earl of Blackwater. He was already cheating on the bargain and hating it; he would never countenance such a massive fraud as presenting a virgin to his uncle as his converted prostitute. There were whores aplenty who would play the charade for him.

She pushed back from his chest, slithering down onto the sofa again. Her eyes were still unfocused, dreamy with desire, her cheeks pink, her ringlets tumbled, but she forced herself to sit up, to compose herself. "I'd prefer not to rush to inevitable conclusions here, sir. May we slow down?"

He pursed his lips as he reached sideways for his champagne glass. "I have agreed to let you set the pace, at least for the moment." He took a sip, regarding her with a degree of puzzlement. "You were as eager as I, then, Clarissa. Why is it so important to delay the inevitable?"

"Anticipation, I have heard, greatly enhances pleasure," she said, amazed at her boldness. She'd heard nothing of the kind but to her amazed relief he didn't seem to think she'd said anything strange. She took up her own glass. The bubbles went up her nose and her moment of triumph ended in a mortifying scramble for a handkerchief.

Jasper watched her struggles with the same puzzlement. Something was so badly wrong with this, and he couldn't for the life of him put his finger on it. She had been within a heartbeat of yielding, her body soft, pliant, ready for his lovemaking, and then something had brought her up as sharply as a curb on a bolting horse.

But his own rampant desire was no longer importunate, and he had time. He would get to the bottom of this puzzle soon enough. And in the meantime he hugely enjoyed her company, when she wasn't succumbing to a fit of sneezes, coughs, or hilarity. Her tongue was too sharp, her wits too quick, for who and what she was supposed to be. There were too many puzzling strands in Mistress Clarissa's narrative, too many contradictions.

Whores did not ride, did not offer critical assessments of a man's driving skills, did not curtsy with all the perfect formality of a debutante at the queen's drawing room.

And they most certainly did not carry themselves with the composure and occasional arrogance of a woman who knew her place in society, a place that was subservient to no one.

So what had driven her to whoredom? If she was as gently bred as he now believed, how had she ended up in Mother Griffiths's nunnery?

CHAPTER TWELVE

Jasper decided to leave seduction to follow its own course for the time being. They dined companionably and he set himself to find out as much as he could about Clarissa's past. "Did you grow up in Bedfordshire?" It was a casual question, asked as he passed her a dish of artichokes. "Is that where your family is from?"

Clarissa helped herself to the vegetable, her mind working rapidly. It was time now to come up with a story, a convincing life story that would explain her choice of profession and her presence at 32 King Street. She racked her brain trying to remember what she knew of Bedfordshire, a county of which she had absolutely no experience. Bedford was the county town, that much she did know.

"My parents had a small farm when I was a baby. I don't really remember much about it. It was in the country outside Bedford.

And then something happened, I don't know exactly what, and my father lost the farm." She sliced into the breast of capon on her plate, looking up to give him what she hoped was a bleak smile. "My parents moved to Bedford, where they thought my father could get work, but then the plague came and they both died."

"How old were you?" He passed her a bowl of crisply roasted potatoes, watching her closely.

She shrugged, taking a potato, hoping that indulging her appetite wouldn't lessen the poignancy of her tale. "Three or four . . . I was put on the parish and sent to the workhouse. They didn't work us little ones until we were five or so, then we worked in the kitchens and the laundry, and every now and again well-dressed women would come and we'd be paraded before them and if they took a fancy to a girl they took her on as a maid."

Jasper's clear gaze didn't waver from her countenance as she spoke. "Did that happen to you?"

"Yes, quite quickly. A lawyer's family in Bedford. The woman wanted a new maid-of-all-work she could train up." As she spun her tale, she kept in her mind's eye the image of the little girl, breakfastless, scrubbing the steps with her chapped hands and cheeks on a frigid morning. "There was a housekeeper, who was kind enough, but the mistress was hard."

"Who taught you to read?"

She looked at him, startled. She hadn't expected such a question. But of course a woman with the life story she was inventing would probably be illiterate. He knew she could write her own name, but that didn't necessarily argue for all-round literacy. "How do you know I can?"

He shook his head with a short laugh. "What do you take me for, Clarissa?"

"Not a fool," she responded, rapidly concocting a convincing explanation.

Jasper was beginning to doubt the truth of that, but he pressed on. "Then answer the question."

"There was one son, seven years older than I was. He took a fancy to me. At first he teased me because I couldn't read or write, and then he offered to teach me." She was warming to her story now, sure of the direction it would take, an embellishment on the tale she'd told Bertha, the baby farmer. "He was sickly much of the time so they didn't send him to school. He had a tutor and after a time he secretly shared his lessons with me."

She sat back, taking a sip of wine, astonished once again at how fertile her imagination was proving to be. She would never have thought she had the capacity to tell such convincing tales. A quick glance at her audience revealed no sign that he disbelieved any of this farrago of lies, but no sign that he believed it either. His expression gave nothing away.

She took another mouthful of capon. It was served with an orange sauce that was quite delectable. "You may be an impoverished nobleman, sir, but you keep a fine kitchen." She poured a little more sauce onto the bird.

He smiled, dabbing at his lips with his napkin. "Your compliments should go to the redoubtable Mistress Hogarth. She rules the kitchen with a rod of iron. She was our parents' cook and woe betide me or my brothers if we should fail to do justice to her culinary creations." He glanced at her now empty plate and flicked an amused eyebrow. "You need have no fears on that score. She will approve of you without reservation."

Clarissa blushed a little, saying slightly defensively, "I've always had a good appetite. Maybe it was because I was always hungry in my early years." *Stroke of genius.*

Who could resist the plight of a famished child?

"No doubt." Jasper reached across to refill her wineglass. "So, pray continue your tale."

"Oh . . . well, it becomes a little more difficult to talk about."

"I imagine it does." His tone was dry. He leaned back in his chair, idly turning the stem of his wineglass between his fingers, his gaze still resting on her countenance. "What brought you to London, Clarissa?"

She chewed her lower lip, gazing down at her plate. "The younger son, my friend, I thought . . . one night he . . ."

"Raped you." He filled the pause with the plain, unemotional statement. It was the obvious conclusion to this tale she was spinning and he was conscious of a flicker of disappointment that she hadn't come up with something more ingenious.

Clarissa nodded and reached for her wineglass. "I found myself with child . . . they threw me out on the street. It was, of course, my fault, not the beloved son's." She was beginning to believe the story herself; the bitterness in her voice sounded utterly genuine. And she realized that, of course, it was a story that so many real women had lived, and she was at this moment experiencing it through their eyes. "I had nowhere to go, no one to turn to. The boy slipped me some money, guilt money, I suppose, so for a while I wasn't destitute."

"What happened to the child?"

"I lost it . . . fortunately for both of us." She glanced quickly across at him, wondering if he was shocked, but his expression was still as calm and unreadable as before.

"I took the stage to London and found a cheap room, but then I lost the child and was ill for several weeks. The money was soon spent on the physician and medicines and then I had nothing to pay for my lodging, or food, or anything." She stopped, feeling that further embellishment would only detract from the power of the narrative.

"A sad story," he said. "But not an uncommon one, more's the pity." He glanced towards the door as the butler and a footman entered.

Clarissa greeted the conversational break with relief. She felt completely drained of all mental and emotional energy and didn't think her powers of invention could be stretched to any further gymnastics tonight. She sipped her wine as the first course was removed, replaced with a bowl of Rhenish cream, a plate of apple tartlets, and a cheese pudding.

"Mistress Ordway wishes to send her

compliments to Mistress Hogarth," Jasper informed Crofton.

"Yes, indeed. Pray convey my thanks and my compliments to Mistress Hogarth, Crofton. Rarely have I enjoyed a dinner so much." Clarissa was behaving quite naturally and missed the effect her warm smile and gracious tones had on the butler, who had never heard a piece of muslin, even one as lovely as this, talk with all the natural ease of a lady of the manor. He glanced at his master, who met his look with an impassive countenance.

"It will be my pleasure, madam." He bowed and gestured impatiently to the footman, who hastily preceded him from the room.

"What may I serve you?" Jasper indicated the dishes on the table when they were alone once more.

Clarissa took a spoonful of the cheese pudding. "Tell me about the house on Half Moon Street."

"It's quite small, but elegant, I believe. The cook-housekeeper will take care of your household needs; Sally is your personal maid. I understand she has a deft hand with a needle and a flatiron, and is quite knowledgeable about the latest hairstyles."

"You've hired this maid already?"

"Some time ago." He took a bite from a fruit tartlet.

Clarissa frowned. "How? I don't quite understand. We met only a very short time ago. How could you have hired me a personal maid before we even met?"

He looked at her with a half smile, saying gently, "The house has had other occupants. I hope that doesn't grieve you, Clarissa."

Of course. What a fool she was. The house on Half Moon Street was where he kept all his mistresses for the duration of their liaison, and presumably the servants simply took care of whichever mistress was in favor.

"Of course not," she stated, sipping her wine. "I wasn't thinking clearly."

"No," he agreed. "But you may rest assured that the house has been furnished specifically for you. There will be no . . . no unfortunate reminders of its previous inhabitant. And my servants are well trained. They serve me and only one lady of the house."

She managed a smile, but it was not particularly enthusiastic.

"The house will be ready for you tomorrow. My carriage will fetch you and convey you there. I'm assuming you have little in the way of possessions?" He quirked an eyebrow.

"A portmanteau with a few things. Nothing heavy."

He nodded. "If you have quite finished, then, I suggest we repair to the library fire." He rose from his chair and held Clarissa's as she stood up.

"I should go back to King Street to prepare for tomorrow's move," she said tentatively, moving ahead of him to the door.

"All in good time," Jasper responded blandly. "It's most impolite to dine in company and then rush off to pastures new, my dear. Although it does seem to be something of a habit of yours."

"It is not," she stated flatly. "Or, at least, only in your company, my lord. In this instance I am thinking only of how much sooner we can be together in Half Moon Street if I'm ready for the coachman early tomorrow."

He gave a shout of incredulous laughter. "Oh, you are utterly outrageous, Mistress Clarissa. How dare you try to bamboozle me like that? What kind of gull d'you think me?" He put an arm around her shoulders, sweeping her ahead of him across the hall and into the library. "That deserves a forfeit, ma'am."

She looked at him warily. The laughter was still in his eyes but there was something else too, a deepening intensity that alarmed her as much as it thrilled her, and she felt herself responding with that sinking, plunging feeling in her belly, a heat over her skin, a swiftness in her blood.

He stepped close to her, taking her shoulders, looking deep into her eyes. "I wonder what you really are," he murmured the instant before he kissed her.

This kiss was slow, deep, as if he would answer his question with the taste of her mouth, the scent of her skin, the feel of her body. His hands were all over her body, moving down her back, pressing into her backside, holding her tight against him, against the hardness she now felt rising against her loins.

Her breath shuddered and her own hands were moving now, slipping beneath his coat to feel the warmth of his skin through the fine lawn of his shirt. They slid around his back, traced the hard, knobbly line of his spine, felt the ripple of muscle across his shoulders and the tight muscularity of his buttocks. The intimacy of this exploration took her breath away, but she didn't want it to stop. Her eyes were closed and she was learning him through her hands, through her fingertips, and she wanted more of him.

She wanted his skin, his body against her own.

And it was Jasper who stepped back first this time. He ran a fingertip over her kiss-reddened lips, a knowing smile in his eyes. He palmed the curve of her cheek, then traced the whorls of her ears with the tip of his little finger in a tantalizing stroke that brought prickles to her skin. "Well, well," he murmured. "What a depth of passion you've been hiding, my sweet. It seems anticipation does indeed heighten sensation."

Clarissa was too shaken, still too lost to respond. He bent and lightly kissed the corner of her mouth. "Perhaps I should send you home now, after all. I think we shall enjoy the consummation of this arrangement much more if it's properly orchestrated. Tomorrow night, Clarissa."

He opened the door. "Crofton, send to the mews for the carriage. Mistress Ordway is going home. Oh, and make sure there's a hot brick and a lap rug in the carriage."

"Right away, m'lord." Crofton's expression gave no indication of his astonishment. He couldn't remember another occasion when his lordship had sent a lady of the night about her business before he'd conducted his own with her.

Clarissa drew a deep steadying breath.

"My hat . . . gloves . . . ?"

"In the hall. Henry will have them for you." He ushered her out with an arm around her, and the footman was indeed standing by the door, ready to hand her the straw hat and kid gloves.

"May I?" Jasper took the hat and set it on her head, adjusting the brim with a tiny smile before he tied the ribbons beneath her chin. "It is a most charmingly frivolous piece of headgear."

Clarissa drew on her gloves, aware that her fingers were shaking a little. She closed her hands tightly and offered him a bright smile. "What time should I expect your coachman tomorrow?"

"What time would be convenient?" His expression was all solemnity.

"I should be ready by midmorning."

"Then that is when he will be there." He moved to the front door, his arm once more around her shoulders. Henry opened it and as they stepped out into the night a carriage drew up. The liveried coachman jumped down from the box and hurried to open the door. He let down the footstep and bowed as Jasper escorted Clarissa down the steps.

"Thank you for a delightful evening, my lord." Clarissa gave him her hand. "I will see you tomorrow."

"Oh, yes, you may be assured of that." He raised her hand to his lips, then stepped back as she stepped up into the carriage. "Sleep well, Clarissa."

A ready response to that did not come immediately to mind, so Clarissa contented herself with a smile and a wave as the door closed, shutting her into the welcome darkness of the closed carriage. A hot brick was at her feet and a warm sheepskin lap robe on the squabbed leather seat beside her. She wrapped herself securely, then leaned back against the squabs, closing her eyes as she faced the morass she had floundered into.

Either she ran from King Street in the morning and ensured that neither Mother Griffiths nor the Earl of Blackwater ever laid eyes on her again, or she gave her virginity to Jasper. Either she abandoned a foolproof plan to keep her brother safe, or she paid for the earl's protection for both of them with her virginity.

Stark choices, but in her heart of hearts she knew there was no choice, and neither did she really wish for one. The wave of lust and passion that had engulfed her that evening had astounded her but had filled her with a deep delight. Her maidenhead seemed like a matter of no importance in the light of those feelings, and since its loss was the one sure way to achieve her brother's safety, then it was best to accept that and work out how this consummation could be accomplished without the earl realizing he had bedded a virgin.

"Thirty-two King Street, madam."

She realized with a shock that the carriage was no longer moving and the coachman stood at the now open door, letting down the footstep. "So soon . . . thank you." She unwrapped herself from the rug, reluctantly took her feet from the hot brick, and accepted his hand to descend to the street. The house was ablaze with light as always, music and laughter drifting into the street as the front door opened to admit a clearly inebriated pair of gentlemen.

She smiled at the coachman, wished him good night, and hurried to the door. The steward admitted her and she ran up to her chamber, expecting to find it cold and dark. Instead it was firelit, candles burning brightly, the bed turned down invitingly. Presumably the house worked on the assumption that a gentleman could accompany a lady to her boudoir at any time.

She cast aside her hat and gloves and sat on the edge of the bed. She needed advice, and who better to give it than Emily or Maddy, or, indeed, any of the other women at work in this house. She pulled the bell rope.

"What can I do for you, miss?" The maid stood in the door, her gaze studiously avoiding the bed.

"Emily . . . or Maddy . . . are they with gentlemen at the moment?"

"Miss Em's not. She's in the salon. Miss Maddy's busy."

Clarissa had learned in her time at King Street that if a girl was not with a gentleman she waited in the salon, where gentlemen who had no specific lady in mind would come in off the street, take a glass of wine, engage in superficial conversation, and then pick a companion from among the available ladies.

"Could you give Emily a message?"

The girl looked doubtful. "Maybe."

"Ask her if she has any free time tonight to visit me here . . . Maddy, too, if she's free later."

"Mistress Griffiths don't close the front door till four," the maid said.

"No, I know that. But if by any chance either of them is free for a while, could you ask them if they would come here to me? It's very important."

The girl shrugged. "If I can, I will. Anything else you want?"

Clarissa shook her head. "No, thank you."

The girl went off and Clarissa undressed slowly. Naked, she stood in front of the mirror, wondering what a man would see when he saw her like this. Would he see what she saw? A slim woman with insignificant breasts, skinny thighs, long thin feet. There was nothing voluptuous about her body, nothing particularly arousing, she thought. But maybe a man might see something that she couldn't.

She wrapped herself in her chamber robe and climbed into bed. Might as well try to sleep until Maddy or Emily was free to answer her summons. But sleep wouldn't come. She lay watching the flames flickering on the high ceiling, listening to the hiss and pop of the fire. What would she be feeling this time tomorrow night? *How* would she be feeling? Her body was filled with a restless energy that made her legs twitch until finally she got out of bed and went to sit on the broad window seat, watching the scenes in the street below. The revelers for the most part were good-natured, but there were one or two scuffles, and every now and again the shrill sound of a watchman's whistle would rise above the sounds of revelry.

Was her little brother asleep? Was he in a

gin-soaked stupor, shivering in the freezing attic, his empty belly cleaving to his backbone? She couldn't get to him until Sunday, the day after tomorrow. She had to have a safe place to take him, somewhere warm and comfortable where he could regain his strength, look once again like her little brother instead of the frightened waif he had become. Her heart swelled with hatred for her uncle. She would kill him given half a chance. But first things first. Francis could survive one more day. He *must.*

She was so lost in her anxious reverie she didn't hear the door open until Emily spoke softly. "Is something the matter, Clarissa?"

"Oh, no . . . not really." Clarissa returned to the present with a start. She jumped off the window seat, crossing the room with hands outstretched to her visitor. "Thank you for coming, Em. I desperately need some advice on a rather . . ." She gave a slightly embarrassed little laugh as she took Emily's hands and drew her to the fire. "A rather delicate matter, and it's quite difficult to explain."

Emily looked puzzled but sat down willingly enough. "Tell me."

Clarissa hesitated. "Would you like a glass of wine? . . . I think I would." A tray with decanter and glasses stood on a pier table against the far wall. She poured two glasses of Madeira and brought them back to the fire.

Emily took hers with a smile of thanks. "Tell me," she repeated.

Clarissa took a deep breath. "This is going to sound very strange, but I need to lose my virginity tonight."

Emily nearly dropped the glass. "What in the world can you mean?"

"There are some things I can't explain, Em, but this is the truth, even if I can't explain it properly."

Emily listened openmouthed. Clarissa kept it as simple as possible, saying nothing about her true background, or about Francis and Luke, merely implying that she had agreed to the contract with Lord Blackwater for compelling family reasons of her own and now found herself obliged to fulfill the terms of the contract without his discovering that she was not what he believed her to be.

"Does Mother Griffiths know you're a virgin?" Emily was still staring in wide-eyed astonishment.

Clarissa shook her head. "If she ever believed it, I'm sure she doesn't now. Why would a virgin agree to a brothel contract to be a man's mistress? But I do have my reasons, Em," she added quickly. "I'm sorry I can't explain them."

"Well, we all have our secrets in this business," Emily declared with a tiny shrug. "And we don't pry." She stood up. "We need reinforcements. Trudy is not busy at the moment. I'll fetch her." She whisked herself out of the chamber.

Clarissa sat down, sipping the Madeira, and waited, unsure whether she was right to trust the inhabitants of 32 King Street with so much of her secret, but she could think of no alternative.

Emily returned in five minutes, accompanied by a very curious Maddy and a somewhat skeptical Trudy. "Maddy's gentleman had just left, so I brought her too," Emily said. "I haven't told them much, there wasn't time, so you'd better tell them what you just told me."

Clarissa did so, watching their faces somewhat anxiously. Their expressions ran the gamut of disbelief, astonishment, and finally amusement. When Clarissa fell silent, Trudy began to laugh. She had a deep laugh that seemed appropriate enough booming forth from her broad-shouldered, big-boned frame. After a moment, Emily and Maddy joined in.

Clarissa looked for the humor in the situation and couldn't find it, so she waited patiently until their laughter ceased. Trudy dabbed at her eyes, which shone with tears of laughter, and her shoulders still shook as she pronounced at last, "Well, this is a new one, isn't it, girls?" She picked up Emily's wineglass and held it to the light. "Madeira . . . I'll have a glass, Mistress Virgin, if I may."

Clarissa filled a glass and handed it to her. "So, do you have a solution?" Her tone was a touch impatient; their laughter had galled her a little, although she wouldn't admit it.

"We're more used to solving the reverse problem," Emily explained. "Often we have to re-create virginity if a client demands a virgin. We all know how to do that, but this is quite different."

"How do you re-create virginity?" For a moment Clarissa forgot her own problem in this fascinating subject.

"The midwives have ways of creating an artificial barrier, just some fine webbing. And there's a little cubbyhole in the bedpost where we keep a vial of blood. The men are all so wrapped up in their own lust that as soon as they feel the barrier, they push like a ramrod through a portcullis and when their cocks break through, you should hear 'em crow."

Trudy shook her head with a scornful chuckle. "Fools, all of 'em. We open the vial and smear the blood about while they're still crowing, and oh, how it suits their manhood to think they've spoiled a virgin. Some of 'em actually believe a woman will remember her first for the rest of her days. Makes 'em so proud." Her lip curled in disdain for the entire male sex.

Clarissa listened, wide-eyed in her turn. The world was full of tricksters, it seemed. And she was no better and no worse than the rest. "So, how do I achieve the opposite, Trudy?"

"Simple enough." Trudy got to her feet. "I'll be back in a moment."

"Have either of you ever done that?" Clarissa asked after the other woman had left. "Pretended to be virgins?"

"Oh, I did, once," Maddy said. "At first I wanted to laugh so hard, instead of gasping and shrieking so that they think it hurts, but then I remembered my real first time, and that made it easier." Her expression darkened, her usually merry eyes suddenly shadowed by memory. "He was a brute."

Emily laid a sympathetic hand on her knee. "I was luckier. Mother Griffiths sold my virginity in an auction, but the man who bought it was a real gentleman. He kept me as an exclusive for a year after that."

Clarissa began to wonder how she had spun her tale of hardship to Jasper so glibly when the true tales were so filled with suppressed pain and horror. She looked up with relief as Trudy came back into the chamber.

"You just use this," she said, holding out a slim pointed object.

Clarissa took it and looked at it blankly. "What is it?"

All three stared at her. "It's a dildo. Have you never seen one before?" Maddy asked.

She shook her head. "What does it do?"

"Use your imagination," Trudy told her briskly. "You need to break the maidenhead . . ."

"With this?" She turned the slender object around. It was made of ivory, very smooth and cool. "I put it . . ."

"Yes, exactly," Maddy said. "One quick thrust and it'll be over. It'll hurt, but at least you'll be doing it to yourself."

"Unless you want me to do it for you." Trudy held out her hand. "It'll take but a second."

Clarissa shook her head. "No . . . no, thank you. I appreciate the offer, Trudy, but I'd rather do it myself."

"Then we'll leave you to get on with it." Trudy went to the door. "Come on, ladies,

Mother's on the prowl and she's going to want to know why we aren't in the salon."

The other two followed her to the door. Emily hung back long enough to murmur a whispered "Good luck" before closing the door behind them.

Clarissa examined the ivory dildo. She drank another glass of Madeira, and then she climbed onto the bed.

CHAPTER THIRTEEN

There was very little blood, Clarissa was relieved to discover, and really very little pain, just a quick stab. She expected to feel a sense of loss, of finality at the change she had made in herself, but amazingly she fell asleep quickly once it was done, and to her astonishment slept deeply and dreamlessly until an hour after sunrise. She awoke filled with a pleasant languor, her limbs heavy and relaxed in the featherbed, wondering why she felt a sense of anticipation, a strange thrill of excitement.

And then she remembered. She sat up against the pillows and peered at the clock on the mantel. Eight o'clock already. She rarely slept so late, but then the house was deadly quiet around her and there was still little noise from the street below, so perhaps it wasn't surprising, particularly after the excitements of the previous night.

She got out of bed and stood up slowly,

tentatively taking a step towards the washstand. She felt no different this morning,
just a slight soreness, and that would be
eased by a hot bath. It seemed to have been
weeks since she'd had that luxury. She
contemplated the bell-pull, but then thought
of some poor maid hauling endless jugs of
hot water upstairs to fill the copper tub in
front of the fire and decided that in good
conscience she couldn't expect it. But one
jug of hot water wasn't too much to ask.
She pulled the rope.

It was answered surprisingly quickly. "You
rang, miss?"

"Yes." She smiled at the young girl standing hesitantly in the doorway. "Could you
bring me a jug of hot water, and some hot
chocolate, perhaps, and some breakfast?"

The girl nodded and vanished, reappear-
ing in ten minutes with a steaming jug that
she set on the dresser. "I'll fetch up that
breakfast now." She disappeared again.

Clarissa pulled her chemise over her head
and poured water into the basin. She dipped
the washcloth and sponged herself from
head to toe. There were smears of blood on
her inner thighs but no other visible evidence of her lost maidenhead. The girl came
in with a breakfast tray and immediately
went to rekindle the fire.

Clarissa slipped into her chamber robe and poured hot chocolate in a fragrant stream into a delicate china cup. Thirty-two King Street was undeniably a den of iniquity, but it provided a most elegant and charming environment for the sinning. She had no reason to believe that Half Moon Street would be any less so.

Her father would turn in his grave if he knew she was about to become a kept woman, the mistress of a philandering earl, and about to keep his son and heir hidden in the earl's love nest to boot. But there was no safer place for Francis. He would be under the earl's protection as much as she was, although Jasper would not know whom he was protecting. Luke would never think to look for his wards under his very nose in the center of fashionable London. And the idea that his niece was the mistress of the Earl of Blackwater was so farfetched there were no circumstances in which it could enter his head.

Today had to be devoted to Jasper, to the business of becoming his mistress. The prospect sent shivers up her spine, part terror, part thrill . . . or were the two indistinguishable? However deeply she looked into her soul, she could find not the slightest reservation over the step she was about to take. Maybe she was truly a harlot at heart after all. The thought brought a grin to her face until she reflected that while she had taken care of the physical obstacle to a non-virgin state, she had no idea how to behave, harlot at heart or not. She had no idea what a woman experienced in the ways of lust would do or say. Surely it would be obvious to any experienced man what a novice she was?

Then she told herself there was no point worrying about something she could do nothing about. She would just have to rely on instinct, and hope that some things were simply ingrained from birth and would come naturally. She had to keep her eye on the reason for this deception. One more day, and she would have Francis out of that cesspit.

But what if something happened to him in this one day? She felt the familiar nut of anxiety in her chest, a ripple of nausea in her belly. She couldn't think like that. She *mustn't* think like that. One false move today and all would be lost. She had to keep her eyes and her mind on the goal and somehow present the man who was about to become her protector with an untrammeled countenance and a light heart.

But she was no longer hungry for her

breakfast when she looked at the boiled eggs and bread and butter. She could think only of her little brother making do with a small piece of gingerbread given him by a kindly itinerant packman.

One more day, Francis. One more day. She imagined that with a sheer effort of will she could project her thoughts across London to Francis's wretched attic. Somehow he would hear her promise that he had only to hold on for one more day.

The earl's coachman arrived punctually at ten that morning. Clarissa was just closing her small portmanteau when Mistress Griffiths came into her chamber. "So, are you ready to leave us, my dear?"

"I believe I have everything, ma'am." She turned to face the woman. "I thank you for your hospitality, Mistress Griffiths." *Not that she hadn't paid for it,* she thought, but kept the thought to herself.

"Not at all, my dear." Nan ran an experienced eye over her. "Good, you're wearing the gown Jasper gave you. I would offer you the sprig muslin, but I doubt you'll need it. Blackwater is generous to a fault, and you'll have no need of something so plain."

Clarissa was under no illusion that Nan would really have parted with the sprig muslin. The sale was complete and she'd been paid for her part in it; there was no need to be overly generous. The gown would remain to dress up some other innocent for the right customer. She merely smiled and adjusted the set of her hat in the mirror.

"I would like to make my farewells to Emily and the others. They were very kind to me."

"You'll be kind to them if you leave them to their rest," Nan declared. "But you're welcome to visit anytime. My door is always open to you, and if you need any advice, I am always here. Don't hesitate should there be any issues that you are perhaps a little uncomfortable with or uncertain about. I know his lordship well and can advise you to good effect when it comes to pleasing him."

"I don't doubt it, ma'am." Clarissa's smile was neutral. "And I promise I won't hesitate to take advantage of your kind offer should the need arise." She picked up her portmanteau.

"And when his lordship tires of you, there'll always be a place for you here," Nan reassured her as she escorted her to the door. The steward took her portmanteau and carried it to the carriage. He gave it to the coachman, who stood at the open carriage door, then offered Clarissa a half salute and returned to the house, closing the door to 32 King Street on its erstwhile occupant.

Clarissa climbed into the carriage, where a hot brick and the fur-edged lap robe awaited. The coachman put her portmanteau onto the opposite seat, closed the door, and the carriage moved off at a brisk clip. Clarissa leaned forward to look out of the window as they crossed the Great Piazza and passed through the surrounding streets of Covent Garden. She would be back, she was certain, but not as a supplicant. She would be back to attend the theatre and the opera with the rest of fashionable London. She would be back on the arm of the fifth Earl of Blackwater. Again she was aware of that little prickle of excitement along her spine.

Half Moon Street was a small, pretty street running between Curzon Street and Piccadilly. It was in the heart of fashionable London and yet seemed like an oasis as Clarissa stepped down from the carriage. She could hear the bustle of Piccadilly behind her, and see a carriage bowling down Curzon Street just ahead of her, but she stood on a quiet street lined with narrow houses. Most of the windows were graced with boxes displaying autumn greenery.

A man stepped out of a house across the street. He doffed his hat and bowed to Clarissa as he walked towards Piccadilly. A maid was polishing the brass on a house two doors down. A small boy with a nursemaid came from the direction of Green Park. He was bowling a hoop along the side of the street and Clarissa saw Francis doing the same thing. Francis playing in Green Park, bowling a hoop, sailing a toy boat on the pond. She blinked rapidly and resolutely turned back to the door of the house, where the coachman was banging the shining brass knocker.

The door opened the instant Clarissa reached it. "Good morning, Mistress Ordway." A young maidservant curtsied. "We was expectin' you. His lordship said as how you'd be along afore noon." She stepped back, allowing Clarissa entrance into a small square hall. A narrow staircase rose from the rear.

"You must be Sally." Clarissa smiled at her.

"Aye, ma'am." Sally was regarding her with ill-concealed curiosity. "Should I show you around the house?"

"Yes, if you please. But I should like to meet the housekeeper first." Clarissa wondered if she should consider the conspicuously absent greeting from the woman responsible for the smooth running of the household some kind of a statement on her own parlous social position. She drew off her gloves, looking around the well-appointed entryway.

"Oh, Mistress Newby's having a bit of a barney with the butcher, ma'am. Trying to pass off a piece of scrag end for best end of neck, he was. Should 'ave known better," Sally confided cheerfully. "No one can put one over on Mistress Newby. I'll just show you what's what down 'ere, and then we'll go upstairs. Mistress Newby'll be along as soon as she's told off the butcher."

"I'll be leaving Mistress Ordway's portmanteau 'ere then, Sally." The coachman set the valise down inside the door. "If that'll be all, ma'am." He touched his forehead in a half salute in Clarissa's general direction.

"Yes, thank you." Clarissa dismissed him with a smile. This was all familiar ground and she was already beginning to feel like herself again, in charge of her own establishment. She may not have known how to behave like a whore, but she did know how to conduct herself in these circumstances.

"This here's the dining parlor, ma'am."

Sally opened a door to the right of the front entrance. " 'Tis not very big, but his lordship doesn't do much entertaining here."

Clarissa absorbed that in silence. It sounded as if the current occupant of the house on Half Moon Street was not expected to entertain guests for herself. But what did she know of the mores of kept women? She peered dutifully into the room. It was pleasant, neutral, furnished as one would expect of a dining parlor. She followed Sally, who had hoisted the portmanteau, upstairs with rather more interest.

"This here's the drawing room, ma'am. Looks a bit different now, it does." She opened the door onto a room at the front of the house.

"A bit different from what?" Clarissa walked past her into the room.

"Oh, from when Mis—" Sally stopped abruptly, blushing to the roots of her hair. "Beggin' your pardon, mistress."

"That's quite all right, Sally." Clarissa looked around and liked the room instantly. It was furnished with a mixture of understated elegance and comfortable simplicity. The curtains at the long windows were a rich blue damask, held back by gold tasseled ropes, and the colors in the Axminster carpet echoed the blue and gold. "What did

314

it look like before?" She couldn't resist the question.

"Oh, it was all a bit Turkish," Sally said. "Silk cushions everywhere and gold scrolls on the sofas. And there were little things everywhere. The devil to dust, it were. Madam took all that stuff with her; good riddance is what I say."

Clarissa hid her smile. The house might have been sophisticated but the servant was down-to-earth enough. She was about to express again her wish to meet with the housekeeper when the woman herself came into the room, slightly breathless, wiping her hands on her apron.

"Oh, I beg your pardon for not greeting you, Mistress Ordway, but the butcher —"

"Was trying to pass off scrag end as best end of neck," Clarissa finished for her with a warm smile. She held out her hand. "Mistress Newby, isn't it?"

"Aye, that it is." The woman took the proffered hand somewhat hesitantly as she bobbed a curtsy. "He's a new butcher . . . he'll know better next time." The declaration was accompanied by a firm nod and a grim smile.

"I'm certain he will." Clarissa looked around the room. "Who else helps out in the house, Mistress Newby?"

"Oh, there's just Sammy. He does all the odd jobs, cleans the shoes, brings in the coal, black-leads the range. If we need help with the heavy work, his lordship sends one of his own servants to help out. Sally and me manages the rest quite well."

A cozy little nest indeed, Clarissa reflected. "I hope I won't add too much to your burdens."

The woman looked at her in gratified surprise. " 'Tis no trouble, Mistress Ordway. You just say what you need." She added in a whisper, "That last madam was a right tartar an' no mistake."

Clarissa hid a smile and, curious though she was, let the statement lie. "Could I see the rest of the house?"

"Sally'll show you. I'll be getting on with your dinner. If you'd like a pot of coffee send Sally down for it." Mistress Newby bustled away.

"So, where to now, Sally?"

"The bedchamber is across the hall, mistress." Sally led the way to the door directly opposite the one to the drawing room. She opened it with a flourish.

Clarissa stepped inside. It was furnished in very much the same style as the drawing room, comfortable, luxurious even, but lacking in flamboyance. The pale rose damask of the bed hangings matched the curtains at the windows; the carpet was a deep emerald green. A daybed beneath the window was upholstered in apple-green silk, with emerald-green cushions, and the two armchairs on either side of the fire matched the cushions.

"Is this room different too?"

"Oh, yes, ma'am. Quite different. The whole house is different. They was workin' all day yesterday, from dawn to midnight. Pretty though, innit?" Sally beamed as if she had been solely responsible for the transformation. "The dressing room's through here."

She opened a door in the far wall. Clarissa followed her into a small, intimate chamber, furnished with a chaise longue, a washstand, a mirrored dresser, a linen press, and an armoire. Clarissa's first thought was that it would be perfect for Francis. He could sleep on the chaise, or better still, a cot. That would be easy enough to furnish. Quite how she was to explain the urgent need to keep a rescued urchin at her side at all times, she hadn't worked out, but she was beginning to trust her powers of invention.

"This is lovely, Sally. When my wardrobe from Madame Hortense is delivered, it will

317

be most handsomely housed."

"Oh, that it will, madam. And I'm a dab hand with the flatiron and needle and thread, so I'll look after everything all right and tight."

"I'm sure you will, Sally." Clarissa untied her hat, setting it down on the dresser, before she went back into the bedchamber. "I would like a bath," she said. "Could that be contrived, Sally?"

"Oh, yes, ma'am. There's cauldrons on the range already. I'll get Sammy to bring up some jugs." Sally opened the door of a recessed cupboard and pulled out a copper hip bath. She hauled it over in front of the fire. "It'll be nicer in 'ere, rather than the dressing room. I'll just fetch the sheets for the floor."

Clarissa sat on the long bench at the bottom of the bed as Sally spread thick sheets on the floor beneath the bath. A young boy came in, touched his forelock with an embarrassed smile at Clarissa, and poured water into the bath. He made four journeys with steaming jugs before Sally told him to go back to the kitchen and heat more water, she'd call him when they needed it.

Clarissa allowed Sally to help her undress and then with a little sigh of pleasure she stepped into the bath, sliding down into the

318

hot water, closing her eyes.

"There's lavender oil, if you'd like." Sally pulled the stopper out of a small vial. "An' there's rosemary too. An' if you was wantin' to wash your hair, there's orange flower water for the rinse."

"All of those, thank you," Clarissa said dreamily, sliding into the water to wet her hair.

Jasper spun on the ball of one stockinged foot and pressed his advance with a thrust in tierce. Steel rang on steel and his buttoned foil slipped beneath his opponent's blade, sliding under his arm to press lightly against his flesh. His opponent stepped back, raising his épée in surrender. "Touché, Jasper. Well placed. I'm a damn fool not to have seen that coming, it was always your favorite thrust."

"A matter of saving face, dear boy. You had me on the run a few minutes ago with that feint and counterfeint." Jasper wiped the sweat from his brow with a towel and tossed it to an attendant. He fitted his foil into the rack on the wall of the fencing salon and rolled down his shirtsleeves.

His opponent followed suit, and they sat side by side on the bench running the length of the long narrow room to put on their shoes. "Where to now, Robert?" Jasper stood up, reaching for his coat, which was held by the waiting attendant.

"I've a thirst on me after all that exertion." Robert Delaney shrugged into his own coat. "I'm for Whites and a gallon of claret. Will you come?"

Jasper shook his head. "Not this afternoon, m'dear. I've a more pressing matter to attend to." A tiny smile touched the corners of his mouth and Robert's eyes narrowed.

"I know that look, you sly devil. Some lady's waiting for you, I'll be bound."

Jasper laughed, saying airily, "Oh, maybe." He took his own sword from the wall rack, sheathing it at his hip. Unlike the previous weapon, it was no prettily buttoned fencing sword but an épée that was meant for business. "I'll walk with you to Piccadilly." He took up his hat, gloves, and cane.

The two men went down a narrow flight of stairs and out onto Albemarle Street. A brisk wind whistled around the corner from Grafton Street and Jasper glanced up at the gathering clouds. "Looks like rain."

His companion merely grunted an acknowledgment. "So, who's the lady, Jasper? Are you setting up a new mistress?"

"What makes you think that, Robert?"

"It's common knowledge you'd tired of

320

the little Mallory."

"Oh, more likely she had tired of me," Jasper amended.

Robert chuckled. "She had a roving eye, I grant you that. I understand young Lassiter is her latest victim."

Jasper shrugged. "It's nothing to me, Robert." There was a note in his voice that Robert marked well. His old friend had a very strong code of honor and could never be drawn into a derogatory discussion, most particularly when it concerned a woman who had once lived under his protection.

They reached Piccadilly and parted company, Robert to walk to his club on James Street, Jasper to stroll down Piccadilly to Half Moon Street. He walked briskly but barely felt the biting wind. His mind was pleasantly occupied in contemplation of the final steps in the seduction of Mistress Ordway.

He let himself into the house and Sally burst from the door to the kitchen regions as soon as she heard his step. "Good afternoon, m'lord."

"Afternoon, Sally." He smiled at the curtsying girl as he unfastened his sword belt. "Did Mistress Ordway arrive safely?"

"Oh, yes, sir. She's above stairs . . . in her chamber, sir. I'll run up and tell her your lordship's arrived."

He held up a hand. "No, don't do that. I'll announce myself." He laid his sword on an oak bench by the door.

Sally looked nonplussed. "Oh, but Mistress Ordway's in the bath, m'lord."

Jasper raised a speaking eyebrow as he handed her his hat and cane. "I hardly think that's a matter of any moment." He drew off his gloves, slapping them lightly into the palm of one hand. "Do you?"

"No . . . no, of course not, sir." Sally hastened away with her burdens and Jasper, smiling, took the stairs two at a time. He paused for a moment outside the door to Clarissa's bedchamber, listening. His smile broadened; she was singing in her bath. He lifted the latch soundlessly and stepped into the room.

A screen stood in front of the fire protecting the bather from drafts from the door, and also from prying eyes. The room was bathed in candlelight from the branched candelabrum on a table by the window and two others on either side of the mantel. Jasper walked softly across the room and peered over the top of the screen.

The bather had her back to the door and was at first oblivious of the unseen observer. His gaze followed the sweep of her back as it curved beneath the water. Her bent knees broke the surface of the water, and he thought distractedly that they were as beautiful as the rest of her. She raised her arms to pour water over her hair, which hung in damp strands to her smoothly sloping shoulders and halfway down her back. He gazed in delight at the lovely line of her arms, the elegant curve of her forearms.

If Bathsheba had given David this much voyeuristic pleasure, Jasper reflected, it was no wonder he sent the woman's husband into the jaws of death. Suddenly Clarissa's movements stilled, her arms came down. "Is that you, Sally?"

"No, but I venture to suggest I could serve you just as well," he responded, resting his forearms on the top of the screen, smiling down at her as she slowly turned her head to look at him.

A hot wave of embarrassment flooded Clarissa and instinctively she ducked down further into the water. It was impossible to achieve full immersion in a hip bath and she was conscious of her breasts, fully exposed above the water. What else could he see? Somehow she had to hide her embarrassment. A true whore wouldn't give a second thought to her nakedness in these circumstances.

"I can manage quite well, thank you." Her voice sounded stiff to her ears and she had to fight to keep her hands from covering her breasts. He'd seen them before, after all. Instead she let her hands drift under the water to cover the dark tangle at the apex of her thighs, drawing her knees up even further.

"I could wash your back." He didn't move from his casual position leaning over the screen, but his black eyes devoured every visible line of her body.

"No . . . it doesn't need . . . I have already . . ." With a sense of futility she let the stammering muddle of protest die and reached sideways for the towel that Sally had hung over the fire screen. If she could somehow manage to stand up while wrapping herself in the soft cloth, she could maybe preserve some degree of modesty.

Jasper moved around the screen and twitched the towel from her hand. "Stand up, and I'll dry you." He held up the towel invitingly.

There was nothing for it. Clarissa stood up in a shower of drops, keeping her back to him, and reached behind her for the towel.

"Just a minute," he said softly, holding it away from her. His lascivious gaze ran down the line of her back, over the swell of her hips, the delicious curves of her bottom, and the long sweep of her thighs. It had definitely been worth waiting for, he reflected. Anticipatory imagination had not done her justice. He draped the towel over her shoulders, at the same time turning her to face him. Clarissa instantly wrapped the towel tight around her.

"Must we continue to play this game, Clarissa?" He shook his head in reproof and firmly grasped the sides of the towel, opening it. She stood still, frozen beneath the hungry gaze.

"Dear God, but you are lovely," he murmured. "Even more than I had imagined."

He ran a fingertip down from the hollow of her throat, between her breasts, circling her navel, gliding over the flat plane of her belly.

She shivered, but with a strange perverse delight now, as his fingertip burrowed into the tight nest of damp curling hair at the base of her belly, burrowed, found the cleft between the soft lips, moved further, faster. Clarissa gasped at the sensation, a heat, a cold, that sinking plunge in her belly. Her legs felt weak and she tightened her thighs instinctively, and the sensation grew stronger. She stared up at him, at the slight smile on his lips. He knew exactly what he was doing to her, exactly what was happening to her. And she knew nothing except that it was wonderful and she didn't want it to stop.

When the wave broke over her it took her by surprise. She cried out, grasped his upper arms as if they were driftwood in a tempest, and her head dropped onto his chest. At last she became aware of the steady beat of his heart as the wave receded, and slowly she came back to herself, to an awareness of her surroundings, of the warmth of the fire against her back, the glow of candlelight, the scent of lavender from his shirt.

The towel had fallen to the floor but she didn't notice for a moment, until his hands moved down her back in a leisurely caress, stroked over her backside, pressing her nakedness against him. She felt the hardness of his erection through the silk of his britches, pressing against her belly, and it came to her that she should give him something in return for the pleasure he had brought her.

Tentatively she brought her own hand around to cup the hard jut of his penis. It throbbed against her palm. She raised her head from his chest and looked up at him, half-questioningly.

He nodded, lifted her, and carried her to the bed. He laid her on the coverlet, looking down at the white naked body against the rich, rose silk embroidered with a garden of pale green and emerald blossoms, her still damp hair a titian fan framing her face. He undressed slowly, deliberately, removing his coat, his shirt, before he sat on the edge of the bed, bare-chested, to unbuckle his shoes and remove his stockings.

Clarissa gazed with unabashed curiosity at the broad expanse of his chest, the ripple of muscle in his upper arms, noticing for the first time the tensile strength in his wrists, in his long white hands. They were his uncle's hands, she thought irrelevantly. He stood up and unfastened his britches, pushing them off his hips in one swift movement, unlike the slow deliberation of his earlier disrobing.

Clarissa stared at the jutting penis, pushing out from the black hair that ran in a line from his navel to his thighs. She had never seen a naked man before, and was for a moment startled by the sheer size and power of that pillar of flesh.

"Touch me." His voice was husky, impatient almost.

Clarissa sat up, leaning forward to enclose

his penis in her hand. She felt the corded veins pulsing against her palm, felt the life of it as it twitched against her. Instinct at last seemed to have come to the fore. Without prompting she reached between his thighs with her free hand and cupped his balls one at a time, smiling as she heard his murmured intake of breath.

She bent her head and kissed the top of his penis, then she fell back on the bed, raising her arms to him.

He came down to her, moving on top of her, nudging her thighs apart with his knee. Resting on his elbows he looked down into her eyes, a searching scrutiny that seemed to be asking myriad questions, then he slipped his hands beneath her backside, lifted her on the shelf of his palms, and entered her.

Clarissa's body tensed for a second against the invasion, but she was aroused and ready for him, and insensibly began to move with his rhythm. There came a moment when she felt as if she was reaching a peak, as if something wonderful hung on the horizon. She gazed wide-eyed up into Jasper's face, and he smiled, slowing his movements for an instant, his own eyes glowing with a distant light. He withdrew to the very edge of her body, holding himself there, watching the wonder grow in her eyes.

Clarissa put her hand flat against the plane of his concave belly, feeling the responding ripple of muscle beneath the skin. If this was whoredom, she thought, she would never get enough of it.

He sheathed himself slowly within her, inch by tantalizing inch, until he was buried deep inside and she felt her inner muscles tighten instinctively around him. He withdrew slowly again, holding them both breathless on the brink of the wonder hovering just out of reach, but whose coming she knew was inevitable. Her body could not hold this much sensation without bursting apart. And suddenly he moved, faster, ever deeper, and her hips bucked beneath him and she didn't know whether she had crested a peak or fallen into a crevasse. Either way, she lost touch with her self.

Jasper disengaged slowly and rolled sideways onto the coverlet beside her. He lay with one arm flung above his head, the other resting across Clarissa's belly. He turned his head slightly to look at the curve of her cheek. Her eyes were closed and her thick golden-brown lashes formed half moons against the delicately flushed creaminess of her countenance. *Who the hell is Clarissa Ordway?* What was she? Not what she wanted the world to think; he now knew that beyond a shadow of doubt.

Chapter Fourteen

Clarissa awoke just before dawn feeling strangely bereft. She ran a hand over the bed beside her. It was empty, and the bed curtains were pulled back. A single candle burned on the mantel and she rolled onto one elbow, peering out into the room. A shadowy figure was crouched over the hearth, rekindling the ashy embers.

"Jasper? What are you doing?"

The scrape of tinder and flint, and a flame shot up from the hearth. Jasper straightened and came over to the bed. "I was lighting the fire for you. It's cold in here now."

She smiled sleepily. "You're a man of many parts."

His eyes were narrowed as they looked at her. "And you, my dear, are a woman of even more."

She had the uneasy feeling that it wasn't meant as a compliment, but he was smiling, and there was nothing in his demeanor to alarm. Except that he was dressed. "Are you leaving?" She couldn't keep the disappointment from her voice.

"I prefer to start the day in my own bed." He came around the bed and sat on the edge beside her. "It's a strange preference, perhaps." He smoothed the fall of her hair back from her face. "Sleep a little more. I foresee disturbed nights in your future." His teeth gleamed in the flash of a smile. He bent and kissed the corner of her mouth, then the tip of her nose. "Do you have plans for the day?"

One. She shook her head. "Not really. I may go for a walk, find my way around the neighborhood."

"Do you need money? I haven't had time yet to arrange a regular draft on my bank for the payment of your allowance, but I can leave you enough should something take your fancy in the shops."

Clarissa shook her head with more vehemence than she intended. "No. I have no need of your . . ." She recollected herself hastily, seeing the sudden frown crease his brow. "No, thank you. I have all I need for the present. When will you come back?"

The frown remained for a moment, then vanished, and his voice was cheerful as he answered her. "To dine with you. Look for

332

me about four o'clock." He leaned in to kiss her mouth, then stood. "Try to sleep now. My one requirement is that I should find you rested when I return."

"If that's all you require, my lord, the life of a mistress seems rather an easy one," Clarissa murmured, snuggling back under the covers. His laughter echoed after he'd closed the door behind him.

She lay there, wide-awake now, savoring her memories of the night. She had been right to trust instinct, it seemed, but she also understood how fortunate she had been that Jasper was a considerate lover. Even in her naïvety she realized how surely Jasper had led her instinct. She understood now how a rough, urgent, possessive lust could have turned a wonderful experience into a wretchedly mortifying and painful one. And amid her delight at the sensual world he had opened for her, gratitude had its place.

She sat up abruptly. Now was not the time to wallow in glorious sensual memory. She had the whole day to herself and no one to question her absences as long as she was back for four o'clock. Her mind was now free to concentrate on the plan for Francis's rescue. There couldn't be any fuss. The longer it took for Luke to discover the child's absence, the safer they would be.

For that to happen Bertha had to believe that the child was removed from her so-called care on Luke's instructions.

Money was the one sure and certain route to Bertha's heart. Clarissa pushed aside the bedcovers and got up. Her purse was buried at the bottom of her portmanteau. She took it out and laid out her funds. Bertha was paid sixpence a week and she'd implied that she'd been paid in advance for Francis's keep. How far in advance? She fingered a golden guinea. Sixpence a week for a year. Twenty-six shillings. Luke would not have paid Bertha a year in advance — he didn't expect Francis to live that long — so surely a guinea, twenty-one shillings, would be more than enough to win the boy's freedom. But in the final analysis it didn't matter how much it cost; money was irrelevant as long as she had enough.

Once she had Francis safe, she could worry about finding a convincing reason for his presence in the house. She put the money back into her purse and returned it to its hiding place in the portmanteau. Now that she knew exactly where she was going, she had no need to waste time traveling on the river. She would walk to Piccadilly and find a hackney. Jarveys understood money and she had sufficient to pay over the odds for this journey. She would get the man to wait while she fetched Francis, and then he could drop them off again somewhere along Piccadilly. They would take a circuitous route walking back to Half Moon Street and no one would be any the wiser.

Clarissa yawned, suddenly overcome by a wash of sleepiness. She could do nothing in the dark, and she needed to be sufficiently refreshed to have her wits about her. She snuffed the candle and returned to bed.

She awoke to the sound of church bells. Of course, it was Sunday. Daylight showed between the curtains at the windows and she was about to get out of bed to draw them back when a brief knock at the door brought Sally into the room. "Good morning, Mistress Ordway. I've brought your hot chocolate. I wasn't sure if you'll be going to church this morning." She set her tray down and hurried to open the curtains. "It's a cold one, but sunny for a change." She turned to the fire, which, although burning low, was still alight. "Oh, it's kept in all night."

"His lordship relit it before he left a couple of hours ago." Clarissa sat up against her pillows, stifling a yawn behind her hand. "What's the time, Sally?"

"Seven thirty. Service is at nine, in St.

Barnabas." Sally poured her hot chocolate. "It's quite popular with the gentry and his lordship sometimes attends service there, if he stays the night." She handed Clarissa the cup.

"Oh, I understood he doesn't usually spend all night." Clarissa couldn't disguise her surprise as she took the cup.

"Oh, he does sometimes," Sally returned cheerfully. "Often of a Saturday."

"I see. I must have misunderstood." Clarissa sipped her hot chocolate, hiding her unease under a vague smile. Had she done something wrong? What could she have done wrong? Was she not adventurous enough for him . . . not daring enough? She didn't know any whore's tricks. Had he expected them and been disappointed? But he hadn't seemed disappointed. Quite the reverse. But he had left her in the dark hour before dawn.

Sally cast her a quick glance as she moved around the room straightening cushions, adding coal to the fire. "Will you have breakfast in the dining parlor, ma'am, or here by the fire?"

"Here by the fire." Clarissa set down her cup and got out of bed. "I'll attend service with some friends today, but I expect you and Mistress Newby will wish to go to St.

Barnabas. I probably won't be back until early afternoon. His lordship is coming to dine at four o'clock."

"Very well, ma'am. I'll bring up hot water. Should I bring the curling iron?"

An hour later Clarissa let herself out of the house and walked with brisk purpose to Piccadilly. She was dressed in the new gown; freshly curled ringlets framed her face beneath the straw hat. She wore the green kid boots and gloves, and was satisfied that she looked as unlike the dejected, downtrodden pregnant maid as possible. Her posture and manner, not to mention the contents of her purse, would do the rest. She looked exactly what she was, a woman of substantial enough position in the world to have the authority and the means to remove a child from a baby farmer.

Of course, once she had been described to Luke he would know exactly who had Francis, but by that time it wouldn't matter. He'd never find them.

She hailed the first hackney she saw and gave him the address with calm assurance. "I will need you to wait for a few minutes while I collect someone, and then you may bring us back." She opened the door. "Have no fear, jarvey. You'll be well paid."

He looked at her askance. "You sure you

want to go there, ma'am? Particularly all alone. 'Tis a bad part of town."

"Positive," she said firmly, climbing into the carriage and closing the door. Once she was inside he could hardly refuse to take her where she wanted to go.

He shrugged, cracked his whip, and the vehicle rumbled off. Clarissa sat forward, too anxious to lean back and relax as the hackney barreled its way through the streets of fashionable London and then into the increasingly meaner streets of the East End. She watched the passing scene through the window, the river appearing and disappearing as the streets twisted and turned. She recognized London Bridge and the Tower, and knew that they were getting close.

Her heart began to beat faster and her hands were clammy in her gloves, despite the cold. She took off the gloves, flipping them against her knee. The hackney clattered along the river and the jarvey called back, " 'Ere's Wapping Stairs, miss. Where to from 'ere?"

She leaned out of the window aperture. "Up Scandrett Street and turn right along the green. You'll come to Dundee Street on the right."

A few minutes later the carriage came to a stop. "Well, 'ere y'are. You sure this is what you wants?" The driver sounded incredulous.

Clarissa stepped down from the vehicle, drawing on her gloves, her shoulders squared and her head high. "Yes, this is right. Wait here for me, I won't be many minutes. As I said before, you'll be well paid."

"That's as may be," he said, looking doubtfully around. "You just holler if 'n you needs me, miss. This is no place for the likes of you."

"I couldn't agree more." She gave him a grateful smile. It was comforting to think of his brawny presence waiting at her back. "But everything will be all right, I'm certain."

"Aye, let's 'ope so." He still sounded doubtful.

She turned resolutely to the door and banged loudly. After a few minutes the door opened a crack and the same child as before peered at her. Clarissa regarded her unsmiling. "Is your mother in, child?"

"Who wants 'er?"

"That's no concern of yours." Clarissa kept her voice cold and haughty, looking down on the girl with what she hoped was an intimidating glare. There must be absolutely no resemblance to her previous incarnation. "Fetch your mother, if you please."

The child seemed to hesitate. She wiped her nose on her sleeve, then abruptly scuttled away, leaving the door ajar. Clarissa pushed it open and entered the narrow passage. The same snufflings, whimperings, little cries came from above, and it was cold as ice in the hallway.

Bertha appeared in the passage. She looked at her visitor with a degree of hostility. "What d'you want with me, then?"

Clarissa allowed a chilly smile to touch her mouth. "Are you the woman who is looking after a boy by the name of Francis? He was placed in your charge by his uncle some weeks ago."

"What's it to you if I am?"

"I am come to take him away. His guardian sent me to fetch him."

"I don't know nothin' about no guardian." Bertha pointed to the door. "We don't want the likes of you around 'ere. You get goin' now."

Clarissa stood her ground. "I think, Mistress Bertha — I have that right, I think . . . Bertha? You would do well to hear me out. Shall we go into the kitchen? Is it this way?" She gestured into the dark regions at the rear of the hallway.

Bertha's air of confident hostility wavered a little. She turned and shuffled towards the kitchen. Clarissa followed her, her heart hammering. She had felt safer in the hallway with the open door behind her, and the jarvey behind that, but she had no choice except to go further into the den.

The kitchen was much as she remembered it, the gin-sodden man still sitting in his rickety chair by the fire. He looked up and blinked blearily. "Who's this then? Some fine lady come a-visitin'? That's a turn-up." His laugh was a cracked rasp and he had instant resort to the brown bottle, then fell back into his chair, his breathing ragged.

Clarissa stood in the doorway, keeping the comforting sense of freedom behind her. "The boy's guardian has sent me to fetch him home. I am authorized to pay you one guinea in recompense for lost income."

She reached into the deep pocket of her cloak and drew out the golden guinea, holding it so that it winked in the light of the tallow candle on the table. "Should you find it difficult to produce the child, then of course I shall have no choice but to fetch the beadle. He will remove the child on his guardian's authority and you will receive not a penny's recompense. In fact, I would imagine you would find yourself serving time in Bridewell, if there's any evidence that the children in your care are suffering neglect despite the money paid for their keep."

She had no idea whether that was true, indeed she strongly suspected that the authorities wouldn't care twopence for the fate of these abandoned children, but it sounded threatening enough, and she was fairly certain Bertha would do anything to avoid any contact with the law.

She waited, the coin still winking its largesse in her hand, her eyes cold and steady on Bertha's face, praying that the woman couldn't sense her fear, her desperation. They said animals could smell fear; perhaps this dreadful creature had the same ability. And Clarissa was very afraid.

"Oh, give 'er the sprat, Bertha." The man in the chair roused himself as the reality of the guinea broke through his stupor. " 'Tis not worth the trouble, an' you'll never see the likes of that guinea by keepin' 'im. 'Ow long d'you think 'e's going to last?"

Bertha stretched out her hand. "Give it 'ere, then."

Clarissa shook her head. "Bring the child to me first. I need to see that he's alive and well."

Bertha glared, and the man in the chair

pushed back his chair. "If you won't fetch 'im, I will . . . an' I'll 'ave that guinea fer it too."

"Over my dead body." Bertha pushed past Clarissa and headed for the stairs. Clarissa followed her, praying that nothing would go wrong, that Bertha wouldn't try some trick.

She stood at the bottom of the stairs as Bertha tramped up them. Her voice drifted down. "Eh, you, boy. Come 'ere. Yes, you. I'm talkin' to you . . . Francis, or whatever yer fancy name is. You gone deaf or summat?"

Clarissa forced herself to stay where she was, although every muscle strained to race up the stairs and kick Bertha down them, one step at a time. She held herself very still, and finally Bertha reappeared, pulling Francis by the arm. She pushed him in front of her. "There . . . someone's come fer you. Get down them stairs."

Francis's scared eyes gazed down at his sister and at first he didn't seem to know her. Wordlessly she held out her arms to him and with a squeal that made her heart turn over, he hurtled down the stairs and jumped into her arms. He was so light, so frail beneath the ragged shirt and britches, she wanted to kill someone. Luke first, very slowly. And then the large woman descending on her with her powerful forearms and her face red with gin blossoms.

Clarissa tossed the guinea to the bottom step and turned and ran from the house, Francis held tight in her arms. What if the hackney had gone? But of course it hadn't. The man wanted his fare. He was sitting on his box, smoking a corncob pipe, as if he had not a care in the world.

"Get in." Clarissa thrust her brother up into the dark interior of the carriage, still terrified something would go wrong . . . Bertha would explode from the door yelling for a hue and cry . . . the streets would fill with angry faces, all intent on stopping her.

But it didn't happen. She climbed in after Francis, pulled the door shut, and the carriage started off immediately. There were no sounds of pursuit, no angry cries. Just Francis's soft sobbing in the opposite corner of the hackney.

She reached for him with trembling hands, pulled him across onto her lap, holding him tight, smoothing his ragged, ill-smelling hair, crooning softly as she rocked him.

After a while his tears ceased and he pushed himself upright, looking at her. "Why didn't you come before?"

The accusatory tone made her want to weep herself but she said gently, "I couldn't, love. I came as quickly as I could. Luke wouldn't tell me where you were. It took me a long time to find you."

He seemed to consider this, chewing his lip, which was already red and sore. "I'm hungry."

"Yes, I know. As soon as we get out of the hackney, we'll find a pieman." She cradled him against her again, hardly daring to believe that at last she had him safe, and he seemed content now to lie close to her, as the carriage clattered over the cobbles.

"Where d'you want me to let you down, miss?" The jarvey leaned down from his box and shouted through the window aperture.

"On Piccadilly . . . where you picked me up."

"Right y'are. Comin' up in a minute."

Francis sat up again. "What's going to happen to Uncle Luke? He's evil, 'Rissa. Why did he take me to that place and leave me?"

"We'll talk about that later, darling." She lifted him off her lap as the carriage came to a halt.

The jarvey opened the door for her and lifted Francis out, holding him for a moment in the air. "Poor little mite, what 'appened to 'im then? He's just skin an' bone."

Clarissa bit back a sharp retort. The man

345

had been kind, and without knowing he was at her back she would have had much less courage on Dundee Street. She smiled instead. "I know, but he'll be all right now. Thanks in no small part to you." She handed him a gold sovereign.

He bit it, nodded, and touched his forelock. "Good luck to ye, then, ma'am. An' to the little lad. He needs to put some flesh on 'im."

"I intend to see to that immediately." Clarissa took Francis's hand. "We're going in search of a pieman."

"That'll set you up good an' proper, laddie," the driver said, patting the boy's bony shoulder before climbing back onto his box. He clicked his tongue and the hackney moved off down Piccadilly.

The streets were relatively quiet, as befitted a Sunday, but Clarissa steered them across Piccadilly into Green Park, where they found a man selling pasties and a milkmaid tending two cows, her yoked wooden pails filled to the brim. She bought a pasty and a cup of milk for Francis and watched as he devoured them both. Then she had the cup refilled and watched him drain that, before gently guiding him into the trees in search of a private spot where they could talk. They found a bench under the bare branches of a copper beech.

"I'm still hungry," he complained.

"Yes, and you shall have a proper dinner very soon. But now I have to explain some things to you."

Francis perched on the bench, shivering in his thin shirt. "What happened to your clothes?" Clarissa asked, wrapping him in her cloak.

"Don't know. That Bertha took 'em off me an' gave me these instead. They smell," he added with a wrinkled nose. "They always did."

"Well, we'll find you some decent clothes soon enough." She looked at him, trying to think of how best to start . . . where to start, indeed. "We have to hide from Luke, Francis, you understand that."

He nodded vigorously. "I told you, he's *evil.*"

"Yes, he is, and as soon as he knows you're gone, he will be looking for you . . . for us both. Now, I have found us a place to stay where he will never think to look. But you have to be clever, Francis. As clever as I know you can be."

Francis watched his sister intently, listening. He was no longer famished and was warm enough now to concentrate. Some of his old spirit that had not been extinguished by the hardships of the last weeks was returning. His sister was telling him that he would live with her in a house near here. It was owned by a gentleman, but he would not know the gentleman, might not even meet him, and if he did he was to bow and disappear quickly.

"Who is the gentleman?"

"He's the Earl of Blackwater, darling."

"But how d'you know him, 'Rissa? He's a lord."

"Yes, and so was your grandfather." Clarissa immediately regretted that. The last thing she needed was for Francis to behave like an earl's grandson. She took a deep breath and started again.

Francis listened. "I was a chimney sweep?" He interrupted the narrative with a tiny squawk of laughter that warmed his sister's heart even as it accentuated the need to impress upon him the gravity of the situation.

"You almost were," she said. "You have to understand one thing, Francis. Luke *must* not find you again. You have to keep quiet about who you are, who I am, about everything to do with the family. Do you understand that?"

Francis nodded, serious now. "If he finds me I'll go back to that place. I'm not going back to that place." He kicked his legs thoughtfully. "Per'aps I should be dumb, pretend I can't speak. That would work, wouldn't it?"

"It would," Clarissa agreed with a smile. "But I doubt you could keep it up for long, and once you drop the act it'll cause more questions."

"I suppose so. I might accidentally speak, almost without knowing it, an' then everyone would wonder."

"They would." She stood up, holding out her hand. "Come on, let's go home."

As they walked she told him about Sally and Mistress Newby. "And there's a boy called Sammy who does the rough work in the house. You'll need to help out a bit, love. It might seem strange at first, but just imagine it's like helping Silas with the tack in the stables. If you do as you're asked cheerfully, and don't make a fuss about anything, we'll brush through this somehow."

A niggling little voice told her she was probably being overly optimistic about her brother's ability to turn himself into something he wasn't, but she would be on the lookout and forestall as much as she could. And if the worst came to the worst, then they would have to leave and find somewhere buried in the country where she could keep him hidden until she gained her majority.

"Here we are." She stopped outside the house. "I'll have to take back the cloak for a moment, love." She slung it around her shoulders and took a step to the door, then stopped, realizing for the first time that she didn't have a key to the door. That would have to be remedied, unless, of course, the privilege of keys to this house was not as a matter of course accorded to temporary occupants. If that was so, Jasper would have to make an exception in her case. She banged the lion's-head knocker.

Sally opened the door almost immediately. She opened her mouth on a greeting, but the words didn't come. She stared at Clarissa's companion. Francis stood holding his sister's hand tightly, and dropped his eyes, squirming closer to Clarissa, trying to make himself as small and inconspicuous as possible.

Clarissa stepped into the hall, bringing Francis up beside her. "Sally, this is a lad I found on the street. He says his name's Frank. He was being abused most horribly by his master because he wouldn't go up the chimneys. I thought perhaps we could use him to help out Sammy."

Sally looked at the boy, eyebrows raised. "A bit scrawny, isn't he?"

"He won't be, once we fatten him up."

"Please, ma'am, I'm hungry," Francis murmured, gazing up with liquid brown eyes. "Me belly's rattlin' somefink awful."

Sally's face softened. "Well, we can fix that easily enough. Looks like he could do with a bath, though."

"Yes, in my chamber, Sally. Then he won't be in Mistress Newby's way in the kitchen. Could we find him some fresh clothes though? The rags he's wearing wouldn't keep out a summer breeze."

Sally regarded him with her head on one side. "I've a little brother about his size. Maybe me mam could spare his second-best suit."

"Oh, I'd be happy to pay for a new suit for your brother." Clarissa began to wonder how much longer she would be able to survive without the earl's promised allowance. "Just so that we can get this boy warm and respectable again quickly."

"I'll fetch up the bath first, ma'am, then I'll run over to me mam's. It won't take but an hour an' his lordship's not expected before dinner."

"Then do it, Sally. Come along, Frank." She hustled him up the stairs and into her

351

own chamber. "That was quick thinking, love. Can you talk like that all the time?"

"Course," he said somewhat scornfully. "Just like the lads in the stables at home, an' just like they all talked in that horrible place."

"Good, well try not to let it slip except when you're alone with me. Let's get you out of those filthy clothes."

It was hard not to weep at the sight of her little brother's half-starved body, where grime was ingrained into every crease and fold. Francis splashed happily in the hip bath and didn't object even when his sister pulled a fine-tooth comb through his hair, looking for lice. Amazingly she didn't find any. Once bathed and swamped in her chamber robe, sitting beside her fire, he ate a bowl of bread and milk, a plate of coddled eggs and toasted bread, and a thick slice of fruitcake. Mistress Newby had responded to the tale of the rescued chimney sweep with motherly concern, and after one look at the child in the bath had professed herself disgusted and disappeared to her kitchen to set about the process of remedying the situation.

Clarissa, curled in her chair by the fire, felt the last strains of the terror that had accompanied her ever since she had learned of her little brother's fate slide away from her as she watched him eat, watched his cheeks almost visibly plump out under the effects of good food and warmth. She would never let him be taken from her again. Luke would have to kill her first. It occurred to her that that was probably not beyond his capabilities, but she found she could almost smile at the thought.

This was the scene that met Jasper's eyes when he entered his mistress's bedchamber at three o'clock. He was already put out by the lack of ceremony that had greeted his early arrival. Neither Clarissa nor Sally had come down to his cheerful hail from the hall and he'd been left to make his own way upstairs. There was no sign of Clarissa in the drawing room, where he'd expected to find her, fresh and eager, dressed to please him.

Instead this. His eyebrows crawled into his scalp. There was a small child wrapped in a chamber robe, sitting by the fire consuming an enormous piece of fruitcake, a milk mustache adorning his upper lip. And Clarissa, the earl's mistress, was ensconced cozily in the chair opposite, watching the boy with a possessive fondness that made the hairs on Jasper's neck prickle.

"What the devil is this?"

CHAPTER FIFTEEN

Clarissa jumped, her eyes darting to the clock on the mantel. "Oh, my lord . . . Jasper . . . I wasn't expecting you so soon."

"No," he agreed aridly. "So it would seem. Who's this?"

Francis, from the folds of his sister's chamber robe, regarded the new arrival with wide-eyed curiosity and a hint of anxiety. The man didn't seem very happy to see him.

"He's just a child I found on the street." Clarissa uncurled herself from the chair and stood up, feeling that she would be more in control of the situation on her feet. "He'd run away from his master, a chimney sweep who had abused him most dreadfully. Poor little thing is afraid to go up the chimney because of the rats . . . I couldn't leave him to that man's fists. For heaven's sake, he's only a child. He can't stand up for himself. He's half-starved into the bargain. Look how thin he is."

Jasper frowned at this impassioned speech. "That may be so, but you can't take a legal apprentice from his master."

This struck Clarissa as as heartless as it was absurd. "Maybe *you* couldn't, my lord, but I most certainly can," she declared. "Anyway, how can you know it was a legal apprenticeship? I've heard these chimney sweeps just take children off the streets, anywhere they find them. I'm sure that's what happened to Frank."

Jasper shook his head. "What do you intend doing with him?"

"Feed him up, for a start. Stand up, Frank." She took his hand and pulled him to his feet. "Just look at how thin he is, Jasper." She unwrapped the folds of the chamber robe. Francis shivered as the air hit his naked body, but he made no sound, gazing stoically at the earl, keeping his skinny arms at his sides. It seemed important that this man feel sorry for him.

Jasper's frown deepened. It was no surprise to him that children in this state of neglect were loose in the city, but the actual reality of a child so thin you could count every rib and knob of his spine did shake his equanimity somewhat. He shook his head again. "For God's sake, wrap him up, before he catches his death."

Clarissa did so and installed him in the chair again. He curled up in the swaddling robe and resumed his consumption of fruitcake. "Sally's gone to fetch him some clothes, her brother's second-best suit."

"I see. I can assume then that my entire household is involved in the care and nurturing of this pathetic scrap of humanity?"

Clarissa's jade eyes burned, and her voice was frigid. "You can assume, sir, that this household has a degree of human compassion that you so conspicuously lack. Would you throw him back on the street?"

Jasper held up his hands in a defensive gesture. "I didn't say that, Clarissa. If you want to keep the boy, then do so. I can afford to feed and house him, I suppose, and he should be able to make himself useful. As long as his master doesn't bring the beadle to the door."

"Don't be absurd," she said sharply. "How could his master even know where he is?"

"I hope you're right. And I hope you know what you're doing. The boy's probably a thief."

"I ain't," Francis declared with indignation through a mouthful of cake.

Jasper quelled him with a look before turning back to Clarissa, who was struggling to master her own indignation. "If things start disappearing you'll know where to look."

"I see," she said furiously. "Judged and sentenced out of hand. Well, my lord, I beg leave to tell you that I don't think much of your sense of justice."

"Oh, for God's sake, Clarissa, be realistic. It stands to reason the only way the child's survived thus far is by stealing. I'm not blaming him for that, but I am saying that old habits die hard. But on your own head be it." He turned away and left the chamber, going into the drawing room.

He poured himself a glass of Madeira and went to the fire, standing with one foot on the andiron, one arm braced against the mantel, as he stared into the flames trying to master his irritation. If he hadn't just spent the best part of the day in a state of mental turmoil he probably wouldn't have been so irritated at Clarissa's philanthropic rescue of a starving waif. In fact, if he weren't so thoroughly put out already, he probably would have applauded it. But he needed his mistress to himself this evening, and he needed all her attention.

He'd left her bed in the early hours of the morning, not knowing what course of action to take. The startling revelation that the so-called whore he'd just made love to was as virgin as on the day of her birth had shaken him to his core. But oddly enough not as much as the idea that Clarissa herself thought she could deceive him about something so vitally important. The naïvety of such an idea was laughable. Did she really imagine that an experienced man would not know instantly that he was making love to a virgin? There had been no maidenhead to breach, certainly, but no other man had touched her body in the ways of love, no other man had entered that tight virginal sheath.

It seemed that everything she had presented to him about herself had been a lie. He had become convinced she was not what she seemed, and it had intrigued him, but he hadn't considered the extent of her deception. And for a few moments he had found himself doubting her passionate response to his lovemaking. Had that also been a lie? But in his heart he knew that she had responded with true passion; no one, however expert a whore, could counterfeit such a response. And whatever else she was, Clarissa Ordway, if indeed that was her name, was no whore. Or hadn't been until he bought her services. He had already asked himself what had turned a seemingly gently bred young woman into a denizen of a Covent Garden nunnery, and now he couldn't begin to untangle his confusion. If she wasn't working for Nan, why was the tough-hearted businesswoman giving her shelter? And *what* in the name of all that was good lay behind this elaborate charade?

He had been a poor companion all day, distracted enough to lose two bouts at the fencing salon and to cause his friends in his club to abandon him with good-humored mockery when it was clear he had no interest in either conversation or cards. And he was no nearer now to solving the conundrum.

Clarissa spoke softly behind him. "I'm sorry to have discommoded you, Jasper. I didn't think a small child under your roof would upset you so much."

He turned away from the fire. She stood by the door, her expression composed, her eyes glowing with only the embers of their earlier angry fire. Her hair hung loose, held back from her face with a band of velvet ribbon. "There's really no reason for you even to notice him."

He took a sip from his glass, regarding her over the lip. "As long as you promise not to fill the house with waifs and strays, I daresay that's true." He set down his glass and held out his arms. "Come here."

She came readily enough. He grasped her head between his hands, his fingers twisting in the red-gold hair, and he realized as he kissed her that despite his confusion, his irritation, or perhaps because of it, he wanted, no, needed to reassert a sense of exclusive possession. Somehow that sense had been shaken by the child's presence, by the way Clarissa had been looking at the boy, the atmosphere of easy, settled companionship that surrounded them. Where had it come from?

Clarissa responded to the fierceness of the kiss with her own need. The intensity of the kiss was a burning brand against her lips; his tongue was savagely possessive in her mouth, fencing with her own, establishing its presence within her. She could sense the residue of his anger as she could sense her own, and the kiss became a battleground of sorts, scouring their shared ill feeling in the heat of passion.

At last the fierce grip on her face eased and his hands moved down her back to hold her hips. His lips softened against hers, and his tongue explored her mouth gently, no longer invading. When he raised his head, his eyes held a rueful smile as he stroked her swollen lips with a fingertip.

"I don't know quite what that was," he

said softly. "But I have been thinking of you all day." Which was entirely true, he reflected wryly, although his thoughts had not been particularly loving.

She leaned into him, resting her head for a moment on his chest, listening to the steady beat of his heart. Somehow she seemed to draw strength from his closeness. "I have missed you all day." Only as she said it did she realize how true it was. Even though she had been completely absorbed with Francis, at the back of her mind had been the sense of unease she had felt when he had left her that morning . . . a need to see him again, to reassure herself that things had not changed between them.

"When you weren't rescuing stray chimney sweeps," he said lightly, tucking a stray tendril of hair behind her ear. "Where's the boy now?"

"Still in my bedchamber. I'm going to make up a bed for him in the dressing room."

"Oh, no, that is not going to happen," Jasper stated firmly. "You may hurl accusations of brutality at my head if you wish, but I will not have that child — any child — sleeping in the room adjoining the bedchamber. He can sleep in the servants' quarters. They're comfortable enough, and

I'm sure he'll think them a palace compared to any bed he has slept in hitherto."

Reluctantly Clarissa acknowledged to herself that Jasper was right. Francis's presence in the dressing room would be inhibiting to say the least. She raised her head from his chest and took a step back. "I'll talk to Sally."

Jasper reached for the bellpull. "If we're going to continue this evening as originally intended, then it's time we started afresh."

Sally answered the ring with a parcel in her arms. "Here's the clothes, Mistress Ord— Oh, my lord, I didn't know you was here already."

"Since you weren't here to greet my arrival, it's not surprising," he said with a dry smile. "I trust you're now prepared to resume your duties."

"Jasper, that's not fair," Clarissa protested, seeing Sally's discomfiture. "It was my fault Sally was not here, and anyway, you arrived an hour earlier than you'd said."

"Clearly something that should not become a habit." He smiled suddenly, the smile as always transforming his countenance. "Forgive me, Sally. I was just teasing you a little."

Sally curtsied, still blushing. "Yes, m'lord. Here's the clothes, Mistress Ordway." She held out the parcel.

"Thank you, I'll get him dressed straight-away." Clarissa took the bundle.

"No, you won't." Jasper took it from her and handed it back to Sally. "Sally, would you mind seeing to the child? Take him down to the kitchen fire, and make him up a bed in the servants' quarters."

"Oh, the poor little mite can sleep with me." Sally took the parcel. "I sleep with my little brother at home. I'll look after him, don't you worry." She hurried to the door, saying over her shoulder, "Oh, Mistress Newby says dinner will be served in five minutes, sir, if that's convenient."

"Well, that seems a satisfactory solution," Jasper said as the door closed behind the girl. "I trust you think so?" He raised an interrogative eyebrow.

Clarissa smiled vaguely. "I'm sure he'll be very comfortable with Sally."

Jasper frowned a little. "Should I expect any more lost souls?"

"Maybe you think it strange in me to want to help him, but when I saw him I thought of the child I lost. I thought how I would hope that if my child was in trouble some-one would be kind to him." It wasn't entirely an untruth, Clarissa told herself. It was certainly how she would have felt in those

363

circumstances.

It would have been plausible enough, Jasper reflected, if he didn't know that this lost infant was a fantastic invention. What *was* she trying to hide? Was she a runaway? Wanted by the Bow Street Runners? It seemed ludicrous when he looked at her, but since pretty well everything out of her mouth seemed to be a vivid construction of her imagination nothing was too absurd.

Should he confront her? But every instinct told him that if he wanted to keep her with him, then it was too soon to challenge her. And the one thing he had no confusion about was the fact that he didn't want to lose her. She intrigued him, and she delighted him. And, most importantly, she was still the answer to the condition of his uncle's will. He would bide his time and see how the dice fell. So he merely nodded in apparent acceptance and offered her his arm. "Shall we go down to dinner, ma'am?"

The carriage that drew up outside 32 King Street early that evening was of a bygone era. A large, cumbersome vehicle drawn by four horses, it was not made to negotiate the narrow crowded streets of the city. The coachman perched on his high box cursed at every corner, every dog cart, every pedestrian who stared and pointed, laughing, as he fought to guide the carriage around the Great Piazza without scraping the gold paint or the coats of arms on the panels.

Within, comfortably unaware of his coachman's difficulties, Viscount Bradley sat ensconced beneath fur rugs, his feet on a hot brick, his hands tucked into a bearskin muff. When the carriage finally stopped, the footman jumped from his perch at the rear of the carriage and ran to open the door and let down the footstool. Despite the biting wind, the driver wiped sweat from his brow and grimly contemplated the return journey.

Lord Bradley descended with some difficulty, trailing lap rugs that the footman hastily bundled back into the vehicle's interior. His lordship wore a thick muffler, a hat with earpieces, and a heavy fur-trimmed cloak. "Get the door open, fool," he snapped at the footman, who ceased his bundling and ran to the door, pulling the bell rope vigorously.

The viscount, leaning heavily on a stout, silver-knobbed cane, hobbled on gouty feet up to the door just as the steward opened it. He pushed past his footman and the steward and entered the house, where he stood expectantly while the steward closed the door.

It was the steward's misfortune not to recognize the old man immediately. "What can I do for you, sir?" he asked, regarding the newcomer with some curiosity. The usual clients of 32 King Street tended to be rather more vigorous in body than this frail old man.

The viscount glared at him. "I'm Bradley, you fool. Tell your mistress I'm here, and bring me a cup of negus." Without invitation he turned aside to the small parlor.

Nan was in the drawing room entertaining a pair of young men who were trying to make up their minds how to choose among the young women waiting to service them. The steward whispered in her ear and her eyes widened in surprise. "Good God, Lord Bradley . . . here?" she murmured. "Where have you put him?"

"He went into the small parlor, madam. He asked for negus."

"Then fetch it immediately." She turned back to her prospective clients. "Gentlemen, you must excuse me . . . urgent business. I'm sure Eloise and Natalie will take care of you admirably." She sailed from the room, the fringe of a paisley shawl wafting behind her.

"My lord Bradley, what a delightful surprise." She spoke as she entered the parlor.

The viscount was sitting by the small fire, still wrapped in muffler, hat, and cloak. "Nan . . . I'll wager you never expected to see me darken your doors again." He chuckled, holding out his hand to her.

She took the hand and curtsied. "Believe me, my lord, I am gratified." She hesitated, then asked, "May I bring some of my young ladies for your selection?"

He chuckled again. "You flatter me, Nan. Alas, I doubt I'd get my money's worth these days, and the young lady in question certainly wouldn't. Ah, but in the old days, I could satisfy three at once, and then another three in the course of a night." He shook his head in reminiscence. "Where's that fellow with the negus? Paltry drink, but all the leeches will allow me."

"I'll fetch it myself." Nan went to the door just as the steward crossed the hall with a steaming goblet on a silver tray. She took it from him and brought it back to the viscount. "Can I take your muffler, perhaps . . . your cloak . . . it's quite warm in here, my lord."

"Is it?" He shook his head. "I'm never warm these days. You can take the muffler and gloves." He handed both to her, then took the goblet between his long white hands, inhaling the spiced fragrance. "Well, it'll warm me, at least."

Nan sat down and waited for the purpose of this visit to be revealed. The viscount sipped his negus, then said, "M'nephew came to see me the other day . . . brought a rather fine piece with him . . . understand he got her here."

"Clarissa Ordway, you mean." Nan nodded. "Lord Blackwater has taken her under his protection. I believe she is living in the house on Half Moon Street."

"Mmm." The old man nodded. "Bright young thing, she seemed. Not in the common way."

"She's certainly lovely, and has a fine figure," Nan agreed cautiously.

Bradley waved a dismissive hand. "Oh, that's true enough I daresay, but there was something else, something I couldn't put my finger on. Where'd she come from?"

Nan chose her words carefully. "She came to me from the streets, looking for employment in a Covent Garden house. I took her on for her looks. She's not as experienced as most of my girls, but there are men who like that. I thought it was worth giving her a trial."

"You always knew your own business, Nan." The old man looked at her, and his eyes were sharp and shrewd. "What's her history?"

Regretfully Nan shook her head. "I don't know, my lord. She said she was up from the country, had fallen on hard times . . ." She shrugged. "It's the usual story, I hear it ten times a day. She had something unusual about her, so I took her on. Your nephew saw her in the Piazza and was struck by her."

"So I gathered." The old man rocked a little in his chair. "Well, what my nephew does is none of my business, but I'd like to discover more about the girl. D'you think she might have confided more about her history to the other girls here?"

"I don't know, my lord. She wasn't here very long before Lord Blackwater took her away. I doubt she had time to find a confidante."

"Well, ask around, Nan. And anything you discover, send it to me. I'll pay well for any information."

Nan rose to help the viscount as he began to struggle up from his chair. She was intrigued herself now. Why was the viscount, whose wealth was fabled, taking such an interest in the country lass his nephew had taken as his mistress? Jasper was a grown man, master of his own independence.

The viscount wrapped his muffler around

his neck. "Did your other clients find her satisfactory?" he asked, inserting his fingers into his gloves.

Nan hesitated. If she admitted that Clarissa had had no other customers except the earl it could lead to uncomfortable questions about whether she had had the right to claim commission for the girl's sale to Jasper. "I didn't hear any complaints," she said, temporizing.

He gave her another sharp look, then shrugged and picked up his cane. "Tell that footman of mine to come and help me out."

Nan curtsied and hurried away, hoping she hadn't said anything inadvertently to jeopardize her ownership of Clarissa Ordway's services. It would have helped if she'd known more about the girl, but in the haste of the transaction with Jasper she hadn't thought it important.

Viscount Bradley climbed back into his coach, swearing at the footman when he jogged his gout-swollen foot as he removed the footstool. He settled into his corner, frowning. It wasn't particularly surprising that Nan knew so little of the girl's history; it wouldn't have interested her in the least, as long as the whore did her work well and brought money into the house. But there was something smoky about the girl. She looked the part, for the most part acted it, but the look she had given him as she stalked from the room after he had admittedly and quite deliberately insulted her had not been the look of a whore, however outraged.

Jasper slid from the bed and padded soundlessly across the room to put more wood on the fire. A single candle still burned on the mantel.

Clarissa spoke suddenly. "Are you leaving so soon again?"

He turned, his naked body illuminated by the spurt of flame from the fire behind him. "I hadn't thought to do so." His eyes roamed over her as she leaned back, resting on her elbows, gazing at him with those huge jade-green eyes. The sheet was tangled around her ankles and her skin was peaches and cream in the glow of the candle, the pink crowns of her breasts drawing his gaze.

"Would you wish me to?" He came over to the bed, leaning over her to trace a fingertip down between her breasts, to circle her nipples, smiling as, instantly responsive, they peaked and hardened.

She shook her head. "No, but you did last night. You said you preferred to wake in your own bed."

"That is sometimes true," he agreed. "But not always."

She looked relieved. "I was wondering if something was wrong . . . if I'd done something wrong, when Sally said you often stayed the night, and you'd told me something else."

He straightened. He had been angry then, but now he no longer felt deceived by her. He had been angry at the sense of being manipulated, but now he was in control of the situation. For the moment he would let her continue to believe that her deception was unchallenged.

"I was awake and restless this morning. I didn't want to disturb you." He made his tone light. "But now I have an urge for a bowl of punch. Will you join me if I fetch the makings from the kitchen?"

"A midnight feast." She kicked away the sheet, swinging her legs off the bed. "I'll come with you. I'm hungry."

"From what I've seen, you and that brat have similar appetites," he observed, turning to pick up the chamber robe that lived permanently in the armoire. His back was turned to her, so he didn't see the startled flush flooding her cheeks.

Clarissa slipped her arms into her own robe, keeping her own face averted until she felt the flush die down. She was going to have to learn not to react to innocent remarks of that kind. It wouldn't take long. It *couldn't* take long. "The difference being that he's half-starved and I'm not. I'll probably end up fat as a pig."

He gave her a mocking smile over his shoulder as he opened the door. "On the whole I'd rather you didn't. At least until you've worn out your new wardrobe."

She laughed and followed him down to the kitchen. He seemed to know his way around the shelves and pantry, fetching the punch bowl and ladle, an orange and lemon, the cloves, nutmeg, and brandy bottle.

"Are you an expert at punch making?" she asked, rummaging in the pantry.

"I've made many a bowl in my time." He took a paring knife and began to peel the zest from the fruit. "My father was partial to it. He taught me to make it when I was quite small, and then when he became an invalid he would insist I make it for him whenever I was home from school. No one else would do."

"How old were you when he died?" She emerged from the pantry with two cold chicken legs, regarding him curiously.

"Twelve." He shrugged. "Rather too young to ascend to an earldom, however impoverished, but fortunately my brothers were able to prevent it giving me an inflated sense of my own consequence." He put the freshly peeled zest into the punch bowl.

"What about your mother?" She perched on the edge of the kitchen table, absently gnawing on a drumstick.

"She died a couple of years later." He began to squeeze the juice from the fruit into the bowl. "She had been ailing for a long time, really a shadow in her children's lives. Her death didn't make a lot of difference to our day-to-day existence."

"So you and your brothers were left quite alone?"

"We had each other," he said with a quiet smile. "It was enough." He began piling his ingredients on a tray. "We were luckier than you in that respect. Your parents' deaths left you without any family." He threw out the comment, not expecting a response, since she had already told him her parents had died when she was little more than a baby. He had no idea whether that particular fact amongst the farrago of invention happened to be true, although he rather doubted it.

"Yes, I suppose so" was all she said as she grabbed a hunk of cheese before following Jasper back upstairs. She cast a glance towards the attic stairs, hoping that Francis was sound asleep, warmly nestled next to Sally's comfortable frame.

Jasper stirred the punch slowly over the fire. "I expect your wardrobe will arrive in the morning. I acquired a well-mannered lady's horse for you at Tattersalls this afternoon, so if you feel comfortable riding, I would like us to ride in the park tomorrow afternoon. Again I don't wish you to engage in conversation with anyone, only this time you should acknowledge a bow with one of your own. Just a slight inclination of the head. Do you think you can manage that?"

"It sounds simple enough." She couldn't quite keep the hint of derision from her voice.

Jasper contented himself with a raised eyebrow. He stirred nutmeg into the bowl. "In the evening we shall go to the theatre. There, again, we shall avoid any introductions. We'll arrive just as the first act begins, and we'll leave in the interval before people start visiting the boxes." He smiled. "The whole town will be abuzz with speculation."

Clarissa was aware of a little frisson of excitement at the prospect. They were playing a game, a game with high stakes, and she knew she could play her part to perfection. "Is anyone to know that I'm supp—" She broke off, chose her words again. "That

I came from a nunnery?"

"They will know that," he said smoothly, pretending he hadn't noticed her slip. "I shall make sure it gets out, but you have no need to behave as you did with Lord Bradley. You will show the world only the impeccable demeanor of a lady of taste and breeding."

"How else will they accept me as a reformed whore?" she murmured, setting aside a well-gnawed chicken leg.

"How else indeed?"

Clarissa looked sharply at him but his expression was calm as he stirred the punch, before ladling it into goblets.

He raised his goblet in a toast. "To our venture, Clarissa."

"Our venture." She drank. Francis was safe upstairs; she would do her part here for as long as necessary.

A carriage delivered Clarissa's wardrobe late the following morning. Jasper had left after breakfast, saying he would be back with the horses later. Two footmen obeyed the instructions of the two young women who had helped Hortense with the fittings, carrying the gowns up to the bedchamber, where the women hung them in the armoire, smoothing down the folds with reverent hands.

Clarissa was astounded at the quantity of garments. She had listened to the catalogue that Hortense and Jasper had considered necessary for life in the Polite World, but hadn't quite managed to envision what that meant.

Sally entered into the spirit of it with boundless enthusiasm, helping to hang the gowns, folding away shawls, placing hats on shelves. Francis stood in the shadows, gazing openmouthed at the proceedings. He was dressed in a shirt of good homespun, jacket and britches of a coarse but serviceable woolen cloth, good stockings, and a pair of boots that were a little too small for him, so he kept scrunching his toes. But he was perfectly happy in his new situation, and rapidly learning his way around the kitchen and servants' quarters. He knew exactly how to cajole a piece of cake from Mistress Newby, and he and Sammy had already developed a friendly rivalry over who could fill a coal scuttle quickest.

Hortense's assistants had left when Jasper once again let himself into the house to no greeting. This time, however, he merely gave a mental shrug, discarded his sword and his outer garments, and mounted the stairs, following the sound of voices to the bedchamber.

Clarissa was standing in front of a pier glass buttoning the waistcoat of a riding habit of dark green wool. She saw Jasper in the mirror, as he stood in the doorway surveying the scene, and said with a seductive smile, "So, my lord, what do you think? Will I disgrace you on the tan this afternoon?" She held out her arms so that Sally could help her into the tightly fitted jacket.

He laughed and came into the room. "Is everything here?"

"Oh, you've never seen the like," she said, waving an expansive hand. "There must be at least forty ball gowns, forty-four day dresses, a hundred walking dresses —"

"Absurd creature." He caught her up against him, holding her in the air for a moment. "It's no laughing matter, I'll have you know." He let her slide down between his hands until her feet touched the floor again. "Finish dressing and we'll go for a little ride in Green Park."

Her eyes narrowed. "Do you doubt my expertise, sir?"

"No," he said calmly. "But I would still like to satisfy myself before we try it in public. The horses are below. Finish dressing. I'll wait in the drawing room." He turned to leave and his astounded gaze fell on Francis. "What the devil are you doing in here?"

Francis, head down, shot out of his corner and through the door without a word. Jasper looked across at Clarissa. "How long has that brat been in here?"

She shrugged carelessly. "Oh, I don't know. He probably followed Sally in. He's only a child, Jasper. He means no harm."

"I don't give a damn what he means. But I'd better not see him outside the servants' quarters again. I suggest in his own interests that you impress that upon him."

Clarissa bit down on the words of protest that bubbled to her lips. She said quietly, "As you wish, my lord. Sally, would you make sure Frank stays below stairs?"

"Aye, Mistress Ordway. I'll look out for him next time." She cast a scared look at the earl, who merely nodded and stalked away.

"Oh, dear," Clarissa murmured. "I don't think his lordship cares overmuch for children . . . pass me the boots, Sally." She sat down in front of the dresser mirror and extended one slender foot.

"I daresay his lordship isn't accustomed to them." Sally knelt to help Clarissa into the tight-fitting leather riding boots, lacing them up with deft fingers.

"Well, perhaps we can accustom him

gently." Clarissa held out one foot after the other, examining the boots with a critical air. "They feel comfortable. How do you think they look, Sally?"

"Most elegant, ma'am. The last word," Sally said in admiration. "And here's the hat." She took up a high-crowned black beaver hat with a handsome green plume. She ran the plume through her fingers. "Madame Hortense has a perfect eye."

"So it would seem," Clarissa agreed. She swiveled on the stool to face the mirror and set the hat on her head. The clustered ringlets beneath the brim were most attractive, she decided, turning from the mirror to take the gloves from Sally. "Now, we'll see what kind of riding horse my lord has selected."

After what Jasper had said about mild-mannered ladies' horses she was rather expecting a broad-backed, sedate old mare, and was pleasantly surprised by the pretty dappled mare in the care of the groom on the street outside. The groom also held the reins of a handsome black gelding, who tossed his head when Jasper appeared, and pawed the ground.

"The gelding's feeling his oats," Clarissa observed as she went to the mare's head. She stroked the velvety nose and ran a hand over the animal's neck. "She's pretty, Jasper. Does she have a name?"

"Dancer, I believe. Do you like her?"

She turned her head against the mare's neck and smiled at him. "She's lovely, very dainty. 'Dancer' suits her."

"Well, let's put you up and see how she goes." He cupped a palm and tossed Clarissa into the saddle, his eyes sharp as he watched to see how she handled the maneuver. It seemed second nature to her, he decided, watching covertly as she settled into the saddle, slipping her booted feet into the stirrups, taking up the reins with practiced hands. "How are the stirrups?"

"They need shortening a little."

He nodded. "See to it, Tom." He swung onto the gelding and took up the reins.

The groom adjusted the mare's stirrups and checked the girth. "That better, ma'am?"

"Yes, perfect, thank you." She nudged the mare's flanks with her knees and the animal started forward. Clarissa was aware of Jasper's watchful eyes as they rode towards Green Park. When they crossed Piccadilly, he moved the gelding up close beside the mare, and she could see that he was ready at any moment to seize the bridle should her mount take fright at the traffic.

"I am quite competent, you know," she said mildly. "If she starts, I can hold her."

"Mmm." It was a noncommittal sound. "Where did you learn to ride? Your illicit childhood tutor perhaps?"

"When I wasn't working I used to hang around the stables a lot. I've always liked horses. It amused the grooms to teach me," she said with a casual shrug. "And, yes, I did go out riding with the son sometimes. Is that so strange?"

"Unusual, certainly."

Clarissa sucked on her lower lip. She was beginning to feel perilously as if she'd bitten off far more than she could chew with this deception. But as long as Jasper didn't challenge her outright, then she could muddle through it one invention at a time.

CHAPTER SIXTEEN

Ed sat comfortably in Bertha's kitchen, his feet propped on the fender, an ale pot cradled in one huge fist. "So, when's your old lady due back then, Dirk?"

"Said she'd be back in 'alf an hour. Some lass needs 'elp wi' a birthing down by the docks. Bertha'll bring the babby back 'ere like as not." Dirk tipped the gin bottle to his lips. The shrill wail of a baby pierced the kitchen and he swore, yelling, "Eh, Jude, you lazy bitch . . . do summat about that racket."

"All right, Pa, all right." A young girl staggered in from the kitchen yard with a scuttle of sea coal, which she set down with a thump in front of the fire. Her hands were thick with coal dust, and she brushed lank hair out of her eyes with her forearm. "It'll shut itself up in a minute."

"Jest get up there an' shut it up yerself," her father growled, raising a threatening fist.

The girl ducked away and headed out of the kitchen towards the wail, which had now been joined by a chorus of others.

"Damned brats," Dirk grumbled to his brother-in-law. "Screechin' all day an' all night. A man's entitled to some peace an' quiet in 'is own 'ome, seems to me."

"Aye, right enough." Ed took a deep draft of ale. "But 'tis a good little business our Bertha's got goin'. Keeps you in gin an' idleness, lucky bugger." He grinned.

The kitchen door flew open, letting in a blast of freezing air. Bertha came in on the gust, carrying a tiny bundle in a thin, ragged blanket. "Well, this one'll not last long. Its mam's gone." She set the bundle in a wicker basket beside the fire. A thin cry rose from the blanket, then died away. "We'll be buryin' it by morning." She nodded at Ed. "Not seen you in a while, Ed."

"No, been busy," he said. "How're you doin', our Bertha?"

"Can't complain. You?"

"Nah, can't complain. I jest come about that lad what the gent placed wi' you. " 'Ow's 'e doin'?"

"Lor', Ed, 'e's bin gone since yesterday, as your gent knows full well, seein' as 'ow 'e sent fer 'im."

"What?" Ed looked startled. "Why'd he

send me to check up on 'im then?"

" 'Ow should I know?" Bertha shrugged. "Alls I know, this fine, lardy-da lady comes visitin', says 'e wants the lad back, an' I give 'im to 'er." She cast a warning glance at her husband. If her brother found out about the golden guinea, he'd demand his share as payment for having placed the boy with them in the first place.

"You give 'im to 'er. Just like that?" Ed looked incredulous. "Didn't she 'ave no letter or summink?"

Bertha turned to the dresser, taking up the ale jug. "Fat load o' good that would do, seein' as I can't read a word."

"Well, the gent's goin' to be in a right state when 'e 'ears this." Ed held out his tankard. "Give us a drop more then, lass."

Clarissa took Jasper's hand and stepped out of the carriage outside the Drury Lane theatre. The crowd of theatregoers jostled at the doors, which stood open to the foyer. The strains of music from the orchestra drifted from deep within the theatre.

Jasper glanced at her, wondering if she was nervous at this first seriously public outing. If she was, she gave no sign of it. Of course, if she had been an established member of one of the nunneries, she would

385

have spent many an evening in the pit of the theatre, touting for custom from those playgoers whose main interest was the whores rather than the play itself. "I daresay you've spent many evenings here?" he observed, taking her arm to ease her through the crowd to the doors. He was curious as to how she would deflect the assumption.

"No." Clarissa shook her head. "Never. Why would you think so?"

"It's a popular spot for whores to find customers and customers to find whores."

"Oh, well, yes, of course, but as it happens I never found myself looking for custom here." She thought she'd made a quick recovery, and a covert glance at his expression gave her no reason to think otherwise.

The theatre was a blaze of light from the many chandeliers and sconced candles around the gilded walls. The buzz of noise was almost deafening as people talked and shouted across rows of the audience, and the calls of the orange girls, pamphlet sellers, and whoremongers rose above the cacophony, while the orchestra gallantly tried to make itself heard.

Jasper steered Clarissa up a curving flight of stairs, along a corridor, and through a small door, which opened onto a box high above the pit, looking directly down at the stage. He took her opera cloak and pulled out one of the velvet-covered seats with gilded arms that were positioned just behind a broad cushioned balcony rail.

"Sit down and look out into the theatre," he instructed softly, "but try not to make eye contact with anyone. Remember we're after mystery tonight. I want you to be the subject of every supper table after the play. Use your fan . . . yes, exactly so." He nodded his approval as she unfurled her fan and partially covered her face with it, leaving only her eyes clearly visible.

"What if someone decides to visit us?" she murmured, leaning forward to rest one hand on the padded balcony.

"There's no time before the first act. And we'll leave before the interval." He raised a hand in greeting to a woman in a box opposite who was waving her fan at him.

"Who's that?"

"Lady Mondrain. An inveterate gossip, but a useful woman to have as a friend. You'll meet her soon enough." Jasper's smile was fixed to his lips as he acknowledged the smiles and waves directed their way from around the theatre. He watched with satisfaction as heads bobbed in conversation interspersed with covert glances. The orchestra fell silent, and the buzz in the theatre died down somewhat, but not completely, as the first act of the play began.

Clarissa lost interest in the audience and turned her attention to the stage. She was among the minority. The theatre was as brightly lit as ever, and the actors had to fight for the audience's full attention. Conversations continued; orange girls moved up and down the rows throwing fruit to buyers, who passed the necessary coins along the row. And every now and again one of the actors would have to shout to make himself heard.

"It seems very unfair," Clarissa muttered indignantly from behind her fan. "Why do people come here if they're not interested in the play?"

"They come to see and be seen," Jasper returned. "And to ensure that they're up to date on the latest play, actor, opera, musician. It's human nature, my dear. But when Garrick plays, then you can hear a pin drop."

"I should like to see him onstage." She sounded wistful.

"And so you shall," Jasper stated. "All in good time."

Clarissa wafted her fan and took another glance around the theatre. Her wafting fan wavered. She drew back a little into the shadows of the box. Luke was in the pit, looking around the boxes, quizzing glass to his eye. Her heart lurched, then resumed its normal rhythm as she reminded herself that he would never recognize her, dressed as she was with her hair piled high in an extravagant coiffure, decorated with plumes, and her fashionable evening gown of gold-embroidered black taffeta. And, of course, her escort.

She told herself again that the best place to hide was always right under the nose of the seeker. Most people saw what they expected to see. And Luke would never expect to see his countrified niece in a theatre in Covent Garden under the auspices of the Earl of Blackwater. She leaned forward with more confidence and let her gaze roam around the audience.

Jasper had noticed the quick withdrawal, her sudden pallor, then the recovery. He leaned forward, resting his arms on the balcony, and swept the scene with his quizzing glass. He could see nothing out of the ordinary. So what had caused that? He glanced at his companion, who gave him a bland smile.

An instant before the orchestra struck up for the intermission, Jasper took Clarissa's arm. "Come now." He hurried her out of the box, down to the foyer, and out onto Drury Lane. His coachman was waiting a few yards up the street and Jasper swept Clarissa ahead of him. "Others will be leaving and I don't wish to be detained."

Clarissa climbed in, but to her surprise Jasper didn't follow her. "I have another engagement. Jake will drive you home."

"Oh." She felt rather bereft. "Will you come later?"

He shook his head. "No, not tonight. I am engaged with friends, but I'll bring you some visitors tomorrow morning. Dress accordingly." He blew her a kiss, closed the door, and stepped back as the coachman set the horses in motion.

Clarissa leaned back, watching the lights of Covent Garden flicker past the window. There was no reason why she should expect him to spend every night in her bed, and she was quite surprised that she had. A mistress could no more expect her lover to live in her pocket than a wife could her husband. Of course Jasper had friends, a life outside the house on Half Moon Street, but she couldn't deny how much she had wanted another night in his arms. His company filled her with a pleasure as deep as did his body. The prospect of lying alone in the bed that had brought her so much delight in the last two days brought a wash of dismay and a disgruntled sense of loss.

Jasper waited until the carriage had turned the corner, then he strolled to 32 King Street. It was time to ask some serious questions of Nan Griffiths.

Luke left the theatre in the interval in the company of friends. "Women or cards?" the Honorable Lucien Talbot asked, sniffing the air of Covent Garden like a scenting foxhound. "Greek shop or bagnio?"

"Why not both?" a lanky young man asked, casting an eye up and down the street. "Let's to Archer's on Charles Street. The faro tables play high and the women are better than most." He passed his hands through the air in a lewd illustration.

Luke took mental inventory of his present funds. The stakes at Archer's were too rich for his blood; most tables insisted on stakes of fifty pounds or more. But one solid win would set him up for the month. And faro was his game. He acceded with a nod and the small party surged down Russell Street and into Charles Street.

They were greeted by the liveried and bewigged footman at a discreet house on

Charles Street. "Gentlemen, welcome." He took their cloaks and hats, and waited while they divested themselves of their swords. Weapons were not permitted at the tables, with good reason. He ushered them into the first of the gaming salons.

Luke strolled around the tables, looking at the play, listening to the groom porters calling the odds, trying to get a feeling for which one would bring him luck. He took a bumper of rum punch from a waiter's tray and finally settled in to play.

The rest of the evening passed in a haze of rum punch and a gradually seeping knowledge of disaster. He laid down one IOU after another. The banker accepted them all without demur, and Luke watched the little pile of paper grow. He became aware of one of his friends standing at his shoulder.

"Odd's blood, man. Call it a night. It's enough," Lucien remonstrated. "We're all rolled up for tonight, it's time to drown our losses between a pair of sweet thighs. Come, Luke. Give it up now."

Luke waved him away. "One more. I can smell a win in the next hand. You go on, and I'll see you later."

The Honorable Lucien shrugged and left. Luke won the next hand and, emboldened, played three more. He lost them all and finally rose from the table unable to comprehend the extent of his losses, but vaguely aware in his befuddled brain that he faced disaster.

He staggered out into the cold night air and immediately felt dizzy. He leaned against the wall until the world stopped spinning. As soon as the brat was dead, everything would come right. As soon as it was known he was heir to the Astley fortune, his creditors would step back. They would be only too happy to offer him as much credit as he wanted.

True, gambling debts were debts of honor. He couldn't expect them to be extended. But once he had firm expectations the moneylenders would be more than happy to accommodate him. He walked through the Piazza, seeing little of what was going on around him. If Francis hadn't yet succumbed, then he was going to have to do something more to encourage it . . . and that quickly.

He hailed a hackney. His house was in darkness when he stepped out of the carriage. He paid the driver and let himself into the hall. A guttering candle was all the light available and he cursed at the negligence of his servant. He took up the candle stub and stumbled up the stairs to his bedchamber, where he lit a candle by the bed from the stub in his hand and sat down heavily to remove his shoes. He didn't get much further before falling back on the bed in a stertorous sleep.

No one disturbed him until he awoke at midday to his customary pounding head and dry mouth. He sat up, looked down in disgust at his crumpled clothes. Staggering to his feet he shrugged out of his coat and yanked the bellpull.

"You rang, sir." His manservant appeared in the doorway, shrugging into his own coat. It was clear he had been recently roused from his own slumber.

"Help me out of these clothes."

The man did so. "Late night, was it, sir?"

"If you'd done your job and waited up for me you'd know the answer to that," Luke said savagely.

The man responded with a derisive sniff. No one else would work for the paltry wages he received, if, indeed, he received them at all. And who could blame a man who worked for next to nothing taking as much time away from the job as he pleased? "Ed was here last even." He took his master's waistcoat, shaking out the creases.

"What did he want?" Luke turned from

the basin where he was soaking a cloth in cold water.

"He didn't come to speak to me, sir, so I wouldn't know. He just said it was urgent."

Luke placed the cold cloth on his forehead. "Urgent?" Could that mean he was bringing the one piece of news that would make everything all right? "Send a message to the stables . . . tell him to come at once."

"I'll see if he's free, sir."

"And bring me some hot water, and the brandy bottle." Luke stripped off the rest of his clothes and put on a chamber robe. His headache was improving by the minute, and he could feel optimism creeping into his blood. It was time for this to be over.

The servant returned with the brandy bottle and a jug of hot water. "I sent the boy up to the stables, sir. Should I shave you?"

Luke tilted the bottle to his lips, feeling the steadying warmth returning sense and stability to his mind and limbs. "Get on with it then."

Half an hour later Ed arrived and was shown up to Luke's bedchamber. "The boy's not there no more."

Light sprang into Luke's dull eyes. "Good. He's gone then."

"Aye. Why'd you send someone to fetch

'im and then tell me to find out 'ow's he doin'?" Ed's aggrieved tone puzzled Luke as much as the strange words.

"What do you mean? Speak clearly, man."

Ed looked at him pityingly. "I means, sir, exactly what I says. Bertha said you'd sent fer the boy an' she give 'im up."

"*What?* I never sent for him . . . who would I send?"

"Some hoity-toity lady, she said. Took the boy, said you'd sent her to fetch 'im."

Luke's world began to fall apart, piece by piece, like a tumbling jigsaw. "What did she look like, this lady?"

Ed shrugged. "Don't rightly know, sir. Like a lady, that's all Bertha said."

Clarissa? Could it have been Clarissa? But how on earth could she have found Francis? It was not possible. No one knew where he was except his uncle and Ed.

Luke turned on the groom. "What have you done? Who have you told? You betrayed me, you cur. I'll have you locked up . . . I'll have you transported . . . dear God, I'll see you hang for this."

"Whoa." Ed held up his hands, half curled into fists. "Hold yer 'osses, sir. You ain't got no call to threaten me like that. I done nuthin' but what you paid me to do, an' that was small enough. Took the lad to our

Bertha's an' left 'im there." His eyes narrowed. "If you asks me, y'are the one the law'd be interested in . . . wantin' to do away wi' a poor scrap like that . . . yer own nephew an' all."

Luke spun away from him. He couldn't afford to anger the man; he knew too much. "Well that's as may be," he said with difficulty. "I didn't mean to accuse you of anything, Ed. I know you've done me good service. Did your sister give you any real description of this woman? Her hair color, her stature, anything at all? Did the boy go with her willingly?"

Ed shook his head. "No . . . didn't ask and she didn't tell. You want me to go back?"

"Yes, today . . . at once. No . . . wait. I'll go myself." He could find out much better for himself, he decided. He needed to know how the woman arrived there, if she left any clue as to where she was going . . . how the boy greeted her . . . what she was wearing . . . and most particularly, her hair color. He couldn't rely on Ed to ask all the right questions, and neither could he bear to sit chewing his nails waiting for the man to return.

"Tell me how to get there." He picked up his sword belt, fastening it at his hip.

"You owe me a sovereign," Ed reminded him without answering the question.

"Later." Luke picked up his cloak. "Give me the direction."

"Not wi'out the sovereign." Ed folded his arms and regarded Luke placidly. "If I don't get it now, I doubt I'll see the color of yer money this side o' next Christmas."

Luke burned with fury and mortification. Even this stable-hand questioned his honor.

Ed continued to regard him in silence and Luke swallowed, turned his back, and dug into the recesses of his armoire, where he kept a small purse of emergency coins. He took out a sovereign and slowly held it out to the man.

Ed took it, tossed it in the air, and caught it deftly. He bit it, then nodded, shoving it into his pocket. "Ye'll be wanting the stairs at Wapping. Ye'll find our Bertha on Dundee Street, third 'ouse from the top. Ask anyone, they'll tell you right enough . . . I'll be off now." He headed for the door.

Luke ran down the stairs after him, shouting for his servant. "Send to the mews for my horse."

It took him an hour with several wrong turns to reach the mean streets of east London, but at last he found Wapping Stairs, and after two queries drew rein outside the house on Dundee Street. He stared up at the house. For some reason he hadn't expected anything quite so foul and forbidding as these ranks of crooked houses, the stinking kennels running to the river, the tumbledown roofs and glassless windows.

He didn't dismount — he was too afraid to leave his horse — and instead banged on the door with his riding whip. The small girl who opened it a crack peered up at him. "What d'you want?"

"Bertha. Ask her to come out here." He spoke impatiently, looking up and down the street, expecting a group of ruffians to descend upon him at any moment. "At once, girl."

She ducked back, closing the door again, and he leaned over and banged with his whip again, keeping it up until the door opened and a brawny woman stood there with folded arms glaring at him. "You wantin' to wake the dead then?"

"Are you Bertha?"

"Depends who's askin'."

"I left a boy with you and paid you three months in advance for his keep. Ed tells me you gave him to a woman. I want to know about her."

"It'll cost you."

"It damn well will not," he exclaimed. "I paid you in advance, and now you don't have him anymore. Tell me what the woman looked like, before I call the watch on you."

Bertha seemed to consider this, then she gave a scornful laugh. "Much good that'll do you." But she relented enough to give him as near a detailed description of her visitor as she could manage, and Luke listened in growing rage and despair.

He rode away from the woman's door knowing without a shadow of doubt that Clarissa had taken her brother. He couldn't begin to imagine how she'd found him, but find him she had. So where the hell was she now? His wards were somewhere in this city, unless she'd gone back to Kent, back to the protection and support of her father's friends. Danforth and the physician. That would be her most logical step. She would rely on them to support her. But however black the picture she painted Luke still had the law on his side. He was still their legal guardian. Not even Danforth could overset the will, and he had absolute control and authority over his wards until Clarissa came of age. He could post into Kent and assert his authority there and no one could gainsay him.

But what if Clarissa never came of age?

The freshness of the idea was so startling he drew rein involuntarily and his horse reared up with a loud protesting whinny. If something happened to Clarissa before she reached her twenty-first birthday, then his guardianship of Francis would continue until the boy reached his own majority.

He would have eleven years in which to milk his ward's inheritance. Charges for care and feeding . . . for schooling . . . oh, there were many ways in which he could live quite well off young Francis without doing away with him in the short term. And it was so much less risky, so much less obvious. He could play the devoted uncle and guardian for the world to see, and removing one young woman from the earth's surface should not be that difficult. Once he knew where she was.

He would post into Kent at once and would assert his authority more in sorrow than in anger. He would be the misunderstood, falsely maligned guardian, and he would insist on bringing them both back to London with him. If the lawyer and the physician protested, he would remove his wards with the full force of the law.

CHAPTER SEVENTEEN

The Honorable Sebastian Sullivan ran his cane along the railings as he sauntered down Half Moon Street in the company of his twin. "When d'you think Jasper will make his announcement, Perry?"

"I don't know . . . and really, Seb, I don't think we should be visiting her without Jasper's say-so. She's his business, not ours."

"Nonsense," Sebastian declared, playing a robust tune on the railings. "We used to visit Gwendolyn whenever the urge took us; he never objected to that. Besides, Mistress Ordway's going to become part of the family, if Jasper has anything to do with it. It's only natural we should visit our brother's betrothed; of course we'd be interested in looking her over."

Peregrine shook his head. "She's not yet his betrothed, and you know it. And if you think Jasper's going to be interested in your approval, you have windmills in your head.

I'm certainly not going to submit my prospective bride for your or Jasper's approval."

"Who is she, anyway?" His brother turned his head against his high starched cravat to regard his twin with a quizzical grin.

"I'm not ready to say just yet. Who's yours?"

Sebastian's grin broadened. "Oh, a positive winner, Perry. I'll snatch her from a den of iniquity just as she's about to forfeit her immortal soul."

"Has Uncle Bradley seen her yet?"

Sebastian looked mysterious. "Well, maybe he has, and maybe he hasn't. It rather depends."

"On what?" Perry demanded.

"On what he remembers. Have you shown him yours?"

Peregrine shook his head. "Not yet. It's hard for her to find the time."

"Why? What occupies her time otherwise?"

Perry shook his head again. "Not telling you yet. We're here." He stopped at the door of Jasper's house. "Are you sure it's not discourteous to descend upon her without warning?"

"Why should it be? It's a perfectly respectable time for a morning call. If she's going to make a passable countess, she's got to be able to show to advantage in a social setting. What more ordinary a social setting than receiving visitors?"

"Well, I hope you're right. I don't want to be in Jasper's black books."

"We won't be." Sebastian ran lightly up the steps and banged the knocker.

Sally opened the door, expecting Lord Blackwater. She blinked in surprise at his lordship's brothers. "Good morning, sirs. His lordship isn't here."

"We didn't come to see him," Sebastian said cheerfully. "We came to pay our respects to Mistress Ordway."

"Oh." Sally looked a little doubtful. "If you'll wait in the hall, sirs, I'll let my mistress know you're here."

"Oh, we'd like to surprise her." Sebastian half lifted Sally out of the way. "Is she in the drawing room? Come, Perry." He started for the stairs just as a small boy catapulted into the hall from the kitchen.

"Sally, I'm goin' to find the peddler down the road. He just left an' Mistress Newby forgot to get some pink ribbon she wants for 'er Sunday bonnet, so I'm goin' to get it for her. Will you tell my s—" He swallowed the word in the nick of time, just as he took in the presence of strangers. "Tell the mistress?" he finished in a rather more subdued tone. "In case she wants me." He was already struggling with the door latch.

"Yes, I'll tell her, but don't be long. I've work for you to do," Sally said. "And go out the back door, the front door's for the gentry. Surely you know that?"

The child bit his lip, then turned and scampered back through the rear door to the kitchen.

"He's new around here," Peregrine observed. "What happened to the other lad?"

"Oh, he's still around," Sally said with something of a martyred sigh. "And the pair of them are always up to no good. Encourage each other, they do."

"Best not let Jasper catch 'em," Sebastian said with a chuckle. "Small boys can annoy him. Remember Cousin Julia's boy, Perry? He took Jasper's gun out of the gun room at Blackwater Manor and then dropped it in the pond because it was too heavy for him. Oh, that was a ruckus. Cousin Julia standing in front of her ewe lamb with her arms outstretched to defend him, and Jasper, black as thunder, threatening all kinds of retribution."

"We never seemed to annoy him," Peregrine observed.

"Oh, I don't know about that. Don't you remember when we got stranded on Dough

Crag that time we set out to climb it and it was too late in the day . . . God, he was as mad as fire when he found us."

"We'd scared him silly, that's why." Peregrine ran lightly up the stairs ahead of his brother.

Clarissa was sitting at the secretaire composing a difficult letter to Lawyer Danforth when the brothers entered the drawing room. Hastily she covered her composition. It was the devil's own task to reassure the lawyer that all was well with both herself and Francis, without telling him any details, but in good conscience she couldn't leave her friends worrying any longer. And she knew they would probably be frantic by now. She had to give him an address to write back to, and the only possible one was Half Moon Street, so she'd constructed yet another fantasy about a kindly woman who ran a lodging house, where she was staying to be close to her brother, since her uncle's house was not really big enough for all of them, and as it was a bachelor's establishment she didn't feel too comfortable living there. It all made perfect sense, and she could see no reason why anything in that narrative would disturb the lawyer.

She had been so deeply immersed in her

complicated task that she hadn't heard the door knocker and now looked in startled surprise at the unceremonious arrival of her visitors.

She stood up, looking automatically for Jasper, who had surely come with his brothers. He'd said he would be bringing her visitors this morning. "Gentlemen . . . is your brother not with you?"

"No, ma'am. We took the liberty of visiting you alone. Must we go away again?" Sebastian's smile was endearing.

"No . . . no, of course not. You are both most welcome. Pray, be seated." She gestured to a sofa. "What may I offer you? Sherry . . . Madeira . . . or claret if you prefer?"

"Oh, a glass of Jasper's claret, I think. What about you, Perry?"

"The same, thank you. Allow me, ma'am." Peregrine lifted the decanter. "Will you join us, Mistress Ordway?"

"Not at present, thank you." She sat down in an armless chair opposite the sofa and regarded them thoughtfully. "So, I am honored, sirs. Is there a special reason for this visit?"

"Not a bit of it," Sebastian declared. "But we saw you at the theatre last evening, and, I have to tell you, ma'am, the town is abuzz with the question of the hour: Who is the beauty on Blackwater's arm?

She shook her head. "You flatter me, sir." Jasper had been right, it seemed, about her carefully orchestrated debut.

"I can't speak for my brother, Mistress Ordway." Peregrine smiled at her. "But I would have chosen the same words, and without the intention of flattery. Since you have been seen in public with my brother, and we have been introduced previously, we thought we could without any breach of etiquette take the liberty of visiting you."

"Oh, you would put me to shame, Perry," Sebastian declared with mock annoyance. "Believe me, Mistress Ordway, I meant every word."

She smiled. These two were so different from their elder brother, but they were also, apart from their identical physiques, quite different from each other.

"You do me too much honor, sirs." She was about to say something else when she heard more voices from downstairs. "Your brother, I believe, gentlemen."

The twins exchanged a glance. The door opened and Jasper came in, accompanied by two others. "Sebastian . . . Peregrine . . . what an unexpected pleasure," he murmured. "My dear Clarissa, I trust these rattles haven't been boring you to tears."

"Indeed, my lord, they haven't been here long enough to do so," she returned, smiling. Her smile extended to the two men with Jasper while she waited for an introduction.

"Ma'am, allow me to present Lord Varley and Lord Delaney." Jasper gestured to his companions, who both bowed with a murmured "Honored, ma'am."

Clarissa curtsied. "What may I offer you gentlemen? I understand the claret is particularly fine."

"Yes, it is," Jasper said, "and far too good for those good-for-nothing brothers of mine." He went to the sideboard and filled glasses. "Clarissa, will you take a glass of Madeira?"

"No, thank you, sir." She rang the bell. "I would prefer coffee." When Sally appeared Clarissa asked for coffee, before saying casually, "I trust the boys are behaving themselves, Sally. They were rather boisterous this morning." For some reason she felt the need to check up on her brother's whereabouts at frequent intervals. If she'd had her way she'd have kept him beside her at all times, but it was hardly practical, and particularly now when Jasper was in the house.

"Oh, that they were, but young Frank's gone on an errand for Mistress Newby, so he'll be out of the house for a bit."

Clarissa paled. "What . . . what kind of errand?"

"Mistress Newby sent him after the peddler. She forgot her ribbon when he came by this morning," Sally said cheerfully. "I'll fetch that coffee now, ma'am."

Clarissa held herself very still. Francis was running around the streets. He could run into Luke on any corner. Every muscle strained to race outside, to chase after him, call him, bring him back. But she couldn't. Not at this moment. She turned slowly back to her guests and realized Jasper was looking at her, in puzzlement certainly, but with that strange reflective gleam in his eye that made her so uneasy.

She gave a light laugh. "Oh, the child's always up to mischief." She sat down, folding her hands into her lap. "Did you see the play last evening, Lord Varley?"

Jasper said little, leaving her to entertain his brothers and his guests. It was abundantly clear to him that she was more than accustomed to this kind of intercourse. He hadn't learned very much from Nan the previous evening, except that she had finally and very reluctantly confirmed his conviction that Mistress Ordway had not been employed in the usual fashion at 32 King Street. But Nan knew nothing concrete about her erstwhile lodger, except that although she seemed to be alone in the city, she was not without funds.

So who was she? And what the hell was it about that boy that touched her so nearly? Her face had shown pure terror for a moment at the thought of his running loose in the streets. She'd recovered quickly enough but Jasper had seen the struggle it had cost her. Part of him wanted to shake the truth out of her, but that wouldn't give him what he really wanted. She had to tell him the truth herself, because she wanted to, because she couldn't bear lying to him any longer.

He couldn't hide from himself how badly he wanted her to reach that point. The point when her trust overcame her fear, when she would acknowledge that only open honesty would serve between them . . . that something was happening between them that could not flourish if she continued to lie to him. He had not expected to fall in love with the woman who would bring him his fortune, but he could no longer hide the truth from himself. He was rapidly losing his heart to an enigma.

Clarissa glanced up at him and, as if aware of his reflections, gave him a tentative smile, her head slightly on one side in silent question. He shook his own head ruefully and turned to refill his guests' glasses.

Clarissa wondered what that head-shake had meant. It seemed like a resigned dismissal of his reflections . . . troubling reflections judging by the gravity, almost wistfulness, of his expression. She had the urge to go to him, to touch his hand, ask him what was the matter. But she couldn't do that in this room full of visitors.

Her head began to ache and she wished they would all take their leave. Jasper's concerns aside, she was desperate to find out whether Francis was back yet. If he hadn't returned, why not? She needed to impress upon him that he mustn't go out again under any circumstances. Maybe it was a long shot that Luke would happen to be walking up Half Moon Street as his ward was running down it, but it was not an impossibility.

At long last, her visitors rose to take their leave. She curtsied, shook hands, thanked them for coming, all the time keeping her smile in place, her voice composed. Jasper left the drawing room with them and as soon as the door was closed on them, she slipped out into the corridor. Their voices rose from the hall, Jasper's among them. Clarissa took the back stairs to the kitchen.

Sweet relief flooded her at the scene of quiet domesticity that greeted her. Her brother was standing on a stool earnestly peeling potatoes at the kitchen table. Mistress Newby was busy at the range, Sally was working with a pile of ironing. Young Sammy was polishing silver.

"Eh, Mistress Ordway, is there something I can do for you?" Sally looked dismayed at Clarissa's sudden arrival in the kitchen. "You should've rung for me."

"No, I don't need anything, Sally. I wanted a word with Frank."

"Oh, I could've sent him up to you." Sally exchanged the flatiron she was using for one heating on the range. "No need for you to traipse all the way down here, ma'am."

"It's hardly a marathon walk." Clarissa smiled. She beckoned to her brother, who climbed off the stool and came to her, eyes wide with curiosity. "Let's go out here for a minute." She led him into the back corridor that ran between the kitchen and the front hall and bent down to eye level. "Listen, darling, you mustn't ever leave the house like that. Supposing you should run into Uncle Luke when I wasn't there?"

Francis's eyes widened even more, but this time with fright. He shook his head vigorously. "I won't . . . I won't ever go outside again, 'Rissa, promise."

"See that you don't." She straightened slowly. "You gave me such a fright."

"How long're we going to stay here?" the boy asked. "That man doesn't like me."

"What man? The earl you mean? That's nonsense, love, of course he likes you."

"He doesn't like boys, Sally said so to Mistress Newby. Just a little while ago."

"I expect he doesn't know much about them," she said crisply. "Anyway, keep out of his way and everything will be all right."

"But how long're we staying here?" he repeated.

"I don't know yet. We have to stay here until it's safe. A few months maybe."

Francis looked crestfallen. "I want to go home. I want to see Silas an' my pony. I want to go to school in the vicarage again. I don't like it here." His voice rose alarmingly and Clarissa shushed him with a finger to her lips.

"I know, love. It's hard for you, and you've been so brave, but you have to trust me. We have to stay here just for a little longer." She bent to kiss him, hugging him close to her.

Jasper stood in the hall, just beyond the door that stood slightly ajar. He'd seen his visitors out and returned to the drawing room, to find both it and the bedchamber deserted. There was no sign of Clarissa in the dressing room, either. Reasoning that the only other place she could be was the kitchen, odd though that was, he descended to the hall again and was about to push open the baize door to the kitchen regions when he heard Clarissa's urgent whisper. He stepped back instinctively, unwilling to eavesdrop, then, quashing scruple, he inched the door open a little further.

Why the devil was Clarissa hugging that scrawny little boy?

He stepped back and moved towards the staircase. Was this yet another piece of the puzzle to be fitted into the whole, or was it just a manifestation of a natural, if overdeveloped, maternal instinct? She'd rescued the child from the streets; perhaps she'd been afraid that away from the safety of the house he might run into his old master or be kidnapped by some other ruffian. Except that the boy no longer looked like a street urchin. Clean and dressed as he was in sturdy respectable garments he obviously belonged to someone, and no ruffian would

risk abducting a child who belonged somewhere.

"Jasper, I didn't realize you were down
here. I thought perhaps you might have left
with your brothers and your friends." She
spoke from behind him and he turned on
the stair.

"I would not have left without telling
you." He looked at her closely. She seemed
unflustered. "What were you doing in the
kitchen?"

"I wanted to make sure Frank was back."
She smiled, shrugged. "It's probably foolish
of me, but I had visions of him being
snatched by that brutal chimney sweep
again."

It was reasonable enough; he'd thought of
it himself. And yet, Jasper was not wholly
convinced. However, he said only, "I missed
you last night."

"I missed you." She came up the stairs to
him. "I kept hoping that you would suddenly appear and I'd wake and find you in
bed beside me." She stood just below him
on the stair, her lips curved in a seductive
smile, her eyes aglow. Her tongue flicked
over her lips and he put aside the conundrum. There were many pleasanter ways to
occupy his time.

He reached down to touch her face, to

trace the curve of her full mouth with a fingertip. "Perhaps we should make up for lost time."

"In the daytime, my lord?" Her eyes widened in mock horror. "Isn't that very decadent?"

"Maybe, but why else would a man keep a mistress?" He slipped his hands beneath her arms and lifted her up onto the step above him. "Into bed, mistress mine. I find I have a most powerful hunger." A hand on her rear encouraged her upwards.

Clarissa jumped ahead. "You'll have to catch me first." Laughing, she ran for her bedchamber. Jasper followed her, kicking the door shut behind him. He caught her up, holding her high against him. "Caught you."

"So you have." Her gaze held his. "So what now, my lord?"

"An interesting question with a multitude of answers." He let her slide down his body until her feet touched the floor. His eyes took on a smoky hue as his fingers moved over the laces of her gown, opening the bodice. He spread the sides wide and bent to kiss the soft, sweet-scented swell of her breasts over the neckline of her thin muslin shift. His tongue dipped into the cleft between them, and she sighed with pleasure.

He pushed the shift off her shoulders, baring her to the waist, and, kneeling now, cupped her breasts in his hand, kissing her nipples, suckling them, his teeth lightly grazing the hard pink crowns.

Clarissa ran her fingers through his hair, traced the shells of his ears with her fingertips, feeling the heat rise in her belly. Jasper pushed her gown off her hips and with rough haste did the same with her shift, so that she stood in a puddle of ruffled silk and pale muslin. He kissed her belly, tasted her navel, pressed his thumbs into the hard points of her hipbones. With a soft moan she shifted on the carpet, her thighs parting for the heated exploration of his tongue as it painted a path down her inner thighs. He held her hips, grasped her bottom, his fingers kneading the firm flesh. Her own fingers twined in his hair, and she thrust her hips forward for the caress of his tongue.

His mouth found her core, his tongue teased the hard little nub of flesh, and he held her, his cheek pressed to her belly, his hands firm on her hips, as the storm ripped through her.

She fell forward, her hands resting on his shoulders, her body curved in surrender, until he rose to his feet and moved her backwards until the edge of the bed caught her behind her knees and she fell onto it. He stood over her, stripping off his clothes, his hungry gaze fixed upon her body, naked except for her gartered stockings. For some reason he found the erotic allure of those white silk stockings and the black lace garters against the cream of her nakedness more powerful than anything he could imagine.

He came down to the bed beside her, kneeling, his penis hard and demanding. Clarissa took him in her mouth. She let her tongue circle the moist tip as her hand moved up and down the shaft. His breathing quickened, his hips moved, and she reached both hands between his thighs, stroking his balls, grasping the hard muscular curve of his backside as her mouth moved along his penis, her lips pressing firmly, her teeth grazing.

It was a shock when he spoke, his voice strangely husky. "Turn over."

She moved her head away from his engorged flesh, her eyes glinting with excitement, and rolled onto her belly. He slipped his hands beneath her belly and lifted her onto her knees. His hands gripped her hips and she gave a little gasp as he entered her. She had a moment to think that the feeling was quite different from this position, and then coherent thought was no longer possible as the exquisite spiral of sensation coiled ever tighter. His hands were hard on her hips, holding her tightly, and she rocked on her knees to meet his thrusts, her cries of delight muffled in the coverlet. And when it was over, she rested her forehead on the bed and fought for breath as wave after wave of sweetness flooded her loins.

Jasper kissed the nape of her neck, his body molded to her damp back as he came back to his own reality. There was something about making love with an enigma that transcended the ordinary, he reflected with an inner smile. Slowly he disengaged and rolled onto his side, letting his hand rest on her bottom.

After a minute, Clarissa turned onto her side to face him. She rested her cheek on her arm and with a free hand touched his face. "I still seem to be flying around the room in little pieces. Do you think they'll all come back together again eventually?"

"I certainly hope so," he responded with appropriate gravity, belied by the dancing smile in his eyes that matched her own.

It was on the tip of Clarissa's tongue to ask him how many other positions he knew for this delightful activity, but she bit her tongue in the nick of time. A whore would surely know everything there was to know.

"What were you going to say?"

"Nothing," she denied. "I wasn't going to say anything."

The smile stopped dancing in his eyes and he became reflective. "Why do I so often think that you're not telling me the whole truth, Clarissa?"

"I can't imagine." She sat up on the edge of the bed, so that he could see only her back. "You know everything relevant about me. Everything relevant to this game we're playing." How she wished she could turn to him, tell him everything, but there was too much at stake. She had to keep up the lies for Francis's sake. But it was tearing her apart; every time she had to come up with yet another lie, another twist to the fabrication, she seemed to lose a little bit of herself, her essential integrity.

Jasper pursed his lips. Once again he wanted to shake her, tell her that the game was no longer the point, demand that she admit she understood that. But instead, he swung out of bed and began to dress. "We're going to pay a visit this afternoon." He wandered over to the armoire. "Let's see what you should wear."

"A visit to whom? Not your uncle again, I hope."

"No." He opened up the double doors and examined the contents. "Lady Mondrain; you saw her at the theatre last night."

"And will you present me as your mistress?" Their lovemaking had been spoiled and Clarissa felt dejected, out of sorts.

"I won't need to." He took out a driving dress of rich dark brown velvet. "This, I think."

"You mean they'll automatically assume it?" She watched with little interest as he laid the garment over a chair.

"Of course. But these things do not need to be spoken. While they're not spoken, they can be ignored. It's much more comfortable all around, if they're ignored."

"And if . . . when I become your wife, they'll still be ignored?"

"Certainly. The marriage will be a quiet affair, discreetly noted in the *Gazette*."

"And your uncle will be satisfied with that? Aren't you supposed to shock society?"

"No, only the family," he said with a wry smile. "Uncle Bradley doesn't give a fig for society, but he wants to rub the family's nose in the dirt, as they've tried so often to do to him.

"Besides," he added, giving her a covert glance, "your position as my wife will be much more comfortable if society is able to ignore the truth. Of course, there'll be some holdouts, some sticklers, but I have every hope, my dear, that in time you'll win them over."

"In time?" She stood up slowly. "But this marriage is not to last."

"Why?" he said, looking at her directly. "It doesn't have to be annulled, Clarissa. Not if we don't wish it."

She swallowed, tears pricking behind her eyes. She couldn't think of anything she'd like more than to spend the rest of her life with this man. He completed her. When she was with him she felt whole, as if all the little disparate bits that made the whole Clarissa Astley were fitted neatly together. When he wasn't with her, she was bereft, lonely. But without giving him the truth, she couldn't possibly marry him except as a charade. She couldn't live a lie for the rest of her life. After they were married and Francis was safe, she would tell him the truth, but that would be the end of any feelings he would have for her. How could he love someone who had deceived him just to achieve her own goal? It would be different if he had deceived her, but he had never been anything but honest.

Jasper waited for an answer, and when he didn't get one, he reached for the bellpull.

Maybe he was wrong and she didn't feel what he did. If she didn't there was no point hoping she would confide in him. He'd pressed as far as he wanted to. He didn't know whether anger or disappointment was uppermost as he said curtly, "Sally will help you dress. I'll wait in the drawing room."

He left her and went into the drawing room, waiting until he heard Sally enter the bedchamber. Then he left, going downstairs and into the kitchen.

Mistress Newby nearly dropped the trivet she was carrying from the range to the table when his lordship appeared in her kitchen. "Oh, lord love us, m'lord. What can we do for you? Sally's gone to Mistress Ordway."

"I am aware, Mistress Newby." His gaze fell on Frank, hovering near the back door. "My business lies with this young gentleman."

"Lord, what's the lad done, sir?"

"Nothing, to my knowledge," Jasper said. "But I'd like a word." He approached the child, who looked ready to run. "Let's go into the yard, Frank." A hand on his elbow, and he had the boy through the door and into the enclosed yard.

Frank looked up at him, his eyes scared. "You don't like me."

"I don't know you. I'm not so unreasonable I dislike on sight, child." Jasper tilted the boy's face with a finger under the rounded chin. The eyes were hazel rather than jade, the hair brown rather than titian, but a ray of sun caught a glint of gold in the thick thatch. The features were still childishly unformed, but the bone structure was there, the determined line of the jaw, the broad forehead under the widow's peak.

Everything about the child shouted breeding, despite his slovenly speech. Just as everything about Clarissa bespoke breeding and education.

"Sally said you don't like little boys."

"I can't imagine why Sally should consider herself qualified to make such a statement." He frowned, wondering how the maid could have come up with such an idea. In general he neither liked nor disliked children. "As it happens I have nothing against small boys unless they annoy me. How old are you, Frank?"

"Ten." Francis tried to twitch his chin away from the earl's grip. The intent scrutiny made him very uncomfortable.

What was the child to Clarissa then? Certainly no scrap of human flotsam rescued by chance from the street. He could probably force the truth out of the boy, but that would do his cause no good at all. Clarissa clearly adored Frank, whoever he was, and whatever had happened to reduce a sturdy boy to this pathetic scrap of humanity had certainly been brutal. He needed no more coercion in his short life. If he was going to coerce the truth from anyone it was going to be Clarissa. But he had one piece of the puzzle in place now. Frank's presence in his house was no accident.

"Very well." He released his grip and Francis raced back to the kitchen. Jasper watched his departure with a half smile. He had a sudden memory of himself at the same age, fleeing the wrath of his grandfather's head gardener after he'd stripped the raspberry canes one glorious June afternoon.

CHAPTER EIGHTEEN

Luke Astley dismounted in the yard of the Coach and Horses in the small town of Sevenoaks. He looked around impatiently. A knot of men were throwing dice over by the horse trough and it took a few minutes before they acknowledged the rider's arrival in the yard. One of them stood up reluctantly and came over to Luke.

"You puttin' up at the inn, sir?" He sucked on a wisp of hay as he took the reins of Luke's horse.

"Probably," Luke said. "See he gets a bran mash and a good rubdown. I've ridden him from London."

"Aye, looks like it too," the man muttered, running a hand down the animal's damp neck. The horse was sweating and breathing heavily. He'd clearly been ridden hard.

"What's that supposed to mean?" Luke demanded, bristling.

The groom shrugged, spat his wisp of hay

onto the cobbles at his feet, and led the horse towards the stables.

Luke cursed his impudence as he strode to the inn door. He knew he had ridden the horse hard for longer than the animal could comfortably handle, but he hadn't the money to change his mount halfway through the journey, and by the same token he didn't want to pay for an extra night on the road.

The landlord came out of the taproom, greeting him with a bow. "Welcome to the Coach an' Horses, sir. How can we serve you this evening?"

"Dinner," Luke commanded curtly. "I'll take it in the ordinary."

"Aye, sir, there's a toothsome rabbit pie in the oven." The landlord opened the door to the common dining parlor, where a group of men were already seated at a round table, drinking ale. "Dinner'll be on the table in ten minutes, sirs." The landlord bowed Luke into the parlor and returned to the taproom.

Luke nodded at his fellow diners and took a seat. He poured himself a tankard of ale from the pitcher on the table.

"You come far, sir?" one of the men inquired. He had the look of a farmer in homespun britches, leather waistcoat, and heavy riding boots.

"From London." Luke buried his nose in the tankard.

"Oh, aye? Long ride that. 'Tis market day in Sevenoaks, so we're takin' our dinners afore goin' home," the farmer offered. "You goin' far?"

Luke shook his head. "Not tonight. I'm heading for Shipbourne in the morning. Visiting some friends there."

"Oh, aye." One of his fellow diners looked up from his own tankard. "I heard tell there was some trouble, Shipbourne way."

Luke looked sharply at him. "What kind of trouble?"

The man frowned. "Summat to do wi' a missing lass. One of the gentry folk." He shook his head. "Can't rightly remember."

The conversation was interrupted by the landlord's arrival with the promised rabbit pie. He set it in the middle of the table. "There you go, gents. Best rabbit pie this side of Canterbury. An' there's a suet puddin' to follow, better'n any your mams ever made, I'll wager."

Luke waited impatiently while his companions helped themselves before saying, "There's the squire's family in Shipbourne — Artley? Ashby? Something like that."

"Astley, that's it," the farmer declared, slurping gravy. "Aye, I think 'twas that lass what's gone missing. Quite a brouhaha, there was. Talk of setting the runners onto it."

"*Was* — is she back then?" He buttered a piece of bread lavishly.

The man shrugged. "Not as far as I know . . . but I haven't been that way in a while. Anyone else know?" He glanced interrogatively around the table.

"The housekeeper's a friend of my missus," a man offered. "Last I 'eard the lass had still not turned up. They was talking of draggin' the village pond."

Luke nodded. *Where the hell was she then?* If she hadn't come home with Francis, then it stood to reason they were still in London. But how was he to find them? Perhaps she had written to Danforth or to the doctor.

He spent a restless night at the inn and left first thing next morning, riding the short distance to the village of Shipbourne. The squire's stately manor house stood at the end of the main village lane, surrounded by a redbrick wall. Iron gates gave entrance to the long driveway that led straight to the long, low, thatched-roof house. Everything seemed in order, the lawns well tended, the flower beds free of weeds, the shrubs neatly trimmed. But there was a strange air of desolation about the place, as if it was

430

empty, although of course it was not. A full staff of servants kept it running smoothly.

Luke hesitated, then he turned to the gatekeeper's house and banged on the door with his whip. It opened promptly and the man looked at him in surprise. "Why, Master Astley, we wasn't expecting you."

"I see no reason why you should be," Luke declared. "My movements are hardly the business of a gatekeeper. I'm going up to the house. Open the gates."

The man retreated into his house and returned with the great brass key. He unlocked the heavy gates and pushed them open, standing to one side as Luke rode through them.

Luke dismounted at the front door and banged the knocker. It was opened by a footman, who stared at him first in surprise, then in hope. "Master Astley, sir? Is there news of Mistress Clarissa?"

"What do you mean, news?" Luke, his story well prepared, looked astonished. "Is she not here? She and her brother?"

The man shook his head. "No, sir. Mistress Clarissa disappeared some weeks ago, and we haven't seen Master Francis since you took him away."

"But that can't be. I saw them off myself, just two days past. In a hired postchaise.

431

They were coming here."

The footman shook his head again. "We haven't seen hide nor hair of them, sir." He stepped back. "Will you be coming in, sir?"

Luke frowned. "If they're not here, there's no point. I'll see if Master Danforth knows anything. This is very worrying." He turned back to his horse.

He rode back into the village and stopped at the lawyer's house, which was also his place of business. A substantial house on the outskirts of the village, it sat in a well-tended garden. It was a gray, overcast morning, and welcoming lights showed in the windows. Luke rode up the path and dismounted. He tethered his horse to the hitching post conveniently situated to the side of the door and banged the knocker.

A plump, rosy-cheeked maidservant opened the door and bobbed a curtsy. "Good mornin', sir. Are you here to see Master Danforth on business?"

"I am."

"Who shall I say, sir?"

"Master Astley. It is a matter of some urgency." Luke stepped past her into a square hall.

"He has a client with him at present, sir. Will you wait in the parlor?"

"No, I'll wait here. Go at once and tell

him I am here on a matter of grave importance." Luke flicked his whip against his boot, as if to underscore the urgency of his errand.

The girl scurried to a door to the right of the hall and knocked. On invitation, she popped her head around the door. "I beg pardon, Master Danforth, for disturbin' you, but there's a gentleman to see you, says 'tis very urgent . . . name of Master Astley, sir."

Danforth himself came out into the hall, his expression wreathed in anxiety. "Master Astley, has something happened?"

Luke looked worried. "Indeed, sir, I don't know how to answer you. I was hoping you would have news of Clarissa and her brother. They left by postchaise two days ago to come home for a while. Francis was homesick and I thought it necessary for his health that he spend a week here with his sister." He looked around as if expecting them to materialize from the paneled walls. "They are not up at the manor. Are they here?"

Dismayed, the lawyer shook his head. "Indeed, no, sir. I had assumed they were still with you, or with the tutor in Bath. I own I am surprised Clarissa has not written — it's so unlike her — but I assumed that her life in London was so full of amusements that like so many young people these days, she forgot her old friends. Doctor Alsop is very troubled."

Luke looked very grave, even as his mind raced. He had hoped that the man would have some news, some clue as to Clarissa's whereabouts, but clearly he was as ignorant as Luke himself. Which left him squarely back where he'd started from.

"A hired chaise, you said." Danforth was pacing the hall, pulling at his chin. "Well, it should be easy enough to trace. They would have taken the London road to Sevenoaks, so they would have changed horses probably at the Rose and Crown at Orpington. How did you come? Horse or carriage?"

"I rode." Luke didn't want this energetic gentleman to take action on his own. "I'll ride back at once and make inquiries at the coaching inns along the London road." He turned back to the door. "I'll send word when I have news."

"Do, m'dear fellow. Please do. Alsop and I will be in a fever of anxiety until they're found. The whole village has been concerned ever since Clarissa left home without so much as a word." The lawyer followed him outside and waited as he mounted his horse. "Godspeed, sir. Godspeed."

Luke raised a hand in farewell and rode fast until he was out of sight, then he reined in his horse to a more gentle trot. There was no need for a breakneck speed, since there was no need to make inquiries at the coaching inns about a nonexistent postchaise. Where were they? Where to look next?

Lady Mondrain was delighted to receive Lord Blackwater and Mistress Ordway. She had been as curious as everyone else about the elegant, beautiful young woman in the earl's box at the theatre, and when inquiries had produced the information that the lady in question was in residence in the earl's house on Half Moon Street, she happily drew the universal conclusion. Jasper had set up a new mistress.

"How delightful of you to bring Mistress Ordway to visit me, my lord." She smiled at Clarissa, putting up her quizzing glass. "Your gown is exquisite, Mistress Ordway. It has the look of Hortense."

Clarissa, who had been brought up to think such personal comments and such calculating scrutiny to be the height of vulgarity, hid her surprise with a demure curtsy and a cool smile. "Indeed, Lady Mondrain, I hadn't realized that her designs are so easily identified. Thank you for pointing it out to me. I believe I must in future look for a dressmaker a little out of the common way."

Jasper bit back a reluctant grin as her ladyship's eyebrows crawled into her scalp. Meg Mondrain prided herself on speaking her mind and didn't give twopence whom she offended. The eldest daughter of a duke, she considered herself well above the mundane social constraints of lesser mortals. But her self-consequence was mitigated by a rich sense of humor that could as easily be directed at herself as at others.

"Well, when you find her, my dear, I daresay she will quickly cease to be out of the common way," she said, continuing to examine Clarissa through her quizzing glass. "Anyone who dresses you will immediately find a following." She dropped her glass and turned back to Jasper. "She's quite charming, Jasper."

"You are too kind, ma'am." Clarissa spoke with an edge to her voice. She didn't care for either the quizzing glass or a conversation about her that excluded her.

Lady Mondrain turned back to her. "Oh, dear, now I have offended you. Forgive me." She held out her hands to Clarissa with a warm but rueful smile. "I do like to speak my mind."

Clarissa took her hands with her own smile. "I have something of the same failing, my lady. So I should be the last to take offense."

Jasper gave a shout of laughter. "Meg, my dear, I think you might have met your match."

"Indeed, maybe I have." Meg laughed and put an arm around Clarissa's waist, urging her to a chair by the fire. "Come, you shall tell me all about yourself. Jasper, go and play piquet with Mondrain. He's moping in the library."

Jasper bowed and promptly took his congé. Clarissa had proved she could look after herself.

"So, you are residing on Half Moon Street, I understand?" Her ladyship rang the little handbell at her side. "How do you like it? A pleasant part of town, I always find . . . ah, Bateman, champagne, if you please." She gave Clarissa a smile. "I do find a glass of champagne in the afternoon to be most invigorating, almost as much so as a little nap. I am most partial to napping in the afternoon."

"Indeed, ma'am." Clarissa could think of no other comment.

Meg laughed. "You, of course, have far

too much energy to find that appealing. You are very young, my dear."

"I am ten months shy of my majority, ma'am. Not so very young."

Meg gave her a shrewd look. "That rather depends on the life you've led hitherto . . . ah, thank you, Bateman." She took the glass of champagne offered by the butler. "To you, my dear." She raised the glass and sipped.

Clarissa took a sip of her own, wondering if Jasper had been wrong and she was now about to be subjected to a barrage of questions about her history. But her hostess began to talk of the concerts at Vauxhall Gardens and she relaxed somewhat, listening attentively, prepared to pick up whatever useful nuggets of information about society life that were dropped.

Their tête-à-tête was interrupted after half an hour by the arrival of an elderly dowager and her two daughters. Clarissa had an instant's panic. Would they know she was Blackwater's mistress? Not every lady would be as broad-minded as her hostess. She curtsied as she was introduced to Lady Morecombe and the ladies Eleanor and Emily.

"You're new to town," Lady Morecombe declared, waving away the offer of champagne. "No . . . no, I'll take tea. Ordway . . . don't know the name. Where's your family from?"

"The Ordways are from Bedfordshire," Clarissa responded. "A small village some way outside Bedford." She silently prayed she wouldn't be asked to name the village in question as she didn't know any.

She needn't have worried. Lady Morecombe sniffed and waved a dismissive hand. "Oh, a small village. Country folk, I daresay." She turned her attention to her hostess, who was listening with a half smile that had just a hint of malice. Lady Morecombe was a stickler for convention and if she realized that not only was she chatting amiably with Lord Blackwater's mistress, she had placed her daughters in close proximity to the debauched creature, she would have fainted dead away.

"Lady Mondrain, I most particularly wanted to ask you to support the effort to save those poor carthorses. The brewers drive them into the ground, and then sell them to those dreadful knackers' yards for pennies. It's a disgrace. I am collecting funds to establish a nice pasture where they can end their days in peace." She nodded her head with complacent satisfaction.

Clarissa wondered how many chimney

sweeps' boys had been sent up her lady-ship's chimneys, fires lit behind them to keep them moving through the bewildering, soot-choked network of black passages barely wide enough for a starved child to negotiate. Presumably her ladyship thought her chimneys swept themselves. She sipped her champagne and wished Jasper would come and rescue her.

He did come eventually. His gaze took in the scene, the look of barely suppressed boredom on his mistress's countenance, a look that was matched almost exactly by her hostess. He controlled his laughter and bowed solemnly to Lady Morecombe and her daughters.

"My lady . . . Lady Eleanor, Lady Emily . . . your servant."

"Blackwater, I need your support for my poor carthorses." Her ladyship launched instantly into a repeat of her diatribe.

Jasper listened in silence, and when she had fallen silent, said with a bow, "They have my sympathies, Lady Morecombe, but there are neglected children, wounded soldiers, and cast-off girls roaming the streets without a roof over their heads, a coat to their backs, or a crust for their bellies. I believe they deserve my sympathies more." He extended a hand to Clarissa. "If you are ready to leave, Mistress Ordway, I have asked for my carriage and will escort you home."

She rose, astounded at his speech, but her radiant expression told him exactly how she felt. She made her farewells with a demure curtsy and, as soon as they were out in the hall, laid a hand on his arm. "Oh, bravo, Jasper. I didn't think you'd even be aware of such dreadful misfortunes. That woman is odious. I hope I never find myself in the same room with her again."

"That, my dear girl, is a fond hope. The Morecombes are to be found everywhere." He was as surprised at his own earlier speech as he was at the deep pleasure he felt at Clarissa's approbation. He hadn't spoken to please her, or he didn't think he had. But then, perhaps he had. He handed her into the coach and followed her in.

She turned instantly into his embrace, reaching up to stroke his face as he kissed her in the swaying gloom of the vehicle. "Do we have to go out again this evening?" she murmured against his mouth.

"We are not going to leave the bedchamber before morning," he declared, pulling her sideways onto his lap, sliding a hand beneath her cloak, slipping his fingers into her décolletage to caress her breasts. He loved how responsive they were to the slightest brush of a touch, the nipples rising hard against his fingers, the silken skin warming against his hand.

"But we might be hungry," she whispered, turning her body so that her hip pressed against his erection, pushing against his britches.

"Fear not, sweetheart, we shall satisfy all our appetites." He slid a hand up beneath her skirts, smoothing over her calves, her thighs, up into the deep cleft between them. She shuddered against him.

"No . . . Jasper . . . not here . . . you know what happens when you do that."

It was a faint protest and he chuckled, continuing his knowing exploration, relishing how quickly he could bring her to ecstasy, topple her over into insensate joy whenever or wherever he wished. It gave him a sense of pure masculine power that he'd never before been interested in wielding. But perhaps it was because this woman was so different from others, so private, so composed, so full of her own secrets. By compelling her to an open, honest response with no defenses he felt less diminished by those secrets.

She lay across his lap, trying to catch her breath, as the carriage drew up outside the house. Jasper withdrew his hand, adjusted her skirts, and helped her to sit up. He smiled at her disheveled hair, her pink cheeks, the dazed and slightly indignant glaze in her eyes. "I'll give you your revenge later," he promised, opening the door and stepping out.

He held up a hand to her and she took it, conscious that it was the hand that had a few minutes earlier been working such illicit magic on her helpless body. She raised it to her cheek and inhaled her own scent. Her eyes met his.

He swept her in front of him to the door and unlocked it with his own key. "That reminds me," she said, remembering a grievance with a degree of relief. Anything to regain a sense of control. "I would like a key to the door."

"Why?" He sounded genuinely puzzled. "Sally will always be here to let you in."

She shook her head in frustration. "I need to feel that it's my house . . . that I can come and go as I please. It doesn't feel right to have to knock on the door. I have keys to my own house and have had since I was twelve years old." She stopped, her eyes stricken. What had she just said? The urge to pour out the truth was almost irresistible; the words hovered on her lips. "You must think that's rather strange," she said with difficulty.

"As you say." His eyebrows flickered as he watched her countenance.

"Perhaps . . . perhaps I should tell you that . . . well, that not everything I've told you about my past has been the whole truth." She cleared her throat. "There are . . . there are some things it's too difficult for me to talk about." She tried a tentative smile, knowing how inadequate that nonexplanation was.

"I see." He looked at her steadily and in silence for a moment as he waited for more. When it didn't come, he said, "Perhaps you'll find it possible to talk about them at some other time."

"Perhaps," she said, biting her lip.

He nodded and turned aside to greet Sally, who had come into the hall at the sound of their arrival. Soon, he thought. Soon it would all come out. But he would not press her. She would tell him because she wanted to, not because he'd taken advantage of a slip of the tongue.

"We'll be supping in the bedchamber later, Sally. We'll ring when we're ready." He turned back to Clarissa, who still stood like a statue in the hall. "If it's that important to you, then I'll have another key cut."

He gestured with an inviting arm to the stairs. "Shall we go up, madam?"

CHAPTER NINETEEN

Two days later, Clarissa was sipping her morning hot chocolate by her bedroom fire when she heard the sound of carriage wheels in the street below her window. The sound stopped at the front door and, curious, she took her cup to the window. A massive, old-fashioned carriage seemed to take up most of the width of the narrow street. The coat of arms on the panels was unfamiliar, and she watched with interest as the liveried footman jumped down from the box at the rear of the coach and came up to the front door.

There was something faintly familiar about the livery — it was as old-fashioned as the carriage — and then it came to her. She'd last seen it on Viscount Bradley's footman. Was that unpleasant old gentleman sitting in the carriage, waiting for something . . . someone? Perhaps he thought his nephew was here. But Jasper had not spent the previous night. He'd escorted her to the opera for another round of "see and be seen," but on this occasion they had not left before the interval, and a procession of curious gentlemen had visited their box. One or two had escorted their lady companions, but for the most part their visitors were single gentlemen, openly fascinated to meet the earl's new mistress.

Clarissa had rather enjoyed the attention, fluttering her fan flirtatiously, offering provocative smiles and murmured comments, playing her part to the hilt. They had had a late supper in the Piazza with several other couples, and Jasper had sent her home in the carriage when he went off to continue the evening with his friends. She hadn't enjoyed coming home alone, had missed him in the big bed as usual, but there was also relief for the brief respite from watching her words constantly, trying to maintain the lies.

She turned as Sally came into the chamber. "There's a message for you, ma'am. The footman's waiting below." She gave Clarissa a folded, sealed paper.

Clarissa looked at the seal. She remembered the heavy signet ring on the slender white finger, and for some reason it made her shudder. Her name was inscribed in elegant penmanship on the front of the sealed paper, so it had clearly been delivered to the right place. But why in the world was Viscount Bradley writing to her? There was one way to find out.

She took the paper to the secretaire and slit the wafer with the paper knife, unfolding it carefully. The message was short and succinct.

Viscount Bradley begs Mistress Ordway to do him the honor of visiting him this morning. His carriage awaits her convenience.

Clarissa read it several times, but it was too clear a message for misinterpretation. Should she go? Should she ask Jasper first? Bradley was his uncle after all, and also the reason for this elaborate charade. What could he want of her? He knew what she was, or thought he did; he knew she'd come from Mother Griffiths's nunnery. Did he want to torment her in some way? Insult her as he had done before?

"The footman said he'd wait until you was ready, ma'am," Sally said somewhat hesitantly, seeing Clarissa's frown. "Should I lay out a driving dress for you?"

"I'm not sure . . ." Then she made up her mind. "Yes, but first tell the man I'll be ready in an hour — oh, and please bring me up some breakfast, Sally." She was not going to hurry to obey this summons, and it *was* a summons, however courteously phrased. This time she was not going to allow Viscount Bradley to disconcert her. And if he was rude, she would leave immediately.

She had another thought as Sally ran down to give the man the message. When she returned with a breakfast tray Clarissa said, "I would like you to accompany me, Sally. It is customary for a lady to be accompanied by her maid." She would present an utterly respectable appearance on this occasion, and she would have Sally's unimpeachable escort if she was obliged to walk home.

Sally nodded cheerfully, setting the tray on a table. "Oh, yes, ma'am. I was used to accompany my previous mistress when she went visiting. There's coddled eggs, and bread and butter." She went to the armoire. "Will you wear the gray velvet driving dress? The one with the black ribbon trim." She drew it forth and laid it on the bed, smoothing the folds, before stepping back admiringly. "It's very fetching. And with the sable pelisse . . ." She gave a firm nod.

Clarissa, dipping bread into her egg in a most unladylike fashion, agreed with a vague smile. She reached for the coffeepot. "The half boots of gray kid, I think, Sally."

It was quite amusing, this dressing-up business, she thought as she finished her breakfast and contemplated the outfit laid out for her. She would miss it when it was all over and she was once more ensconced in her country-mouse existence.

But it didn't have to be over. Jasper had said so. *If they didn't want it to be over, it didn't have to be.* Sometimes she allowed herself to imagine that perhaps that could be true, but she knew it to be a fond hope. When he knew the truth — and she would tell him the truth once the danger for Francis was past — he would want nothing to do with her. He would believe he would never be able to trust her. And she wouldn't know how to convince him otherwise.

She had no choice but to continue the lie. And she would stand by that lie in the face of anything that nasty, evil-talking old man threw at her. Resolutely, she pushed away her breakfast tray. "I'll dress now, Sally."

Half an hour later she was ready. A careful examination of her appearance in the mirror showed her an elegant young woman, her hair coiled in a neat braid around her head, the severity softened by clustered ringlets framing her face. The driving dress presumably bore all the hallmarks of a Hortense creation, as Lady Mondrain would no doubt point out. If the viscount happened to recognize it as such, then so much the better.

"Are you ready, Sally?"

Sally, in cloak and bonnet, nodded. "Quite ready. Young Frank wanted to come with us, said he could be your page." She laughed. "Quite the imp he is."

Clarissa wondered if she needed to impress anew upon her little brother the absolute imperative that he remain within doors. It was hard for him, she knew. He was too young and energetic to accept this confinement easily. She'd talk to him when they got back, and maybe she could take him to Green Park, where he could run around, play with a ball, or bowl a hoop.

The liveried footman was standing to attention in the hall, and she had the impression he'd been standing like that for the entire hour she'd kept him waiting. She had a moment's guilt but dismissed it as he handed her into the carriage. It was his own master who was responsible. Sally climbed in after her, and the cumbersome vehicle started off.

"That'll be all, Father." Viscount Bradley waved an irritable hand at his father confessor. "You look as miserable as a nun in need of swiving."

The priest winced. "I must protest, my lord. Such language. You talk of the church, of our sisters, in such disrespectful terms . . . I don't know how much longer I can continue to serve you as your priest and confessor."

"Don't be absurd, man. I'm giving you the opportunity to reform the blackest heart in the most recalcitrant sinner it'll ever be your Christian misfortune to meet. Do your duty, Father. God will show his gratitude, I'm sure." The old man's laugh became a wheeze, and Father Cosgrove held a cup of water to his lips. "Not that, you crow!" The viscount dashed his hand away. "You'll kill me with that filthy stuff. Bring me a glass of cognac."

The priest did so. If it killed the old man quicker, he wouldn't be sorry. For a few minutes he didn't regret the ill thought, then resigned himself to doing penance for it later.

"Where is the girl?" Bradley said fretfully. "How long's it been since I sent for her?"

"Over an hour, my lord."

"So where is she?"

"Maybe she wasn't home, sir."

"Nonsense . . . where else would she be at ten in the morning? Whores don't leave their beds till noon."

Father Cosgrove closed his lips firmly. After a minute the viscount muttered, "Of course, she's m'nephew's mistress now, so maybe her habits have changed."

"No doubt, sir."

"Look out of the window. Is there any sign of the carriage?"

The priest went to the window, peering out into the street. "I see it, sir. Just drawing up."

"Good." Bradley settled back into his chair with his cognac. "When she comes in, you may leave. I'll spare you a whore's company. We don't want to endanger your immortal soul, now, do we?"

Father Cosgrove said nothing, but as soon as the footman announced Mistress Ordway, he slipped from the room as she stepped into it and curtsied to her host.

The viscount put up his glass and examined his visitor. "Hmm. My congratulations, Mistress Ordway."

"On what, sir?"

"On a remarkable transformation. Last time you were here, you looked the perfect whore . . . an unmistakable denizen of a nunnery. Whereas now, you have the appearance of . . ." He waved a hand.

"A mistress?" she inquired, her eyebrows

lifting. She came up to the fire.

He gave a crack of laughter. "Precisely, my dear. My nephew's mistress. Has he talked to you of marriage?"

Clarissa looked astounded. "Of marriage, sir? Men do not marry their mistresses."

"Oh, it has been done, believe me." He waved a hand again, this time to a low, armless chair on the other side of the fire. "Pray take a seat."

Clarissa did so, drawing off her gloves and folding her hands in her lap, regarding the viscount with an air of calm inquiry. "What was so urgent that you needed to see me, sir?"

"Who said it was urgent?"

"Forgive me, but it was certainly the impression I received."

"I wanted to see you, take another look at you."

"And now you have done so, if you'll excuse me, I'll be on my way." She made to rise, but he waved her down.

"Sit . . . sit, girl. I haven't finished yet." He frowned at her, bushy white eyebrows forming a crooked line across the bridge of his nose. "How long have you been whoring?"

Clarissa plaited her fingers in her lap as she considered her answer. "It was forced upon me, my lord, a year or so ago."

"Oh, how so?" He leaned forward to pick up his glass again.

Well, Clarissa reflected, the story that had done for the nephew would do just as well for the uncle. She told her tale, watching his reaction. At its end he only grunted, which left her wondering whether it had had any impact on him. At least he had no reason to disbelieve it. It was a common enough story.

"Bring me those papers." He gestured to the pile of closely written pages on the secretaire by the window.

Puzzled, Clarissa obeyed, handing him the sheaf before returning to her seat.

He riffled through them, a smile on his face now that she found chilling. Not only was it humorless, it radiated malice. "Ah, here it is." He leaned forward, holding out a few pages to her. "Read that, my dear. One of my fondest memories. I wonder if you've participated in such an amusing game yourself. Go on . . . read it. Read it aloud."

Clarissa, instantly on her guard, dropped her eyes to the first page. Slowly she realized what the old man was up to. She held a thoroughly obscene account of a sexual encounter he'd had with three women and a young boy, no details spared, and he was watching closely to see how she reacted. She read it to the end, allowing a small smile to touch her lips even as they formed some of the most vile words to describe the perversity of these sex acts. Then she looked up and laughed.

"You appear to have had a most amusing evening, my lord."

He looked at her through narrowed eyes. For a moment he appeared disconcerted and she felt a savage satisfaction. "It was, indeed. Those houris know exactly what pleases a man. Nothing is forbidden. They train them from children, you know. The boy there was only in his second year of training, but he was an adept student."

"It certainly appears so," she said with a placid smile, even as her stomach recoiled in revulsion. "Such a night makes the entertainment offered by Mother Griffiths seem rather tame by comparison."

"Oh, I daresay I could arrange such a spectacle for you, my dear. One in which you could participate if you were so inclined. There are several establishments in the Piazza where a man can request a tableaux vivant, offering any activity that appeals to him. Alas, my days of participation are long gone and I can only watch these days. But I still find such spectacles quite enchanting. Would you care to participate in such a one? You would find it well worth your while."

"As it happens, I might have something to say about that, sir."

They both turned to the door. Jasper stood there, his expression unreadable except for his black eyes, which were as hot as hell's own inferno. "Forgive me for disturbing your tete-à-tête." He came further into the room, his gaze sweeping over Clarissa, who sat still as stone, her face pale, her eyes fixed upon the viscount as she tried to conceal her overwhelming relief at this timely arrival.

After a moment, once she was sure she had herself well in hand, she said lightly, "Oh, his lordship has been entertaining me most amusingly, Jasper." She touched the pages in her lap. "Such daringly shameless adventures, you wouldn't believe."

"I'm sure I would. Give those to me." He took them from her lap and dropped them disdainfully onto the table beside his uncle. "I trust you've amused yourself adequately for one morning, sir."

His uncle gave a crack of laughter. "Oh, very much so, my boy. She's delightful, this whore of yours."

Clarissa rose from her chair. "If you have

no further need of me, my lord, I will take my leave. Did you see Sally downstairs, Lord Blackwater?"

"Yes, she's waiting. Let us go." He bowed her to the door, waiting until she was out of earshot on the stairs, before saying quietly over his shoulder, "Be careful you don't set too high a price, uncle."

The old man laughed again. "That's unlikely, dear boy. Besides, I was merely assuring myself that my conditions are being honestly met."

Jasper closed the door on the viscount's laughter and went down to the hall. Clarissa was very pale now, her hands shaking a little as she drew on her gloves. "Why does he so enjoy insulting me?"

"Oh, he enjoys insulting anyone who can't fight back." He looked closely at her. "You, I think, fought back."

"He didn't win, if that's what you mean."

"That's exactly what I mean. I doubt he'll trouble you again."

Clarissa shook her head. "I devoutly hope not. Come, Sally." She went to the door as the footman held it open. Jasper's curricle was in the street, his groom walking the horses slowly up and down in front of the house.

"Sally, I'm afraid you will have to walk

back with Tom." Jasper handed Clarissa into the curricle, then jumped up onto the box, taking the reins. "Let go their heads, Tom." The horses sprang forward. "A drive will blow the old man's devilment from your mind," he said lightly. "Unless you'd rather go straight home."

"No," she said swiftly. "I would very much like to air my mind; it feels like a cesspit."

He inclined his head in acknowledgment. "I can well believe it. My uncle is a lover of the midden, and always has been. But it behooves me to keep him sweet. The best revenge will be his fortune."

Clarissa wasn't sure that any revenge would be sufficient short of twisting a knife slowly in the evil old man's gut.

"There's to be a masquerade tonight at Ranelagh Gardens." Jasper turned his horses through the park gates. "Do you care to go? I have it in mind to make up a small party."

"Oh, yes, I've heard so much about the gardens, and the Chinese pavilion. But what does one wear to a masquerade?"

He glanced sideways at her. "Have you never been to a public ridotto before? It's one of the most popular trysting places for ladies of the night."

"This lady of the night has not had that pleasure," she responded a shade tartly.

"The opportunity has never come my way."

"Then we will remedy the situation," he said amiably. "You need a mask and a domino over your gown. The unmasking takes place at midnight. Of course, everyone knows who everyone is, but it's a harmless sport."

"I should like to go."

"Then so you shall. I'll bring the mask and domino when I come for you at ten o'clock tonight."

Clarissa nodded and returned to the subject uppermost in her mind, her interview with Lord Bradley. "Who told you where to find me this morning?"

"That young Frank gave me a very vivid description of the carriage which had taken you away. He sounded a little alarmed at being abandoned by both you and Sally, carried off in such an exotic vehicle." He gave her another sideways glance.

"He wanted to accompany us, but I considered it inappropriate," Clarissa said with perfect composure. "It's not surprising he should have been a little frightened if neither of us was there to protect him. He's still afraid the sweep will find him and take him away." There was a kernel of truth there, she told herself. They were both afraid that Luke would somehow find them.

Jasper nodded. "Well, he's a very observant child. He described the arms on the coach down to the last gilded leaf." He whistled to himself for a few minutes before saying, "Surprisingly for a sweep's boy, he seems to know his letters."

"Really?" Clarissa managed to sound incredulous. "I must ask him how he learned them."

"Mmm. I'd be interested in knowing the answer." He raised a hand in salute and bowed to two ladies in a landaulet coming towards them. He drew rein as they came abreast. "Lady Huffington . . . Lady Susan. How delightful to see you. Are you acquainted with Mistress Ordway?"

Clarissa bowed as Lady Huffington raised a quizzing glass and examined her rather rudely before giving her a stiff nod. Lady Susan, a young woman of timid manner, offered a shy smile and a quick duck of her head as Lord Blackwater bestowed a warm smile upon her.

"Don't be such a great gaby, girl," her mama scolded. "Bid his lordship a proper good morning. What will he think of you?"

Lady Susan flushed scarlet and looked ready to weep. "G . . . good morning, my lord."

Jasper bowed gravely. "It is certainly a

beautiful one. Good day to you, ma'am . . . Lady Susan." He flicked his whip and the horses moved on again.

"Is that one of the young ladies who's set her cap at you?" Clarissa inquired with interest.

"Her mother has certainly," he responded aridly.

"My presence hasn't changed that?"

"In general mistresses are not considered a barrier to marriage. These fond mamas will merely inform their daughters that they must expect their husbands to seek a certain amount of entertainment outside the marriage bed." His tone was sardonic, his eyes flat and humorless. He didn't look at all like the man Clarissa was accustomed to.

"What happens when you announce your engagement?"

"There will be no announcement. The first anyone will know of it will be an after-the-fact announcement of our marriage. At which point we'll retreat to my family estates in Northumberland."

Northumberland. It was the first Clarissa had heard of beating such a retreat. But it would be perfect. Luke would never find them there; it was a wild county, way up north. She and Francis would be perfectly safe up there until she gained her majority.

And then . . . then what?

"What's the matter?" He looked at her sharply. "What did I say to trouble you?"

"Nothing . . . only that . . . well, I didn't know we would be going so far from London."

That was not it at all, he thought with grim conviction. However, he said mildly, "But, my dear, we have to have a honeymoon. It is expected after all. And it will serve to put scandal to rest. Gossip cannot exist in a vacuum and if its objects are not around to furnish more choice morsels, then it dies a death."

"And when will the marriage be annulled? Before we come back to town, or after?"

"A matter for later discussion, I believe. We haven't solemnized the marriage yet, so it seems a moot point at this time."

"Yes," she agreed. "I suppose it does." Her tone was dull.

Jasper fought a silent battle with the increasingly frequent urge to shake the truth out of her. They drove once more around the park, responding to greetings, before he drove back to Half Moon Street, where Tom awaited him outside the house. "Miss Sally's gone in, ma'am." He helped Clarissa down from the curricle.

"Thank you." She glanced up at Jasper,

who was still in the curricle. "Are you not coming in?"

He shook his head. "I don't want to keep my horses standing in the cold." Ordinarily he would have sent them back to the mews with Tom and walked home himself later, but the abortive conversation in the park had exasperated him so much he wasn't sure he could trust himself not to let it infect the next few hours.

"Have I angered you in some way?" She could feel the discordance between them like the intimation of a coming thunderstorm in the air.

"Is there a reason why you should have?" He watched her face, saw the uncertainty flash across the jade eyes, and for a moment had a surge of hope, but it was short-lived.

"I will expect you this evening then?" Her smile couldn't conceal her disappointment.

The smile tugged at his heartstrings, but he wasn't ready to let go of his irritation just yet. Maybe an afternoon alone would provide her with some much-needed reflection. "At ten o'clock." He waited until she was admitted into the house before driving away.

Francis was waiting in the hall, hiding in the shadows of the staircase. "Where's the man?" he whispered, creeping out into the hall.

"He's taking his horses back to the stable. Why are you hiding there?"

"I didn't want him to see me if he came in with you." Francis hugged her knees. "Why did you go with Sally? I was frightened all alone."

"You weren't alone, love. Mistress Newby was here, and Sammy."

"They couldn't save me from Uncle Luke."

"Oh, I daresay Mistress Newby's very fierce with an iron skillet and a rolling pin."

That made him laugh, and she took him upstairs with her. Jasper would not return unexpectedly. He had been angry and she knew why. He knew she had secrets, and he wanted to hear them. And she couldn't bear angering him, any more than she could endure this lack of trust for much longer. Tonight, after the ridotto, when they were home in bed, in the dark, when she couldn't see his face, she would try to give him a little more of the truth. She couldn't risk the end of the charade completely. He must still believe that their marriage would fulfill his uncle's demand, but she could give him a little.

She realized that her brother was speaking

to her, tugging at her skirt. "What's the matter, 'Rissa?"

She shook herself out of her dismal reverie and turned her attention to the child. "You should really do some lessons, Francis." His education was being shamefully neglected, but there was little she could do about it. They had none of his schoolbooks with them. She sat him down on the window seat and gave him some arithmetic problems to solve as a sop to her conscience, then returned to the troublesome business of finishing her composition to Lawyer Danforth, which had been interrupted by her visitors the previous morning. How to reassure him without giving anything away? It was the devil's own task.

She finished it finally. It was not entirely satisfactory but it would have to do. She sanded the sheet, folded it, and sealed it, before writing the address, then she rang for Sally. "Could you take this to the post for me, Sally?"

Sally took the letter, asking in surprise, "You don't want his lordship to frank it for you, ma'am?"

"Oh, no, there's no need. The recipient will be happy to pay the postage," she responded with confidence. "I'd like it to catch the night mail."

"I'll send young Sammy. Fleet as the wind he is." Sally glanced curiously at Frank, sucking the end of his quill as he considered a problem. "What's he doing?"

"Sums. I was thinking we might send him to a dame school or something," Clarissa responded vaguely. "He seems a sharp lad; a little education might help him get on in the world."

Sally looked very doubtful, but it wasn't her place to argue. She took the letter and hurried to find Sammy.

CHAPTER TWENTY

Jasper entered Clarissa's bedchamber just before ten o'clock that evening. She turned on her dresser stool as he came in. She felt that familiar lurch in her belly at the sight of him, a swift racing in her blood. He was wearing a coat of dusky red silk edged with his favorite silver lace. Lace frothed at his throat and wrists, and for once he wore his hair fashionably powdered and fastened in a queue at his neck with an engraved silver clasp. His eyes looked blacker than ever, but they held a deep glow of intensity as he subjected her to a frankly appreciative scrutiny.

"My lord, I didn't realize you were here already." She smiled, immensely relieved that she could detect none of his earlier anger. "How handsome you look."

He tossed a parcel onto the bed. "Be so good as to unwrap that, Sally." He swept Clarissa a flourishing bow. "You are too kind, ma'am. I can only hope I will make a worthy escort for such a beautiful lady."

Clarissa laughed, screwing an enameled stud into her ear. "I am impervious to empty compliments, sir."

"Oh, believe me, there's nothing empty about them when made to you." He came up behind her. "Don't put those in. I have something else for you." He laid a square box on the dresser. "Open it," he prompted when she looked blankly between the box and then himself.

Clarissa lifted the lid. Her mouth opened on an O of wonderment. A pair of diamond studs nestled in the silken interior, with a diamond collar and a matching comb. She looked up at him. "What are these?"

"What do they look like?" He took out the collar and fastened it at her neck. The stones winked and flashed against her pale throat. "Fasten the studs."

She did not immediately comply, holding them on her palm. "They're so beautiful . . . so delicate. Whom do they belong to?"

"They will belong to my wife. They are traditionally the property of the Countess of Blackwater, passed on her death to the wife of the eldest son."

"I don't think I can wear them." Clarissa looked up at him, shaking her head. "Indeed, Jasper, it doesn't feel right."

"It is quite right, and you will wear them." He spoke firmly, taking the comb and inserting it in the plaited crown of her hair. "Fasten the studs now, I would see how they suit you."

Slowly she screwed them in place and gazed at her reflection in awe. The diamonds were magnificent stones, blue light seeming to pour from their depths. "What will people think?"

"Exactly what they're supposed to think." He turned to Sally, who had been observing the proceedings in wide-eyed silence. "Will you place the comb, Sally? I don't think I have it quite right."

"Yes, m'lord." Sally held the comb reverently. Nothing like this had ever adorned the head of her previous mistress. She inserted it with deft fingers, twisting clustered ringlets around her fingers to encourage them to curl more tightly. "Beautiful, madam," she breathed. "They could have been made for you."

Clarissa wondered if finally she had stepped way out of her depth. Her mother's jewelry collection contained some fine pieces, but none as magnificent as this set. She was accustomed to wearing the simplest of adornments herself, hence the enameled ear studs, and now she felt like a usurper.

"Stand up and let me look at you properly."

She did so, turning slowly to face him. Her gown was of gold tissue over a petticoat of celestial blue damask. The elbow-length sleeves ended in wide lace ruffles. The blue of the damask brought blue light dancing in the facets of the diamond collar, which in turn drew the eye to the ivory swell of her breasts over the low décolletage.

"It seems a pity to conceal such enchantment," Jasper murmured. "But a masquerade is a masquerade. Bring the domino here, Sally. Amazingly I chose the perfect color."

The domino was a rich blue silk fastened with pale blue ribbons down the front. The mask was dark blue velvet, concealing the upper part of her face. "How exotic," Clarissa murmured, forgetting her discomfort over the diamonds as she looked at her image. "What color is your domino?"

"Black, of course." He gestured to the garment on the bed. "Black as night. But the mask is gold." He laughed at her expression. "I can enter into the spirit of these games as well as anyone, my dear. Come, shall we go?" He offered her his arm.

His carriage was downstairs, furnished as

always with the comforting fur lap rugs and hot bricks. Ranelagh Gardens was a little out of London in the village of Chelsea and Clarissa felt an ordinary excitement at the prospect of the evening ahead. It was such a normal emotion it took her aback. She hadn't had an ordinary response to anything in months it seemed. But she felt just as Clarissa Astley would have done on her way to her first masquerade in the magical wonderland of Ranelagh Gardens. Except that Clarissa Astley would not have been decked out in a king's ransom of diamonds.

It was a chilly night, but braziers lined the gravel paths leading to the Rotunda and the Chinese pavilion. Lamps spilling golden light were strung between the trees, illuminating the scene in a soft glow. Light blazed from the buildings, from the supper boxes warmed by braziers overlooking the gardens and fountains. Masked people strolled the pathways in many-colored dominos, like a garden of butterflies, Clarissa thought, entranced. Strains of music filled the air. She looked at Jasper and saw that he was watching her expression with a strange look in his eye.

"What is it?"

"Nothing, except that your pleasure gives me pleasure."

She yearned to stop, to touch his face, to kiss his eyelids, to hold his body close. She yearned to tell him how she truly felt, how she loved him with every fiber of her being. For a moment there was a hesitation in his step, as if he sensed her need, as if he was waiting for something, and then when she said nothing, did nothing, he continued down the path, her arm firmly held in his.

"Where are your friends? You said you would be making up a party." It was not the question she wanted to ask. The words seemed as dull and leaden as a shovel of mud. But it was all she could trust herself to say.

"They'll be waiting for us in one of the boxes, where I have ordered supper. I hope it pleases you. Vauxhall is famous for its wafer-thin slices of ham, but at Ranelagh we have breast of pigeon in truffle sauce." His voice was light and inconsequential, as if that instant of intensity had never happened.

Clarissa was aware of a sense of loss, but that moment couldn't be repeated, and she told herself it was better this way, but she couldn't quite convince herself. They entered the Rotunda. The huge circular space was warmed by fireplaces, lit by thousands of candles, and the domino-clad butterflies circled to the music of the orchestra on a high dais.

"Do you care to dance, ma'am?" He offered his hand. The orchestra was playing a country dance and Clarissa's toes were already tapping.

She took his hand and he led her into the dance. Clarissa had loved to dance since she was a small child and for the half hour of this country dance she lost herself completely. All the terrors, the anxieties, the dreadful knowledge of her deception, the dreadful acknowledgment that that continued deception would eventually deprive her of the one thing that would ensure her happiness, faded into the background. Jasper was a worthy partner, light on his feet, sure of his steps, and he knew what every good partner knew, that his task was simply to enable his lady to show herself at her best.

When the music died Clarissa took a moment to catch her breath, fanning herself. "Thank you, it's been a long time since I've danced like that."

Jasper wondered how long it would take her to realize what she had said, what she had revealed. He tried to tell himself that her guard kept slipping because trust was simply seeping in, like the first trickle of water through a pinhole in a Dutch dike. If he was patient, soon it would swamp the low ground and her defenses would finally crumble. Unless, of course, that was pure wishful thinking, which, knowing this woman as he was beginning to, struck him as not unlikely.

He pushed the grim reflection aside. "Shall we go to the supper box now? I think you will enjoy the company. I have invited my brothers, and several others whom you've met. You may not have met all the ladies, but I think you will find them congenial."

The supper box was warmed with a brazier, serviced by liveried footmen, and entertained by a small group of musicians. Three couples were seated at the round table, sipping champagne; Jasper's two brothers strolled up just as Jasper and Clarissa entered the box.

"Well met, Mistress Ordway." Sebastian bowed. "It is I, Sebastian . . . should you not recognize me in this disguise."

"Mask and domino or not, I would recognize you as either yourself or your brother," she said with a smile. "So, as usual, sir, I am grateful for the early identification." She turned to his companion with a curtsy. "Good evening, sir. The Honorable Peregrine, I presume."

Peregrine for a moment said nothing, his gaze fixed upon the diamonds sparkling in the candlelight. Then he recovered, bowed over her hand. "Just so, Mistress Ordway."

Clarissa curtsied and murmured greetings to the rest of the assembled company, and they sat down for supper. She found herself between the twins. "So, have you set the date, Miss Ordway?" Peregrine asked.

"I don't understand. What date?" Once again she was back in the world that governed her. She tried a smile over her wineglass.

"You happen to be wearing the Blackwater diamonds," Sebastian said with a lazy grin. "And damme, how they suit you. Could have been made for you. Thing is, Jasper wouldn't have given 'em to you if he didn't intend to pop the question."

She took a sip of wine and considered her answer. These two weren't supposed to know that she knew all there was to know and was a willing participant. It would be simpler if she could just admit it and they could enjoy each other's company without all this subterfuge. But Jasper had decreed secrecy, so secrecy it would be.

"Your brother has not made me an offer, gentlemen. Or perhaps I should say, he has not made me an offer of marriage." She smiled at them both. "It probably pleased him to set tongues wagging with the diamonds. You know how much he enjoys a game . . . they will be returned to the vault in the morning, I'm sure."

"He does enjoy playing people for fools," Peregrine said doubtfully. He met his twin's quelling eye and fell silent. It would seem that Jasper had not progressed as far as they'd thought with turning his whore into a wife.

"I think we should dispense with this formality," Sebastian announced, lifting his glass in a toast. "You're in some part family, so I intend to call you Clarissa. You shall call me Seb . . . or Sebastian if you insist. And on your other side is Perry . . . or Peregrine if you insist."

"It will be my pleasure, Sebastian." Clarissa lifted her own glass. "Peregrine." She drank to the man on her other side.

Jasper was a little surprised to find how much it pleased him to see the way his brothers and Clarissa seemed to enjoy each other. He hadn't thought he cared much one way or the other about his brothers' opinions of his own life, but now it seemed that he did. His younger brothers were important to him, their well-being something he had always looked out for as a simple matter of fact and family.

On the death of their father he'd somehow assumed in their eyes the role of protector and authority on all matters of importance. Their mother had been their nominal guardian but, always ailing, had had little or nothing to do with the day-to-day upbringing of her sons. Jasper managed to haul himself to adulthood, but he nurtured his brothers and ensured they had as near to a normal boyhood as was possible.

They'd followed him to Harrow when he was in his final year there and he'd made sure they were protected from much of the gratuitous violence that was unilaterally doled out to the young newcomers. He'd had to fight his own battles, and for the most part had won them, and he now used that dominion within the strict and brutal hierarchy to cloak his brothers until they were good and ready to look after themselves.

They'd responded by according him absolute loyalty, respect, and an affection he knew he could not endure to see diminished.

"We should go to the Rotunda for the midnight unmasking," the Honorable Percy Sutton declared as fireworks began to light up the sky. He reached for his mask, which, like the others, he had discarded as they sat down to supper.

"Allow me." Jasper tied Clarissa's mask for her before tying his own. "Are you ready for the grand finale, my dear?"

She nodded, rising to her feet. "Indeed, sir, I'm eager for it." The group spilled out of the box and onto the gravel walk leading to the Rotunda. Fireworks exploded around them, brightly colored lights whirling, swirling, dancing, then falling from the sky.

Jasper tucked Clarissa's hand into his arm as they joined the stream of people entering the Rotunda. The orchestra was playing one of the fashionable French dances and couples joined the thronged floor as they came into the Rotunda. They slipped into the line of dance just as every light was extinguished and the space was plunged into blackness. There was a moment of disorientation when Clarissa reached for Jasper. Her hand encountered a sleeve that felt unfamiliar. She turned in the darkness, people pressing on her from all sides, their breath permeating the darkness, and then the torches were lit again and light flooded the space as laughing people untied their masks and those of anyone close enough to them.

Clarissa felt someone's fingers on the ties

of her mask, assumed it was Jasper, and when the mask was lifted from her eyes found herself laughing into an unknown face. "Oh, forgive me . . . I thought you were my escort."

She turned, looking around for Jasper or one of her own group, and stared straight into Luke's cold brown orbs. Her uncle was standing about ten feet from her, his own mask hanging from his fingers. He looked at her. Incredulity was chased by rage. He took a step towards her, his hands reaching for her. She turned to run and found herself up against Jasper's chest.

He looked at her expression and said swiftly, "There's no need to panic, I know it's bewildering for a moment. Come, we'll get out of this crowd." He swept her ahead of him in an encircling arm and somehow carved a path through the throng out into the cold night air.

Clarissa looked over her shoulder. She could see no sign of Luke. He must be lost in the mass of people behind them. She should never have agreed to attend such a public event when she'd be mingling at close quarters with half of London. At the theatre, or the opera, she was insulated in a box, far enough away from ordinary folk in the pit, but even that she now realized had been an unacceptable risk.

She looked over her shoulder again. Still no sign of him. She had a sudden wild hope that if they could get out of there without his seeing them again, maybe he wouldn't be certain he had seen her in that instant when the lamps were relit. Everyone was confused, dazzled by the sudden illumination.

She was too busy looking over her shoulder to watch where she was going and her foot caught on a stone. She stumbled and would have fallen if Jasper hadn't caught her up. "Steady now. Did you have too much champagne?"

"Maybe," Clarissa said. "I was enjoying myself so much I might not have noticed how many glasses I had."

"Well, the carriage is under the trees. We'll have you home and in bed in no time." The words were a caress, a promise, weighted with desire, but for once Clarissa couldn't match them. She glanced over her shoulder yet again. There were people following them down the lit path. Still no sign of Luke.

Jasper handed her into the carriage, and she shrank into a far corner away from the lighted window. She told herself again that Luke could never be sure he had really seen her as long as he didn't see her again, but she knew she was fooling herself. She'd seen the look on his face when he'd looked at her. He had known exactly who she was, regardless of diamonds and domino. Would he know how to find her?

A great black cloud of dread enveloped her, and even as she forced herself to respond to the slight pressure on her shoulder and turned into Jasper's embrace, she knew it would be a constant companion until she could get her little brother out of London.

Luke, lost in the crowd, moved with its flow, managing to keep the blue domino in his sights. Who was the black domino? He couldn't see the man's face, only the back of his head. His clothing was covered by the plain black domino. Whoever he was, he had a very possessive arm around Clarissa. He watched them climb into a closed carriage and he ducked through the crowd to see the coat of arms on the panel.

He frowned, trying to identify the insignia. And then it came to him. They were the arms of the Earl of Blackwater. *What was Clarissa doing with an earl?* It was ridiculous, insane even. Had he really seen her? But that hair was unmistakable, made even more dramatic by the glint of diamonds. And unless they were fakes, his niece had been loaded with a king's ransom of gems. It beggared belief. It was too fantastic. What had happened to her in the weeks since she'd disappeared?

He stood immobile, staring after the carriage, heedless of the crowd bubbling around him. "There you are, Luke. We lost you at the unmasking." A man with a raddled complexion and heavy-lidded eyes hailed him, pushing his way through the crowd. His scarlet domino hung open over a substantial belly. "What's the matter with you? Look like you've seen a ghost." He swayed slightly on his feet, and his gaze was unfocused.

"I thought I saw someone I know," Luke said, frowning. "But in this rabble it's hard to be sure."

"Rabble's the word." The man looked around disdainfully. "Not a decent doxy amongst 'em. Time was, a public ridotto would be crawlin' with 'em, ready and eager for a tumble. Couldn't find nary a one tonight."

Luke shrugged. "If it's a harlot you want, let's visit the Piazza. Where are the others?"

"Lost 'em too." The corpulent gentleman pursed his lips and hailed a hackney from the line of waiting carriages. "Come on, Ast-

483

ley. I'm in need of brandy and a woman, not necessarily in that order."

Luke followed him into the carriage. "D'you know anything of Blackwater, Arnet?" He pulled the door to behind him and sat in the near corner, nervously pushing a thumbnail between his front teeth.

"The Sullivan family, you mean? Jasper Sullivan's the fifth earl. A bit high in the instep for the likes of us, my friend. Why d'you ask?"

"No particular reason. I just happened to see him get into his carriage. He was with a woman."

Arnet nodded sagely. "That'll be his new mistress. I heard tell he'd finished with the Mallory woman; she got a little too friendly with Henry Lassiter. Blackwater set up a new gal in that cozy little house of his on Half Moon Street. Saw her at the opera the other night. Quite a striking redhead. Not in the usual way at all."

So he hadn't been mistaken. Luke settled back into his corner and smiled grimly in the swaying darkness. Half Moon Street. If Clarissa was there, surely she would have Francis with her. He could go there and remove them both with the full force of the law. Clarissa might be the mistress of an earl, but she was first and foremost his own

484

ward, subject to his authority in every way. He could get a signed warrant from a Justice of the Peace and take a representative of the watch to enforce the law. Not even the Earl of Blackwater could gainsay him.

But did he want to tangle with such a powerful member of Society? The Earl of Blackwater could make life very unpleasant for Master Luke Astley if he so chose. Maybe the straightforward approach was not the best.

"It's very mortifying, but I don't seem to be holding your attention." Jasper raised his head from between her thighs and looked at Clarissa with a quizzical frown. "Why are you distracted, Clarissa? You're jangling like an out-of-tune pianoforte."

"I'm not," she denied. "Please don't stop." She reached down to twine her fingers into his hair.

He circled her wrist with his fingers and firmly removed her hand, then came up the bed to lie beside her. His eyes were filled with concern as he examined her averted countenance. He could feel her distress almost as if she were in physical pain. "What is it, my love?"

The endearment brought a lump to her throat. It was the first time he had ever used the term, and he didn't seem aware that he had spoken it now. She longed to give it back to him, to show him how it warmed her with the deepest pleasure, but all she could manage was a tight smile. "I think I must have had too much champagne. I feel a little strange."

"Ah." He rolled onto his back, gazing up at the embroidered tester. A nugget of cold anger began to expand deep inside him. "I can't dispute that, of course. But I have to tell you, I don't find it convincing. However, if you won't tell me the truth, there's really nothing I can do." He sat up. "I'll leave you to sleep and hope that you feel better in the morning."

"No, don't go . . . please, Jasper." His voice was cold, the words clipped, and it frightened her. She put out a hand to him as he got off the bed. "Couldn't we just sleep tonight? I like to feel you beside me while I sleep."

He stood naked beside the bed, staring down at her, his jaw set. Anger flickered in the dark gaze. It had gone far enough and he could no longer keep up the pretense. She was edging deeper and deeper into his heart, and he was getting nothing back. How long could she go on assuming that he didn't know she was lying to him, had been

486

lying to him from the first moment they met? He just didn't know why.

She offered him a cajoling smile, and his anger became cold steel. He didn't want the bit of her she was willing to share, he wanted all of her, and if she wouldn't give him that, he wanted none of her. He shook his head. "I wish you'd stop playing me for a fool, Clarissa."

"I . . . I'm not," she stammered, taken aback. "I . . . I don't know what you mean, Jasper."

"Oh, I think you do." He bent and flicked the covers back over her naked body, then turned away, dressing swiftly.

Clarissa looked at him helplessly, tears pricking behind her eyes. He was going to leave her like this, and she didn't know how to stop him. She knew he wanted more from her, and she had been intending to give it to him that night, but that had been before Luke had seen her. Now she could take no risks. Even if the risk was minuscule, she dared not take it. She had to play this through; it was the only hope of keeping free of Luke.

Dressed, he came back to the bed and stood looking down at her again. "Very well, we'll play this your way. Bear in mind that I have paid, and paid well, for your services.

But your confidence was never part of the contract, and I accept that. We will go through with the marriage, as agreed, but you need have no fear that I will burden you unnecessarily with my presence. After a certain interval, I will arrange for the annulment and you'll be free to go anywhere you wish. Until that time, it will suit us both if as you once requested you continue to act as my mistress without taking on any of the more intimate aspects of the role. Sleep well; I trust you'll feel better in the morning." He turned on his heel and left the chamber.

Clarissa lay immobile, paralyzed by shock, unable to grasp what had just happened . . . the suddenness of his fury, the bitter cold of his anger. Even the dread that had filled her since she'd seen Luke was diminished by the dreadful knowledge of what she had just lost.

Jasper let himself out of the house, closing the door softly behind him, resisting the childish urge to bang it loudly. His patience had quite suddenly and without any warning finally snapped. He was deeply wounded and frustrated both by Clarissa's lack of confidence in him and by the fact that she could continue to use him for whatever purpose of her own, even when he knew she understood that their liaison had gone way beyond a simple practical contract that benefited them both. But he also knew that, despite his own hurt, he should not have spoken to her in such a manner. He could see her jade eyes widening with pain and bewilderment throughout his nasty little speech, but he hadn't been able to help himself; the words had just spoken themselves. Even now, despite his remorse, he was still angry, frustrated beyond bearing with her obstinacy. *Why wouldn't she trust him?*

He walked quickly through the cold night, hoping to clear his head, cool his temper, return to his customary rational self. But he was still bitter, still angry when he entered his own house, and when he awoke in the morning he was still determined to leave Clarissa to her own reflections for a while.

CHAPTER TWENTY-ONE

Clarissa slept fitfully and awoke with a dull headache and aching limbs. She wanted nothing so much as to stay curled up under the quilt and let the day go on without her, but when Sally came in with her hot chocolate she forced herself to sit up.

"It's a beautiful day, ma'am." Sally pulled back the curtains, letting in pale November sunlight. "Cold and crisp . . . bit of night frost. What gown will you wear?"

"Anything suitable for walking." Clarissa sipped her chocolate. "I'll need you to accompany me, Sally." At some point in the long and restless night she had come to a conclusion. There was only one way out of the present morass. Nothing was more important than her brother's safety; her own concerns must take second place. Francis would not be safe until her marriage to Jasper was solemnized and they were on their way to Northumberland. Of course she'd have to find a way to convince Jasper that they needed to take the child with them, but something would come to her.

That difficulty was minor compared with the present problem of how to persuade Jasper of the need for haste after the night's dreadful confrontation. Even before that, he hadn't seemed to be in too much of a hurry for a wedding. Indeed, if he so wished, he could wait until his brothers had taken their own wives, since their uncle's fortune would be shared only if they all fulfilled the terms of the will before the old man's death.

"Send Frank up to me, Sally," she asked as the abigail finished doing her hair. "I want to talk to him before we leave. Oh, before you go, I'll wear that blue silk hat with the veil."

"Aye, madam." Sally lifted the hat out of its box, turning it on her hand with an admiring look. "Right pretty this is. The veil's a nice touch. He's such a bundle of energy, that boy. He needs to run it off before he gets into any more mischief. Mistress Newby was at her wits' end yesterday with those two lads, egging each other on. 'Tis only natural with youngsters like that; if they don't have enough to do, they get up to all sorts." Sally tutted, shaking her head, and hurried away.

Clarissa had noticed her little brother's restlessness. At home in Kent, apart from the few necessary hours he spent in the vicarage schoolroom, he was never still, running around outside, roaming the estate, haunting the stables, perfectly at home in every tenant's cottage, where he was a great favorite. It was really not fair to keep such an active ten-year-old confined within doors indefinitely. Some compromise had to be reached.

Francis burst unceremoniously into his sister's bedchamber just as she'd reached this conclusion. "Sally said you wanted me, 'Rissa."

"Yes, I did." She turned on the dresser stool and held out her arms to him. She had to put him on his guard without scaring him too much. "Listen to me carefully, love. I think Luke may have seen me last night . . . no, it's all right, don't look so scared. He doesn't know where we are, but we have to be extra careful for the next few days. You understand?"

The child nodded vigorously, his eyes still wide with fear. "I'll never go outside . . . *never*. Not even in the yard with Sammy."

She smiled. "I think you'll be safe enough in the yard, but nowhere else without me." He was beginning to fill out since his rescue from Wapping and she could feel his restless energy as a palpable force in the wiry frame. "I have to go out in a minute, but when I get back we'll go for a walk in the park." It would be safe enough. The last place they would run into their uncle would be strolling decorously through Green Park. It was a place for children and their nursemaids, not men-about-town.

"All right." Francis nodded. "Can I take a ball?"

"If you have one."

"We found one in the shed in the yard."

"We'll go when I get back." She stood up and reached for her pelisse. "Try not to plague Mistress Newby while I'm gone."

He grinned at her and her heart turned over. He was almost back to his old self. She sent him back to the kitchen and adjusted the veil of her hat before going downstairs. It concealed the upper part of her face quite adequately, completely covered her hair, and made her feel less vulnerable.

It was quite a short walk to Upper Brook Street. She walked briskly, her eyes darting from side to side beneath the veil. There were plenty of people on the street, all hurrying about their business, no one taking any notice of anyone else. Sally struggled a little to keep pace with her and was quite breathless when they reached the handsome façade of Blackwater House.

Clarissa began to have doubts even as she raised a hand to the door knocker. Perhaps he would refuse to see her. Or perhaps he would assume she had come to make everything right, to pour out her soul to him. But she couldn't do that. She was into this deception way too deep to wade out of it with a simple confession. She wouldn't blame him in the least if, once he knew how she had used him, he canceled their agreement out of hand. Until Francis was safe from Luke, this miserable estrangement would have to continue.

Resolutely she lifted the lion's head and let it fall with a bang. The door opened within a few minutes and Jasper's butler regarded the visitor with a look of surprise. It was early for morning callers, even of the mistress variety. Clarissa smiled, relieved that she remembered his name. "Good morning, Crofton. Is his lordship at home?"

"I believe so, ma'am. But I don't know if he's receiving visitors as yet."

"Then perhaps you'd be good enough to ask him if he would receive Mistress Ordway." She stepped past him into the hall and Sally scooted up behind her.

"If you'd wait in the library, ma'am . . ." Crofton opened the door to the room. "Your abigail can remain in the hall."

Sally sat down placidly on a bench along one wall as Clarissa entered the library. It was the same shabbily cozy room she remembered, with an inviting bright fire in the grate. Her gaze fell on the sofa where he had first kissed her properly and the memory filled her with longing. Would they ever be so close again? Would he even receive her? She didn't think she could bear another angry attack, when all she wanted was to put her arms around him, press her lips to his, tease him to the peak of desire as she knew so well how to do.

Jasper was finishing dressing when Crofton announced his visitor. He felt a surge of hope. Was she finally ready to tell him the truth? To open herself to him? Why else would she be here after last night?

"I'll be down directly, Crofton. Bring coffee to the library." He slipped his arms into his coat and went downstairs, trying to conceal his eagerness. He crossed the hall and entered the library.

Clarissa was standing in front of the fire, facing the door. Her face was pale but resolute and Jasper felt his hopeful eagerness fade. She was not there to make things right between them.

"You choose an early hour for visiting, ma'am." His voice was cool and dry. "To what do I owe the unexpected pleasure?"

It was worse than she'd expected. In the face of that glacial chill, Clarissa felt the words clog her throat. His black gaze was impenetrable, with not the faintest remnant of the amused warmth she was so accustomed to. His fine mouth was set in a humorless line. But she couldn't break down. If this was how it was to be, then so be it. All she needed was the marriage that would bring her the protection of the Earl of Blackwater and a journey to Northumberland. Just the bare bones of the contract agreed between them.

"I thought, in view of the way matters are between us, my lord, that we should hasten the day of our marriage."

He flipped the lid of a small Buhl snuffbox and took a leisurely pinch. "Indeed . . . in view of the way matters are between us . . . Mmm." He dropped the snuffbox back into the deep pocket of his coat. "Well, let us see how those matters stand."

She could bear it no longer. "Oh, please, Jasper. Don't make things so difficult. You need this marriage, and I need what it will give me." Which was perfectly true, although what it would give her was not what had been offered. "What point is there in delaying something that benefits us equally?"

He said nothing, merely rocked slightly on his heels, regarding her meditatively. "Equally?" he murmured with a faint question mark.

"Last night, you said that you would insist only on the original terms of our contract. As you pointed out, you have paid handsomely for my part in this charade. I am merely asking that we complete it soon, since prolonging the process is not giving us any pleasure."

He raised an eyebrow. "It has given *me* a considerable amount of pleasure on occasion."

She felt herself blush. "And it has me, too. As you well know, my lord. But for some reason that isn't happening anymore, so I would be grateful if we could complete the terms of the contract and go our separate ways."

Never would she have thought herself capable of such an impassioned lie so absolutely against her own will. But it was said, and she saw anger, then disdain, cross his face. "Your arguments are unimpeachable, madam. I will make the necessary arrangements as soon as possible and will escort you to Blackwater Manor in Northumberland, where I must insist you remain for a minimum of six months."

"And you?" Her voice was quiet.

He gave a short crack of derisive laughter. "As I said last night, you may rest assured I will not burden you with my presence, Mistress Ordway." He turned as Crofton came in with a tray of coffee. "Mistress Ordway is leaving, Crofton."

The butler concealed his surprise and curiosity with a bow of acknowledgment. The mistress, it seemed, had seriously offended his lordship. The earl was rarely angry, but there was no mistaking the controlled rage consuming him now. Crofton opened the library door for the lady, who walked straight past him, head up, her eyes fixed ahead.

The abigail jumped up as they entered the hall. "Are we leaving, ma'am?"

"Yes, Sally." Clarissa tapped her foot as the butler opened the door, then she sailed through it with a murmured "Thank you, Crofton."

She walked fast enough for Sally to have to trot to keep up with her. She was furious herself now. Furious with Jasper for treating her with such disdain, for embarrassing her in front of his servant. And furious with herself for getting herself into this convoluted mess. Lies bred like rabbits, it seemed, and she began to wonder if she would ever be able to untangle her tongue sufficiently to start telling the truth again once it was possible.

Luke found the house on Half Moon Street with little difficulty. It was a small street and one inquiry brought him the information he sought. He stood in a narrow alley leading to a mews opposite the earl's house. There were windows on the ground floor to one side of the front door, but an attempt to enter the house through them would easily be witnessed by the houses opposite. The back of the house would presumably be reached by an alley further up the street, similar to the one he stood in now. It would lead behind the houses to the mews. But the idea of breaking, entering, and abducting didn't strike him as particularly feasible. Too noisy for a start, and Clarissa would certainly put up a fight.

He was debating various possibilities when two women came up the street on the opposite side. One of them wore a fur pelisse and an elegant little hat with a spotted veil. The other he guessed was her maid. When they stopped at the earl's door, he pressed back against the alley wall. It had to be Clarissa and an abigail. She had to have Francis in the house with her. She wouldn't have let him out of her sight once she'd snatched him from the baby farmer.

The door closed behind them and Luke remained where he was, tapping his teeth with a fingernail as he considered his next move. In a few minutes the door opened again and Clarissa emerged with her brother, who was bouncing a ball and jumping up and down with excitement. Clarissa took his hand firmly and they walked off in the direction of Piccadilly.

Luke smiled. He had them both now. All he needed was a plan to scoop them up. He waited until they had reached Piccadilly at the end of the street, then walked quickly after them, keeping a good distance back, losing himself in clumps of pedestrians. He reached Piccadilly and caught sight of them across the busy thoroughfare entering Green Park. He didn't follow them. He would be too conspicuous among the nursemaids and their charges frolicking among the bushes and around the pond.

He walked along Piccadilly and hailed a hackney.

■ ■ ■ ■

Clarissa found some tranquillity watching her brother kicking his ball across the grass, running along the pathways, his still-thin cheeks red with cold and exertion. He'd stopped at the pond and watched enviously as two boys played with a wooden boat, pushing it into the pond with sticks.

"Next time, can Sammy come too, 'Rissa?"

"Maybe," she said vaguely. "We'll have to see. It depends on whether Mistress Newby needs him."

Francis nodded and jumped gleefully into a pile of crisp brown leaves, carefully assembled by one of the gardeners. Clarissa smiled and strolled along the path, her eyes ever watchful beneath her veil. It was impossible to imagine Luke here, but she wasn't going to drop her guard for an instant.

She let Francis play for an hour and then called him. "We must go home now, love. It's nearly noon." She smiled fondly. "Aren't you hungry?"

"Starving," he responded, taking her hand and prancing along beside her. "Mistress Newby promised to make apple fritters."

"Then we should hurry." She held his

hand tightly as they crossed Piccadilly, dodging a brewer's dray piled high with beer kegs.

Francis, who, until his uncle had removed him from his own home, had never ventured into a town bigger than Sevenoaks, gazed in wide-eyed fascination at the scene surging around him. Carts, horses, carriages, vendors pushing carts shouting their wares, stray dogs dodging between carriage wheels.

"Can we come out again, 'Rissa?"

"Yes, we'll try to take a walk every day." She turned onto Half Moon Street. A hackney was parked on the opposite side of the street from the house; the two horses between the shafts stood with their heads down, a picture of melancholy.

The carriage began to move as Clarissa and her brother approached. She watched it warily but it was just an ordinary hackney. The horses lifted their heads as the driver cracked his whip and they pulled the carriage into the middle of the narrow street an instant before Clarissa and Francis reached their own front door.

It happened so quickly that Clarissa could never remember the exact sequence of events. The door of the hackney opened with sudden violence just as they were abreast of the vehicle, knocking her sideways against the wall of the house. She hit her head and for a moment saw stars, then she heard Francis scream. Rough hands grabbed her upper arms and dragged her bodily into the carriage. She fell to her knees on the floor as the hackney started moving with a jerk.

She looked up, stunned and bewildered. She could hear Francis whimpering but for a moment she could see only her uncle sitting on the seat opposite, his arms folded, regarding her with a thin smile.

Clarissa struggled up from the floor of the hackney and sat down on the bench next to Francis, who was cowering in a corner. She looked at her uncle. "You'll pay for this."

He reached over and with a leisurely movement gave her a backhanded slap across the face. "Oh, I doubt that, Clarissa. You and your brother are my wards. I have the legal authority to do anything I wish with either of you. If I took you before a judge and laid a charge against you that you had abducted my ward, you would find yourself picking hemp in Bridewell. As it is . . ." He smiled. "I have another solution for you . . . a much neater one."

Clarissa felt cold. Her face burned and she could taste blood from the corner of her mouth where his ring had cut. She touched the lump on her head where she had hit the wall. Francis was still whimpering softly. She reached for him, drawing him against her breast, stroking his face. The child mustn't know she was afraid. She had to ignore her hurts and somehow defy Luke, if only with her manner. But she couldn't ignore her terror at Luke's cold satisfaction, his absolute confidence that nothing would prevent him now.

She glanced at the door, wondering if she could fling it open and tumble out with Francis held tight against her. But she knew it wasn't possible. They'd probably fall beneath the carriage wheels and solve Luke's problems themselves.

She leaned back, still stroking her brother's hair, closing her eyes as if she had not a care in the world. Until the hackney lurched to a stop.

Luke leaned forward and Francis cried out. His uncle held a knife. He hauled Francis out of his sister's embrace and held him with an arm around his throat, the knife pricking behind the child's ear. "Step down, Clarissa, and stand quite still."

She didn't need him to amplify his threat. Francis had stopped whimpering and, dry eyed, looked at his sister in shocked inquiry, the tip of the knife pricking his skin. She gave him what she hoped was a reassuring smile and obeyed her uncle's instructions, stepping down from the hackney to the street. They were outside Luke's house on Ludgate Hill.

Luke descended, Francis held against his chest, the knife still pressed against the soft vulnerable point behind his ear. "Go up to the door and knock."

Clarissa obeyed. Every instinct screamed that all would be lost if they went into the house and that door closed behind them, but she could see no way out. Not while Luke held the knife to the child's neck. The door opened and with a sense of dread inevitability she stepped into a narrow, musty-smelling hall.

Luke and Francis came in behind her and the door closed. The only natural light in the hall came from a fan-shaped window above the door. She looked around, trying to fix her surroundings in her mind.

"Upstairs." Luke jerked his head to the narrow flight of stairs and Clarissa went up them, Luke pushing Francis behind her. At the top he directed them to a further flight, which took them into the attics. He told her to open a door, which led into a garret bedchamber of sorts. Poorly furnished, uncarpeted, with only a bed, a broken dresser, and a stained chamber pot sticking out carelessly from beneath the bed, it was bitterly cold, with wind gusting through an ill-fitting window.

Luke released Francis and pushed him down onto the bed, then he turned back to the door. "You'll remain in here while I arrange your future accommodations." He smiled at Clarissa. "I have the perfect solution for you, my meddling niece, but it will take me a few hours to put in place. Until then, I trust you'll be comfortable." He went out, closing the door, and the key grated in the lock.

Francis looked dry eyed at his sister. A bead of blood stood out against the white skin behind his ear. "What will he do?"

Clarissa forced a smile. "We'll have to wait and see, love." She went to the tiny window. It looked down on a narrow alley three floors below. She could see no drainpipe, no hand- or foothold. There was no way out there.

She turned back to her brother. Sitting beside him, she drew him tight against her, rocking him until after a while he fell into an exhausted sleep, his head in her lap. She stroked his hair and stared sightlessly into the middle distance, for once in her life unable to think of any way out of her situation. Bleakly she wondered what Jasper would think when he discovered she'd gone. He'd never find her, probably wouldn't even bother to look. Of course, if she'd confided in him . . .

CHAPTER TWENTY-TWO

Lawyer Danforth was at his breakfast when his servant brought in the mail. "This come on the night mail from London, sir. Cost threepence postage." He laid a letter on the table. "Can I fetch you another kipper, sir; Cook says she's got two more on the go if you'd like 'em."

"And exceptional kippers they are," the lawyer said, rubbing his hands with a beaming smile. "Thank Cook, and tell her I'd be glad of another one."

He picked up the letter beside his plate and instantly his gaze sharpened. The writing was Clarissa's distinctive script. He had almost given up hope of hearing from her and had assumed that Luke had tracked them down on the road from London; presumably an accident to the carriage had delayed them. It happened often enough on the rough roads. With a sense of foreboding that he couldn't quite explain, he took a knife and slit the wafer, unfolding the single, closely written sheet.

A frown darkened his customarily cheery countenance as he tried to make sense of what Clarissa had written. There was no mention of an aborted journey home with her supposedly homesick brother, no explanation for Luke's search for them. She wrote that instead of staying with her uncle, she had moved into a lodging house on Half Moon Street with a most respectable landlady. Luke's house was too small to accommodate both her and her brother comfortably, and since she wished to remain close to Francis, at least until he was properly settled, this seemed like a good arrangement. The tutor's family hadn't proved suitable for her brother — he had found it hard to make friends with the other children — so he had returned to his uncle's house. They were both well, and she was enjoying London. Her quarterly allowance was sufficient for her present expenses. And she had signed off with all the customary respectful greetings.

The lawyer set the letter aside and turned his attention to dissecting his newly arrived kippers. The delicate activity helped to order his thoughts. After a few moments he rang the handbell beside his plate. "Send to the

stables for my horse, Paul," he instructed
the servant when he arrived in answer to
the summons.

A meticulous man, he finished his breakfast to the last mouthful before draining his
ale tankard, tucking the letter into the
pocket of his waistcoat, and leaving the
table. He collected his hat, whip, and gloves
from the hall and went out to his horse,
which was waiting for him outside the front
door.

It was a brisk, sunny winter morning but
he took little pleasure in it, barely acknowl-
edging the greetings of those he passed as
he rode through the village. He drew rein
outside a substantial redbrick house on the
opposite side of the village. His old friend
Doctor Alsop was deadheading a bush of
late-flowering camellias as Danforth rode
up the drive.

"What brings you so early, George?" John
Alsop waved his pruning shears. "Nothing
wrong, I trust."

"I don't know, John." The lawyer dismounted, tethering his horse to the post at
the door. "A letter from Clarissa . . . rather
a curious missive. I'd like you to take a
look."

"A letter at last . . . thank God for that."
Doctor Alsop hurried to the door ahead of

his friend, stamping his feet on the mat before entering the hall. A fire burned in the grate, and the air smelled of beeswax and potpourri. "Ah, Eleanor, my dear." He greeted his wife, who emerged from the kitchen regions just as they entered the house. "George has come on business concerning Clarissa. At last the girl has written."

"Oh, I've been so worried," his wife said, patting her plump bosom in agitation. "What does she say, John?"

"All in good time, my dear. We'll go into my office. Would you send in some coffee . . . or . . ." John cast a professional eye over his visitor. "Perhaps something stronger would be in order . . . something to keep out the cold?"

He ushered his friend into his office. "A glass of this fine port should do the trick. A bottle from our dear departed friend's cellars. He gave me six for Christmas last year, and I've been drinking them sparingly, savoring every drop." He poured two glasses. "To Francis, may he rest in peace."

Both men drank the toast, then the lawyer drew Clarissa's letter out of his waistcoat pocket and laid it on the mahogany desk, smoothing out the crease. "This arrived by the night mail this morning. What d'ye think of it?"

The doctor put on his pince-nez and read the script. "A lodging house? What the devil's the girl doing in a lodging house? Francis must be turning in his grave."

"My thoughts exactly. This Half Moon Street . . . it's a respectable enough part of town but not given to lodging houses, I would have thought."

"Maybe Astley found it for her. He is her guardian, after all. He'd not willingly see his ward in less than respectable circumstances."

"Maybe not." Danforth looked thoughtful. "But given Clarissa's concerns . . ." He let the rest of the sentence slide and the doctor pulled his side-whiskers and stared down at the letter as if he could read more into it than the simple words themselves.

"Perhaps we should go and see for ourselves." The doctor had little difficulty in finishing his old friend's sentence. "It's a rum business whichever way you slice it."

Danforth nodded. "I've some business to finish up, but I'll be ready to leave this afternoon. We can put up for the night at Orpington and be in Half Moon Street late tomorrow morning."

"I'll ride over at around two o'clock. I've

a few patients to see on my rounds this morning. Ah, Eleanor, my dear . . ." He greeted his wife as she came in with a tray of coffee. "I'll be going to London with George this afternoon. Could you put up a few necessities for me?"

"This is to do with Clarissa?" His wife set the tray on the desk.

"Read for yourself." Her husband passed her the letter.

After a few moments she looked up and said briskly, "The sooner you get up there the better, sir. Something is not right here. We may have no official responsibility for Clarissa and her brother, but we owe it to Francis to have a care for them. Make all haste." On which definitive instruction she hurried from the room.

"Jasper, my friend, it's your play." Charles Ravenswood leaned back in his chair, idly twisting the stem of his wineglass between his fingers as he watched his friend absently fingering his cards. "Where's your head these days, man? I've won three games of piquet, and normally I can barely wrest a single game off you."

Jasper shook his head with a murmured apology and called his card. With a degree of shock as they counted the points he realized he had just missed the utter humiliation of being rubiconed by only ten points. He tossed his cards on the table and pushed back his chair. "My apologies, Charles. I'll send your winnings to your house this afternoon." He walked away, barely noticing the greetings of his friends in the dimly lit card room at Whites.

He had been wrestling with himself all morning and into the afternoon. He was bitterly regretting his harshness, wishing the words unsaid. He was still hurt, still angry, but he was beginning to believe that maybe Clarissa's secrecy, the elaborate deceptions, had a reason that transcended his own need for her trust. He didn't think he could have mistaken her true feelings for him. Not even Clarissa could pull off quite such a monumental counterfeit.

He walked out of the club and stood for a moment on the pavement, then with an imperceptible shrug he yielded to the urge he'd been fighting all day and set off towards Piccadilly and Half Moon Street. He didn't know what he was going to say to her, didn't know whether finally he was going to force her confidence, he only knew that he couldn't continue in this limbo. He turned the corner from Piccadilly onto Half Moon Street just as his brothers came up the street towards him.

"If you're in search of the fair Clarissa, Jasper, you're out of luck," Sebastian called cheerfully. "We've just been turned disconsolate from her door."

"Why? Is she not receiving?" Jasper could well believe that Clarissa was in no mood for visitors.

"Wasn't there," Perry said. "Sally said she and that little lad had gone off to Green Park this morning — why she's taking an urchin to play in the park is anyone's guess, mind you — and haven't come back yet."

Jasper felt something cold squeeze his chest. "This morning?"

"So the girl said." Sebastian looked at his brother with concern. Jasper had gone rather pale, his face suddenly tight and drawn. "What's the matter, Jasper?"

"Nothing," he said shortly. "Why should there be?" He raised a hand in brusque farewell and strode off down the street.

"He didn't look too happy," Peregrine observed. "Odd that she should go off like that without a word, though. Don't you think, Seb?"

"Mmm." Sebastian was staring after his brother. "Something's not right, Perry. Can't put my finger on it, but something's not right."

"Well, Jasper doesn't take kindly to anyone poking around in his business," his twin reminded him. "If something's wrong he'll tell us when he's good and ready."

"You don't think we should go after him then?"

Peregrine shook his head vigorously. "I'm not inviting the rough edge of his tongue. You can, if you choose, but I have a greater care for my skin."

Sebastian shrugged and rather reluctantly turned away from the house, accompanying his brother back to Piccadilly.

Jasper let himself into the house and felt Clarissa's absence instantly. The house felt oddly empty, although Sally appeared the instant he stepped into the hall.

She bobbed a curtsy. "Oh, my lord, Mistress Ordway's not in, sir."

"So I understand from my brothers. When did she go out?" He laid a hand on the banister preparatory to mounting the stairs.

Sally looked puzzled and discomfited. "Just afore nuncheon, my lord. She took the lad, Frank, to the park for a walk. She said he needed to run off the fidgets. We expected them back for nuncheon . . . Mistress Newby made apple fritters for Frank — he's right partial to them — but they're not back yet, sir."

That cold fist squeezed harder in his chest. "Oh, I expect she met a friend in the park," he said lightly, and went upstairs to the drawing room. He could find nothing in the room out of the ordinary, nothing missing. In her bedchamber, everything was in order. The diamonds were in their box on the dresser, and even as he checked he despised himself for even the faintest suspicion. As far as he could see all her garments were in the armoire and the linen press. Her brushes were on the dresser. She had gone, but she had taken nothing with her except the child.

So she had left him. His unkindness had driven her away. He had wanted more from her than she was prepared to give, so she had simply given up on him. He had thought that beneath the surface deception, Clarissa had true feelings for him; he had allowed himself to believe that because he'd wanted to. He'd wanted to believe she returned his feelings. What a fool he was. He'd been so careful, ever since his youthful heart had been broken by Nan's young whore, not to lose his heart to any woman. He'd loved lightly when he'd loved and had accepted the inevitable end of a relationship from the moment of its inception. And he had never been hurt again. Until this enigma had stormed into his life, thrown all his resolutions into chaos, turned his rational self topsy-turvy, and then quite simply walked away from him.

Jasper went downstairs and let himself out of the house. For the first time since his youth he had the urge to drink himself into oblivion. It wasn't an urge he was going to indulge, but he needed his own company, the solitude of his own house to lick his wounds.

"I'm hungry, 'Rissa." Francis spoke in a small voice, lifting his head from his sister's lap. His eyes were still heavy with sleep.

"Yes, of course you are, love. So am I." Clarissa smiled at him, stroking his hair back from his face. "Let's see what we can do about it." She shifted him onto the bed and went to the door. She banged on it with her fist, and when that produced only a resounding silence, she took off her boot and hammered with the heel. Paint splintered. She banged harder and faster. No one in the house could possibly withstand such a racket, she thought, glancing at Francis, who was now sitting on the bed watching her with a mixture of childish delight at the noise she was making and fright.

Finally she heard steps on the stairs and

stepped back from the door, still holding her boot. The key grated in the lock and the door swung open carefully. Luke lounged in the doorway, a glass of brandy in his hand, his eyes bloodshot, his cheeks flushed.

"What the hell are you doing?" His words were a little slurred.

Clarissa's mind worked quickly. Could she manage to knock him aside . . . knock him off his feet long enough to grab Francis and race down the stairs? And then she saw a shadow behind him. A man was standing a few feet away, blocking the head of the stairs. Luke, drunk or not, was no fool. Better to settle for a small victory she was fairly confident of winning. She spoke with icy calm.

"I'm aware that starvation is your preferred method of inflicting a slow death, sir, but I think in this case it's unrealistic. It might have worked when Francis was hidden away in that cesspit in Wapping, but starving someone to death on Ludgate Hill is a different matter. We're both hungry, and unless you want me to go on hammering on the door and screaming out of the window, you'll provide us with some food."

Luke's eyes narrowed and he gave a short laugh. "Hoity-toity, aren't we? But you'll be singing another tune tomorrow, niece." He stepped back, slamming the door, and the key grated once more in the lock. The sooner he got her out of his house the safer he would feel, but his arrangements for her would not be in place before the morning. Until then, he thought, he'd better keep her quiet.

Clarissa looked at the closed door, wondering whether to start up the hammering again, but Francis was weeping and comforting him seemed a priority. "Don't cry, sweetheart." She sat down and lifted him onto her lap. "I'll think of something, I promise." She rocked him, and after a few minutes his tears stopped.

Five minutes later the key sounded in the lock and the door opened a crack. A tray slid into the room pushed by unseen hands, and the door was closed and locked again. "Ah, see, all is not lost," Clarissa said cheerfully, going over to the tray. There was bread and cheese and a carafe of water. Hardly a feast but enough to give Francis some heart, and indeed as he ate hungrily he seemed visibly to cheer up.

"What's going to happen, 'Rissa?"

"I don't know," she said honestly, nibbling a small piece of cheese. "We'll have to see what Luke does in the morning, but for now, let's try to sleep. I'll get us out of here somehow, love. And I'll have a better chance if I've had some sleep."

Francis seemed to find this argument convincing and allowed his sister to tuck him under the thin, dusty coverlet. She climbed in beside him, hugging him close to give him some of her body warmth. It was cold in the attic, the covers were inadequate, and it was not going to get any warmer overnight.

Jasper lay awake most of the night. *Where could she have gone?* He couldn't for the life of him come up with an answer. She had funds, that much he knew. Had she left the city? Stagecoaches went from the Bell Inn at Cheapside to destinations all over the land; she could have been on her way to Scotland for all he knew. He fell into an unrestful doze just before dawn and awoke determined to visit the coaching inn. An elegant young woman and a small boy were distinctive enough to stick in the memory. Someone would have noticed them buying tickets and with luck would remember their destination. If he drew a blank there, then he would try the inns on the main routes out of London that hired postchaises. There weren't too many of them. He had no idea how much money Clarissa had, but she could well have sufficient to hire a postchaise for a few stages at least.

He left the house without breakfast and rode to the Bell at Cheapside, where he drew a blank. The usual posting houses on the main routes out of the city also brought him nothing, and, dispirited, he returned to Half Moon Street at midday, intent on looking again through everything Clarissa had left behind. There must be a clue somewhere.

Sally greeted him anxiously. "Is there news of Mistress Ordway, my lord? She didn't say nothing to me about being called away so sudden like. Could she have 'ad an accident, sir?"

"If I knew the answer to that, Sally, I wouldn't be here now." Jasper went upstairs and began a methodical search through the drawers, the armoire, the linen press, the secretaire, and everything he found made him question whether Clarissa had left of her own free will. Surely, even if she wanted nothing to remind her of a liaison that had ended with so much pain, she would have taken her toothbrush . . . her hairbrushes . . . the portmanteau that she had brought with her from King Street. Her own plain, simple gowns. They had nothing to do with him. They were not tainted by his touch.

It was a bitter reflection and brought him no comfort. He was looking once more through the contents of the secretaire when he heard the front door knocker. Frowning, he went to the window looking down on the street. Did Clarissa often have visitors he didn't know? Or was it his brothers once again? Two strange horses were tethered to the hitching posts that lined the street.

Voices rose from the hall in answer to Sally's inquiring tones. Jasper went to the door and stepped out onto the small landing.

"We are here to see Mistress Astley, my girl. Be so good as to inform her?" The voice was plummy but redolent of authority.

"But, sir, there's no one of that name 'ere." Sally was confused and apologetic.

"Don't talk nonsense, girl." The second voice lacked the richness of the first but was every bit as authoritative. "Mistress Astley wrote to us from this very address. Where is your mistress?"

Jasper felt his spirits lighten for the first time in two days as a glimmer of hope pierced his dread. He came swiftly down the stairs. "Gentlemen, perhaps we may be of service to each other." He bowed as he reached the hall. The two prosperous-looking gentlemen bowed punctiliously, but their expressions were not particularly friendly.

"I don't know about that, sir. Whom do we have the honor of addressing?" Lawyer Danforth asked.

"Blackwater, at your service, sir." Jasper extended his hand, saying over his shoulder, "Sally, you may go."

"Blackwater who?" the other gentleman demanded.

"Earl of," Jasper informed him with a wry smile. "But you have the advantage of me, gentlemen."

They both subjected him to an astonished scrutiny. "You are the Earl of Blackwater, sir?"

"The very same."

"Then perhaps you would be good enough to explain why you are giving orders in the house where Mistress Astley lodges?"

"Astley?" Jasper raised an eyebrow. "So that's her name. Gentlemen, the lady you seek is known to me and my household as Mistress Clarissa Ordway. If we can clarify that, then maybe we can converse to good purpose." The glimmer of hope became a full-blown sunburst.

"*Your* household, my lord?" Doctor Alsop was outraged. "Then permit me to tell you, sir, that you are a blackguard."

"Certainly you may tell me that, although

I would dispute its truth." Jasper gestured to the stairs. "As it happens Clarissa is my affianced bride, just so that there may be no misperceptions at the outset. Will you go up, gentlemen? I believe we need to exchange some information with a degree of urgency. Clarissa, you see, has disappeared, together with a small boy she seemed rather fond of."

"Francis," his visitors said in unison.

"That would be the urchin in question, although I know him as Frank. *Please,* gentlemen . . ." He gestured to the stairs again and this time the two men preceded him up and into the drawing room without demur.

Jasper poured claret for his guests. "I need you to tell me the whole. Who is Clarissa? Who is responsible for her? And who let her loose in London, and why?"

The doctor and the lawyer exchanged glances. Then Lawyer Danforth said, "Before we give you any such information, my lord, as the friends of Clarissa's father, and as such her unofficial guardians, we would like to know why you consider you have the right to ask for it."

Jasper picked his words carefully. "Clarissa, as I said, is my affianced bride. She said she had no guardian, no family, and I thought it right that throughout our betrothal she should reside under my protection . . . in this house."

"And you believed her, sir?" Doctor Alsop made no attempt to hide his skepticism.

"Not necessarily," Jasper responded with a bland smile. "But she would divulge nothing more to me, so I judged it politic to go along with her fabrication." He frowned suddenly. "Gentlemen, this is truly a matter of some urgency. Clarissa and the child — her brother, I assume — are in danger. There's no other explanation." No other explanation for any of it, he thought. For her prevarication, her lies, her manipulation. She had been desperately dodging danger as best she could.

Danforth coughed, sipped his claret, glanced at the doctor, who nodded, and then the lawyer gave Jasper finally the whole picture.

"So this piece of vermin has a house on Ludgate Hill?" Jasper was already at the door before the lawyer had reached his final period. "We'll start there."

"He is their guardian, Lord Blackwater," Danforth put in, as much for form's sake as anything.

"And he will shortly regret that fact," Jasper stated curtly. "You are welcome to remain here, gentlemen, until I return with Clarissa and her brother." He had reached the head of the stairs when the door knocker sounded again and Sally hurried across the hall to answer it.

"Is Mistress Ordway in, Sally?" Sebastian came in on the question and saw his brother on the stair. "Oh, Jasper . . . will we be in the way? We came to see how Clarissa is."

"You will not be in the way, either of you." Jasper nodded at Peregrine, who stood just behind his twin. "As it happens you will be very much to the point. Come with me."

CHAPTER TWENTY-THREE

The morning inched by in the attic bed-chamber. No more food or water had been supplied and Clarissa was hard-pressed to find any kind of comfort for her little brother, who had sunk into an almost catatonic reverie, lying on the bed sucking his thumb, which he hadn't done in years.

She had tried hammering on the door but this time the noise had produced no response. It was just before noon when the door opened at last and Luke stood there, his wicked little knife in his hand. "Well, my dears, I'm sure you'll be happy to hear that my plans are now made." He smiled at them. "Bring that sniveling brat over here, Clarissa."

She hesitated, and with sudden startling speed his arm flashed in another vicious blow across her face that made her reel, her head spinning. At least it wasn't his knife hand, she thought with a strange mordant humor, which seemed to her as absurd as it was out of place.

"Bring him here." The command cracked with the same vicious intent as his hand.

Clarissa went to the bed and gently lifted Francis to his feet. "Start to scream, love," she whispered. She had no plan, could think of nothing except that if she let Luke take the boy without her, she would never see him again. Francis began to shriek, an ear-splitting scream that made her eardrums ache. Luke opened his mouth to speak but his voice had no power against the child's wild screams.

"He'll stop if I come with him," Clarissa shouted. "He won't let you take him without me."

Francis picked up his cue rapidly. He flung himself on the floor, kicking, screaming at the top of his lungs, and when his uncle approached, bending to pull him to his feet, he sank his teeth into his hand. Luke yelled, yanking his hand back.

"He'll come quietly if I come with him," Clarissa repeated desperately. They both needed to get out of this prison. There would be no opportunities for escape if they didn't.

Luke glowered, sucking his hand. He looked down at the screaming, flailing child.

"Bring him," he said savagely. "It makes no difference to me whether you're with him or not."

Clarissa bent to lift Francis to his feet. He looked at her for guidance and she murmured, "Well done," as she urged him to the door.

Luke raised his knife hand. "One false move, Niece, and I'll slice off the boy's ear." Francis shuddered with fear, pressing close to his sister as they went downstairs. Clarissa looked for the manservant, or whoever it was who had been behind Luke the previous day, but it felt as if the house was empty of all but themselves.

"In there." Luke gestured to a door to the right of the small landing. It gave onto a shabby salon. He thrust Francis down onto a sagging sofa and went to a sideboard to pour himself a tumbler of brandy. He turned back to them, cradling the glass in his palm. He surveyed them coldly for a long moment before beginning to speak. "Well, now that I have my wards safely in my guardianship once more, let me explain a few facts to you both."

Clarissa stood behind the sofa, her hands on her brother's shoulders, reassuring him of her presence with the firmness of her grip. Her eyes were on the knife that Luke had laid down beside the brandy bottle on the sideboard. If she could get hold of it, she would kill her uncle without a moment's hesitation.

Luke was continuing to speak. "It seems to me, Niece, that your behavior in recent weeks indicates a certain witlessness, not to mention corruption of mind. My poor, dear brother would be turning in his grave if he knew that his gently bred daughter had embraced a life of such shocking depravity . . . shamelessly selling her body. Fortunately there are places where the depraved and weak-minded can be cared for, and I intend to see you safely committed to such an institution without delay." His thin smile flickered across his lips, as poisonous as the tongue of an asp.

Clarissa stared at him, for the moment unable to make sense of what he was saying, and then as the horror unfolded she thought she would vomit. "Bedlam?" she whispered. "You would threaten me with Bedlam?"

He shook his head. "No, no, my dear niece, you much mistake the matter. I am not threatening you with anything, merely telling you how things will be." He looked down at Francis. "You, my boy, will remain here with me in this house. We shall deal together extremely well, I'm sure. My attempt to educate you outside my house in a congenial family setting met only with ingratitude, so you will stay here. Your education may be a trifle neglected, but for that you have only yourself to blame."

Clarissa wondered if she really had lost her mind, listening to this extraordinary fabrication. No one would believe it; how could they? And yet, only she and Francis knew the truth of the baby farmer, and why would anyone believe such a tale of wickedness when their uncle and guardian smiled and swore the opposite? Besides, she would be locked up in a madhouse, anything she might say construed as the insane ramblings of a weak mind, and Francis would be alone with his uncle.

It couldn't happen. She couldn't let it. She met her uncle's self-satisfied smile with a cold stare, determined that he would not see her fear. "Since we appear to be your guests at present, sir, may we trespass upon your hospitality for some refreshment once again? It's been a long time since that piece of moldy bread and stale cheese you saw fit to provide yesterday. Perhaps some coffee and bread and butter wouldn't be too difficult to find . . . oh, and a glass of milk for Francis. He's a growing boy."

She was rewarded with a flash of uncertainty in Luke's eyes as for the first time a tiny crack marred his air of utter confidence. Then he recovered. "I suppose, since it will in some way be your last meal, my dear niece, something could be contrived."

"Are you saying they don't feed the inmates of Bedlam?" she inquired, raising her eyebrows.

Luke took a step towards her, his hand raised to strike again. She held her ground, meeting his fury-filled gaze steadily. It took every last vestige of courage she possessed, but it worked. Her uncle gave her a look of loathing, but his hand dropped and he turned away to pull the bell rope. When his servant appeared, his curious gaze darting to the boy on the sofa, his master told him irascibly to bring coffee and bread and butter, and a cup of milk.

Luke poured himself more brandy and drained the glass. Clarissa glanced casually around the salon, looking for inspiration. Something she could use, anything that would give her a plan of action. Luke regarded them in silence, that same flicker of a smile on his lips. Francis sat slumped in the corner of the sofa, and Clarissa could feel beneath her hands that he had surrendered his spirit. She couldn't blame him after the dreadful experiences of the last months, but it filled her with a cold fury that added fuel to the determination to do something . . . anything.

The manservant came back with a tray, which he set down on the table in front of the sofa. "That be all?"

Luke waved him away. "Well, what are you waiting for? Avail yourself of my hospitality, Niece."

Clarissa came around to the front of the sofa. "You are very kind, sir." She picked up the milk and gave it to Francis. "Drink this, love, and I'll get you some bread and butter." She turned back to the tray. "Coffee, Uncle?"

He shook his head, refilling his brandy glass for the third time. "Make the most of it. We'll be leaving in half an hour and I doubt you'll see another coffeepot for the remainder of your miserable existence."

Clarissa picked up the coffeepot, spun on her heel, and hurled the pot and its steaming contents at her uncle. "*Run,* Francis." She picked up the poker and swung it at Luke's head as he convulsed, with his hands to his face, hot coffee streaming through his fingers. The poker made contact with bone, and he crumpled to his knees, choking and gasping.

Francis was already at the door, wrenching it open. Clarissa hurled herself after him, grabbing his hand and racing down the stairs. The startled manservant was halfway across the hall when he saw them. He stared, his jaw dropping in surprise, and Clarissa shoved him hard as she ran for the door. He stumbled, righted himself as she tugged at the heavy bolts.

"Hurry, 'Rissa . . . *hurry*." Francis was prancing on his toes beside her while she struggled with the door. The manservant lunged forward and the child ducked and drove headfirst into his belly. The man made a strange sound like air emerging from a deflated balloon, bending double, his eyes streaming.

Clarissa hauled the door open and burst into the street, Francis on her heels, and ran, for the second time in her life, straight into the Earl of Blackwater. His arms went around her and for a moment he held her tightly, her head pressed to his chest.

Francis found himself swept into the arms of a man he'd seen before in the house on Half Moon Street. "Steady now, little man. You're quite safe." Peregrine's voice was soothing as he held the child tightly. He looked at Sebastian over the child's head, and they both looked at their elder brother, who was still clasping Clarissa closely against him.

"I don't know if I've killed him," Clarissa said, her voice muffled. She lifted her head from Jasper's chest.

"We're talking of your guardian, I assume." Jasper moved her a little away from him so that he could look at her properly.

Jasper gently touched the cut on her mouth, the bruise on her cheek, the lump on her head. "Is he responsible for these?" His voice was very soft but nonetheless filled with menace.

"Yes. But I might have killed him . . . with the poker."

"Well, why don't we go and find out." Despite his fury at the cuts and bruises on her face, Jasper was filled with such happiness he could barely contain it. Only now did he understand the depths of his fear that something dreadful had happened to her . . . to the woman he loved more than life itself. She had been hurt, but he had her safe now.

He tipped her chin on his palm, looking deep into her eyes. "I thought I had lost you."

Clarissa looked at him, her eyes still a little wild. And it was as if she hadn't heard him. "If we go back in there and he's not dead, he won't let us go again."

Jasper shook his head. "Believe me, Clarissa. No one is going to keep you from me. No one has that power. Now, let's go in and see if I'm about to wed a murderess."

"I can't understand why you would find that amusing," she protested, although the terror of the last hours was gradually sliding away. "Francis mustn't go into that house again. Perry, will you take him home?"

"Of course, ma'am. Anything you say . . . be my pleasure." Peregrine set Francis on his horse and swung up behind him, circling the boy with a securing arm.

" 'Rissa?" Francis held out his hands to his sister.

She managed a reassuring smile. "I'll be back soon, sweetheart. Go with Peregrine, you're quite safe now."

The child looked over his shoulder at the gentleman riding behind him. Peregrine smiled. "Your sister's right. You're safe as houses with me, and you'll see her soon."

"Perry, take him to Blackwater House, and stay with him," Jasper instructed. "Sebastian, you had best come with us. If this brute of an uncle is not yet dead, we might need two swords. Although, of course, there's always the poker."

"Oh, I do love a mill," Sebastian said cheerfully, pushing the door open wide.

"Dear me, there's some poor soul gasping in the hall. Is that the uncle, Clarissa?"

"No," she said. "The servant. Francis butted him in the belly."

"Good for him," Sebastian said. "You two seem remarkably well able to take care of yourselves."

The brothers were making the whole situation seem surreal with their light amusement, but Clarissa felt the nightmarish terror receding. They might have seemed to treat the situation superficially as a jest, but she was in no doubt as to the deadly seriousness of their intent. It was clear as day in the set of their mouths, in the fierce determination in their eyes. Sebastian was as fair as Jasper was dark, but the family resemblance was there, and never more so than at this moment.

Jasper sensed the tension gradually leave her and was well satisfied. As he'd held her he'd felt her terror and could only guess at this point at what she'd gone through since her disappearance twenty-four hours ago. His deliberately humorous attitude was an instinctive attempt to restore and reassure her, and he could see the wildness begin to leave her eyes.

"So, where's the uncle?"

"Upstairs." She paused, hugging her arms

across her chest. "I hope I have killed him. He was going to have me committed to Bedlam."

Jasper lost all ability to make light of anything. His face went white. *"What?"*

She nodded bleakly. "He's my guardian. He can do whatever he wants."

"Let's get him." Sebastian drew his sword and started up the stairs.

Jasper followed suit. "Wait outside if you'd prefer, Clarissa."

She shook her head. "No. I'm coming." She followed them up and into the salon. Luke was slumped in a chair, his eyes closed, his breathing ragged. A great lump was forming on his temple. His face was reddened by the hot coffee, and his clothes dripped with it. The pot itself lay on its side on the floor.

"Did you throw the coffeepot at him as well, Clarissa?" Sebastian asked with some awe.

Clarissa was standing with her arms folded tight across her chest, looking down at the man who a few short minutes ago had terrified her with his power to harm her. "Yes," she said. "I hope it scalded him. I don't seem to have killed him."

"No," agreed Jasper. He stretched out his sword arm and pressed the tip of the weapon against the unconscious man's throat. Blood welled, and Luke's eyes flew open.

He stared blankly up into cold flat black eyes. His gaze flickered, and he saw Clarissa standing behind the man whose sword was pressed to his throat. He put a hand to his throat. "Who are you? What are you doing in my house?" His voice was a croak.

"I came to see if you were alive, and if you were to remedy the situation," Jasper said amiably. "I understand you had some rather unpleasant ideas about this lady's future." He cast an illustrative glance at Clarissa.

"She's my ward, in my guardianship until she gains her majority." Luke's voice gained strength. "There's not a justice in the land who would dispute my right to make what arrangements I see fit for *my* wards."

The sword point pressed a little deeper, and Luke sank back into the chair as if he could thus avoid the point. Jasper continued conversationally. "Well, there's one small matter you've omitted to mention. Or perhaps you didn't know it. The lady is no longer your ward. She is now my wife, the Countess of Blackwater, and as such lives under my authority, not yours."

Luke's eyes darted wildly around the

room. "She hasn't the right to marry without my consent."

"Maybe not, but she has done so, and it is a fait accompli. If you attempted to challenge it, I would challenge the right of a guardian to commit his perfectly sane ward to a lunatic asylum, and I'd lay odds you would find yourself facing some very serious unpleasantness. The only question that interests me now is what to do with such a loathsome piece of human flotsam."

Clarissa's mind was reeling. Jasper had just told a barefaced lie, without so much as the quiver of an eyelash. She glanced at Sebastian, expecting to see shock on his face. He knew quite well she was his brother's mistress. But he seemed perfectly sanguine, as if he'd heard nothing at all surprising.

"So, Clarissa, what do you want done with this *relative* of yours?" Jasper looked over at Clarissa without moving his sword point.

"He put Francis out with a baby farmer, expecting him to die of infection and starvation in a few months," she said slowly. "If Francis dies, Luke will inherit everything."

"Then I think we had best ensure that under no circumstances can he inherit anything. What d'you think, Sebastian?"

"Without a doubt." Sebastian stepped forward. His own sword point pressed into

Luke's belly and the man gave a strangled scream.

Clarissa closed her eyes. She couldn't let them do this, and yet with every primitive instinct she possessed she wanted revenge for what had been done to Francis, and for what Luke would have done to her. A slow and wretched death for both of them.

"I don't think he deserves a quick death," she said. "He was not prepared to give that to either Francis or myself."

"How true." Jasper nodded. "Now, my dear, I suggest you go downstairs and leave Sebastian and myself to our own devices. You may rest assured we will enact a biblical vengeance, precise in every detail."

Luke moaned and his eyes closed again. Clarissa looked thoughtfully at Jasper, wondering if he was really capable of the kind of savagery he was implying. But when he said softly, "Go, Clarissa," she turned and left. She walked out into the crisp afternoon and breathed deeply.

Jasper waited until he heard the front door close, then he leaned over his victim. "Listen to me very carefully. My brother is going to escort you to the coast, where he will find you passage on some craft heading a very long way from here to a place as barbaric as you. You will be quite at home. And if ever I see you within the borders of this land again, there will be no limit to my vengeance. Do I make myself clear?" His sword point moved in a leisurely stroke across the man's throat, leaving a fine line of blood in its wake.

"Do I make myself clear?"

Luke nodded, trying to keep his Adam's apple still.

"Good." Jasper raised his sword and sheathed it. "Seb, hold him here until I send my coach with Plunkett. He could hold this louse down with one hand, so between you, you should have no trouble getting him to Dover."

Sebastian nodded with a grin. Jasper's coachman was an erstwhile prizefighter and more than capable of dealing with the scrawny figure of Luke Astley. "Never fear, Jasper. We'll have our friend on the high seas by dawn tomorrow."

"Look for a ship sailing for the Indies. They should be big enough and inhospitable enough to hold him." Jasper raised a hand in farewell and left. He found Clarissa on the street, stroking his horses, while Tom stood phlegmatic as always at their heads.

Clarissa turned her cheek against an animal's silky neck as Jasper emerged from the house. "Is he dead?"

"He will soon wish he were." He stroked her hair back from her forehead, smoothing the deep frown lines with his finger. "But, forgive me, my love, killing him out of hand could make my life a little awkward, and I also thought you might have regrets at such a drastic vengeance when matters had settled down, and since such a vengeance would be so very final . . ." He gave an expressive shrug.

Clarissa smiled. "I was already having regrets. But if he stays alive, he will be a threat to Francis until I gain my majority and my brother passes into my guardianship."

"You have no need to worry. Your uncle will be far away for the next ten months. And Francis will be with us."

"Oh, yes." She remembered and was astonished she could have forgotten even for a moment. "That was an amazing lie, my lord, even bigger than the ones I've been telling."

"Oh, I very much doubt that," he said with a dry smile. "However, my particular lie is about to be made truth." He lifted her unceremoniously and deposited her in the curricle, jumping up beside her.

"I don't understand." She grabbed the

side of the curricle as the horses sprang forward, racing down the street. "Jasper, if this turns over, we'll all break our necks."

"Oh, ye of little faith," he scoffed. "It makes a change for you not to understand. I've been existing in confusion ever since I first met you. However, that is about to be remedied. But first, I have a special license and two witnesses back at Half Moon Street, so we shall make a lie the truth."

"I thought it had to be a Catholic ceremony to fulfill the terms of your uncle's will."

"Oh, we shall have that afterwards, for the benefit of the family. For now I am interested only in making this union legal; it seems the only way I can be sure of keeping hold of you." He glanced sideways at her, and his expression was wiped clear of all amusement. "I can only ask your pardon for my harshness, for words that I have regretted every minute since I spoke them, but why, Clarissa? Why couldn't you trust me?"

She looked down at her lap, feeling for the words. "I don't know . . . it wasn't so much that I thought I couldn't, but there was so much at stake I couldn't see how I could rely on anyone but myself. I'm accustomed to helping myself. Francis is my responsibility, and I knew how important it was for you to fulfill the terms of the viscount's will, and I know how honorable you are, and I was afraid that if you knew I wasn't a whore, you'd feel you would be cheating again if you went through with a marriage to someone who didn't qualify." She gave a tiny laugh. "My mother was the daughter of an earl, and my father was a wealthy squire, Master of Hounds, Justice of the Peace. I was a virgin. How could I possibly fit the viscount's criteria?"

"You couldn't. I've known that from our first night together. Did you really imagine you could hide your virginity from me, you absurd creature?" He shook his head in reproach.

"You knew?" She stared at him. "Always. You've known always?"

"Always from that night."

"Oh." She plaited her fingers in her lap. "I'm not very experienced in these matters."

"That would appear to be the case," he responded drily. "But I do think you might have given me a little more credit all around."

"Yes," she agreed. "And I ask your pardon. But if you'd told me what you suspected, it might have helped a little too."

He smiled. "I think we both need pardon,

and I give mine freely."

"And I mine."

He drew rein abruptly, turning on the bench to take her in his arms, his mouth finding hers. He kissed her cut and swollen mouth gently, in benediction and in promise, as he murmured, "I love you, Clarissa. I will always love you."

"And I you, Jasper. For all time."

It was hard to believe the long nightmare was over, but it was. Francis was safe now. He'd take their father's place and fill the squire's shoes admirably. And she . . . ah, well . . . she could see nothing but roses in her future.

EPILOGUE

Viscount Bradley was dozing before the fire one evening three months later when the sound of laughter and merriment, most unusual in this drearily massive mausoleum, reached him from the antechamber to his bedchamber. He opened his eyes and directed a jaundiced glare at the group of gaily dressed revelers who came into the room.

His three nephews accompanied a beautiful young woman. All three were in court dress, the young woman in a ball gown of ivory damask embroidered with seed pearls, her hair powdered and arranged in a most elaborate coiffure, adorned with two ostrich plumes. The Blackwater diamonds sparked blue fire in the candlelight.

"Well, well," the viscount muttered. "So he finally made an honest woman of you, my lady. You've made your curtsy to good Queen Charlotte. You are to be congratulated."

"Thank you, sir." Clarissa curtsied as she had done to the queen a few hours past, expertly handling her long train, dipping her head so that the ostrich feathers seemed to dip and curtsy in imitation.

The viscount chuckled, and for once his amusement lacked malice. "Nicely done, my dear. Nicely done. No one would ever believe you had once been a whore." As he said this his gaze flicked to his oldest nephew.

Jasper smiled and took out his snuffbox. "As you say, sir." He took a leisurely pinch before dropping the emerald-encrusted gold box back into the deep pocket of his emerald-green coat. A massive emerald winked on his finger, its twin nestled in the froth of Mechlin lace at his throat.

"Who presented the girl?" the viscount demanded.

"Our cousin, sir. Lady Hester Graham. It is only right and proper that my wife should be presented under the auspices of the family, wouldn't you agree?" Jasper's smile was smooth, his tone suave, and it was clear to the old man that his nephew was enjoying this little interview. The viscount had insisted that the family that had labeled him their black sheep and cast him beyond the family pale embrace an erstwhile whore as the wife of the family's head. Presenting her at court was the ultimate sign of acceptance.

Jasper had fulfilled the terms of the will to the nth degree.

Or had he? The viscount looked at his nephew's lovely bride again. He would never know, but he would always suspect.

The employees of Thorndike Press hope you have enjoyed this Large Print book. All our Thorndike, Wheeler, and Kennebec Large Print titles are designed for easy reading, and all our books are made to last. Other Thorndike Press Large Print books are available at your library, through selected bookstores, or directly from us.

For information about titles, please call:
(800) 223-1244

or visit our Web site at:
http://gale.cengage.com/thorndike

To share your comments, please write:
Publisher
Thorndike Press
10 Water St., Suite 310
Waterville, ME 04901